THE WAXWORK CORPSE

Charles Holborne Legal Thrillers
Book Five

Simon Michael

SAPERE
BOOKS

THE WAXWORK CORPSE

Published by Sapere Books.

20 Windermere Drive, Leeds, England, LS17 7UZ,
United Kingdom

saperebooks.com

ISBN: 978-1-913335-83-0

To Peggy, with love and thanks. All the themes are here.

ACKNOWLEDGEMENTS

As always, I need to thank my patient friends and beta readers who have read and contributed to this book: Neil Cameron and Carly Jordan for their eagle-eyed attention to detail and historical accuracy; Debbie Jacobs for her deep knowledge of Judaism; and Amy Durant of Sapere Books, for her understanding of structure and her immense patience with a difficult author. As for the law and procedure in the 1960s I have relied on my own knowledge and the invaluable 35th. edition of Archbold, but I am greatly indebted to Simon Worlock and Rex Tedd QC of No 5 Chambers, who filled several important gaps. If any of the law and procedure are wrong, it's my fault and I seek leave to appeal.

Finally, my thanks go to Simeon Maskrey QC. He probably won't remember this, but many years ago we shared a barristers' robing room while we awaited jury verdicts. It was his wonderful telling of this story, his feet up on the dressing table, that persuaded me that, one day, I would have to write this novel.

PROLOGUE

1940, London

'You comin' Charlie?'

Charlie Horowitz looks up from the kitchen table where he's reading that evening's *Standard*. His cousin and best friend, Izzy Conway, known on the Thames as "Merlin", is slipping on his leather jacket.

'Where to?' asks Charlie.

'Thought I'd grab a quick one at the *Prospect*.'

Charlie frowns. His cousin, tall, muscular and possessing matinee idol looks, never goes out in the evening, even to the local, without looking sharp: clean shirt, razor-creased trousers, polished shoes and Brylcreem on his sun-bleached locks. But Izzy is still wearing his working lighterman's clothes, stained baggy trousers, collarless shirt rolled up to the elbows and trademark leather cap perched on the back of his head.

'Dressed like that?' asks Charlie.

'You're not taking Charlie to the pub again, Izzy,' intervenes the matriarch of the home, Beatrice Conway, as she clears the remaining plates and slides the rest of the fish pie into the oven to await her husband's return from his shift. 'Charlie's underage,' she says. 'His mother'd kill me if she knew.'

'Well, she's in Wales, so I don't suppose she'll ever find out. Not unless you tell 'er,' replies Izzy with a wink directed at Charlie.

The remaining person in the room, Jonjo Milstein, swallows his last mouthful of lokshen pudding and speaks as he pushes the bowl away. 'Come on Bea,' he chides gently. 'Charlie does a man's job on the river, better than most men twice his age. Let the boy go; the odd pint won't kill him.'

Milstein is in his seventies, bronzed by a lifetime working the Thames and tough as whipcord. He's the only member of the family who can speak to his formidable daughter like this and get away with it without an earful. He waves his hand at the young men, shooing them out of the room.

'I'll look after 'im,' says Izzy as he disappears into the hall.

Charlie stands, dragging his jacket off the back of the chair. 'I'll be fine, Aunt Bea,' he reassures her. He sneaks up behind the large woman as she fills a bowl from the kettle to wash up, and kisses her loudly on her ruddy cheek. 'Thanks for supper.'

'It's called "tea" in this 'ousehold!' she calls after him, but as usual Charlie's good manners and thoughtfulness have won her round.

Over the last several months she's watched an unhappy brooding teenager develop into a confident and outgoing young man, and she loves having him in her home, despite her sister-in law's thin-lipped fury. Millie Horowitz wants her elder son to return to the safety of rural Wales where the family has been evacuated. Charlie refuses. He's a different person in this crowded house with its noise, laughter and ever-present smell of Jewish cooking, and he relishes the difference.

The shabby family home of his aunt Bea and uncle Jacob, close enough to the river to hear the lapping water in the still of night, is quite unlike the spotlessly clean, rule-bound home of the Horowitz family on British Street — now demolished — where he felt constantly criticised and permanently on edge. In the months since he slipped silently out of the shared Welsh farmhouse to clamber aboard a freight train to London, returning to the rubble-strewn East End streets he knows so well, he has been happier than he can ever remember, notwithstanding the Luftwaffe's bombs and strafing, and the daily diet of a lighterman working long shifts on the river. Charlie is fifteen and, accordingly, invulnerable; surrounded by daily death and dismemberment, he cannot conceive that it could possibly happen to him.

He follows Izzy out of the front door onto the deserted street where the older boy waits. It's only a five-minute walk from the Conways' tall terraced house on Juniper Street to the *Prospect of Whitby* public house at Wapping Wall but, to Charlie's surprise, instead of turning east, Izzy goes the other way, north towards Cable Street.

'Er —' queries Charlie, but Izzy puts his finger to his lips to demand silence and Charlie complies.

Although twice his breadth and almost the same height, Charlie is a couple of years younger than Izzy, and there is a whiff of hero-worship in his admiration for his charismatic older cousin. Charlie has been sharing a room with Izzy ever since he was pulled from the bombed house on British Street where, unnoticed by the authorities, he'd been living rough. Within days he was following his cousin in and out of East End boozers, West End dance halls and no end of scrapes.

They round the corner into King David Lane and Izzy opens the door of a lock-up garage. It usually houses a tangle of ropes, boxes, spare buoys — all the tools and paraphernalia required of a Thames lighterage business — but to Charlie's surprise the space has been tidied sufficiently to make room for a small dark-coloured van.

Izzy gets in. 'Gotta little job to do,' he explains opaquely. He leans across to the passenger door, opening it quietly. 'You coming?'

Charlie shrugs and does as instructed. Izzy starts the engine. They back out onto the road and Izzy re-locks the garage door.

'Where're we going?' asks Charlie as Izzy rejoins him in the cab.

'You'll see.'

They turn north onto Commercial Road. Air raid sirens start wailing five minutes later as they enter West India Avenue.

'Perfect!' says Izzy.

Charlie examines his cousin's face, finding not sarcasm but determination. 'Seriously?'

Five minutes later, Izzy brings the van to a halt on Back Lane outside the docks. The road here is narrowed by enormous piles of rubble and burned-out vehicles, evidence of the previous nights' bombing. Izzy winds down the driver's window and inclines his head, listening intently. River smells and smoke drift into the cab. The sirens are still sounding but the skies seem clear; no sound of approaching aircraft and silence from the ack-ack batteries. Searchlight beams criss-cross the night sky above the buildings, seeking targets.

London holds its breath.

Izzy turns to Charlie and speaks urgently. 'Number Two warehouse on North Quay was hit two nights ago, and the timber they was using to patch it up went up in flames last night. So there's no back wall. Anyone can just walk in.'

'And why would they do that?' asks Charlie, knowing the answer.

''Cos it's a bonded warehouse. I had a scout round this morning. The first floor's full of cases of brandy. Half were destroyed but…'

'Half weren't.'

'Exactly. Look, Charlie, you can stay in the van if you want, but I'm going to lift a couple while the raid's on. It'll be deserted. And the way things're going, them cases probably won't last the night anyway, so where's the harm?'

He's right about that, concedes Charlie silently. Since the Blitz began in September, half the Port of London has burned to the ground and there's no sign of Hitler letting the other half off. For a fleeting moment Charlie imagines his father's expression at the prospect of his elder son, the quiet studious one, looting a bonded warehouse in the middle of an air raid. Honest in every fibre of his being, the little East End tailor would have beaten his strapping son until his arms ached, while at the same time lecturing him on the Seventh Commandment. Probably in Hebrew.

Izzy reaches behind him and lifts two Zuckerman helmets from the back of the cab. He hands one to Charlie who turns the thin steel round in his hands, noting the white "W" painted on the front.

'What poor warden's doing without his tonight?' he asks.

'None,' replies Izzy with a smile. 'I picked them up yesterday. Cost me a bag of coal off that flat-iron.'

Charlie pulls on the helmet, turns to his cousin and grins. 'All right. What're we waiting for?'

Charlie's first experience of looting appears to go as smoothly as Izzy predicted. They drive up to the warehouse, walk through the missing north wall, climb the charred stairs to the first floor and carry four timber cases between them back down the stairs and into the waiting van. Twelve minutes later, with the sound of the approaching Luftwaffe bombers and their escorts building like thunder from the south, and ack-ack shells starting to burst above them, the two thieves are driving back up Commercial Road. Neither notices another lorry, its engine idling as it sits in the shadows between the warehouse and the wharf. Neither notices the men wearing balaclava helmets who occupy it — men with the same idea as Izzy, but who timed their arrival just a few minutes too late.

Despite the sirens and the approaching death from above, Commercial Road, a main artery into the City of London from the east, is surprisingly busy with latecomers running hither and thither towards basements and Andersons. A newspaper seller is still locking up his kiosk on the pavement and there are two toms leaning against the wall of a pub in their high heels and painted-on stocking seams, perhaps hoping for last-minute business in the dark of a nearby shelter.

'Pity about that pint,' says Charlie.

Izzy turns his head towards Charlie and winks conspiratorially. 'Oh, I think we might still —'

'Stop!' cries Charlie, his attention distracted by movement on the periphery of his vision and a familiar *plop-plop* sound. Izzy hammers the brakes and the van skids sideways to a halt.

They have driven into a shower of incendiaries. The bombs bounce off the pavements and tarmac all around them, fizzing like fireworks but not yet alight. Charlie glances to his right; the two young women are trapped against the wall. Before Izzy can engage reverse, Charlie is out of the passenger door, wrenching off his steel helmet. He races across the road towards the women, judging the bombs nearest to them. He selects his target as he runs and spins his helmet sideways. It's a perfect shot; the helmet lands directly on top of the incendiary to one side of the women, continuing to rotate clockwise on its rim as it settles.

'Here!' he shouts, beckoning urgently, and gestures to the path he's made safe. The women clatter toward him on their stiletto heels. Even before the helmet has ceased turning, it glows first red hot, then white hot and then, before Izzy's eyes, it disintegrates as heat and light fan out from it, but the precious three or four seconds Charlie has bought are sufficient. He slides back onto the bench seat of the van, squeezing close to Izzy to make room for both women. They're right on his heels, and the cab is suddenly awash with cheap perfume and flapping skirts.

'Go!' orders Charlie, a stranger now perched on his lap, and Izzy slams the vehicle into reverse, spins it round and accelerates out of danger.

A few minutes later they pull up outside the *Prospect of Whitby*. The cousins have been caught at the pub during air raids before, and are banking on access to its cellar. As long as it's not already full they'll be reasonably safe and, importantly, might even be served a drink or two while they wait for the all-clear. The young women, who have declared their names to be Louise and May, agree to join them.

'I don't like the idea of leaving the van out in the open,' says Izzy. 'You go down, I'll drive to the lock-up and run back.'

Charlie frowns doubtfully. 'Don't risk it, Izzy. Come down with us.'

Izzy shakes his head and Charlie knows he'd be wasting his breath to argue. Once Izzy has made up his mind, no amount of reasoning will ever dissuade him. 'Go on, I shan't be a sec,' he insists, and he engages gear and revs the engine impatiently.

'Don't be long, gorgeous,' instructs Louise, blowing him a kiss before sliding out of the cab.

Fifteen minutes later, Charlie and the two women are squashed shoulder to shoulder with twenty other refugees from the air raid in the cellar of the *Prospect*, glasses in hand. Charlie and his new friends are sitting with several others on the cold flagstones underneath a long oak table on which is stacked a pyramid of empty beer barrels.

One of the oldest waterside public houses in London, for over 400 years *The Prospect of Whitby* has been a favourite haunt of smugglers, footpads and pickpockets, and Charlie likes knowing he's the latest in a long line of humans and contraband to have been hidden here over the centuries.

With every thud of a bomb landing on the streets above them, dust from the ancient ships' beams that now form the low ceiling drifts down to settle on the table and their protruding legs. May, a plump girl with a perfect cupid's bow of a mouth brightly outlined in red lipstick, has taken a fancy to Charlie. Or, he concedes phlegmatically, she'd seen her friend's interest in Izzy and took what was left.

Charlie is a well-muscled young man and he looks a good few years older than he is. His figure, dark complexion, dark eyes and unruly black curly hair attract the glances of many a young woman. But he's a realist; whenever they are up West, Izzy's film-star features are inevitably the centre of attention; women, and some men, are drawn to the young lighterman like moths to a flame.

May's right hand clutches her drink as her left runs down Charlie's massive forearm.

'How old are you anyway?' she whispers.

'Eighteen,' lies Charlie distractedly. Where the hell is Izzy? he thinks; he should have been back long before now.

There's a heavy explosion above them, and the cellar reverberates like the inside of a drum. The single light bulb dims, flickers and dies as power to the street is interrupted. The cellar is plunged into total darkness.

Hot words are breathed into Charlie's ear. 'You was ever so brave,' says May, apparently unmoved by the bombs above, and suddenly her small hands are all over him, touching, caressing and undoing. Charlie nestles his head blindly into the soft angle between the fur collar of her coat and her neck, realising that despite being pressed against total strangers and at risk of imminent death — indeed, perhaps because of that very peril — May … will.

The sound of the Heinkel aircraft engines above them fades to the north. Another few minutes pass in the darkness, but before May's soft little hands have finished their act of kindness Charlie gently and reluctantly pushes them away. It's now almost thirty minutes since Izzy left them and Charlie is seriously worried. He tucks himself away and buttons his flies.

'Back in a sec,' he mutters and, excusing himself, he stands and pushes blindly through the crowd in the direction of the stairs. Ignoring shouted protests, he fumbles for the stair rail, climbs upwards, opens the door and enters the public bar.

Expecting it to be empty, he's surprised to find shadowy figures in the darkness, slivers of light from around the blackout blinds illuminating their movements. The skies are now silent, but the people in the bar seem not to have heard Charlie's entry.

One man is only a pace or two away from Charlie but facing away. He wears what seems in the half-light to be an unusually long woollen hat which descends almost to the nape of his neck. It takes Charlie a second to realise that he's looking at a balaclava, partially rolled up at the front to expose the man's face. The man is intently watching another, one who stands with his back to them both, his feet widely spaced. He's swinging his arms at something, making a *doof-doof* noise reminiscent of that made by Charlie's gloved hands as they thud into a heavy punchbag at the gym. Charlie takes a step to his left to see what the second man is doing and realises with a shock that he's pounding his fists into a third figure whose blond hair hangs in a shaft of light: Izzy.

The lighterman stands in a pose reminiscent of Jesus: arms outstretched at shoulder height, head lolling onto his chest. His

17

knees sag but he is held upright by his wrists which are somehow tied at the height of the bar. The *doof-doof* sound is made by the punches thundering into Izzy's unprotected chest and torso as the man beating him swings his arms powerfully, pivoting from the waist. The bar is silent but for the grunts of the attacker as he lands heavy, methodical, blows to Izzy's unprotected face and abdomen. He is beating Izzy to death. He stops for a second to catch his breath.

'Let me have another go!' hisses the spectator.

Charlie casts around for a weapon, stoops and lifts a wooden bar stool by its feet. As the second man turns at the sound, Charlie brings the stool round in an arc and it crashes against his head. He collapses silently. The stool clatters out of Charlie's grasp and onto the flagstones, causing the other man to pause and turn.

Even in the poor light, Charlie knows him instantly: Alec Bledsoe; a Blackshirt, one of the street-corner demagogues despised and feared by the Jewish community. Formerly one of Sir Oswald Mosley's lieutenants, he's one of the fascist thugs who takes joy in terrorising Jewish families and smashing up their East End businesses. He stands with his fists raised, half-turned towards Charlie, a scowl on his heavy features.

'Best piss off, mate, or you'll get the same. This ain't nothing to do with you.' Charlie doesn't answer. 'Look,' says Bledsoe, indicating with a jerk of his head Izzy's motionless body, 'he's a fucking Jewboy looter on my patch. And he won't tell me where it's stashed. So let me get on, will ya?'

For the first time Bledsoe notices the absence of his companion. His eyes flick round the bar, scanning the shadows and finally land on the crumpled darker heap by Charlie's feet. He does an almost comical double-take and then, with a roar, charges at Charlie like a bull, at the very instant as the all-clear begins to sound.

Charlie's an accomplished boxer, a London schoolboy champion and, after several months working on the River, at the peak of his physical fitness, but Bledsoe is twice his weight and age. However, judging by Bledsoe's puffing and blowing even when attacking a defenceless man, Charlie guesses he's out of condition and is probably a lot slower than he. He sways out of Bledsoe's advance and slams a punch into the other's forehead as he goes past. Bledsoe skids and turns, but before he can position himself Charlie follows up with a combination to the body and dances back on his toes as he would in the ring.

Suddenly all the lights in the bar are illuminated as the electricity supply is restored, and Charlie sighs inwardly with relief, assuming that Bledsoe will now make a run for it. Instead, the older man wipes his face with the back of his hand and launches himself again. Charlie bends under the other's swing and comes up again fast, hitting Bledsoe with another two-punch combination, a jab to the nose which produces a spurt of blood and a fierce punch to the abdomen. The breath whooshes out of the older man's lungs and he bends at the waist, his guard dropping, as if looking for something on the floor.

As Bledsoe tries to force some air back into his lungs Charlie seizes his opportunity, steps back and launches a right-handed uppercut that starts almost at Bledsoe's knees, connects with the underside of his jaw, and ends its arc of travel above Charlie's left ear. It is perhaps the most beautiful punch Charlie has ever thrown.

Bledsoe's body describes a retreating arc, his head slamming on the floor. He's only semi-conscious, his body floppy and his eyes unfocused but, before he can recover, Charlie is astride his chest, raining blows to each side of his face, left to the head, right to the head, left to the head.

A hand grabs Charlie's raised arm from behind but he shrugs it off and continues to punch. More people combine to haul Charlie, still trying to land blows, off Bledsoe's prone body. Charlie turns, struggling, ready to fight whoever has intervened, to find half the people from the cellar, including May and Louise, staring at him.

'That's enough, Charlie,' croaks a weak voice from the direction of the bar.

The familiar voice penetrates the red mist and Charlie subsides. He turns towards the bar. Izzy's face is a mass of bruises and lacerations. There's so much blood, there's barely a patch of pink skin. Blood has stained the front of his clothing from just under his chin to his mid-thighs. But one eye is open, and he is speaking, albeit indistinctly.

'Enough,' he repeats, spitting blood and a tooth from mashed lips. 'Would someone please untie me?'

For a split-second nothing happens, but then the bar comes alive with movement. People rush to each side of Izzy and support him while others untie the ropes binding his wrists. He's half-carried to a chair and someone gets a bar towel to staunch the blood flowing from his cuts. Someone else fills a glass with brandy and holds it to Izzy's lips. People crowd around Bledsoe and his associate. The latter groans from the floor and is helped to sit up. Someone tries to get a call through the overwhelmed telephone exchange for an ambulance. Charlie finds himself crowded to the back of the group. He's aware of May's eyes on him, re-evaluating the stranger with whom she was recently so intimate.

The barman kneels next to Bledsoe's still form. 'It's that bastard, Bledsoe,' he announces, his fingers feeling for a pulse.

More eyes fix on Charlie. Bledsoe's reputation as a tough guy, one with influential and dangerous friends, runs through East London. No one has ever stood up to him before; certainly no one has ever knocked him out. It dawns on Charlie that there are going to be repercussions.

'Can someone give me a hand?' says the barman. 'I ain't too sure…'

A woman with a nurse's uniform visible under her coat pushes her way through the watchers and joins the barman kneeling at Bledsoe's side. She opens his collar further and places a hand under his chin, feeling for a jugular pulse. She leans over, placing her ear close to the unconscious man's gaping mouth. Everyone in the bar is silent. It's a few seconds before she eventually speaks.

'He's dead,' she says simply, straightening up.

All remaining heads in the bar turn towards Charlie.

'I had no choice,' he explains. His voice is tremulous and, despite his size, Charlie suddenly looks like a lost boy. 'Honest! They were killing Izzy.'

CHAPTER 1

The shock of entering the black water is enough to take Julie's breath away. Even in the middle of a warm spring, Wastwater chills to the marrow. She kicks a few times quickly to stir her circulation. A double splash and two champagne bursts of bright bubbles show where her guardians, her boyfriend Neil and an instructor she only met twenty minutes ago, have entered the water, ahead and to her left; only the turbulence and the loom of their lamps reveal their presence.

They have deliberately picked a moonless night. The two beams of light separate and come towards Julie, one on each side, and stand off, waiting for her. The two disembodied light sources are eerie, but she's glad of them. She's been preparing for this first night navigation exercise for months. In the clubhouse she'd joked confidently with the rest of the group about getting lost, coming face-to-face with or, worse still, feeling the black caress of the twelve-foot pikes reputed to live in the lake. But now she's afraid.

Wastwater is the deepest lake in England, carved by glacial action half a million years ago. From gravel beaches, its sides fall steeply for eighty metres until they reach the bottom of a "V" now flattened by millennia of accumulated mud and silt. The sides are steep and regular, except for Tiffen's Rock. Like a decayed molar, the Rock erupts from the smooth side of the lake, its roots lost in the murk and silt, its top levelled by years of deposits. A sinister, freakish excrescence known only to the underwater fraternity, it has been used for years by divers on navigation exercises.

Julie breaks the even rhythm of her strokes to illuminate her console and check her compass bearing and depth, then kicks out again, following the short stab of light from her lamp. Beyond that, blackness. Monstrous pike with razor teeth glide in and out of her imagination, but she pushes them away and concentrates on her stroke and her breathing.

The Rock, when it appears, takes her by surprise. Her navigation has been perfect and, for a second, exhilaration overcomes fear. The three divers descend steeply, parallel to the side of the lake, the leader sweeping his lamp in an arc from side to side. She watches the depth gauge on her console as they descend: ten metres … fifteen … twenty … and with each metre her sense of unease grows. They find the base of Tiffin's Rock at thirty metres, deeper than she has ever dived before. She points her torch away to the east, but the light is soon overcome by the inky blackness that hems them in on all sides.

She swings the lamp back to the front and as she does, something stands out for a second in its beam. She slows her kicks. There, caught in the loom of her torch, is a package. Resting where Tiffen's Rock grows from the walls of the lake, where the root of the tooth disappears into its gum, the package is half-buried in a thick shroud of silt, one corner protruding at an angle. A metre or two in any direction, and it would have rolled all the way down to the lake floor to be lost in millennia of deposits, way beyond human eyes.

Her heart thumping in her chest, she swims over for a closer look, but she's too close, too curious, and suddenly the water is blurred by millions of dancing particles caught in the light. She spins round, realising too late that she's made a mistake, and is suddenly and completely disorientated. The lights of her co-divers, only seconds before just ahead of her, seem to have disappeared altogether. She starts panting, her breath loud in her ears, and she kicks out wildly, anxious to get out of the cloud of disturbed silt and back to clear water.

After a few seconds she slows and turns. She points her torch into the complete blackness, illuminating each quadrant for a second and then turning on the spot to the next, but the silt has spread further than she could have imagined, and it's like driving on high beam through fog. She extinguishes the torch and hangs there in the utter darkness, blood pounding in her ears.

Then: a flash of light, followed by another. She illuminates her torch once, twice, three times quickly in succession, and she's answered: eighty yards away, off to her right, she sees both of her guardians' torches moving simultaneously in slow arcs. Relief overwhelms her, and a giggle bubbles in her chest. She recognises with alarm the light-headedness that signals incipient nitrogen narcosis. She feels her breathing quicken involuntarily, and she fights to maintain control but it slips further away with each breath.

One of the men, the instructor she thinks, is before her now, gesticulating in her face. 'Up!' he points, once, twice, urgently. She nods. He sets off again, close to her right side, Neil on her left. The exertion and regular rhythmic strokes calm her. By the time they reach the top of the Rock, she has control again. They break surface to find a gale howling across the lake. Rain pounds the water so hard it's as if the gods are hurling missiles from the skies.

The instructor is swimming purposefully towards the gravel beach. Neil spits out his regulator mouthpiece and spins in the water. 'Come on!'

'No, stop! Didn't you see her?' Julie says.

'See who?'

A bolt of lightning lights up the sides of the Vale, and the almost instantaneous crack of thunder immediately above their heads almost drowns her reply.

'There's a woman down there!'

'What? Another diver?'

'No! A woman! On the rock! I saw her face!'

'No,' he shouts, 'it was just a boulder. Covered in silt.'

'I saw her, I tell you.'

'It's an hallucination. Nitrogen narcosis.'

'For Christ's sake, Neil, it was no hallucination! That was no boulder. It was a woman, wrapped in plastic. And I'm telling you: I saw her face.'

The detective inspector from London named Abercrombie hugs himself against the wind blowing over Wastwater, stubs out his third cigarette in the car park gravel, and lights another. He bitterly regrets his decision to allow the local sergeant to take the car and go for his dental appointment. But his boss said "Be nice", and so he is being nice. Relations between the Met and the Cumberland, Westmorland and Carlisle Constabulary have become somewhat strained and thus, in the spirit of co-operation, he is freezing his balls off.

He glances at his watch. The divers have been out there for so long, they've had to change air tanks once, and will soon be up for more. The fellow from the Diving Club who bent Abercrombie's ear for fifteen minutes before strolling off to enjoy his hot breakfast somewhere out of the biting wind had opined that that the police divers, who were unfamiliar with the lake, were probably stirring up the silt, making the search more difficult. Abercrombie thinks otherwise; he suspects the entire story of a body-shaped package was either cooked up altogether or exaggerated out of all proportion. If they find anything at all he expects it to be some fly-tipping, maybe an old mattress or a carpet. A student goes missing in a small community and sightings occur everywhere. One imaginative local had even reported seeing a body dropping into the lake from an aeroplane — by parachute! If it weren't for the fact that the missing student happened to be the daughter of some diplomat based in London, he wouldn't even be here.

He shades his eyes and squints over the grey water to the boat two hundred yards out. He can see the man who'd been prevailed upon to row it there, huddled in his coat and trying to shelter below the gunwales. The poor bastard, thinks Abercrombie; he must be even colder than me.

As the inspector watches, the water parts and a black shiny head appears. It is followed shortly by another. They resemble otters, or seals, he thinks, although his knowledge of matters aquatic is limited by his urban upbringing and a detestation of water, boats and everything connected with them. The two divers spin in the water, looking for the shore, and one of them waves energetically.

My God, they've found something! thinks Abercrombie, grinding out his cigarette under foot. Sure enough, the other two divers surface, towing a large muddy object between them. The first two haul themselves into the boat, wriggle out of their apparatus, and lean out over the water. The small craft dips precipitously and for a moment the inspector's sure it's going to capsize, but with two divers pushing and two pulling they eventually get the object into the boat. The oarsman stares at it, and even from the shore the inspector can see his dropped jaw and wide-open eyes. One of the divers prods him into action and he sets to, turning the boat expertly towards the shore, and begins rowing.

DI Abercrombie walks towards the water as the boat grounds on the gravel. He helps pull it up the shore and peers inside. The two divers and the oarsman watch him intently as he bends over the find. Christ, it *is* a body! It's wrapped round and round with some thick plastic material and is bound with yards of wire and rope of differing thicknesses and colours, but the outline of a person can be seen clearly inside. The two divers who were forced to swim back in splash up the gravel and stand by the side of the boat, dripping.

'Well, sir. Looks like we've found her,' says one.

'Call the coroner's office and get a photographer up here immediately,' replies Abercrombie. 'You'd better call your DCI and a police surgeon too. Leave it in the boat and don't touch it till I tell you.'

It takes an hour for the cast to assemble. The body has been carried out of the boat and placed on a large sheet of clean plastic. The area has been taped off and two officers now stand at the top of the road leading down to the car park to prevent unauthorised entry. The local Detective Chief Inspector is the last to arrive, by which time everyone on the beach is hunched in their coats, stamping their feet and blowing on cupped hands. Abercrombie has given up; he lost sensation in his fingers and toes some time ago.

The DCI, a heavy man with the corrugated face of a bloodhound and a Cumbrian accent which, to Abercrombie, is almost entirely impenetrable, wastes few words.

'Let's see what we've got then.'

One of the divers crouches at the head end of the package, a diving knife poised in his hand. At the other end, near its feet, is a detective sergeant with a decade's experience in forensic crime scene investigation. He carries secateurs. This will be his last job in this role because, in an idiotic change he's sure is designed only to save the force money, he and his specialist colleagues are shortly to be replaced by civilians with the grand title of "Scenes of Crime Officers". As the two men begin to cut the cords binding the package, working from its ends towards its middle, the DCI holds out his hand. Abercrombie knows what he wants and hands him a copy of a large fuzzy black and white photograph.

'How was she held down?' asks the DCI.

'Some sort of concrete block with a hole in the middle,' answers the diver between grunts. He is struggling to cut the cords binding the package; they're so tightly embedded in whatever is inside that he's unable to get the blade of his knife under them without risking damage to the corpse.

'The rope's no problem, but this stuff's wire,' comments the detective sergeant. 'It looks like coaxial.'

'Coaxial?' asks the inspector.

'The stuff you use for TV aerials,' replies the DS, slightly out of breath with the effort of sawing through the bindings. He'd just acquired a colour television — the first on his street — and he and a friend from the Post Office had spent the previous weekend doing the cabling themselves.

One by one the bonds are severed. The diver stands, leaving the DS to cut the last cable. The DS takes a deep draught of clean air, anticipating having to hold his breath as soon as the body is revealed. Everyone leans in closer to watch as he peels away several layers of stiff, muddy, plastic. With one to go, the inspector steels himself. He's seen bodies that have been immersed in water for some weeks, and no amount of familiarity can make the sight prettier. The head of a woman is revealed but, to the onlookers' surprise, there is a further plastic bag, perhaps a shopping bag, over it. There is a smell, but far less than anyone expected.

The DS leans and gently wipes a thin layer of silt off the shopping bag. The clarity with which the woman's face appears startles everyone. Her eyes are open and it's as if she's looking at them through a window. She has shoulder-length curly hair and an oval face and so far as they can see, astonishingly, her skin is almost completely intact.

The DS leans a little closer trying to decide what's wrong with the woman's face. It may be the effect of the plastic bag, but despite the almost flawless skin, her features seem somehow blurred; the eyes melt gradually into the nose and it's not quite clear where the mouth begins and ends. She looks like a waxwork dummy that's been left too close to a radiator. Nonetheless the features suggest a Caucasian, despite the coffee-coloured skin. Could the skin colour have been produced by prolonged immersion? wonders Abercrombie.

The plastic sheet is pulled back further. Silt has gathered around her, in the gap between her arms and her torso, in the folds of her ears and in the mesh of the undamaged stockings on her legs, but she seems otherwise perfectly preserved. She wears a pink flowery dress with buttons from the neck to the hem which stops just below her knees. It's tight in the bodice, flared to just below the knee and cinched by a narrow leather belt. Her clothing is water-stained but the colours are still vivid. The silence from the onlookers is broken only by the keening of a bird nearby and the wind over the water.

'I've never seen anything like it,' whispers Abercrombie.

The DCI looks from her to the photograph in his hand and back again. 'Jesus Christ,' he says quietly. 'It's not her.'

'Can't be, sir,' says the DS, kneeling over the corpse. 'This one's been down there months, years probably. I know from the others we've brought up over the years; this silt takes ages to accumulate, especially through so many layers.'

'Then why the hell does she look like that?' asks one of the divers. 'Surely she'd have … deteriorated more?'

'I don't know,' replies the DS.

'Maybe because of the depth,' offers another diver. 'She was a long way down, more than thirty metres. It's at freezing point most of the year.'

'Well, this is all very interesting, gentlemen,' concludes the DCI, 'but we're still looking for a student with white skin and short blonde hair who's only been gone a few days, and we're no further forward. Get this one to the mortuary and see if we can find out who she is. You and your men,' he continues, pointing to the diver with a stubby forefinger, 'get a hot drink inside you, and then get back into the lake and keep looking. God knows how many more we're going to find.'

CHAPTER 2

Charles Holborne needs a big breakfast.

The previous night he stayed up until the small hours smoking and drinking whisky, staring at the silent, glistening city streets below him and ruminating about Sally; specifically about where she was sleeping. And with whom.

Months after their breakup and the sale of their house in Hampstead, he still thinks about her, most days and every night. The nights are the worst, alone in the tiny apartment on Fetter Lane.

So a plateful of bacon, eggs, mushrooms and toast are now absorbing the remnants of the alcohol, and Charles is starting to feel human.

Listening with half an ear to John Arlott commentating on the first few overs of the test match, he reads again the newspaper report of his beloved West Ham becoming only the second British club ever to win a European trophy. They defeated Munich 2 - 0 in the European Cup Winners Cup at Wembley the previous night, and Charles is still cross he missed it. But for the trial that he expected to continue throughout this week, he'd certainly have bought tickets.

He clears up and, a couple of hours later than usual, leaves the flat. He dodges the stationary traffic in the junction with Fleet Street and ducks under the stone arch into Sergeants Inn. It's barely 100 yards from his front door to the Temple, which, in normal circumstances, allows him to wake at seven o'clock, wash, eat a leisurely breakfast and still be at his desk in Chambers before eight.

Charles, now thirty-nine, is as broad as an ox, with enormously wide shoulders, great hams for arms and heavily-muscled legs, and there is a healing cut over his left eyebrow. He looks like a boxer, which is what he is — or was, until his last fight, a few months ago at the relatively late age of thirty-eight. He therefore looks slightly incongruous in a barrister's regulation pinstriped three-piece suit under a light raincoat and battered hat. Slung over his left shoulder, in a red cloth bag closed with a white cord drawstring, are his court robes, and in his right hand he carries a briefcase with the papers from the previous day's case.

The barred gate at the northern end of Kings Bench Walk is manned today by a young official in uniform, the polished buttons of his Inner Temple uniform gleaming in the weak sunshine.

'Good morning, Mr Holborne,' he says. 'Not seen you for a while.'

'Hello Jimmy,' replies Charles.

Charles has known the lad since he first started working in the Temple almost a decade before. He was then employed to direct parking and pick up litter, but despite his difficult start in life (Charles knows he was sent to Borstal for a string of domestic burglaries committed as a juvenile) his cheery disposition and willingness to work hard had seen him promoted gradually through the ranks of Temple employees. Now in his mid-twenties, he's being given greater responsibility.

Inn servants such as Jimmy are largely invisible to Charles's colleagues. Charles, on the other hand, feels more at ease with them than he does the majority of his public school, Oxbridge-educated peers. Most of the minor functionaries in the service of the Law, the employees of the Inn, the clerks and the court staff — in short the people essential to the smooth functioning of the administration of justice — know of Charles. They know that the curly-haired Charles Holborne, Barrister at Law, started life as Charlie Horowitz, boxer and, it was rumoured, criminal. His oldest friends and associates include the Krays and others on the wrong side of the law. He's a Jewish East End lad who had an outstanding war and "made good", and they have a sense of proprietorial pride in him; he's still one of them.

The feeling is mutual. Although Charles has tried to put the Krays and his law-breaking firmly behind him, he likes to pass the time of day with good honest East Enders who share his background and with whom he doesn't have to maintain the cultivated sophistication so carefully grafted onto his Cockney roots.

Charles steps down into the Temple, and as he does so a sudden squall of rain blowing off the Thames hits him square in the face. It carries the familiar aromas of his past life as a lighterman: sea salt and effluence. Taking care on the slippery cobbles, he runs underneath the tall plane trees, their newly-emerged leaves being given an unnecessary shower, and turns the corner into Crown Office Row.

A few seconds later he is bounding up the old staircase into Chambers, creating little puffs of wood dust where his heavy tread lands on every second stair.

This has been Charles's professional home for two years; since he was forced out of his previous chambers; since the murder of his wife; a wife who was, rather inconveniently, the daughter of the former head of those chambers.

He pushes open the door to the clerks' room to find it as frenetic as ever. Barbara, the senior clerk, Chambers' own Edinburgh headmistress, is conducting two calls at the same time, one phone in her hand and the other clamped to the other ear by a tweed shoulder. She looks up from the lesson in good manners being delivered to an unhelpful listing clerk and nods her welcome to Charles. Jennie and Jeremy, the symbiotic junior clerks known throughout the Temple compendiously as "JJ", hover by the door, each with an armful of briefs to be distributed around Chambers. The last member of staff, Clive — a spotty, insouciant Cockney teenager who fills the function of office junior — appears to be elsewhere.

Three barristers juggle for positions by the pigeon-holes, skimming the miscellaneous papers received on existing cases, but in fact more interested in discovering if there might be any buried fees cheques.

'Morning,' says one, a pot-bellied, almost spherical, junior barrister named Knight.

'Morning, Oliver,' replies Charles.

A tall man with his back to Charles turns swiftly. 'Ah, there you are, Holborne,' he says angrily, the use of Charles's surname signifying both formality and condescension.

'Yes, Murray,' replies Charles blandly, scanning his own post without looking up, but deliberately using the taller man's first name.

Murray Dennison, Queen's Counsel, has been a long-term thorn in Charles's side, particularly since Charles's practice took off. Dennison, jealous and ambitious in equal measure, and whose elevation to silk had yet to prove an unqualified success, takes Charles's recent professional ascendancy as a personal insult. His antipathy to Charles's working-class background, his religion, his success — in short, everything about him — had grown swiftly from arrogant antipathy to outright hatred. There's nothing more likely to make a man hate you than his being discovered trying to cause you harm, thinks Charles. It is only a few months since Charles uncovered, and survived, Dennison's plot to have him evicted from Chambers.

'I assume those … *people* in the waiting room are your clients?' says Dennison.

'Mine?' enquires Charles reasonably, in no mood for a fight. 'I'm not expecting any.'

'Well, they're your lot, and they're taking all the space. I've important clients arriving in half an hour.'

'My "lot"?' queries Charles, knowing exactly what Dennison means.

He slips out of the clerks' room and looks through the open door to the waiting room. Sitting silently and uncomfortably on the couch and two of the chairs are four bearded men in dark suits and white shirts, all wearing skull-caps. They are unmistakeably orthodox Jews. Charles smiles and nods before withdrawing and returning to the clerks' room.

'Not my case; not my clients,' he says shortly, making a final effort to avoid a confrontation.

'Aren't they Jews?' says the taller man, narrowing his eyes and jutting his grey lantern jaw at Charles aggressively.

'And because they're Jews, they must be my clients?' demands Charles, his temper slipping.

'It's not an unreasonable assumption.'

'Accordingly, I should assume that, because you defended those two homosexuals last week, you must also be a sodomist?' he replies with a dangerous smile. Charles knows this will provoke Dennison, a Catholic with traditional views on homosexuality.

'Now, now, sir,' intervenes Barbara, now off both telephone calls, 'let's not wind up Mr Dennison.'

Dennison approaches Charles threateningly, almost nose to nose. 'I've just about had enough of you, *barrow boy*.'

Charles tugs his forelock and deliberately exaggerates his native Cockney accent. 'Oh, guvnor, I'm ever so sorry if I forgot me place.'

That produces a suppressed snigger from Jeremy which serves only to increase Dennison's fury, but before the QC can answer, Charles has switched to a thick Yiddish accent. 'On the other hand, perhaps it's because I'm one of the Chosen People?'

Dennison points his bony forefinger at Charles, grasping for an appropriate retort but apparently unable at that instant to decide which prejudice to pursue. He splutters for a moment, changes his mind and strides out of the room. Charles follows him to the door and calls down the corridor after him. 'I'm so sorry *you* weren't chosen, Murray.'

Dennison spins on his heel. 'Why don't you people go back where you came from?'

'This *is* where I came from!' shouts Charles back. 'I can trace my English roots to 1492, Dennison. Can you?' Charles turns to Barbara with a triumphant smile but finds her face stony.

'You're your own worst enemy, Mr Holborne,' she says, shaking her head sadly.

'Yes,' replies Charles heavily. 'So I've been told.'

'What're you staring at?' Barbara says, turning on Jeremy, still by the door. 'Go on, scoot!' The young clerk scuttles out of the room. 'And in case it improves your mood, sir,' says Barbara to Charles sardonically, 'I've just put a nice cheque in your pigeon-hole.'

'Have you?'

'That case from Fletchers, the two-handed rape at Aylesbury.'

'Oh yes.'

'They've cut you down, but not by much. Have a look at the breakdown and let me know if you want to appeal.'

Charles picks up the cheque and the other papers waiting for him and makes to leave the room.

'Oh, by the way, sir,' adds Barbara, 'Clive took a call for you from a Mr Jones.'

'Yes?'

'Mr Jones was rather mysterious. He announced that he was new to the Met police prosecuting service and asked if you'd passed the Scotland Yard Test.'

'And you told him that I had?' Charles asks.

The "Scotland Yard Test" is essentially a list of barristers deemed fit to prosecute cases on behalf of the Metropolitan Police. Charles has now been instructed in several high-profile murder trials for the Crown, so it's surprising the caller was unaware that he's considered acceptable counsel.

'Of course. I asked him if he had instructions for you but he seemed evasive; said he was very anxious to speak to you. Immediately. When I said you weren't in yet, he refused to leave a number and said he'd call back at noon. He asked particularly that you'd be available to take his call.'

'If he's employed by the Met prosecuting service, why on earth didn't he ask one of his colleagues if I was on the list?'

'That's what I thought. I did wonder if it wasn't some sort of practical joke. And…'

'And?'

'Well, he sounded strange.'

'Strange?'

Barbara shrugs and her smile has a trace of embarrassment. 'He sounded like Bugs Bunny!'

Charles laughs. 'Are you sure the call didn't come from inside Chambers? This sounds like one of the junior barristers pulling your leg.'

Barbara pauses, thinking. 'You know, I never thought of that. Maybe that's all it was. No doubt we'll find out soon.'

Charles climbs the stairs to the first floor where his room is situated. It is empty. Peter Bateman, his former pupil, is at court, and the third occupant of the room, a recent addition, is also absent. Charles has yet to meet her, but she represents the welcome face of change: Roberta Gough is a pupil barrister, the first woman pupil to be taken on by the set of barristers in its 150-year history.

Charles makes himself a cup of tea in the area laughingly referred to as the "upstairs kitchen" — a converted cupboard — and takes it to his desk.

His room isn't large, but it's well-lit and comfortable, housing three battered leather armchairs and a small coffee table as well as two leather-inlaid desks loaded with briefs and Miss Gough's small, and still empty, desk tucked into a corner behind the door. What makes the room special to Charles is its view over the manicured lawns of the Inner Temple and thence across the Embankment to the River Thames. On more than one occasion Charles has returned from court to find a temporarily unemployed member of Chambers relaxing in one of the chairs, feet up on Charles's desk, idly surveying the river traffic and the lawyers strolling the gardens.

Charles begins by opening his post. At noon precisely, the telephone rings.

'Mr Jones for you, sir,' says Barbara, and Charles, who knows his senior clerk very well, detects suppressed mirth in her voice.

'Charles Holborne?' asks a clear high-pitched voice.

'Yes,' replies Charles. 'How can I help you?'

'Are you available this afternoon, Mr Holborne?'

Charles smiles in recognition of Barbara's characterisation of the voice. It's not Bugs Bunny, but it is unusually high-pitched and, oddly for a solicitor practising in the Metropolis, Charles detects a definite North American accent.

'Available for what?'

'A conference in a criminal matter.'

'For the prosecution, I assume.'

'That is correct.'

'Certainly. What's the name of the case?'

'I am sorry, but I can't tell you that at present,' replies the solicitor officiously.

'Oh,' says Charles. 'Why on earth not?'

'You'll understand when we meet. Just call it "In the Matter of a Possible Prosecution".'

'Very well,' replies Charles, curbing his curiosity. 'When can you let me see the papers?'

'I won't be sending you any case papers. You'll be instructed by myself and two police officers.' Then Jones's formality slips slightly. 'Sorry about the mystery, Mr Holborne, but you'll understand when we speak in person. I assure you, this is no joke.'

'Very well,' repeats Charles. 'What time would be convenient to you?'

'Your clerk said two o'clock.'

'Fine. I'll see you then.'

'Good. One last thing: the matter is to be mentioned to no one at all. Both you and your senior clerk will be asked to sign the Official Secrets Act before anything of substance is discussed. Goodbye.'

Charles almost laughs as he hangs up. He wonders again if the entire conversation is a hoax. He's never heard of a barrister being required to sign the Official Secrets Act before being instructed in a case. The whole idea is bizarre. He looks forward to the meeting, if it occurs at all, with interest.

CHAPTER 3

At ten minutes past two, Barbara shows three men into Charles's room. Unusually, Barbara remains, closing the door behind her. A diminutive man holds out his hand.

'Good afternoon, Mr Holborne,' he says. Charles recognises the clear piping voice from the telephone. 'My name's Jones. This is Superintendent Brown and this, Detective Inspector Smith.'

Charles shakes hands with the two policemen in turn.

'Jones, Smith and Brown?' asks Charles with a smile. One of the two police officers, the younger one named "Smith" grins at him. The older one, "Brown", makes no eye contact.

'At my request,' replies Jones. 'This matter is extremely delicate, as you will hear.'

'I assume you mean that it must involve someone who is very prominent,' says Charles.

Jones studies him carefully. 'That is correct.'

'And that means I can't know your real names?'

'For the present, it does.'

Charles shrugs, unable to suppress a smile. 'Well, take a seat, gentlemen. Can we get you some tea?'

Smith opens his mouth to accept the offer, but without looking at the policemen Jones vetoes the suggestion. 'No, thank you. We shan't be here long.'

The policemen sit. Jones remains standing, digging into his briefcase. 'I have asked Mrs McIntyre to come in for a moment so we can deal with the formalities.'

He hands a slip of paper to each of Charles and Barbara. They are identical and are headed *The Official Secrets Act*. Charles skims his as Jones explains.

'In short, anything learned while this case is discussed will be covered by the Act. To reveal it to anyone — anyone at all — will constitute a breach of section two and will result in prosecution. I shall be obliged, Mrs McIntyre, if you would ensure that you and you alone deal with this case in the clerk's room. Will that pose a problem?'

Barbara and Charles exchange a glance, but she shakes her head. 'I don't see why it should.'

'Fine. Are you both prepared to sign?'

Charles nods to Barbara and they both sign their declarations and return them to the diminutive solicitor. He replaces them in his briefcase.

'Thank you, Mrs McIntyre,' says Jones, dismissing her. Barbara waits until Charles nods again at her, and departs. The men hear the "Engaged" sign being slid open on the outside of the door. Charles cannot resist the impulse to open the door again, stick his head out into the corridor and look up and down furtively for eavesdroppers. He closes the door again and turns to the men awaiting him.

'Just checking,' he says with a completely straight face. The two police officers stare at him in astonishment until Charles winks. Jones, busy unpacking his suitcase, misses the entire performance. Smith supresses a smile; Brown is stony-faced. Charles takes his seat behind the desk.

'I know that it's the Act which binds us, not a signature,' says Jones, 'but it does focus everyone's mind on the paramount need for confidentiality.'

'Of course,' replies Charles with great seriousness.

Jones finally sits and addresses Charles. 'Three weeks ago, in Wastwater in the Lake District, the police found a body. They were looking for the French student who went missing —'

'I read about that,' confirms Charles. '"*The Mystery of the Waxwork Corpse*",' he says with relish, reciting the newspaper headlines.

'That's right. Wastwater's the deepest lake in England. Under normal circumstances, a body dropped into it would never be found. In this case, by pure chance, it landed on a rocky outcrop known as Tiffen's Rock which sticks up like a finger from the bottom of the lake. It's invisible unless you're thirty metres down. Furthermore, the body came to rest on a small ledge on the Rock — just high enough so it wasn't completely covered in silt, and just deep enough that the temperature was within a degree or so of freezing year-round. As a result, she was almost perfectly preserved. Hence the "waxwork" tag in the newspapers.' The solicitor shakes his head sadly. 'I still find it incredible what your papers are allowed to write,' he says.

'Do I guess from your accent that you're American?' asks Charles.

'No,' replies Jones, bridling slightly. 'Canadian. But I was born here and have a British passport. Anyway, back to the matter at hand. It was a chance in a million that the body was ever discovered.'

'So it sounds. Someone was very unlucky,' says Charles ironically, referring to the supposed murderer. Jones misunderstands him.

'Yes, terribly sad to end one's days in such a fashion.'

Charles groans inwardly. Mr Jones evidently takes himself and his professional duties very seriously; he's not going to be much fun to work with. Charles takes a deep breath and asks another question. 'What do we know?'

Jones hands Charles a document. It's a draft statement. 'Read that.'

Charles pulls a clean sheet of paper before him, places his fountain pen on the desk next to it, and sits back to read.

Draft deposition of Dr Marcus Butcher
Occupation: *Home Office Pathologist*

Magistrates' Court Rules 1952: *This deposition of Marcus Butcher, approved Home Office Pathologist, of West Cumberland Hospital, was sworn before me, Maj. Percival Fitzherbert, Justice of the Peace, on [   ] at [   ] Magistrates' Court.*
Signed: *Maj. Percival Fitzherbert*
Signature of deponent: *M. Butcher*

Marcus Butcher WILL SAY AS FOLLOWS:
I am Dr Marcus Butcher, and I am on the Home Office List of approved forensic pathologists covering Cumberland and Westmorland.

On 30 April 1965 I was asked by Det. Superintendent Wake of the Cumberland, Westmorland and Carlisle Constabulary to conduct a post-mortem examination on the body of a young woman identified by Tag No. 64/CW396 bearing the name "Jane Doe". The examination was carried out at the new pathology wing of the West Cumberland Hospital. The body was that of a well-developed, well-nourished and quite unusually tall woman of about 35 years, weight 10 stones 7 lb, height 5'10".

The body was completely encased in thick plastic sheeting tied with diverse pieces of cable and rope. The head was additionally in a clear plastic bag, possibly a shopping bag. Plastic shopping bags were introduced to the UK market in the early 1950s, which suggests an earliest possible time for the deceased to have been placed into the water.

Examination of the body revealed a female, age approximately 35 years. Her features were Caucasian although her skin colour was light

Negroid, typical of South American countries. The skin colour and hair texture together suggested possible Amerindian ancestry. The body was wrapped in two separate sections of plastic sacking material. There were initials or words embossed into the plastic, namely, "Dillons Shipbuilders". There was then a hole, but the writing continued "YM 245…" which may be a manufacturer's code.

The head, still attached to the torso, was in what remained of a separate clear plastic bag with a name in blue on it saying "Barkhurst", possibly "Bathurst", or even "Barthurst" and then "Green Village Store."

The body was fully-clothed in a pink dress with darker pink flowers. The dress was fastened. Although two of the buttons were missing, there was no sign of damage to the material. The two missing buttons were not contiguous, which one might expect if force had been applied to the front of the garment, and in my opinion the cotton fastening the buttons to the dress had simply deteriorated.

The deceased wore stockings and suspenders, both of which were intact. Their style suggested the late forties or early fifties.

The deceased's knees were bent up to the abdomen, her right arm angled across her chest with the hand near the left side of the chin, and the left arm straight with the hand near the left calf. There was a hole in the plastic and the right foot was partially missing. The structures of the remaining ankle were merely powder and paste, which suggested not that the foot had been cut off but that it had deteriorated over time where the water had penetrated the plastic at that point.

The body was tied in a complicated manner around the ankles, legs, trunk and neck with the following material. One, television aerial wire, two, black electrical wire, three, bluish rope, four, white rope with black thread in it, five, white clothes cord type of rope.

The deceased's full list of clothing is as follows: pink flowered dress with white cuffs, disintegrating. Underclothes: black suspenders and stockings. No underpants and no brassiere. No damage was found to any of the clothing. In particular although the stockings were clogged with silt, they were completely undamaged and still fastened by their clips to the suspenders.'

Charles reaches for his pen and makes a few notes.

'It's very difficult to get the underpants off a woman who is resisting without damaging her stockings,' he says in answer to Jones's enquiring glance. 'The weight of the body makes it difficult to lift the hips clear of the ground. And the suspender belt clips were still attached to the stockings. All of which suggests that she was not the victim of a struggle to remove her underwear.'

He continues reading.

The corpse had been preserved by the development of a condition known as adipocere, in which the fat of the body is changed to a waxy substance due to prolonged immersion in cold water. The external features were all fixed and to a certain extent preserved by this process, although the skin surface was dirty, and brown/black patches had developed on the neck and upper chest due to putrefaction. The skin in those places was disintegrating. The body itself was hard to the touch, but was very friable and disintegrated completely on movement.

I found faint black discolouration around the nose and mouth. The hair is shoulder-length, dark and very curly. I removed the jaws, which were washed. The flesh fell off with the pressure of the tap water, leaving two clean jaw bones in which the teeth stood out clearly. There was an upper partial denture present, bearing two upper right incisors and two left molars. The left central incisor is crowned. Several teeth had been filled and some removed, none recently before death. Twenty-four teeth remained. The workmanship was of a very high standard, suggesting private orthodontic treatment.

I could find no external injuries. In particular there was no evidence of bruising on the upper thighs or around the genitalia.

The brain had retained its form but disintegrated upon touch. It was greenish in colour and extremely soft. No sign of cerebral haemorrhage, two halves equal in size.

There was a distinct area of brown discolouration about half an inch in diameter in the tissues of the left side of the neck over the hyoid bone, which might have been a bruise. There were no fractures to any bones. In particular there was no sign of fracture of the hyoid bone or of the larynx which might have suggested strangulation.

There was a large quantity of fluid in each side of the chest around the lungs. The lungs were soft, greyish in colour and degenerated due to putrefaction.

There were no obvious internal or external injuries.

There were no signs of drugs having been taken but a full laboratory analysis is awaited.

'So,' says Charles, looking up. 'No clear cause of death.'

'It's a preliminary report, but that's right. Dr Butcher was not able to identify any obvious cause of death.'

'So why am I signing the Official Secrets Act over an unidentified female corpse without a clear cause of death?'

'The code on the plastic mentioned by the pathologist. We've been able to trace it to a manufacturer of boats and boating equipment in Kent, long since out of business. We've checked the records of missing persons in Kent for a span of ten to twenty years, and have come up with an alarming possibility. The deceased matches the description of the wife of an eminent judge of the Court of Appeal. The judge reported his wife missing in 1953. It was presumed at the time that she went off with a lover.'

Charles interrupts, addressing himself to the police officers. 'Any evidence there *was* a lover?'

Jones leafs through his papers for the details, but it is DI Smith who answers. 'Yes, sir. Certainly one, and possibly more. Whether the others were current at that time we are still investigating.'

Smith has a soft Geordie accent. He's a good-looking man, Charles notes, with a warmth in his wide eyes and a ready smile that Charles thinks many women would find attractive.

Jones continues, 'You will appreciate that there are two principal suspects at the moment: the lover and the judge. Preliminary investigations suggest that the lover has an alibi for the days immediately before the deceased went missing.'

'Are we talking about any old Court of Appeal judge, or a special one?' asks Charles. There's a long silence. 'I see,' says Charles.

'It is critical that the name of the suspect is not revealed.'

'At all? Are you suggesting that if there's evidence, the Crown won't prosecute?'

'Absolutely not!' protests Jones, his shrill voice rising half an octave further in outrage. 'If the evidence is there, we will certainly prosecute. The point is that until we're sure the evidence exists, and that a prosecution stands the necessary chance of success, the name of the suspect must remain confidential. Otherwise, incalculable harm could be done to the administration of justice. For that reason, all the witness statements you'll see will have the names and addresses of the witnesses removed. It's likely however that the identity of the suspect will become known to you.'

'If it hasn't already,' replies Charles dryly. 'Why are you coming to me?'

'It's not unheard of for counsel to be involved, to assist in directing enquiries, even at this early stage. Look upon it as preliminary advice on evidence. We'll be asking you to suggest avenues of enquiry but, more importantly, to consider the evidence and ensure it's as firm and conclusive, one way or the other, as possible. We can't afford to make any mistakes.'

'No, you misunderstand my question. I mean, why me as against any other barrister? My reputation's been built defence work, certainly until recently. I'm not in silk, and I'm hardly an establishment figure.'

'There's your answer. It *can't* be an establishment figure. There can be no suggestion of sweeping this under the carpet. We want an entirely independent and thorough investigation. If it turns out our suspicions are unfounded or there's insufficient evidence, we'll all be very relieved. On the other hand, if there *is* the evidence, we will certainly go to trial. Members of my department also felt that to go to one of the recognised prosecution sets would risk a breach of security. The suspect was of course a barrister for years before going to the bench, so many of the senior silks know him personally. I took my colleagues' advice. I'm new to the team and didn't know the personalities involved. In fact, that's why this file landed on *my* desk.'

Charles nods. 'OK. What do you want from me today?'

'Well, let's assume that this *is* the judge's wife. Dental checks are due in any day. What we need however is evidence proving — or disproving — the judge's involvement. At the same time, we have to proceed with caution.'

'If this were an ordinary suspect,' intervenes Smith, 'we'd simply arrest him and squeeze. We can't do that here, so we need to approach the case with rather more...'

'Finesse?' suggests Charles.

'Precisely, sir. Furthermore, we don't want to alert him yet to the investigation.'

'Does the judge have any connection with the Lake District?'

'None we've established yet,' answers Jones.

'So it's possible that this isn't murder, merely concealment of a death.'

The Detective Superintendent makes a scornful scoffing noise. He's a large man in his early fifties with an impassive face, wobbling jowls, deep grooves beside his nose, and small deep-set darting eyes.

'Possible, but unlikely,' says Jones. 'Someone went to an awful lot of trouble just to avoid an inquest.'

'Is he or was he a sailor? Member of a sailing club? Did he live near the coast?' Charles sees Jones frowning. 'Well, how do you get a body to the centre of Wastwater? He must have used a boat, right? Not easy to do without being seen. I guess the place is usually swarming with tourists, climbers and divers. So it was probably done at night — more difficult still. That suggests some skill with a boat.'

'Of course,' answers the Superintendent with obvious irritation, still not making eye contact with Charles. 'D'you think we've not thought of that?'

'And I suppose you've already contacted the manufacturer of the plastic to see if the judge ever bought anything from them?'

'Yes,' replies Smith. 'But the company went bust years ago; very few documents still in existence. The ex-M.D. is looking though.'

The Superintendent tuts audibly and looks none too surreptitiously at his watch.

Charles smiles, studying the bloodhound without rancour. *I'll bet you didn't want to be dragged all the way down from the Lake District to see some flash London barrister, did you?* he thinks. *You're being kept away from your investigation. And, to be honest, I can't blame you.* Charles steeples his fingers, closes his eyes for a moment, and starts thinking seriously. *Time to earn your corn, Charlie.*

'He didn't live particularly near the coast,' adds Smith in a less aggressive tone, 'but we could certainly look into boat clubs. Maybe there were lakes or rivers near where he lived.'

Charles can't decide if the suggestion follows from his questions or if Smith is just being diplomatic to dampen the tension in the room.

'Have you searched his home?' asks Charles.

Smith shakes his head. 'He moved to his present home some years after she disappeared.'

'I meant the one he shared with the missing woman,' clarifies Charles. 'Most domestic murders occur in the home, don't they?'

'What would we be looking for, so many years after the event?' asks Jones.

'Bloodstains might be nice,' replies Charles, 'but that's rather hopeful.'

'But the new owners would have reported anything suspicious,' insists Jones. 'Especially bloodstains. And he didn't move for some years after the wife went missing, so there would've been lots of visitors to the house in the interim.'

'Yes, that's right,' says Charles quietly, thinking to himself. 'But the variety in the ropes and cables used to truss up the body suggests it wasn't planned. If it *had* been planned, he'd have got himself prepared, rather than rely on whatever he could find lying about. Where do people keep odds and ends of rope and cable? In the garage or garden shed. But when my parents moved to their present home, they found all sorts of odds and ends up in the loft, especially in the dark corners where it's easy for the people moving out to miss something.'

For the first time the Superintendent looks directly at Charles.

'And you tell me that the rope and cord included a length of coaxial?' continues Charles.

'Yes,' answers the Superintendent.

'That's the stuff used to connect televisions to their aerials, isn't it? Well, if he used an off-cut when wrapping up the body, perhaps there's a larger quantity of matching cable still there. It might even still be running from the roof down to the TV. And back then, it was much rarer than it is now. So easier to make a match.'

The inspector looks across at his superior and smiles. He takes out a notebook and makes some notes. 'Good idea,' he says quietly.

Charles senses that this last contribution is an avenue not thought of by the visitors. *What else can I add?* he wonders. He's never been involved at the ground floor of an investigation before; he's starting to enjoy himself. 'What do we know about their relationship? The judge and his wife.'

'Not much,' says Jones. 'More or less what's in *Who's Who.*'

'We should remedy that. If a man in public life is going to risk all to murder his wife, he must have good reasons. Maybe he did it for money — a bit unlikely, I concede —'

'Very unlikely in this case,' intervenes Smith. 'If the ID holds up, she was black and from a very poor family in Martinique, most of whom are now dead. Her maiden name was Lise Bonseigneur.'

Charles's eyebrows rise in surprise and he pauses for a moment, picturing the Court of Appeal judges one after another, wondering which of them might have once been married to a poor black woman. Even now, in the mid-sixties, that would be extremely unusual; back in the forties it must've been positively scandalous. Charles half-smiles with respect for the unknown judge; whatever he may have done, he was obviously no racist, and to Charles — the daily butt of racist and religious prejudice — that's a mark in his favour.

'Well,' continues Charles, 'if not for money, then, perhaps, for love? Or maybe he hated her. Whatever; we need to establish a motive. For example, did he know about the lovers? We need to interview the neighbours, servants, gardeners, window cleaners — anyone who saw them in their ordinary lives. I don't suppose we can interview his colleagues if we're being all cloak and dagger, but what about hers? If she was working, someone will surely be able to say something about her relationship with her husband.'

There's another pause while the inspector's pen scratches away.

'How's that for starters?' asks Charles.

Jones looks to the two policemen. DI Smith smiles with approval; the Detective Superintendent nods reluctantly and his thick lips twitch into what might, possibly, have been the muscle-memory of a smile.

'Thank you, Mr Holborne,' concludes Jones, shutting his briefcase. 'That's given us some fresh ideas. I shall be in touch by telephone in the next couple of days. Then we may need to meet again.'

Charles shakes hands with the three men again and shows them out. *Money for old rope*, he thinks to himself.

CHAPTER 4

Charles clears a space on his desk and drops the new bundle of papers, tied with white ribbon, with a thump. In centuries past, briefs would arrive in ribbon of one of many colours — green, blue, pink, white — a different colour for each field of law. Now there were only three. Charles's top desk drawer is stuffed with a tangled spaghetti of pink ribbon, testament to the building of his reputation as a defence "brief" over the last fifteen years. Recently, however, he has begun to move into a much more establishment practice, prosecuting a selection of high-profile murderers, rapists and armed robbers for the Crown, and it is no longer a surprise to receive briefs tied in white ribbon. This one is headed, as promised, *In the Matter of a Possible Prosecution* and the actual Instructions are short and to the point.

Counsel is aware of the facts of this matter having advised in conference. Statements taken from the witnesses suggested by Counsel will be found herewith. When Counsel has had the opportunity to read and digest the same, would he please telephone Mr Jones to discuss?

Charles smiles to himself. The brevity of the Instructions and the careful avoidance of any names of witnesses is scarcely warranted. Charles takes out a new pad, sharpens his pencil, opens the bundle of witness statements and settles down to read. At the top of each statement is a section normally completed with the witness's name, address and date of birth. Unusually, however, the witnesses are shown here as "Witness A", "Witness B" and so on, and where their signatures should have been inserted, there are the typed words "Signature verified". Charles flicks ahead. The last one is headed "Witness T". He returns to Witness A.

I used to live at [   ] with my wife and three children. Quite shortly after we moved in, a family by the name of [   ] moved into the house which adjoined the end of our garden. They had one child at that time, a son. He was the same age as our oldest, and so we came to know them quite well. As I worked away a lot, I saw less of the family than my wife did, but Mr [   ] seemed to be a quiet pleasant man, devoted to his son. I knew he was a barrister and was away on cases quite a bit. My recollection of Mrs [   ] was that she was always rather loud and excitable. My work meant that I was sometimes at home in the afternoons, and I would often see her arrive at her house in a red sports car with a man who looked younger than she. These visits were always when Mr [   ] was out. They would go up to the bedroom for several hours. I was able to see this because all the bedrooms of their house overlooked the gardens and I would see her draw the curtains. Not long after they moved into the house, Mrs [   ] started bringing their son round to us in the evenings for us to babysit for her. She used to say that her husband was away and that she had to go out. We were at first happy to do it, but it became such a frequent occurrence (three or four nights a week) that once I made the comment that she should bring his birth certificate round too and I would adopt him.

This situation continued until shortly before she gave birth to their second child, a girl. I must say that I didn't think it was right from the boy's point of view, and I was very alarmed once when I learned that she had taken the child with a friend only a year or so older for a camping holiday and had returned, leaving them both in a tent on their own overnight. In fact, Mr [   ] returned from a case the next day and went to fetch the boys back. This showed me that she had no sense of responsibility, and I clearly remember on a number of occasions her saying that she hadn't wanted the children, and that they were a hindrance.

After their daughter was born, the family had a succession of nannies and housekeepers to look after the children. None but the last stayed very long, and my wife and I used to joke about whether there was any job in the world we would like less than being an employee of Mrs [   ]. My wife used to say that Mrs [   ] was a man's woman and that she did not like or get on with other women. In the years during which we were neighbours, we and they held numerous parties to which the other family would be invited. Mrs [   ] would always like to be the centre of attention, and if other women were about, especially those she did not know, it was like a challenge to her. She would play up to their husbands and flirt with them. Sometimes she went too far and there would be a row. After a while, my wife and I decided not to invite them to our parties anymore, although we did stay on talking terms. I was then posted abroad and we moved away.

Charles makes some notes, marks two or three passages in the statement, and turns to Witness B.

I used to be employed as a housekeeper to Mr [   ] and his wife. At that time, they had two children, a boy and a girl aged 5 and 1. I worked for the family for six months. I left because I was unable to get on with Mrs [   ]. She was a very difficult person to work for. She used to have temper tantrums for no reason at all and would throw things around the room and scream at me. I did not think that that was a proper way to treat staff. There was one occasion when she complained that a cake I had baked had too little fruit in it, and she threw it at me and wrecked the kitchen. It was not long after that incident that I gave my notice. I only stayed on as long as I did because I liked Mr [   ] and the children. I felt particularly sorry for the little boy, as the wife seemed to hate him and used to treat him terribly. I never saw her hit him, but she was very sarcastic and hurtful to him and blamed him for everything that happened in the house, even when it was nothing to do with him. It was a real shock to see a mother treat one of her children in that manner. On more than one occasion I saw her hit her husband. He never retaliated at all. He used to hold her by the wrists until she calmed down, which she would do after a while. Then she would apologise, and kiss and hug everyone, even me, and she would be all right until the next time.

In the six months that I worked at the house, I know that Mrs [   ] had affairs with at least two men. She was completely shameless about them. One of the men worked at a local pub and I knew him by sight. I came home from shopping one afternoon and found this man in the bath. Mrs [   ] walked up to me in her underwear, as bold as you like, and announced she had a guest. Then she closed the bathroom door and I went to collect the boy from nursery school. I never met the other man, but he used to telephone asking for Mrs [   ]. He had an Irish accent.

Witness C:

My name and address are as above, and I live there with my husband. When we moved in, about ten years ago, there was a family called [   ] living opposite us at number [   ]. They had only been there for a year or so, having moved from somewhere closer to London. They had three children, two boys and a girl. The youngest was a baby, only a few weeks old. I did not know the husband very well, but I knew the wife. She made our lives a misery for two years, and we were very pleased when she ran off. In the months before she left she was frequently drunk, and the noise of her screaming and shouting and throwing things around her house could be heard throughout the street. She and her behaviour were the subject of gossip in the village. She had a succession of boyfriends, but with one she always seemed to be in trouble of one sort or another. She claimed that he beat her up, although I never saw any signs of it on her. She was always saying things to make herself the centre of attention, and so I was unsure whether to believe her or not. I said to her once that if any man hit me, I'd stop seeing him and tell the police, but she laughed and said that she loved him and that I wouldn't understand. Matters came to a head when she had a fight with this man in the street outside our house. Someone did call the police. She assumed it was my husband and me, which it was not, and from then on she conducted a feud against us. On one occasion a brick came through our living room window, and on another she let down the tyres on our car.

I have been asked about the character of the husband. I felt sorry for him. He was a quiet type, and he seemed terribly embarrassed by his wife's behaviour. My husband and I used to wonder why he didn't leave her. Then she disappeared. It was rumoured in the village that she'd gone off with a boyfriend, not the one who was supposedly violent to her, but another local man. I don't know his name, but I knew his wife to say "hello" to from church. When she finally left, the street returned to normal. The husband stayed at home more, and the children seemed much happier. The older boy who had been at boarding school came home, and I used to see him cycling to the village school. After about a year the family moved to [   ], a nearby village. We stayed in touch with them and were invited to the party given by the husband when he became a QC, and you could see how happy the family was by then.

Witness D:

I am the person named above, and I live at the above address. About fifteen years ago, I retired from full-time employment. However, I soon found that I was bored, and I thought about doing some part-time work. I saw an advert in a local shop for a part-time assistant in an antiques business, in which I had many years' experience. The advert wanted someone available two days a week to work in a small shop owned by Mrs [   ]. The job was very convenient and so I applied and was appointed. My understanding was that the shop had been purchased for Mrs [   ] by her husband, but he took no part in running it.

After I'd started I mentioned the job to my brother, who was a retired county court judge and he said knew of Mr [   ]. My brother warned me that Mrs [   ] was a difficult woman and that she had been a thorn in Mr [   ]'s side, even to the point that she was holding back his career. It was rumoured in the village that before the family moved into the area, Mrs [   ] had been having an affair. In fact, people used to say that the youngest child was not the husband's and, after I got to know her a bit, Mrs [   ] actually confided to me that she had indeed been having an affair and wasn't sure who the child's father was. She said that the move away from their previous area had been her husband's idea so as to make a fresh start.

I soon realised that Mrs [   ] was not in the least interested in the business. When she took me on, she told me that the job would be temporary as she expected the shop to fail. I thought at the time that she was joking, but after a few weeks it became apparent that she was quite serious, as she made no effort to run the shop, and on the days I didn't work, it remained closed.

After a while, however, I began to make the occasional good sale and Mrs [   ] allowed me to do some purchasing on her behalf. At that stage, she began to show an interest in the business, but only to the extent that she would spend everything we made. On more than one occasion, she ran into the shop in high spirits and raided the till, once leaving me with no money in it at all. After a while I discovered she was conducting an affair. She even gave her lover a job in the shop for a short while and it was apparent that he knew nothing about antiques or running a shop. He would sit about all day talking on the telephone until Mrs [   ] came in and then they would disappear, ostensibly for lunch, but more often than not for the rest of the day.

I met Mr [   ] on several occasions as he would frequently come to the shop to look for his wife. When, as was more normal, she was not there, he would stop for a cup of coffee and discuss how the business was running. I found him to be a quiet, polite man, who seemed resigned to his *wife's attitude. I only heard Mr [   ] and Mrs [   ] argue on one occasion, and that was when Mr [   ] arrived unexpectedly to find his wife and her friend in the small room at the back of the shop. I heard things being thrown around the room and I thought a fight was going on, so I looked in to see if the police should be called. The boyfriend had gone and the rear door was still open. Mrs [   ] had thrown all the things that had been on my desk at her husband. He was surrounded by broken pieces of clock, stationery, correspondence and other odds and ends. He was holding his nose, which was bleeding profusely. When she saw me, Mrs [ ] walked past him to the door and left, but not without hitting him on the side of the head first. He did not respond or retaliate in any way.*

 I found the entire scene astonishing. Mr [   ] was very apologetic and said that his wife was excitable, and asked me not to hold it against her. He begged me to stay on, but I wasn't prepared to work for a woman like her, and I told him so. I helped him staunch the bleeding, and then I left. I did not go back.

Charles laughs. 'I wonder why not?' he asks himself out loud.

Witness E:

My name and address are as above. I am the Headmaster of [   ] School, a private boarding school for boys from age 7 to 18 years. Until 1960 I was Housemaster of Churchill House, one of the schoolhouses, and in that capacity I knew [   ], the elder son of Mr and Mrs [ ]. He was with the school for two years. I fear that he did not have a happy time with us. I gathered that there were problems at home, and although Mr [   ] was reluctant to send him, Mrs [   ] was very keen. The boy showed definite signs of emotional problems and was referred to the educational psychologist. He suffered from a stammer which was markedly worse towards the beginning of term, and which I took to be related to whatever had transpired at home during the vacations. He was clearly an intelligent child, with a particular gift in art and music and

60

some ability on the playing field, but he was never able to reach his potential. He only returned here for one term after the separation of his parents, but by the end of that term he was a different child. His stammer had almost disappeared, and his academic results in every subject had improved beyond recognition. He had also begun to take part in more of the school's social activities. I was sorry in the circumstances that his father decided to remove him from the school at that stage.

Charles reads on for another hour, but the story is always the same, from neighbours, business associates, parents of the children's friends, even her own G.P: this woman was an absolute cow. Charles knows, from bitter personal experience, how a festering, unhappy marriage breeds hatred, and how irrationally and despicably otherwise perfectly well-balanced people behave. This woman however seemed to have had a propensity for being indiscriminately unpleasant to everyone.

Two things seem clear to Charles: firstly, he is sure that the more the prosecution digs into the evidence, the more potential murder suspects they'll find; the woman could make enemies as easily as he makes sandwiches. Secondly, and more importantly from Charles's point of view, if her husband didn't kill her, he was a saint.

Charles now turns to a second bundle of papers. These are the statements of the police officers who found the body, the experts already instructed and, finally, the pathologist's final deposition. The last he reads very carefully, making notes in the margins and on his notebook, but it is almost word for word the same as the draft he was shown in conference and tells him nothing new.

An hour later he gets up and makes himself a cup of coffee, which he takes back to his desk. Then, as requested, he telephones Mr Jones.

'Good morning,' says Jones as Charles is put through. 'Have you read the statements?'

'I have,' replies Charles.

'They make interesting reading, don't they? Let me bring you up to date on the fresh evidence. There are further statements on their way to you by courier, but I'd like your immediate opinion.'

'Fine. Fire away.'

'We have two important developments. Firstly, we've tracked down the last boyfriend. He's moved to Manchester. He says that they spent two days together immediately before the deceased disappeared, in some cottage in the West Country. They drove home and arranged to meet that evening. He claims that he was going to tell her it was all over, and that he had actually done it several times before but she'd always persuaded him to give it one more go. These two days were a sort of farewell, although he was a bit vague as to whether she was aware of it. He says she had a great ability to ignore what she didn't want to know. You're not going to believe this, but the boyfriend's wife knew all about the affair! Had done for ages. She even knew about this last holiday together.'

Jones seems astonished by these revelations, and his cartoon voice reaches an even higher pitch than usual.

'Ever been married?' asks Charles.

'Er … well, no. Why?'

Charles, who has discovered that marriage does not always deliver the advertised bliss, finds the facts rather less surprising. 'Just wondered.'

'Anyway,' continues Jones, 'the best is yet to come. He says, and his wife confirms, that that evening they *both* went to the place where he was to meet the deceased to break it off. The wife went to make sure he didn't lose his nerve. He'd tried ending the relationship more than once before. Apparently, the deceased was able *"to wind him round her little finger"* — the wife's words; you'll be getting a statement from her too. Well, the deceased never showed. They waited several hours and went home. He expected a call from her over the next few days, but heard nothing. He eventually concluded she'd thrown him over, done him a favour he said, so he never called her. He has a pretty good alibi for the rest of the week too, as they had family arriving from South Africa, and they all went off to the Continent for five days.'

Charles says nothing for a while as he continues to make notes. 'Were you present at the interviews?' he asks finally.

'Part of them, yes.'

'What did you make of the couple?'

'I thought he was telling the truth. He's a professional man, slick and handsome, but I get the impression the deceased dominated him, and he liked it. He was in thrall to her … sexually … you know? The wife was more difficult to judge. I can't really understand why she put up with it for so long, but I don't for a moment think she's an accomplice to murder. Very earnest. Pillar of the local church.'

'Prima facie evidence of guilt, in my book.'

'You're not serious, are you?'

Charles sighs silently. 'No.'

'Good. Anyway, we're still checking the alibi for the following days, but I've seen dated photographs with them standing under the Eiffel Tower, so I expect it'll all check out.'

'Very well,' concludes Charles. 'For the moment, let's assume they're in the clear. What's the second piece of evidence?'

'Before I go into that, one last point about the boyfriend. He remembers some of the clothes the deceased was wearing when he last saw her.' Charles hears Jones leafing through some papers. 'Yes, here it is: *"...a pink dress with darker pink flowers, white collar and cuffs, black suspenders and stockings"*. He claims it was his favourite outfit of hers, and she wore it specially for their dirty weekend. He says he bought the dress for her, on a New York business trip. Note, no other underwear. Used to stop off and have sex in a field, apparently. Which means that if he didn't kill her, someone else did within a reasonably short time.'

'Why? Because she was wearing those clothes when the body was found? Not necessarily. She could've left home wearing them. Or packed them when she left, for later use. In fact, she could've been wearing them at any future time, especially if they were her favourite manhunting outfit. Still, I take your point. It's an interesting possibility. What's the second piece of evidence?'

'The body. It's definitely the judge's wife. The dental records leave no room for doubt.'

'Any news from the lab about those bruises?'

'The ones on her neck? No, nothing yet. I'm due to chase them up this afternoon. So, what next? Can we arrest him, do you think?'

'No. It's still far too tenuous. Not only is there no evidence of murder yet, but there's no connection to him.'

'She didn't tie herself up and jump in.'

'No. But have you thought of the possibility that one person might have killed her, and another disposed of the body?'

'Unlikely, and that's still two crimes for which he's a reasonable suspect.'

'I'm afraid I disagree. You told me you didn't want to act until you were sure. Yes, there's evidence of crimes, but there's still nothing to link him to either one. The fact that she didn't turn up to meet the boyfriend doesn't help us, other than to exclude *him*. She could have left the matrimonial home wearing that outfit, or with it packed, and been picked up in Cumberland by the murderer. We know she liked to live dangerously, and she had no trouble picking up men. It's easy to see a woman like that attracting danger from any number of sources.'

The line goes silent as Jones considers these possibilities. 'All right, I take your point. Any other suggestions as to the evidence then?'

'I'd like to wait and find out what you discover at the house.'

'Fine.' There's another pause. 'What's your gut feeling?' asks Jones.

'I don't have one yet. Sorry.'

'If he didn't kill her, he's a saint. I'd have murdered her,' says Jones, betraying the first, albeit injudicious, evidence of a sense of humour since Charles met him.

'Would you, now?'

Jones is surprised by the sarcasm and bitterness in Charles's voice. The line falls silent for a third time.

Charles can almost hear the cogs in Jones's head clicking slowly into gear as he remembers some of the gossip surrounding Charles. Indeed, Charles can detect from Jones's sharp intake of breath exactly the moment the little Canadian solicitor remembers how Charles's wife was murdered and who was charged with the crime. 'Oh, goodness, I'm sorry, Mr Holborne ... Charles ... I completely forgot.'

'It's OK. Forget it.'

'No, it was terribly tactless, please forgive me.'

'Forget it.'

'Yes ... well ... anyway ... according to the friends of the family and the neighbours, he *was* a saint. There are other statements. They're almost unanimous: he wasn't the type for violence.'

'There's no such man in my experience. Everyone can be violent, given the right circumstances, the right provocation. And the more I read, the stronger the motive becomes. This woman had a black belt in provocation.'

'I agree there. God spare us from women like her.'

'Amen to that,' replies Charles.

CHAPTER 6

The Johansens watch, speechless, as the policemen methodically, unemotionally, destroy their lovely home. Anke Johansen is too upset, too astonished, even to cry. Tears will come later, in the following weeks and months as she slowly attempts to rebuild the beautiful Danish home she's painstakingly created during their three years in this alien country. The Johansens know nothing of a judge, his missing wife or their marital difficulties. They can answer none of the detective inspector's relentless questions. All they know is they purchased a house from a man who they were told was a lawyer. They've never met him, never spoken directly to him, never found anything unusual in what was his house, and never, *Gud forbyde!* had to wash blood off walls.

The couple sit in their kitchen, finding it almost impossible to focus on the questions fired at them while, all around and above them, banging and crashing can be heard as, piece by piece, their home is taken apart. There are men in the loft lifting the insulation that Erik laid only the previous winter; men in the garden shed, decanting all the old garden implements and discarding them onto the smooth green lawn; men in the bathroom taking the white panels off the bath and the emersion heater and leaving dents and scratches all over them; men in the lounge peeling back layers of wallpaper, and men in the bedrooms lifting the carpets. Erik sits next to his wife on the tall pine stool at the kitchen bench, clasping her hand in his, knowing in his heart that no matter what receipts the inspector offers, no matter how many times he promises that everything will be replaced in perfect order, they will never again feel secure in their lovely home.

After half an hour of questions, a young police officer in uniform puts his head round the door and raises his eyebrows.

'Got something?' asks the man known to Charles as "DI Smith", putting his pen down on the bench and sliding off the stool.

'Maybe.'

Smith speaks as kindly as he can to the Johansens. 'It might be as well if you wait here. I expect there's quite a mess. I'll only be a moment.'

He disappears after his young colleague, and for a moment the Johansens wait in the kitchen. There is then a particularly loud bang from the room above them and Anke tears her hand from her husband's grip and runs upstairs. He follows. They find the inspector kneeling in the middle of the floor of their bedroom. The furniture has been moved to one side of the room and the carpet lifted and rolled back to reveal shiny floorboards. Anke has always liked polished wooden floors, but these were stained a dark oak colour, darker than any of the other floors in the house, and they hadn't matched their light pine furniture. So she had the room carpeted in a lovely light green colour which complemented the greens and blues of the patchwork quilt her mother had sewn and given to them as a moving-in present.

That carpet is now rucked and creased, partly pinned down by a wardrobe moved from the side of the room and made grubby by the loose floorboards that she sees have been removed and discarded on top of it. As she will discover, it'll take weeks for the creases to disappear and professional cleaning will never manage completely to eradicate the marks.

The Johansens watch unnoticed from the door as a group of men in a tight circle peer into the space, now revealed, between the removed floorboards and the ceiling of the dining room below. The young policeman is showing the inspector something on the joists and on the underside of several of the floorboards. Erik leans into the room to get a closer look and sees irregular black stains. Some dark liquid seems to have been spilled on the floor and soaked through the floorboards, staining their undersides. Little rivulets of dried liquid can be seen on the joists and, on the top of the plasterboard that forms the ceiling of the dining room below, there is a large irregular stain. The colour is different from that of the wood stain, more red, more beautiful. Had the entire floor been that colour, Erik doubts that his wife would have wanted to carpet the room at all.

One of the men, one not wearing a uniform, has taken out a scalpel and is carefully scraping the top layer of the staining into a tiny plastic bag.

'Look here,' says another man, and the tight circle of men shifts on its haunches, a crab-like creature with a single mind, to the right. The speaker is pointing to some cable that disappears down through the ceiling, part of the lighting circuit. Below it, on the other side of the boards, is the ceiling rose and the beautiful brass chandelier in the centre of the dining room ceiling. That belonged to the former owners. The dining room has not been decorated at all since the Johansens moved in; they know few people in England and entertain infrequently, so that room was their last priority when moulding the new home to the personalities of its new occupants. In any event, the dining room and the bedroom above looked as if they'd been redecorated more recently than the others and so the Johansens felt justified in leaving them to last.

Another man speaks. 'It runs right down the wire.'

'Is there enough?' asks Smith.

'Well, the stuff on the boards has soaked right in. I doubt that it'll be possible to do much with it. But where it's on plastic, it's simply dried on the surface.'

'Let's have a look downstairs,' says the inspector, getting up.

He and two of the others push past the Johansens and descend to the dining room. Erik follows them, his curiosity pricked, while Anke remains upstairs. In the dining room, the Inspector takes a chair and stands on it underneath the chandelier. It is a lovely piece of metalwork, with six graceful brass arms spreading from a central sphere. The wire from the bedroom disappears down into the sphere and then splits to serve the bulbs at the end of each arm.

It jangles slightly at the inspector's touch. His hands move around the sphere gently, probing, twisting, trying to find if it comes undone. Suddenly it separates, and the top half moves upwards along the cable as if someone had sliced the top off a hard-boiled egg.

The inspector peers into the lower half of the sphere. There's a plastic junction box from which the cable divides. The junction box sits in black crusty material almost a quarter of an inch deep.

'Get another chair, and look at this,' he says excitedly to one of the men not wearing uniform. The other does as requested, and looks.

'Perfect,' he says, reaching into his pocket for another plastic bag. 'He was bloody lucky the house didn't burn down. This could easily have shorted.'

The inspector descends from his chair and is about to speak when another officer appears at the door. 'Look what I've found,' he announces proudly. In his gloved hand is a length of cable. 'It was under the water tank in the loft.' He brings it forward and the Inspector studies it without touching it.

'Mr Johansen, would you mind having a look at this, sir? Don't touch it, please.' Johansen moves forward. 'It's co-axial cable for a television aerial,' says Smith.

'Yes?'

'Did you bring this into the house?'

'No. I have no such cable. The television outlets were already installed when we arrived. I have done no work to them.'

'Thank you. Bag it up please, Robert.' The policeman leaves carrying the cable. 'And don't forget to log exactly where you found it!' calls Smith after him. He turns to Mr Johansen. 'I don't suppose you have any idea what that red staining on the underside of your floorboards upstairs is, do you?' Johansen shakes his head. 'No, I didn't think so. Perhaps you would like to take your wife back into the kitchen, sir? It'll be less distressing for her. We may be some time still.'

Discoveries come thick and fast thereafter. Under the wallpaper in the bedroom are found splashes of the same reddish black stain as in the floorspace. Removal of the coving around the bedroom ceiling reveals more. The police officers, so good-humoured and light-hearted when they arrived, slowly become grim and silent as they realise that a bloodbath has occurred in the room.

Three hours later they depart, filling two vans with their plastic-bagged prizes, and leaving Mr and Mrs Johansen standing in the wreckage of their home, clutching Kent County Constabulary Property Receipts.

CHAPTER 7

Charles closes the outer doors of Chambers, double-locks them, and walks downstairs into the courtyard. It's almost ten o'clock, dusk is falling, and the Temple is silent.

The gas lamps have just been lit and they glow like warm yellow candles, as yet casting no light on their surroundings. This is the time of day when Charles loves the Temple most. The sky over the River Thames glows with phosphorescent pinks and blues, and the red brick of the buildings, the green of the lawns and the pitted white stone of the Temple Church all seem to vibrate with colour. He walks through Sergeant's Inn and hesitates as he passes the rear door to *The Clachan*. The rise and fall of animated conversation and the smell of alcohol strike him simultaneously, and for a moment he's tempted to push open the door and step into the showy drinking establishment to see who's holding court. He can guess the "regulars" who will be there lingering over "one last bottle" — the criminal Bar in particular is infamous for its poseurs, storytellers and claret conversationalists — but he's not in the mood to join a party that's already well on its way to inebriation.

He crosses Fleet Street, half-deserted by this time in the evening, and walks the hundred or so yards to the block that houses his pocket-sized home. Dennis, the concierge cum porter, has left for the day and Charles reaches over the reception desk for his post before climbing the stairs to his flat.

The place is so small he can throw his briefcase and robes bag onto the couch from the front door. He crosses the lobby in a single step, enters the kitchen and pours himself a large scotch. He drinks most of it in a single swallow and then tops up his glass. He then joins his briefcase on the couch. As he is about to reach for the television switch, the telephone rings.

'Mr Holborne? It's Mr Jones.'

'Good evening, Mr Jones,' says Charles, taking another sip of scotch.

'Forgive me for tracking you down. I called your clerk at home, and she gave me the number. It's urgent, I'm afraid. I'm at Maidstone police station now with two of the officers involved in the investigation, one of whom you've met. They wish to arrest the suspect, but before they do so I would like your input.'

'Fire away.'

'Time is of the essence, as we believe the suspect may now be aware of the enquiries. The police have spent the last six hours executing a search warrant at the address where he lived at the time of the wife's disappearance. In the loft we found co-axial cable identical to that used to tie the plastic sheeting round the body. That's not all. The entire house has been redecorated, probably more than once. However, in the main bedroom, under the carpet, are boards that have been heavily stained and re-varnished. We lifted them up, and on the underside of the boards, over a large area, there is bloodstaining. It's even dripped through into the light fitting below. There are splashes all over the bedroom. We've no match yet, but it tests as human blood. If we're going to move, I think we should do it now. The question is: is there enough to arrest him?'

'There is now. But do it voluntarily if at all possible. "Helping with enquiries".'

'Understood,' says Jones, and he hangs up immediately.

Charles does the same and turns on the television. He's hungry, but just wants five minutes before rousing himself to start cooking.

Ringing suddenly fills Charles's head. He reaches blindly to the telephone beside him and puts the receiver to his ear.

'Charles?'

Charles sits up further, trying to collect his wits. For a second he can't work out where he is, but then realises that he must have fallen asleep in front of the TV. It's dark outside the floor-to-ceiling window.

'Yes?'

'Sorry, did I wake you?'

'No, not really.' He reaches to turn off the TV, the scotch tumbler falling off his lap to the floor. 'How are you, Davie?' he asks. 'And Sonia?'

'We're both very well, thank you. And you? I wondered if perhaps you were on a case out of town.'

'No, I'm here. And fine.' Charles draws a deep breath. He'd been meaning to call his younger brother for several weeks but had been finding excuses to put it off.

'So...?'

'I'm sorry, David, I know I've been a bit...'

'What's going on, Charles? Ever since you and Sally split up, you've become some sort of recluse.'

Charles starts to offer denials, but gives up. 'I couldn't face it. Sorry.'

'Face what?'

'The knowledge that I'd let mum and dad down. Yet again.'

'You haven't let them down. It's all in your head.'

'Really? So I imagined that sad, wistful shaking of the head I got from mum last time, did I? Two hours of sighing and tutting?'

'You know what she's like. She just wants you to be happy.'

'Oh, is that what it is?' says Charles wearily.

David watched his older brother and his mother fight throughout his childhood. The arguments, shouting, tears and recriminations were constant until Charles volunteered for the RAF and left home. Charles couldn't have blamed David had his younger brother been jealous, for Millie Horowitz and her elder son were so locked in battle that David was frequently neglected.

Fortunately, David was blessed with a sunny disposition and an understanding heart and always saw the best in everyone. In his quiet and respectful way, he stood up for Charles against the constant drip-drip of their mother's bitterness which, for as long as he could remember, had been directed at the older brother he admired so much, and over the years found himself cast in the role of the family peacekeeper.

'Look,' says David. 'Forget mum for the moment. Sonia and I would like to invite you to us for Friday night supper. It's important.'

'Are they coming?' asks Charles. 'Because I don't think I can face another evening like the last.'

'I've invited them, but on the strict condition that mum tries to be nice.'

'Oh, well, that's OK then,' replies Charles with thick sarcasm. 'A great time is guaranteed for one and all.'

'Please, Charlie?'

Charles pauses, trying to find a way to decline without hurting David's feelings.

He and David were very close as youngsters. That ended abruptly during Charles's second year at Cambridge, when his parents learned he'd married Henrietta. They convened the entire family and friends from their congregation and "sat *shiva*" in their front room — held seven days of prayers to mourn Charles's death. Thereafter his name was no longer mentioned.

Following Henrietta's murder, a tense reconciliation had been brokered and Charles is no longer entirely persona non grata, but by an unspoken accord neither he nor David had found it necessary to inform their mother that they met occasionally for lunch when both were in London. Charles's name could still produce thin-lipped moodiness from Millie Horowitz.

'Important, huh?' asks Charles.

'We haven't seen you for ages. So, yes, it's important for me and Sonia,' replies David, although there is something in his tone which makes Charles wonder if there isn't something more. Charles's brother and sister-in-law, married a couple of years, are blissfully happy, and although David's a very private man and wouldn't discuss it even with Charles, Charles suspects they've been trying for a baby. In which case, they might have an announcement.

'Fine. I shall be delighted to accept.'

'Good. Mum and dad will make their own way.'

Millie and Harry Horovitz are strictly observant and would never consider travelling in a vehicle on the Sabbath, even if Charles offered to collect them from Golders Green on his way north from the city, but they are still capable of making the twenty-minute walk to David and Sonia's house in Hendon.

'See you Friday, then,' says Charles.

CHAPTER 8

The unmarked police car draws up outside the dark house. The night is warm and still; barely a breath of wind stirs the tops of the trees surrounding the building. The house is set back from the road with its own drive, but it's not ostentatious. The swing and a discarded football in the front garden reveal it as a family home and the car in the drive, although a Mercedes, is six years old.

The tall thin man in the passenger seat flicks off the torch by which he has been reading the papers on his lap, and looks up.

'I expected something rather more substantial,' he says.

The driver, known by Charles as "Smith" but who is in fact Detective Inspector Spencer Carr, doesn't answer. Carr is still wondering what the hell he's doing in rural Kent in the middle of the night, four hundred miles from his home force in Cumberland, and when he hasn't slept for over twenty-four hours. Having established the identity of the deceased and where she met her death, the investigation would normally pass entirely to the local police force, the Kent County Constabulary. His boss had managed to get off the hook; somehow he hadn't. So, apparently in the cause of continuity and liaison, he is stuck on a case that is now based the length of the country away from his heavily pregnant wife, and one where there's a high risk that he and his colleagues will end up with egg on their faces.

Right now, he can see no upside. And to cap it all, this new Superintendent Hook, who point-blank refused Jones's suggestion that he be re-christened "Superintendent Green" for the purposes of this investigation (and what a fucking joke that was!) is now polluting his car with cigarette smoke without permission. Carr only managed to stop smoking a month ago.

'Here we go then,' says Hook as he gets out. 'Leave the talking to me.'

Carr follows him and they crunch together down the gravel drive to the house. As they approach, they trigger an electronic beam and bright light floods the garden, shining directly into their faces and forcing them to shield their eyes from the glare. The interior of the house remains in darkness. Hook rings the bell. It takes a second ring to elicit a response, but an upstairs light is finally illuminated. A few seconds later, a figure can be seen through the obscured glass struggling into a dressing gown as it descends the staircase, and the door is opened.

The Superintendent recognises Steele immediately from the photographs he has just placed on the passenger seat of the car, but he hadn't appreciated how tall the man was. Superintendent Hook is himself over six feet in height, but even in his slippers the judge is half a head taller. Further, the black and white file photographs didn't reveal how intensely blue were his eyes, made all the more penetrating for being framed by very fair eyebrows. Steele also squints against the brightness of the floodlit garden.

'Yes?' he asks.

'Sorry to trouble you, sir,' says Hook, showing his warrant card to Steele as he introduces himself. 'I'm Detective Superintendent Hook from the Kent County Constabulary, and this is Inspector Carr from Cumberland and Westmoreland.'

'And?'

Carr hears irritation in the judge's voice but no suggestion of nervousness. If being woken in the middle of the night by police officers from two different forces, one four hundred miles away and in an area where he might have dumped his wife's body, makes the judge nervous, there's no sign of it in his response.

'You really shouldn't have opened the door to me like that, sir. Didn't Special Branch give you instructions when you were … what? … promoted?'

'The phrase is "made up", superintendent, and the answer is yes they did, but one forgets in a village like this. And would you mind telling me what the bloody hell you're doing giving me lessons in home security in the middle of the night?'

'Sorry, sir. Can we come in? We have some news for you.'

'Won't it wait till a more civilised hour? We're all asleep.'

'I'm afraid not.'

Steele sighs. 'You'd better come in then.'

A woman appears at the head of the stairs. Carr looks up at her, approving of the way the light behind her shows off her full figure through her thin nightdress. She is, he guesses, in her late thirties, perhaps forty, but she is extremely handsome, with very long light brown hair flecked with grey that reaches her waist. Steele sees the direction of Carr's glance and turns to the woman.

'It's all right, Jenny,' he says, 'a police matter. Why don't you go back to bed?'

Jenny does as she is bidden without speaking.

'Your wife, sir?' asks Hook.

Carr casts a swift glance at the superintendent, unsure if the question is designed to elicit a response in the judge or if Hook simply hasn't read the papers fully in the short time available to him.

'No. The children's nanny. Go into the lounge.'

Steele points to a room to the right and closes the front door. Carr finds the light switch and the two police officers sit in armchairs facing the door. Steele follows and takes a seat facing them.

'Right. What's up?' he asks.

'Yes, sir. Now, this may come as a shock.' Hook pauses. 'We have found the body of a woman. It seems to be that of your wife.'

The police officers' scrutiny of the tall man sitting opposite them intensifies as this news is delivered. His eyes widen slightly and his mouth falls slightly open. 'Good God! After all this time.'

There is surprise there, thinks Carr, but no fear.

'Yes sir,' says Hook.

'Are you asking me to identify her? Is that possible after, what, twelve years?'

'Closer to thirteen, actually, sir, but no, it's not that. When I said "it seems to be your wife" I wasn't being really accurate. There's no doubt it's your wife. Dental records confirm it beyond any doubt.'

'Then what do you want from me?'

'Well, sir, there are a few matters that require further clarification.'

'Surely it'll wait till the morning? She's been gone years. One night won't make any difference, will it?'

'I have instructions to take you to Maidstone police station tonight. We've set up an incident room there.'

'I see.' Steele pauses, his elegant hands pressed together before his lips as if in prayer. If he killed her, thinks Carr, he's as cold as ice. There hasn't been the slightest flicker of fear from the second we identified ourselves. 'What are you saying to me? Am I under arrest?'

'I'd hope to have your co-operation.'

'But if I refuse?'

Superintendent Hook leans forward, meets Steele's gaze, and holds it. 'Then I would have no alternative but to arrest you.'

'And, in that eventuality, what would the charge be? You have to tell me of what I am suspected, you know.' Steele is smiling, leaning back in his chair, perfectly relaxed, as if debating an interesting point of law.

'I do know that, sir. The charge would be suspected murder, my Lord.'

There is a gasp, but not from Steele. Both men look up. Jenny is standing in the doorway, now dressed in a bathrobe. She obviously heard the last exchange. Steele turns back to the policemen.

'No, it's only "My Lord" in court, superintendent; "sir" will do fine.' He unfolds his long legs, rises and addresses Jenny. 'You heard that, I gather. It seems that I shall be "helping police with their enquiries".'

Carr is still looking at the woman standing by the door, her eyes wide with fear and her hands clasped to her mouth. That gesture, in which a hand is apparently employed to stifle the organ of speech, has always intrigued him. He continues to look at the woman, something about her reaction, something that he can't quite define, bothering him.

The judge is still speaking. 'I'd better get dressed. Will you get these men a cup of tea, my dear? I'm sure they'd appreciate it. And when you've done that, please would you see if you can get hold of Mr Bell? I assume I am entitled to contact my solicitor?' he asks.

Carr tears his eyes from Jenny. 'Yes, sir.'

'Very well. I shall not detain you long.'

Steele walks swiftly from the room. Hook is about to turn to the nanny when she too slips silently through the open doorway. The policemen hear a fluorescent light bulb hum and click into life and bright light is thrown into the hallway. Hook indicates with his head that Inspector Carr should follow her.

Carr takes a deep breath and hauls himself out of the comfortable chair, his body aching with fatigue, and follows the woman. He finds himself in a large kitchen with a scrubbed pine table in its centre. Someone's homework, exercise books, a set-square and protractor are tidied neatly at one end, and the other end is already laid for breakfast. The room's curtains, bright and colourful, are closed, and Carr can smell the previous night's cooking. The wooden floor is covered in rugs and along one wall is a comfortably worn sofa. A cuckoo clock on the wall above the table ticks reassuringly. Carr is surprised at the warmth and cosiness of the room, unexpected for a house inhabited by a single professional man and his children. He guesses that the nanny had a hand in the choice of furnishings and the ornaments that line the window sills. Jenny is standing at the sink, filling the kettle.

'I'm sorry you've been disturbed so late,' ventures Carr.

'Keep your voice down, please,' she replies sharply. 'The least you can do is let Bobby sleep.'

'Sorry,' replies Carr. 'I don't have children,' he offers by way of excuse. 'Do you?'

'What do you mean? Of course I do.'

'No, I meant children of your own.'

'Sir Anthony's children have had no mother but me since they were very small.'

'Yes, of course. You've been part of the family for a long time. Did you know Mrs Steele?'

'Of course.'

'Did you get on with her?'

She turns sharply towards him. 'Are you going to arrest me too?'

'No, of course not —'

'Am I "helping you with your enquiries" too?'

'No, I was just —'

'Then, if you don't mind, I don't want to talk to you. You can pour the water in when the kettle boils,' and she indicates a teapot. She walks swiftly past him and he listens to her light footsteps going up the staircase.

CHAPTER 9

By the time the judge is dressed (and, the policemen note, shaved) it is almost 2.00 a.m. Steele walks down the gravel drive towards the waiting car, the policemen flanking him. As he ducks to get into the rear seat, Steele turns to look back at the house and waves to Jenny whose silhouette can be seen in the upstairs window. Carr notices the judge's movement and also turns to look up, but by the time he does so there is nothing to be seen except the bedroom curtains swinging gently.

The traffic on the road to Maidstone is almost non-existent and the journey takes no more than an hour. Steele is silent throughout which, thinks Carr, is just as well. Every word spoken to and by Lord Justice Steele, Sir Anthony Steele, QC, during the course of this investigation is to be faithfully recorded, and Hook has given strict instructions: no small talk. It's an instruction for which Carr is grateful. A displaced Geordie lad from a terraced house in Sunderland whose hobbies include fishing, soccer and real ale has little conversation to share with a knight and a justice of the Supreme Court.

The police station is also quiet. Steele is directed to wait on an empty bench as Hook engages in a hurried whispered conversation with the desk sergeant who has a *"No one told me anything about this"* expression, and appears to have been completely unaware that the day shift had allocated space for an incident room. Carr also waits, as lost in this unfamiliar police station as his suspect. Eventually, they are shown to an empty interview room and Hook rushes off somewhere.

'Take a seat, sir,' says Carr. 'We'll start shortly. I'm going to find someone who'll make us a drink. Would you like something? A cup of tea perhaps?'

'Tea?' asks Steele, looking up as if distracted. 'Yes, please.'

Carr slips out of the room, leaving a police woman standing uneasily by the door. She tries not to look at the man sitting only arm's reach from her, but finds it difficult. His manicured hands, silver-grey hair, freshly-pressed cotton shirt and elegant Savile Row suit are completely out of place in the grubby room usually inhabited by sweating policemen and lank-haired suspects. Steele seems unaware of his surroundings. He sits comfortably on the wooden chair, his legs crossed and his hands resting in his lap. His eyes are closed. The door opens briefly a few minutes later for another young officer to place a china mug containing steaming brown liquid on the table before Steele, who doesn't open his eyes. A glance passes between the two police officers before the newcomer departs.

Twenty minutes later, the door opens and Superintendent Hook enters followed by Inspector Carr. Hook places two manila files on the table and the policemen sit. Both take out pens and notebooks.

'You understand that you're not under arrest?' confirms Hook.

'I do.'

'You may therefore leave at any time, if you wish. I hope, however, that you'll assist us in answering a few questions.'

'I shall do my duty as a responsible citizen.'

'Firstly, however, you asked at your home about contacting a solicitor. Has that been done?'

'Jenny tried but, of course, there was no answer. I don't have his home number. But further attempts are being made on my behalf.'

'Very well. In the circumstances, perhaps it would be best to defer this interview until your solicitor can be contacted. I'm not very happy to start at this hour. You're entitled to some sleep now. So we'll start in the morning.'

Steele stares at Hook, uncomprehending. 'Are you serious?' he demands angrily, for the first time revealing some emotion. 'Are you telling me you've woken me in the middle of the night to drive me for an hour to a police station, with no intention of conducting an interview now? You're going to make me wait here until tomorrow morning?'

'Well, sir, it *is* tomorrow morning, if you take my meaning, but I do wish to wait until office hours when your solicitor may be present.'

'Which means that I shall have to sleep here.'

'Yes, I'm afraid it does.'

'This is deliberate harassment! You're trying to create maximum distress, to intimidate and humiliate me. Why on earth bring me in at this hour if it could've waited until morning?'

'I assure you, sir, we had no such intention. One of the reasons for seeking your help at this unusual hour was to protect you from adverse publicity.'

'I don't believe that, superintendent. I can think of no good reason for arresting me now simply to keep me here overnight. You could just as easily have come during daylight hours.'

'I repeat, sir, you are not under arrest.'

'Well, if I am not under arrest, I wish to be returned to my home immediately. Or you can start the interview now. If the matter reaches the point where I feel I want a solicitor here, I shall let you know and we can reconsider.'

Superintendent Hook flushes slightly. He looks across at Carr with raised eyebrows, inviting his opinion. Before setting off to Steele's home, the inspector had tentatively suggested to his superior that perhaps they should defer the whole thing until the following morning, but he'd been peremptorily overruled. Having met the tall superintendent for the first time only half an hour earlier, Carr didn't feel on safe enough ground to argue his corner. Hook's face gives nothing away and he speaks little; when he does, it's through lips that barely move. Carr is reminded of Sydney Greenstreet's description of a "close-mouthed man".

From the tactical perspective as well, Carr would far rather have conducted the interview after getting some sleep. Lord Justice Steele is reputed to have one of the finest intellects of his generation, which is presumably why he's tipped for promotion to the House of Lords in record time. He'd also had over a decade to plan his answers. So the officers would need their wits about them, and it would have been sensible to get a few hours' kip before launching into this particular duel.

Carr weighs his answer carefully, acutely aware that his working relationship with this unknown superintendent probably hangs in the balance. If he agrees that the judge should be taken back home, it will be an obvious snub to his boss, tantamount to saying "*I told you so*." So Carr shrugs and nods, trying to look more awake than he feels.

'I'm happy to proceed if Sir Anthony is,' he says.

Hook addresses the judge. 'Very well. The inspector here will be asking these questions. I have also asked for a solicitor advising the prosecution to attend, unless you have any objections. He'll be here shortly.'

'I have no objections.'

'Then let's begin, inspector,' says Hook, taking out his notebook and pen.

Inspector Carr opens a file before him, leafs through some notes to collect his thoughts, closes the file again and begins.

He deals first with how Steele and Lise Bonseigneur met, when they married, where they honeymooned and where they lived for the first years of their married life. Steele answers every question simply, neither embellishing his answers with extraneous detail nor hiding anything relevant. He sits completely still in his chair, his hands clasped lightly together on the table before him as he speaks, often with his eyes closed, the mug of tea untouched and now cold.

Superintendent Hook, who observes from slightly above the fray, can easily see how the man had been a success at the Bar. His voice is calm but powerful. Facts, such as dates, names and places, are given in a simple, matter-of-fact way, sometimes after a pause, but never seeming to evade or obfuscate. Indeed, it is only rarely that Steele needs to pause for thought, for his memory of places, dates and names — even of neighbours and colleagues whom he hasn't seen for fifteen years — is excellent.

Then Carr moves to more personal but still very general matters. It is now, as he deals with the birth of the couple's children, the milestones in their lives and their schooling, that the superintendent can hear surges of emotion in the answers, and it is these responses, rather than the clarity and simplicity of the others, that begin to convince both policemen that the judge is doing all he can to recount events truthfully.

Carr changes tactics slightly, deliberately jumping quickly from subject to subject, giving his suspect no time to guess the direction or purpose of the questioning.

'Have you ever owned a boat?'

'No,' answers Steele after a short pause for reflection.

'Do you sail?'

'I have sailed, if that's your question, but if you mean do I sail regularly, as in some form of hobby, no I don't.'

'What decorating did you do, or did you have done at your last address?'

'I should think the entire house was redecorated at least once. Probably more. We also had an extension built, which would have entailed redecorating throughout.'

'Have you ever varnished or applied stain to wooden floors at that house?'

'Me personally? I doubt it. I can't swear to it, but I have no recollection of ever doing so. Not the sort of thing that I would do for pleasure. I'm not a handyman.'

'Do you know the Lake District?'

'No. I've never been there, except when driving on my way to Scotland.'

'Did your wife?'

'I don't know. I don't think so, but she might have been there with any of her boyfriends and not told me.'

'Did you have a television at your last home?'

'Yes. Two.'

'Did they have portable aerials or fixed, as in run by cables up to the roof?'

'The latter.'

'When did you do the cabling, or have it done?'

'I did neither. I believe it was installed shortly before we moved in.'

'Did you have a mistress or lover at the time when your wife was killed?'

'Ha!' laughs Steele, with genuine amusement. 'Well, firstly, I have never had a mistress or lover. I don't believe in that sort of thing. And secondly, I don't know when my wife was killed, or if she was at all. All I know is when she left our home. Are the two necessarily the same?'

'That's what we're trying to establish, sir,' replies Superintendent Hook.

Now, having gained some insight into Steele's life and what sort of man he is, Carr feels confident enough to move gradually to the heart of the interview.

'Would you say that yours was a happy marriage?'

'It was for some years. After the children were born it deteriorated rapidly.'

'Deteriorated?'

Steele pauses, collecting his thoughts. 'My wife had an unhappy childhood. She was not shown much love or affection herself. It made her very selfish, and it gave her no idea of how to nurture young children. She had no role models.'

There's a knock on the door and Jones slips into the room. Carr looks up, irritated at his flow having been broken. Jones looks apologetic, Hook makes the introductions and the little solicitor takes a seat in the corner of the room to observe from a distance.

'You were saying that your wife had an unhappy childhood and had difficulty nurturing your children. How did that affect your marriage?'

'She became very unhappy. She knew she wasn't a good mother and, worse, she knew others knew it. She tried quite hard for short periods, particularly at the beginning, but she hated the entire thing. From then on she was … defiant, I suppose. She still cared what others thought of course, but she told herself that she didn't. She started drinking and having … relationships outside the marriage. We became estranged — not in the sense that we lived apart, but in the sense that we couldn't communicate anymore. We lost our way.'

'Did you still love her?'

'Very much.'

'Even when she had affairs with other men?'

'Even then. She was a lost child, looking for … something … love perhaps? In any event, something she believed we, as a family, couldn't give her. I felt that I'd failed her, do you see?'

In truth, Carr is having some difficulty seeing. Steele still speaks with apparent candour and sincerity, but the inspector begins to wonder if Steele's selfless understanding isn't a pose. From where he comes, if your wife starts behaving like a whore, you give her a good hiding. If that doesn't do the trick, you divorce her. The idea that it might be your fault, especially if you never drink, gamble, screw around or beat her up … well, that's difficult to grasp.

'Were you really not jealous?' he asks.

'Of course I was. But I knew that none of these men were important to her. I sometimes thought that she was only doing it for my benefit.'

'Your benefit?' interjects Hook with evident disbelief.

'I'm not certain, you understand, but much of what she did seemed designed to prompt a response in me. When I didn't respond, her behaviour would become even more outrageous. By contrast, on the few occasions I was finally goaded into a row, she would calm down very quickly and be very affectionate afterwards.'

'Were you often goaded into a row?'

'Very rarely. I can remember three such events.'

Steele has himself brought the questioning around to the point which the police particularly want to probe, but at this point Carr shies away from it and changes tack.

'I am curious about something, Sir Anthony. We wake you in the middle of the night, thirteen years after your wife disappears, and ask you to drive for an hour to a police station. You do the journey in complete silence. Then you sit here and answer, what, an hour's worth of questions, yet not once have you asked me why you're here. Why is that?'

Steele smiles, and Carr bridles at the condescension of a man who is at least two moves ahead of him.

'You tell me you have found my wife's body. Clearly, she didn't die on an alcoholic ward or in the throes of some desperate lust in a hotel bed, either of which, frankly, I would have expected, but neither of which would have involved me. At the least, she must have died in unexplained circumstances, or *you* wouldn't be involved. Further, she must have died some considerable time ago, as if it had only been recent, you wouldn't have wanted to question *me*, when the most basic of detection work would have shown that she's had nothing to do with me or the children since the day she walked out. I therefore deduce that you've found her body and that she appears to have died a considerable time ago, when she *was* still involved with me. So you have to interview me to investigate the circumstances of the last time I saw her. Correct so far?'

Carr glances at Superintendent Hook and Jones, both of whom nod. 'Very good, sir,' answers Carr.

'Of course, I'd be surprised if you could say precisely when she died,' continues Steele. 'My experience of forensic pathology is limited, but I guess that after this length of time, a year or two either way is perfectly possible.'

No one answers, and Steele realises that he's hit on a real problem for the police.

'Anyway,' he continues, 'you want to know about the last time I saw her. Shall we get onto that subject? Then you may return me to my bed and continue your enquiries elsewhere.'

Carr smiles, trying to look more confident than he feels. Steele's summary has somehow shifted the balance of power in the room away from him.

'As you say, sir, let's move on. You claim you only had two or three rows with your wife. Was one of those on the day you last saw her?'

'It was.'

'What caused this row?'

'She'd been away for a couple of days with her friend.'

'When you say "friend" do you mean lover?'

'Yes. Her lover.'

He repeats the word not with anger nor even embarrassment, but to the police officers' surprise, with sadness. Steele pauses and, for the first time, appears temporarily lost in his private thoughts.

'I hope he was her lover,' he adds quietly, 'but I suspect he was not. She desperately needed someone to love her in the way she found so ... elusive, yet by all accounts theirs was a pretty stormy relationship.'

'What are you saying?' asks Superintendent Hook. 'You think her lover killed her?'

'No, that is *not* what I'm saying,' retorts Steele with some irritation. 'The fact that she argued with this man — and made his life a misery at times, just as she did mine — is no more likely to make him kill her than it is to make *me* kill her. She was a difficult woman, that's all. She infuriated almost everyone at some time.'

'Where were you when you last saw her?'

'At the house. She returned from this trip late in the afternoon.'

'Was anyone else in the house?'

'No. I think the children were at a friend's house or at the park. Somewhere with the nanny, anyway.'

'What happened?'

'We had a row. I'm not sure of the details now, but I remember there was something about her sheets.'

'Sheets?'

'She took linen away with her to this place, a farmhouse or cottage or something where she used to meet him … Roddy Batchelor, that was his name. She went there quite often. She threw the sheets at me, in the kitchen. Told me to wash them for her.'

'I expect that made you pretty angry,' says Carr.

'I expect it did,' replies Steele. 'I remember a shouting match followed, and she stormed off.'

'Just like that?'

'More or less. The argument carried on upstairs while she fixed her makeup, then she picked up her keys and left.'

'Where to?'

'I have no idea. To meet him, I suppose. That's where she said she was going.'

'And she took her car?'

'No. When they went off together, he'd often pick her up at the end of the road.'

'Did she take anything with her?'

'Her handbag, I suppose.'

'No clothes, personal possessions…?'

'No, nothing like that.'

'Didn't that surprise you?'

'Not at all. She was like that — very histrionic. She loved the drama of it all. We hardly had a friend out of whose house she had not stalked in high dudgeon at some time or another.'

'But when she didn't come back, didn't you think it odd? My wife wouldn't go anywhere without her makeup, hair drier and so on.'

'She would frequently disappear for days on end but, yes, after a few days I began to get worried, so I reported her missing.'

'Where?'

'At the local police house in the village. I'm sure they'll have the records if you check.'

'And what efforts did you make to trace her after that?'

'None. To be honest, I'd had enough of her. And the children were much happier without her. I took the view that we were better off without her disrupting everything.'

'But you said that you still loved her?'

'So I did. But I couldn't make her happy. I hoped someone else could.'

'That's very understanding of you,' says the inspector, his tired voice displaying more disbelief.

'I'm an understanding person,' replies Steele, without arrogance, but with a gentle smile.

Hook leans forward and speaks softly in Carr's ear. Carr nods. 'Can you tell us about your movements during the two days that followed your wife's disappearance?'

'I'll try. That evening, I remember, I stayed at home with the children. I thought she might come back and start smashing things up — she'd done that before — and I wanted to be around. The next day, we all went out to a fair on the heath. The following day I remember very well, as I went with my

95

eldest son to his school near Taunton. I had made an appointment to see the headmaster. I drove down with my son, but the head was away on some emergency, and I decided to stay overnight and see him in the morning.'

'Why?'

'I felt that it was important. I'd fixed a number of other appointments, but either my commitments or his prevented us from meeting. I was worried about my son's progress at the school, and seeing I was down there, I thought I'd make sure I saw the headmaster by waiting overnight.'

'Where did you stay?'

'At a local hotel. I can't tell you the name, although it might be in one of my old diaries. I'd stayed there once or twice before.'

'What did you do the following day?'

'I saw the head and stayed at the school. I hadn't intended to, but my son was pretty upset, and it was the day of his inter-house rugby tournament. He was playing, pretty reluctantly in fact, so I stayed to cheer him on. He scored the winning try in fact.' There's unmistakeable pride in Steele's voice.

'So there would've been a lot of people there who could corroborate your account?' asks Hook.

'There were many people there, but whether or not they'd remember whether I was there, thirteen years on, I doubt. My son would remember.' He pauses. 'Oh, but there *is* a photograph showing him holding the cup in one hand and shaking my hand with the other. In fact, come to think of it, as I was there, the head asked me to present the cup. I was the nearest thing they had to a celebrity. So perhaps someone *would* remember my presence.'

'And where is that photograph?'

'Hanging on the wall in my study at home.'

'Would you have any objection to our searching your home?' Steele doesn't answer. 'Sir?' prompts the superintendent.

'I think I should speak to my solicitor about that before I answer. Of course, if you have grounds, you'll no doubt be able to obtain a search warrant. But I think, for the present, that I'd prefer to decline. If I agree, I can tell you that I'll certainly want to be present when the search is conducted.'

'What do you have to hide, sir?' asks Carr.

'Inspector, if I'd killed my wife, which is something you evidently suspect, do you think I'd have hoarded incriminating evidence for over thirteen years, cart it from one home to another, just so you could find it now? No. It's just that I know what sort of mess your chaps can make, and I don't want my family to be distressed needlessly.'

'Did you kill your wife?' asks Hook.

The question is posed so suddenly and in such a conversational manner that, when Steele grins, it seems perfectly natural.

'No, superintendent, I did not,' he replies, meeting his interrogators' eyes with what seems absolute candour. 'I tell you, there were times when she'd have tried anyone's patience to the limit. She provoked me to the point where sometimes … I didn't know *how* to cope with her. She was vicious, hurtful — to me and to the children — and unreasonable, but I never so much as raised my hand to her.'

'You don't seem particularly sorry that she's dead,' comments Carr.

'Perhaps I'm not. She made our lives an absolute misery for a long time. I've always been worried that she'd suddenly reappear on the doorstep, which would've caused dreadful distress to everyone. As far as I'm concerned, it's as if we'd been divorced for the last thirteen years. Whatever love I bore her has died, I suppose.'

'Can you explain then why the floorboards of what was your bedroom have been saturated with human blood?' demands Carr.

Coming at what appears to be right at the end of the interview, and with no warning, the question is deeply shocking and the room rings with the silence that follows.

'Blood?' whispers Steele, his eyes wide. He disengages as he pauses, his eyes losing focus for a moment. His attention slowly returns to the room and he shakes his head. 'No, I can't. We only lived there for, what? Six or seven years I suppose. The house is over a hundred years old.'

'Did you not see the blood, on the floor, the walls, the ceiling?'

'Obviously not, or I'd have reported it.'

'But when you were decorating, you would have taken the carpets up.'

'No. *Someone* would have taken the carpets up, but not me. I don't like that sort of thing, and I have better things to do. Either I or my wife would have employed decorators.'

'Are you able to give us the names of the people you used?'

Steele shrugs. 'Possibly, but I doubt it. They were probably locals. I might still have some bills at home, but I expect everything relating to the old house was thrown out when we moved.'

'So you never stripped off wallpaper in your bedroom, or applied new wallpaper?'

Steele shakes his head.

'I'm sorry, sir, but may I have a verbal answer?' asks Carr.

'The answer is "No".'

'You never stained and re-polished the floor in your bedroom?'

'No.'

'Did anyone you employed for that job inform you that there were stains on the floorboards?'

'No.'

Steele leans back in his chair and stretches. 'You have to understand, gentlemen; I was away on circuit a great deal. My wife, for all her faults, was very house-proud, certainly in the first few years. I would frequently return to find decorations changed, new carpets or curtains, new lights, rooms changed round and so on.'

'That sounds expensive,' comments Hook.

'Not for a barrister with a busy practice,' says Steele simply. 'I earned double then what I do now.'

'Is that so?' asks Hook with some doubt.

'Ask anyone in the Lord Chancellor's department what judges in the Supreme Court earn. I gave up a very good practice.' Steele watches the Superintendent's face, and laughs again. 'Destroyed one of your theories, have I? That I killed her for money?'

'Not at all, sir,' replies Hook with great politeness. 'I didn't think that. But having a wife such as yours could not have been an advantage when seeking promotion.'

Steele answers more seriously. 'I really don't know how the Lord Chancellor views these things. Some of my brother judges have appalling wives, no doubt, while others are angels. What difference that makes to a chap's ability with the law or in deciding issues of fact, I really don't know.'

Hook looks at Carr, and then at Jones. Jones nods. 'I think we should have a short break,' says Hook.

Jones speaks for the first time. 'We shall leave you here for a moment, if you don't mind.'

'Not at all,' replies Steele. 'I would like a fresh cup of tea though. I never got round to drinking this one.'

'Certainly.'

The three interviewers troop out and enter an adjoining room. Carr picks up a telephone and asks for a cup of tea for Steele.

'He's extremely confident,' says Jones.

'More than he was,' replies Carr. 'You weren't in at the start, but he was concentrating hard then, very cautious, very careful not to make a slip.'

'But so what?' says Hook, impatiently. 'That could be explained by nervousness, or his training, or both. This isn't much fun, even if you're innocent. I'd want to keep a cool head.'

'Do you have anything else you want to ask now?' asks Jones of the superintendent. The close-mouthed man shakes his head. 'You?' asks Jones, turning to Carr.

Inspector Carr shrugs. 'I feel like I'm wrestling with one arm behind my back. In all my time in the force, I've never been so polite during an interview!'

'How often have you interviewed one of England's top judges? OK. Let's call it a night, let him have a few hours' sleep, and come back to it fresh. If nothing else occurs to us by then, we'll thank him for his assistance and get him taken home. I'll speak to Holborne in the meantime, see if he's got any ideas.'

They return to the interview room. The judge has been provided with a fresh cup of tea which, this time, he is drinking. He lowers it to address Jones.

'We've not been introduced,' says the judge, standing formally, and towering over the diminutive solicitor.

'My name's Jones. I'm a solicitor employed by the Metropolitan Police.'

The two men shake hands and the judge resumes his seat.

'Essex, Cumberland and now the Met? Surely the involvement of three forces is hardly an efficient use of resources?'

'I'm sure you're right, Sir Anthony,' replies Jones in his squeaky North American voice. 'Kent is in the process of creating its own internal prosecution department, but presently has to outsource legal advice from one of its local solicitors. My superiors offered my services to Kent as I've been overseeing the case since your wife's body was discovered.'

Jones resumes his seat and scans the faces in the room. The judge looks the freshest of all of them. No doubt he's relieved at the way the questions are going — anyone would be relieved at the end of a long interview on a subject as dangerous as this, acknowledges Jones to himself — but he fancies he can detect something beyond relief. Something in the mocking angle of an eyebrow, the slightly too-ready smile and the relaxed posture, speak of triumph.

'I have decided to adjourn this interview until later this morning,' says Superintendent Hook. 'I would like you to have some sleep, and while you do we shall be taking legal advice.'

'Are you asking me to stay in the police station?' asks Steele, the smile now as conspicuous by its absence as it was moments earlier by its presence.

'I am prepared to have you taken home, if that is your wish. However, I want to start again soon, so I doubt you'd get much sleep before being collected again. Alternatively, you can remain here in the interview room. We can find you clean blankets and a pillow,' replies Hook.

Steele takes a deep breath and looks around him. 'I'm sure I could manage,' he says uncertainly. 'I slept in worse places in the Navy.'

Inspector Carr leans towards Hook and whispers.

'Yes,' says Hook. 'Good idea. I'm prepared to authorise the obtaining of an hotel room for the rest of the night. You could have a few hours' sleep, eat breakfast, and return refreshed when your solicitor is available.'

'That's a better solution,' agrees Steele. 'Thank you, superintendent. I would appreciate that.'

CHAPTER 10

Charles is again woken by the telephone. At least this time he's in bed. As he reaches for the receiver, he looks at the alarm clock on the bedside cabinet: 6:50 a.m.

'Sorry to disturb you so early, Mr Holborne,' says Jones's voice, 'but I didn't want you to remain on standby.'

'Not to worry,' replies Charles, his voice still gravelly from sleep.

'I didn't call back last night because we didn't have the suspect until very late.'

Charles sits up. 'Did you interview him?'

'We did. He's at an hotel at present. His solicitor's been in touch and will be here at eight. We plan to resume then, although I think we've run out of questions. He'll have been advised not to answer anyway.'

'What did he have to say?'

Jones repeats quickly the important parts of the judge's interview. 'Also,' he adds, before finishing, 'some further statements came in yesterday evening. I'm sending copies to chambers but there's not much to them, just stuff about the plastic sheeting and the blood.'

'And?'

'Both dead ends. The blood's human, but can't be grouped. It's too old. We can't even say with any degree of precision when it was spilled.'

'Define "precision".'

'It might have been there before the deceased died. On the other hand, it might have got there some time afterwards.'

'So we have a body with no obvious marks of injury which used to live in a house with bloodstains of indeterminate age and source,' concludes Charles.

'Yes.'

'And what's more, we can't even prove that the bloodstains occurred before or after the deceased died.'

'Yes. What do you think?'

'Bloody hopeless. It's suspicious, but no more than that. It could be a complete coincidence. If you're asking me whether I would recommend a prosecution on this evidence, the answer's definitely "No". The character of the deceased and her risky behaviour make that a double-no. George Carman would tear it to shreds.'

'That's what I expected you to say. We're going to have to release him.'

'Probably. Did you pursue a search warrant for his present home?'

'I decided we'd be unlikely to persuade a magistrate we had enough to issue a warrant. He didn't move there until a year or so after the wife went missing. As he pointed out, he's hardly likely to have preserved damning evidence all this time just for us to find.'

'I agree.'

Jones falls silent for a moment. 'You know, the two policemen in the interview found him very convincing.'

'You didn't?'

'I don't know. I have a gut feeling there's more about it than he's telling. That doesn't necessarily mean I think he did it, but … something's not quite right.'

'But "*Something's not quite right*" won't persuade any judge or jury.'

'Exactly. So, I think that's it. We'll start looking elsewhere. Maybe there were other boyfriends we can interview. In any case, get your clerk to send in a fee note.'

'I will. Thank you.'

'No, thank *you*, Mr Holborne. Your views have been very helpful. I'm just sorry there's to be no brief in it at the end of the day.'

He says his farewells and hangs up. Charles thinks about trying to grab another hour's sleep, but the sun is pouring through the windows, the traffic noise is building and he's now completely awake. He has a committal starting the following Monday and making an early start on the prep would probably be a good idea. He climbs out of bed and pads to the kitchen to make coffee.

By just after half past seven, Charles is walking under the arch into the Temple and is the first into Chambers. The rooms are unusually quiet and it is almost lunchtime before he hears any other voices on his floor.

Feeling virtuous for having worked solidly for five hours, he decides to treat himself to lunch in Hall and wanders over to Middle Temple. It takes his eyes a few seconds to adjust from the bright afternoon sunshine to the gloom inside the Tudor hall. The long trestle tables gleam with glass and silverware, and the smell of roasting meat makes Charles's mouth water.

He installs himself on an empty bench at the far end of Hall with his back to the wood panels bearing the coats of arms of distinguished sons of the Inn and gives his order to the waitress. Hall fills with gossiping barristers, many still in court robes grabbing a quick bite during the short adjournment before rushing back to the Royal Courts of Justice. The spaces on the benches next to and opposite Charles are taken by a group of planning barristers all involved in the same case. Charles smiles at a couple whom he knows slightly but other than to pass water, wine and condiments when requested, he doesn't communicate with the group. He finishes his meal swiftly and returns to Chambers.

By afternoon tea he has finished preparing his brief, and after a quick word with Barbara he slips away.

Two hours later, Charles sits in his battered MG sportscar outside his brother's home in Hendon. He's been there for fifteen minutes, not moving from the car. He's seen his mother through the lounge window and so knows his parents have already arrived. Eventually he takes a deep breath, leans across to the glove box and takes out his yarmulke, the same one in which he was bar mitzvah over twenty years before, reaches behind him for the bunch of flowers to be given to Sonia, and climbs out of the car.

As he walks up the path, the door opens to greet him. David stands on the threshold, grinning.

'I'd been wondering how long it was going to take you to get out of the car,' he says. 'Sonia and I have been laying bets on whether you'd drive off again.'

'Really?'

'No, not really. No one but me knows you've been lurking.'

'"Lurking?" I've not been lurking,' protests Charles, laughing.

He hugs his younger brother with warmth and stands back to appraise him.

Charles's build, olive skin and dark colouring proclaim his Semitic heritage. David, on the other hand, is taller, slimmer and fair-skinned, with grey eyes and light brown hair which, as a boy, had been almost white-blonde. His Aryan looks had even raised eyebrows at the Horowitz's synagogue when he was first taken in to be shown off. One blabbermouthed woman, no longer welcome in the Horowitz household, had been heard to joke that Millie Horowitz must have been raped by a Cossack, but two of Millie's uncles had similar colouring, as she swiftly points out to anyone who comments.

'You look happy,' says Charles, fishing.

'Coming in?' replies David, not taking the bait.

Charles follows David into the kitchen, bypassing the door to the lounge from whence he can hear his father's voice, and delaying the inevitable meeting a few seconds longer. Sonia, wearing an apron, is loading a tray with food to be taken into the dining room. The room smells of warm bread and freshly fried fish. She turns to greet her brother-in-law.

'Hello Charles,' she says softly, and kisses him on both cheeks.

Sonia is more handsome than beautiful, with a full figure, dark hair and soft brown eyes. Charles is envious of his younger brother's luck. Charles would not have wanted to marry a Jewish girl — he is still too conflicted about his parents' religion and stifling culture which he long ago rejected — but he sees how perfectly suited are David and Sonia, how comfortable together. When speaking to one another, they frequently have no need to finish their sentences because each knows the other's mind so well. That's what happens, thinks Charles ruefully, when you pick someone with the same background, attitudes, expectations and interests.

More than once, particularly after Henrietta's death and more still after David and Sonia married, Charles had toyed with the idea of looking within his parents' community for a partner, and each time had rejected the idea. He knew he couldn't fake an interest in a god and in a religion, especially one with such all-pervasive festivals, customs and rituals. He would have left any committed Jewish wife deeply disappointed and isolated. So all of Millie and Harry's hopes and expectations for the next generation have shifted from their first-born son to their second. If there are to be joyous Jewish celebrations, high days and holy days, Charles will only ever be a guest, never a celebrant.

Charles hands Sonia the flowers. She inclines her head to the voices of her parents-in-law which can be heard from the adjoining room.

'Want me to hold your hand?' she asks, with a wink.

Sonia knew Charles by reputation before the Horowitzes and her parents decided that she and David should meet. The East End Jewish community is small, and everyone knew of the local tough guy who won the DFC in the war flying Spitfires, won a scholarship to Cambridge, and then turned his back on his community. He was the one who had married out — the daughter of a Viscount, no less! — and with whom the family had broken all contact.

It had concerned her; what if the younger brother was the same? But then she met David, who proved to be tall, handsome and kind. He was the gentlest of men and deeply devoted to his family and his religion.

Sonia hadn't understood at first when people said that Millie Horowitz was scary; she met only a small, upright, well turned-out woman with eyes of flint that missed nothing. However, in the months before the marriage arranged by their parents, she was able to observe for herself the bile directed by Millie Horowitz at her firstborn, even in absentia, and began to understand it all too well. Millie was not a person to whom one could warm easily. Intelligent, articulate and capable of reducing those around her to helpless laughter, she harboured a deep lake of bitterness whose only expression appeared to be disappointment with Charles and all his life choices. She would never let it go; Charles had committed an unforgivable and personal betrayal at which Millie worried and fretted constantly, like a terrier with a rag.

At the same time Sonia began to see the errant brother through her beloved David's eyes too, and so it was with open-minded curiosity she finally met Charles the week before her wedding. She discovered a man who had rejected the religion and culture which had sustained his forebears for millennia but who, paradoxically, lived his entire life according to one of its most essential principles, that of *tzedakah*, the ethical obligation to do what is right and just. Charles had in him the same kindness as his younger brother, but in Charles it was expressed as a fierce drive to help those in trouble and at the bottom of the pile. It puzzled Sonia that Millie couldn't acknowledge that, despite Charles's rejection of the formal religion, he was the living embodiment of one of its most admirable tenets. Surely that was something of which to be proud? And Charles was funny and good company; he shared with David the same twinkle and susceptibility to uncontrolled giggling they both inherited from their father, Harry.

So although Sonia keeps her own counsel and could no more turn her back on her community than cut off her legs, her sympathies lie with Charles. She admires the courage and patience it takes for him to expose himself to the whips of his mother's sarcasm and emotional manipulation week after week.

'*Courage, mon brave,*' she says, giving Charles a gentle push in the small of his back to usher him out of the kitchen.

As Charles enters the lounge, there's a sudden silence and both his parents turn to look at him. Millie is scowling and Harry stands with his arms and his eyebrows raised in supplication. Millie turns from her husband and sits.

'Hello, son,' says Harry, hugging Charles and kissing him on both cheeks. Charles holds his diminutive father at arm's length, a quizzical expression on his face. Harry Horowitz is a reserved, soft-spoken man, not given to emotional displays, so this greeting is unusual.

'Everything OK, pops?'

'Why shouldn't everything be OK?'

Charles smiles. 'No reason.' He turns to his mother and bends to kiss her. She receives the light brush of his lips on her cheek without quite flinching but makes no movement in response. It's like kissing a statue. 'Hello, mum.'

'I'll see if Sonia needs a hand,' she replies, and she stands and walks directly out of the room. Charles watches her departing back and turns to his father, who he finds studying his shoes.

'What's going on, dad?' Charles asks quietly. 'Did I cause that?'

Harry smiles sadly and shakes his head. 'No, of course not.' He sits, patting the seat beside him on the couch. 'Sit. Tell me what you've been up to.'

Charles hesitates and looks at the open doorway through which his mother has just departed. Millie and Harry have been married for over forty years, and in all that time he has never seen them row.

Charles distractedly spends a couple of minutes telling Harry something about the cases on which he working, but neither is really paying attention.

There's a pause in Charles's flow. Then:

'And how are things with the boys?' asks Harry.

Charles knows exactly to what his father is referring: his long-running and complex relationship with the Kray twins.

'Quiet,' replies Charles, simply.

'Resolved?'

Charles shakes his head, and lowers his voice. 'Not really. They're still *broigus* over the Izzy thing.'

Charles almost never uses Yiddish. It's another marker of his Jewishness to which he'd prefer not to draw attention, but in the company of his brother and father it occasionally slips out. It's familiar and comfortable; moreover, there are some expressions the nuances of which cannot be conveyed in English. To describe the Kray twins as *"broigus"*, loosely, offended or "miffed", is a significant understatement. Ronnie Kray has more than once tried to have Charles killed for both real and imagined wrongs. Most recently Izzy Conway, Charles's cousin, was manipulated by the Twins into attempting to murder Charles. Charles won that battle, but at the cost of Izzy's life. The setback only reinforced Ronnie's determination to settle scores. On the other hand, Charles's relationship with Reggie is more nuanced; faint childhood bonds still join them. Accordingly, an undeclared armistice now exists; the Krays have material on Charles which would end his career and land him in prison and, for the present at least, they consider the blackmail potential to be more useful to them than having Charles dead. The debt has yet to be called in; it's the suspense, waiting for that particular axe to fall, that's responsible for Charles's insomnia, night after night after night.

David puts his head into the room.

'We're ready.'

The family gathers around the Shabbat table in the dining room and Sonia says the ancient prayers to usher in the sabbath and bless the bread and wine. The family sits to eat, chicken soup with dumplings followed by roast chicken and vegetables, all prepared before the sabbath began. David and Charles exchange news, Harry and Sonia contributing occasionally, but Charles notes that Millie is even more tight-lipped than usual.

The soup and main course finished, Sonia and David collect the plates and return to the table with bowls of stewed fruit for dessert. They sit, and Sonia smiles at David as he takes her hand.

'We have an announcement,' he says.

He pauses, looking into the faces of those he loves around the table, savouring the moment. His eyes are shining and Charles's memory goes back to the moment in synagogue when, blessings completed and glass stamped upon, his brother took his new bride in his arms. The same radiance fills David's face now, and Charles guesses what's about to follow. David turns to Sonia and nods encouragement.

'We're expecting,' she says simply.

'In early January,' adds David.

The room fills with exclamations, hugs, kisses and congratulations. David points behind Charles at a bottle of champagne on the sideboard and indicates that he should open it. Charles complies while everyone else chatters, pouring five glasses and handing them around the table.

'I'm so proud of you, David,' says Millie, toasting the couple to her left. 'A real *mensche*, you've become. And you, Sonia, a *balabusta*.'

Charles can't disagree that his brother is an honourable man, a man of integrity, nor that his sister-in-law is a good Jewish homemaker. It's the scornful challenge on his mother's face as she turns defiantly towards him that reveals the subtext to everyone in the room, which falls uncomfortably silent. Charles is neither a *mensch*, nor has he married a *balabusta*. Charles fixes a good-humoured smile to his face and says nothing.

'Now, now, Mum,' soothes David. 'This is a time for celebration.'

'What did I say?' Millie protests. She turns back to Charles. 'Did I say anything?'

'You didn't need to,' says Charles quietly. 'We all know exactly how you feel.'

'So now you're a mind reader?' challenges Millie, her voice rising. 'My oh-so-clever barrister son, the successful professional man.' She is almost shouting. 'Now he's a mind reader too!'

'Millie,' intervenes Harry softly.

'What?'

'Don't start.'

'Well, something should be said. It should have been said years ago. And if you won't —' and she flashes an angry glance at Harry, and Charles wonders if she's inadvertently revealed the subject of their disagreement earlier — 'I shall.'

'Not now —'

'Please —' say Harry and David simultaneously, but Millie's fuse, smouldering even before Charles arrived, is aflame. She's worked herself up into a righteous fury and cannot hear. She bangs her champagne glass on the table, shifts in her seat and squares up to Charles. Here we go, he thinks, and maybe it is time for some honesty. A showdown has been brewing for months, years in fact; he just wishes she'd chosen some other occasion.

'A succession of *shiksas,* you inflict on us. First the hoity-toity one, God rest her soul. Then a bunch whose names people show me in the papers but, thank God, you never brought home. And then finally, little Sally.'

'So?'

'Did we make her welcome?'

'Sally? Yes, Mum, you did,' replies Charles, still attempting conciliation. 'You were very kind to her.'

'You'll never know what that cost me … us!' she says, her voice full of bitterness. 'But we did it, for you, for our great and mighty son, the one who's in the papers every day already! Just to keep the peace.'

'No, Millie,' intervenes Harry softly. 'We did it because we love him, even though he … he…'

'Even though he broke our hearts. Say it, Harry! It's time he heard the truth!'

Harry looks away as his wife continues her attack.

'We made her welcome, treated her as if she was your wife, instead of some cheap *shiksa* you were shacked up with!'

'And I was grateful, Mum. So was she. I know it was hard for you.'

'And now what? You throw it back in our faces!'

'Throw it back in your face?' asks Charles, finally goaded into raising his voice. 'What on earth do you mean by that?'

'You just dumped the poor girl.'

Charles, astounded, looks to the others, baffled at his mother's logic. 'That's not what happened at all, Mum. We split up; it happens.'

'You're a fool!' Millie throws out.

'Maybe. But if so, it has nothing to do with you. It was between Sally and me. I threw nothing back in your face.'

'For you, we broke our principles —'

'Is that how you see it? Well, it looks different from where I sit! You cast me out of the family because I refused to marry "a nice Jewish girl"! I wouldn't do as you wanted so, to punish me, you pretended I was dead. For over a decade! Henrietta had to be murdered before you'd acknowledge my existence!

What right have you to tell me how I live my life? And then, when I finally found someone I loved, I was again in the wrong for "living in sin" with a *shiksa*. But you, so *gracious*, so *forgiving*, deign to invite Sally and me to your home … for tea!' continues Charles, his voice dripping with the sarcasm he'd learned at the knee of the master.

Out of the corner of his eye Charles sees Harry shaking his head sadly, but now the brakes are off and he doesn't want to stop. 'Well, thank you for that, your Majesty. And now*, now* I'm in the wrong because I'm *no longer* living in sin with her?' Charles raises his hands to the heavens in exasperation.

'Charlie,' implores David.

Charles casts a glance at Sonia, who now sits with her face in her hands, barricading herself against the typhoon of emotion raging around her. David has his arm round her shoulders which heave with emotion.

Charles's own shoulders slump in defeat. 'I'm sorry Davie, Sonia. Really I am. I told you this would happen.'

Charles drags his jacket off the back of his seat as he stands.

'There's someone you should really meet, Mum, a chap from my Chambers,' he says, now more sad than angry.

'Oh yes, why is that then?' demands Millie, knowing a trap when she sees it but defiant to the last.

David raises his voice for the first time. 'Enough, Mum! You've already spoiled what should've been a special evening.'

'You'd get on well with him,' continues Charles. 'You're both contemptuous of me — in his case 'cos I'll always be too Jewish, in yours 'cos I'll never be Jewish enough. I'd like to see that bout.'

'Please don't go, Charles,' says Sonia, her tear-streaked face lifting.

'No,' says Millie. 'Let him go, already. I've had enough of him.'

Charles pauses. 'It's probably best, Sonia. I'm sorry. *Mazeltov* to you both. It's wonderful news and I couldn't be happier for you.'

Charles navigates round the dining table. As he reaches the dining room door, he turns. His anger has evaporated. What remains is a deep well of unhappiness but, also, clarity.

'Whatever I do, Mum, it'll never be enough. Instead of trying to bully me into being who you *want*, why could you never just love me for who I *am*?'

CHAPTER 11

Charles spends another largely sleepless night, his mind teeming with white noise and vivid dreams that he can't remember on waking, but which leave him tense and moody when he finally drags himself from bed. He decides to go into Chambers where, he hopes, the tranquillity of the Temple and the view over the river will soothe him.

He walks though the deserted courtyards and climbs the steps to Chambers. The outer doors are still locked, so he'll be the only person in the building. Some papers have been rolled into a tube and squeezed through the letterbox which is substantially too small for them. The result is that the outer pages are torn and marked. Charles extricates them from the letterbox and then realises with surprise they bear his name. He unfurls the damaged envelope. Inside are the additional statements from Jones. He throws the papers onto his desk and his hat onto the hook behind the door (a perfect shot, for once), tunes his transistor radio to Radio Caroline to catch the last hour of the Gary Kemp show, and returns to the kitchen to make a cup of coffee.

The Beachboys are belting out *Help Me Rhonda* when he returns to his desk and the joyous song helps lift Charles's mood. It climbs further as he opens the new evidence from Jones. The first statement confirms what he expected: the co-axial cable was generic and could have been purchased from most electrical stores. The second is not actually a statement, but a summary of the absence of evidence compiled by Inspector Carr. No boathouse had been found and no shed. No boathouse, therefore no boat; and if there's no boat, how could the judge have got the body into the centre of Wastwater? Furthermore, if he had any connection with the plastic used to wrap the body, it can't be proven. All that can be proven is that the plastic sheeting emanated from a company that used to trade in Kent and that it, with the body, ended up four hundred miles away in Wastwater: perhaps a coincidence, perhaps not, but not enough.

Charles turns to the third, and last, new document. It's a short statement from a scientist at the Central Research and Support Establishment at Aldermaston, dealing with the plastic bag in which the deceased woman's head had been encased. The lab had succeeded in completing the wording on the side where the ink had been obliterated by examining the plastic bag for minute indentations left during the printing process.

It is the final sentence which makes Charles's heart beat faster. The statement concludes that the bag came from a village food shop in Somerset. Charles leaps to his feet and reaches for a road atlas from his shelves. He turns the pages to the map for Somerset, pores over it for a moment and then punches the air. He leafs frantically through the documents on his desk for the scrap of paper on which he scribbled Jones's telephone number. After throwing most of the contents of his desk onto the threadbare carpet, he eventually finds and dials the number.

'Jones?'

'Who's speaking?' The voice does not belong to the diminutive Canadian solicitor.

'My name's Charles Holborne. I was counsel instructed on a recent … to advise on evidence.'

'I'm sorry sir, but he's not in today. Can I take a message for him?'

'What about the police officers who were working with him? There was an Inspector Carr from Cumberland I think, and a local superintendent.'

'Yes, sir, that would be Superintendent Hook. I'm afraid he's not in today either, and I believe Inspector Carr has returned north.'

'Shit!'

'Sorry, sir?'

'Never mind. Please can you get a message to Mr Jones as soon as possible and tell him to contact me? He has my numbers both here in Chambers and at my home.'

'Will do, sir.'

Little more than an hour later, Charles hears the phone ringing in the clerk's room downstairs. He races out onto the landing, leaps down the stairs two at a time, and bangs open the door to the room just in time to catch the call.

'Holborne,' he announces breathlessly.

'Mr Holborne, this is Superintendent Hook. I saw a note on a colleague's desk to the effect that you need to get in touch with Jones urgently. Can I help?'

'Yes, Superintendent, thank you for calling. I think I can get you a search warrant of the judge's present home.'

'How come? I thought we were dead in the water. If you'll excuse the pun.'

Charles smiles grimly. 'Well, we have blood at the former matrimonial home. The body was wrapped in plastic from a factory twenty-two miles from that property. Not enough on its own, I agree. But the plastic bag found over the deceased's head comes from a village store only two miles from the oldest boy's school. That's where the judge says he was the day after his wife disappeared. We now have a connection with every stage on the body's potential journey: Kent, then Somerset, then Wastwater. Not enough to persuade a jury to convict on its own perhaps, but I think it's enough to get us a warrant to search his present home.'

The line goes silent as the Superintendent considers Charles's theory.

'Would you feel confident arguing that before a magistrate?'

'Definitely.'

'Under normal circumstances I'd be perfectly happy to take this decision myself but, given the identity of the suspect… Leave it with me and I'll see if I can dig up Jones. How's your diary for tomorrow?'

'Well, by chance, I'm going to be at Maidstone Assizes anyway. If Jones goes with it, have him speak to my clerk about timing, but it should certainly be possible.'

'It is enough to arrest the suspect?'

'Yes, I think it is.'

'On what charge? Disposal of a corpse with intent to prevent an inquest?'

'No. Once he's arrested we don't want him communicating with anyone in that household, the children or the nanny. If it's just disposal of a corpse, maybe even perverting the course of justice, he'll still probably get bail.'

'Therefore…'

'Arrest him on suspicion of murder.'

'Sure?'

'Bloody right I am.'

CHAPTER 12

With perfect synchronicity, Mr Jones and Superintendent Hook descend the court steps, warrants in hand and smiles on faces, just as Inspector Carr, refreshed after a weekend off and two proper nights' sleep, pulls up outside the judge's house in Kent with a policewoman he has collected from the station en route. They are to wait there until joined by Hook and Jones, unless Steele tries to leave the house, in which case he is to be intercepted. Having ascertained that he's at home, Carr moves his vehicle to a discreet distance from the driveway which provides a vantage point from which they can see both the front door and the side entrance.

It takes an hour for the others to arrive in the village. Carr watches in his rear-view mirror as the squad car approaches and the man who is, once again, his boss, descends. The two policemen and the young WPC approach the front door. Steele must have seen the cars outside because it is he who opens the door and he already wears a raincoat and hat. He stands silently on the threshold as Hook formally arrests him and closes the door behind him. Carr takes his handcuffs from his back pocket and puts them on the judge's wrists. Steele says nothing and is escorted to the waiting police cars.

As bad luck would have it, as Steele is assisted into the back of the police car, Mrs Harrison, the next-door neighbour but two is pushing her bike up the hill from the pond and is passing the end of the drive. Her head turns, open-mouthed, as she follows the judge's pale face through the window as the car drives off. It takes her less than five minutes to return to her home and another five minutes to finish a hurried telephone call to Tom and Edna Noakes, who, being on the parish council, usually know everything that goes on in the village.

Edna Noakes likes to call herself a realist. Forty years a nurse until her retirement earlier that year, she reckons she's seen every aspect of human nature, and by and large it isn't nice. In Edna's opinion most people are petty, dishonest and malicious to their fellow men. She'd always suspected that the widowed judge and the beautiful nanny were up to no good. She'd accepted the invitation to their parties, of course, like everyone else in the village, but only to confirm her conclusion that the nanny was no better than she ought to be and the judge was obviously keeping secrets.

Tom Noakes doesn't share his wife's scepticism of all human nature, but he can think of no reason why the judge should be led unwillingly to a police car and so, curiosity aroused, he walks down to the house to see what's going on. He is confirmed in his view that something must be, as he is told firmly to go away by a policewoman stationed at the front gate. Sensing a story, he gets onto his brother-in-law who does the ads at the local newspaper, and shortly thereafter a reporter turns up.

By early evening, a large crowd of villagers and reporters from the national press and the BBC have gathered at the front of the house. They watch, fascinated, as numerous police officers and scientists arrive at the property, some departing again armed with plastic bags full of household contents. Then the nanny is led away to a car in tears, and a relative arrives to look after the children.

Inspector Carr is unknown in the area and for a while is able to get through the crowd and in and out of the cordon without attracting too much attention. Eventually, however, he is addressed by one of the local police officers within earshot of the gates, and by the time he emerges again all the reporters have realised that he is one of the officers in charge of the investigation. Microphones and cameras are thrust into his face as he leaves the house.

'Are you able to give us any information, Inspector?'

'Is Sir Anthony under arrest?'

'Has he been charged yet?'

'Is this anything to do with his wife's disappearance all those years ago?' asks one who had taken the trouble to do a little research before getting on the train from London.

Carr says nothing and pushes his way through the questions to his car. He drives back to Maidstone where Jenny is being interviewed by Superintendent Hook. By the time he arrives, the nanny is sitting in the outer office awaiting a lift back to the house. Her eyes are red and heavy and it's obvious she's been crying. Carr is buzzed past the counter and taken through to a tiny interview room where Hook is sitting at a table reading a statement.

'Is that it, sir?' asks Carr.

'Yes. We've just finished.'

'Well?' asks Carr, sitting down.

'Not much we don't know already. She says the wife was an absolute bitch, but the judge never laid a hand on her. "*He was always extremely patient, even under the greatest of provocation*" is how she puts it.' Hook runs his finger further down the handwritten statement to read another section. "*He was a devoted father and I think the only reason he didn't divorce her was because of the children.*" She says the affair with Roddy was an open secret. Everyone in the village knew. That's about it.'

'And the events of that afternoon?'

'She says she was at the park with the children. By the time she returned, the wife wasn't there, and she got on with making tea.'

'What did you make of her, sir?'

Hook pauses. 'Very distressed, more so than I would've predicted — for an employee I mean. I know she's been with them for years, and I expected her to be close to the children, but…'

'I saw something of that, the night we first went to the house,' comments Carr.

'Yes?'

'I couldn't put my finger on it at the time. Protectiveness of him, maybe. She acted more like a wife than an employee.'

Hook nods. 'I'm not really surprised. Think about it. She's, what? late thirties? Early forties? She's been with the family for fourteen or fifteen years. She a looker, too. She's given the best years of her life, her marriageable years, and probably lost the chance of having her own kids. You don't do that for someone else's children. Not only for that.'

'What do you think?' asks Carr.

'I think she's in love with him, that's what I think.'

'I agree. Which means she might be protecting him.'

'Maybe. Maybe they've been having an affair for years. Maybe *she* killed the wife.'

The door opens and a uniformed sergeant puts his head round the door. 'Something for you, sir; just arrived. Thought you'd like to see it.'

He hands two pages to Hook who takes them and reads them quickly. His thin face creases into a smile as he hands the pages over to Carr. They are the two pages of a further statement by Dr Butcher, the pathologist. After the declaration at the top, it continues:

Further to my first statement, during the post-mortem examination of the body, I removed skin from the forehead and neck of the corpse for microscopic examination. There was found to be a brownish discolouration of the tissue beneath the skin in both of these areas. Microscopic examination of the tissue from each side of the forehead showed deposits of crystalline material which in my opinion is the substance haematoidin, which is produced by the breakdown of haemoglobin, a principal constituent of blood. This indicates that there was bruising of the forehead which would have been produced by a blow. Similarly, there was found a similar brown crystalline material in the tissues near the hyoid bone. This also indicates bruising. Such bruising to the side of the hyoid bone is consistent with, and highly characteristic of, strangulation, especially when it is present on both sides. The discolouration in this case was found only on one side (the left).

However, considering the fact that there was no evidence of organic disease which could have caused or contributed to death, nor any evidence of injury of sufficient severity to cause death, it is my opinion that the bruising at the site of the hyoid bone demonstrates that death resulted from: manual strangulation.

'You know, when I first looked at this I thought we'd be wasting our time,' comments Hook. 'Seems I might have been wrong. Was the nanny still outside when you came in?'

'Yes.'

'Then I think we should interview her again. We can't put any pressure on him, but maybe…'

'Would you mind if I had a shot at it, sir?'

Hook studies the inspector. 'Think you can do better than me, do you?'

'No, sir, not at all. I just think that … maybe … I think I can make a connection with her.'

Hook considers this and then nods in agreement. 'Fine. I need something to eat anyway. Shall I get the sergeant back?'

'No. At least, sir, not unless you particularly want him present.'

'It's a "her" not a "him", but it's your call.'

Jenny is still sitting outside when Carr goes to get her. He explains that there are one or two further questions. She sighs deeply, but rises without speaking and precedes him back to the interview room.

She *is* a looker though, thinks Carr as Jenny takes a seat opposite him. Even tired and with bloodshot eyes, she is strikingly attractive. Her long hair, which he first saw flowing freely to her waist, is now plaited and tied up in a complicated manner that he finds intriguing and inviting, like a bra strap asking to be undone. And her way of moving. He remarked that on the stairs, an almost imperceptible sway of her rounded hips, not a wiggle which a girl in her twenties might have affected, but a slow, languorous movement that reminds him of a ship rocking gently at anchor. I could get into older women, thinks Carr — rather unjustly, as Jenny is only four years his senior. It is the tenderness with which he is thinking of her that colours his first question and his tone.

'You're very fond of him, aren't you, Jenny? You don't mind if I call you "Jenny", do you?'

She tucks a stray strand of hair behind her ear, a gesture he finds charming and slightly erotic.

'I don't care what you call me. I'm fond of all of them. I've been part of the family for fifteen years.'

Her voice is cultured, what he'd have called "very Home Counties". Normally that would've aroused Carr's lifetime prejudice against all things and all people south of the Watford

Gap, but he finds that for her, he's prepared to make an exception.

'Aye, sure, but it's more than that, isn't it, pet?'

Jenny stares hard at him for a moment and then looks away. 'That's none of your business.'

'Oh, but it is, pet,' replies Carr, his Geordie accent soft and trustworthy. 'I don't think you're telling us everything you know, you see, because you care for him and think you're helping him. You don't realise it but, by trying to help, by holding back, you might very well be harming him.'

She looks at the table. 'You do love him then?' he presses, leaning in closer over the small table.

'I'm not going to discuss that with you, a complete stranger, when I've never discussed it with him.'

'Never discussed it with him? All this time?' There's mixed incredulousness and sympathy in his voice. 'All those nights in the house, all those family holidays? It's hard to believe.'

'Believe what you want.'

'You poor lass! All those years, loving those bairns and their father, the man who might've been — should've been — your husband.'

'Don't patronise me, inspector,' she says, her voice more sad than angry.

Carr sits back, irritated. Both the ex-wife and the new accuse him of the same offence. 'Sorry,' he says, but his voice has lost some of its soft beguiling tone.

'I'm not your pet or your poor lass, and I don't want your sympathy.'

She stands.

'Look, I don't understand the procedure here, but I was told I could leave at any time, right? Well, it's getting late and I'm tired. I've told you everything I can. I want to go home now. Bobby needs a meal and his cricket whites for tomorrow.'

'Bobby?'

'The judge's younger son.'

'You're doing more to help them here, believe me,' says Carr carelessly.

'How is that, then?'

'Think about it. There were only four people living there when Lise Steele disappeared, not counting the baby.' He pronounces the last word "*babby*". 'We need to know what happened that day. So, I can ask you or … I can ask them.'

'They were small children! You can't possibly interview them.'

He shrugs. 'I can. This is a murder inquiry. So you'd better believe me; I will if I have to.'

Her eyes open wide. 'Murder? What do you mean? No one said anything about murder.'

'Perhaps you'd better sit down, Miss Sullivan.' She slowly resumes her seat. 'What do you suppose he was arrested for?'

'No one's told me. One minute he was sitting in his study and the next he was being bundled out of the house. Then your lot start taking the place to pieces.'

Carr speaks slowly, locking eyes with her. 'Well, perhaps you should understand now. He's been arrested for the murder of his wife.'

She stares at the inspector, her eyes and mouth making a triangle of "O"s as she assimilates the information. The strand of hair has escaped again and the Inspector has an urge to tuck it back in place for her. She drops her eyes to the corner of the tiny room, looking unseeingly at the marked linoleum and cigarette ends lying like oblong goldfish on the floor. The

Inspector tries to interpret her expression but can discern only distress and indecision.

'The more information we can obtain elsewhere, in other words from *you*, the less chance we'll need to interview the children. No one wants to have them dragged in here. Less still through the courts.'

'The courts?'

He gives her a few moments to allow that scene to play out in her mind. Jenny shakes her head, her lips open as if she's going to speak but then close again. Now Carr is almost sure she knows more than she's said.

'Tell me what happened?' he asks directly. She shakes her head again. 'If he's innocent, what are you trying to hide?'

Carr watches as the woman's eyes fill with tears and now he knows. There's an internal battle raging inside her.

'I think I need to see a solicitor,' she concludes.

'Why's that then? Have you done something wrong?'

'I don't know,' she says, a fat tear emerging from each of her wide eyes and running down her cheeks. She wipes one away with the back of her hand but the other plops onto the table top. She reaches into her jacket pocket and pulls out a handkerchief.

'You don't know?' he asks, surprised.

He tries to imagine Jenny's white knuckles squeezing Lise Steele's neck. He tries to imagine her kneeling over the dying woman fighting for her last breath, hands grabbing and flailing like windmill sails before gradually dropping to her sides. He tries to picture her dragging the bloodied body to an open car boot, bundling it in and fastening it to a concrete kerb.

It's no use; the pictures refuse to coalesce in his imagination. Whatever this woman did, he'll need some convincing that it was murder.

'No, pet,' he says, shaking his head. 'I don't think you've done much wrong, 'cept maybe loving the wrong man.'

'The wrong man? He's not what you think at all,' insists Jenny vehemently. 'He couldn't kill her, or anybody for that matter. It's just not in him.'

'That'll be for a jury to decide.'

'Are you going to charge him with murdering her?'

'That won't be my decision, but I expect so. We now have evidence of strangulation. That plus the blood all over the bedroom … well…'

Carr's mention of the blood is a deliberate attempt to shock her, but again her response surprises him. She looks away from the table as if something disgusting had suddenly landed there. Either she didn't hear him correctly or she already knew about the blood.

'Well, now,' he says, his voice soft again, 'now you really *do* surprise me. That wasn't news to you was it, Jenny? If you knew nothing about it, you'd have asked "*What blood?*"'

Jenny doesn't answer. Carr lets the silence lengthen. Her tears come thick and fast now. He watches the woman before him crying quietly, twisting and untwisting the now sodden handkerchief gripped tightly in her hands.

'You're no good at this, pet. I don't think lying is something you like doing, or something you've any practice in.'

Jenny does not reply.

'Let it out, Jenny. Believe me, you'll feel better. Secrets have a way of burrowing in deep. I've seen it all me career. They lodge, inside you, and grow. Like a cancer.'

She looks up at him, chewing her lower lip. 'He didn't murder her,' she insists with intensity. 'I *know* he didn't!'

'How do you know?'

'I just know.'

'If you love him and you know he's innocent, why on earth won't you tell me what happened? Why are you keeping it to yourself?'

'I don't know what to do!' she cries, tears dripping freely onto the table where they form two slowly expanding pools. 'Can I talk to him?' she pleads, her face an agony of indecision.

Carr shakes his head. 'I want to know what you have to say, not what he wants you to say. If you've information to give about what happened on the day Lise Steele left — or was taken out — of the house, you've a duty to give it.'

Inspector Carr reaches into his jacket pocket and pulls out a small packet of tissues, placing them on the table before her. She stuffs the useless handkerchief back in her pocket and uses a tissue to blow her nose noisily.

'Now, what's it to be? Do you have anything more to say? If not, I'll have a car take you home, and we'll bring in Stephen and Charlotte.'

She closes her eyes, forcing herself to breathe deeply. Then she takes three controlled intakes of air, holding each for a count of five before exhaling slowly. He watches her regain control of herself, and it's an impressive display. She continues to sit with her eyes closed as her breathing calms even more. When she opens her eyes again it is to stare directly at Carr. He sees that a decision has been taken.

'Well, pet — Miss Sullivan? What's it to be?'

'I know he didn't murder her,' she replies, her voice firm.

Carr nods, his face earnest, conveying that he's ready, waiting, eager even, to believe anything she says.

'I know, because he told me,' says Jenny.

She pauses, selecting and testing her words, seeking exactly the right ones to convey her account. More than once Carr opens his mouth to prompt her and each time he decides against it. Eventually she continues.

'OK. He came to me. The day after she got back from her last trip with Roddy. I had never seen him in such a state. He's always calm, controlled. He came to my room, late, and broke down. He said she'd come at him with a knife. He'd been forced to defend himself, and in doing so had killed her. Accidentally. You must believe me, inspector, because I know him!' She stares Carr straight in the eye, beseeching, seeking confirmation that he believes her. 'He would've been utterly incapable of killing her deliberately. He'd sat in the room with her for a whole day, trying to decide what to do.'

She pauses again. Hook desperately wants to start taking notes — his open pocket book is on the table before him and he has a pencil in his hand — but his instinct tells him that if he moves or says anything he might break the spell and she could stop talking. A memory of something said during his training at Hendon comes back to him. An inspector was talking about interview technique.

'Most often you have to prise the story out of them with a jemmy, and it comes out fractured and in pieces. Then it's up to you to put it together. But sometimes the story comes out so fast and with such force that all you can do is get out of its way.'

Inspector Carr puts his pencil down and sits back to listen.

'Over the next six hours, until the next morning, we talked it back and forth. He picked up the telephone a dozen times to call you — the police — and each time he put the phone down again. It was the children! He's a lawyer, through and through, he believes in it, his life is dedicated to it. He knew he should report the whole thing immediately, and the longer he left it, the worse it looked. But he'd seen mistakes made in the courts the whole time, and he was terrified you wouldn't believe him. He kept coming back to the fact that she was an absolute bitch to him, and everyone knew it. He kept saying *"I've prosecuted weaker cases, and won them"*. Then what would happen to the children? They were so young. Stephen was about eleven, Charlotte six, and the baby only a few months. The thought of them going into an institution was just too much for him. He was so scared. I've never seen a man so distressed — it made me think of the Bible, you know? Renting his clothes and tearing his hair, it was like that — at his wits' end. After hours, just as it was getting light, he decided. He shaved and bathed, put on a suit. He was going to drive to the police station.'

Jenny lowers her head and seems unsure how to continue. The pause lengthens to a minute, then two. Carr takes a chance.

'Why didn't he?' he asks, almost so softly that she doesn't hear him.

Her reply is almost whispered. 'Because I persuaded him not to.'

'You?'

'Yes. You see, *I* was frightened. I thought I was going to lose everything, him, the children, my home, everything I loved.'

He nods, understanding.

'What happened then?'

'That decided it for him. He told me to take the children away for three or four days, and everything would be fine when I got back.'

'Did you go?'

'Yes. To friends on the coast. We'd been there several times before for long weekends. They were fine about it.'

'And that's all. You did nothing else, just went away?'

'He asked me to buy him some do-it-yourself things before I left, paint, wallpaper and so on, and I did that.'

'What was it for?'

'To redecorate, I suppose.'

Silence descends on them once more.

Now it is the inspector's face that reveals a difficult internal debate. He shakes his head to himself, trying to reject the conclusion that forces itself on him. He wants to ignore it, to pretend he hasn't heard the last answers, but he's been a copper too long. Contrary to all his expectations, she's crossed the line separating a witness from a suspect and he has no alternative. He stands and she gazes up at him. He sees relief in her eyes, relief that the truth is finally out. He also sees trust. Jenny Sullivan has trusted him with her most preciously guarded secret in the belief that doing so will help the man she loves.

When Carr speaks he can't meet her eyes. 'Jennifer Sullivan: I have no alternative but to arrest you on suspicion of being an accessory after the fact contrary to common law. You don't have to say anything if you don't wish to do so, but anything you do say will be recorded and may be used against you in evidence. Do you understand?'

CHAPTER 13

Mikey McArthur opens the front door of the tiny cottage in Borrowdale, Cumberland. The usual aromas of stale cooking and faeces hit him between the eyes.

'Hello?' comes a tremulous voice from the front room. 'Hello?'

'It's me,' replies McArthur.

'Hello?' repeats the voice.

'It's me, you deaf old scarecrow,' says McArthur, raising his voice impatiently.

He bends to pick up the post delivered in his absence and flicks through the envelopes. All are addressed to "William McArthur". Mikey drops most of them back to the floor, but one looks interesting, an official-looking window envelope. He slides a grubby forefinger under the gummed flap. It's his father's seaman's pension, and McArthur smiles and pockets it.

He walks to the door of the front room and looks in.

'What did you say?' asks the old man.

William McArthur sits in his accustomed armchair next to the wireless. The stained seat, capable of taking its occupant's bulk when he still weighed eighteen stone, now dwarfs him; he looks lost in it. Mikey reckons that his father must have shed over half his body weight in the last year alone. Can't be long now, he thinks; the old geezer looks like a skeleton. On the small table next to the armchair is an empty plate bearing the crumbs of a long-eaten snack and a thermos flask, the lid off, apparently empty.

William peers up at his son, a puzzled expectant expression on his face.

'Remember me?' asks Mikey.

The sick old man's brow wrinkles with effort, but whether he's having trouble remembering his son's name or just passing wind Mikey can't tell.

'Yeh, course I do. Where you been?' Despite twenty years of living in the Lake District, William McArthur still speaks with a thick Cockney accent.

Mikey ignores his father's question. 'Shat yourself again, I see,' he says. The old man looks away, shamed but helpless. 'Well I ain't cleaning you up.'

'Please, boy,' pleads William. 'I've been like this since last night.'

Even with assistance William McArthur can no longer climb the steep and narrow stairs to his bedroom, so he now lives in the front room, being helped to the lavatory in the backyard and being washed down every day or so in the kitchen by the district nurse.

'It'll wait a couple of hours more, then. The nurse'll be along before lunch.'

Mikey turns to leave.

'At least make us a cuppa,' William asks. 'I'm really parched.'

'If I've got time before I go. But I'm busy; things to do, people to see.'

'What? You're off again? You ain't been here for days! What you come back for at all, then?'

'Mind your own fucking business,' says Mikey, turning away.

'You wouldn't treat a dog the way you do me!' quavers William, his voice rising.

'Oh, I don't know,' says Mikey over his shoulder. 'Don't much like dogs; can't stand the *whining*,' and he points at his father, laughing loudly at his own joke.

'Someone's gotta to teach you a bit of respect,' says William, a long-ingrained reflex prompting him to reach for the leather belt that holds up his stinking trousers.

Mikey turns back to his father with a sneer. 'Yeah, well it ain't gonna be you, is it? You can't even raise that belt anymore can you, you old cripple?'

He leaves the old man weeping with frustration and climbs the staircase to his father's bedroom. There he opens all the drawers to the dressing table one after another, searching for something. Unsuccessful, he stands with his hands on his hips, scanning the other furniture in the room. He goes to the wardrobe, pulling back musty clothes and opening shoeboxes. Finally, he looks under the bed.

'Hello, hello,' he mutters to himself.

He drags out a bound leather suitcase. It's covered with ancient labels from all around the world, evidence of his father's former life in the merchant marine: Rotterdam, Aden, Hong Kong — William McArthur has been everywhere. Mikey sits on the bed with the suitcase beside him. He blows off a thick covering of dust and loosens the frayed leather straps. Inside, alongside bundles of handwritten letters tied with string, his father's war medals and other personal memorabilia, he finds what he's looking for. He opens the old blue passport in his hands to check: yes! Staring up at him is his father's photograph, taken when he was fit and healthy and still looked strikingly like Mikey does now. There's a bonus, too: inside the back cover, folded for so long that the creases have browned, is William McArthur's birth certificate. Mikey pockets both documents; you never know. One thing's sure: William McArthur won't be taking any more foreign holidays.

Mikey throws everything else back into the suitcase, chucks it under the bed and thumps down the stairs, shutting the front door behind him and leaving the house without another word to his father.

Three hours later, having cashed the pension cheque, Mikey steps, blinking, into bright afternoon sunshine outside Ladbrokes. He'd been counting on *Lucky Strike*, a supposed 10 – 1 dead cert at Southwell, the tip for which had itself cost five pounds, but the fucking nag came in fourth. So he's back to square one.

He sets off in search of a boozer to work out his next move. He walks through the Co-op car park, paying little attention to his surroundings, and is about to cross the road when a heavy hand lands on his left shoulder, a split second before another lands on the right. Before Mikey can react, a punch comes thundering into his left kidney which doubles him up.

'Boss wants to see you, Mikey,' says a man behind him and to his left.

Mikey is now in his mid-fifties and a lot of his former muscle is now fat, but he's still a big man with a bulldog neck and hands the size of plates. He also spent a lot of time keeping fit at HM Prison Durham on his last stretch, and he reckons he's still quite handy. It was a decent punch but Mikey's adrenaline is running fast, and he's only momentarily aware of the pain. He takes his time to turn and straighten up, slightly more time than he actually needs, and by the time he's upright he's tensed, ready for flight or fight.

Two men face him. The man who spoke, the one who presumably hit him, is six inches taller and probably twenty years younger than Mikey himself, and has the build of a weightlifter. His companion is about the same height, although Mikey notes that he is slimmer and a bit older. For a moment Mikey identifies him as the weaker link, but then he sees the flattened nose and the tangle of scar tissue over both eyebrows.

This bloke was a boxer; maybe still is. Mikey relaxes, deciding that bullshit, rather than fists, are required to extricate himself this time.

'But 'e gave us a week,' protests Mikey. 'And it's only Friday.'

'Yes,' says the taller man with a grin, 'but I'm taking tomorrow off, so it might as well be now. Anyway, where you going to get it before the morning?'

After twenty years living up here, Mikey still finds the Cumbrian accent almost impenetrable.

'I've already got it, ain't I?' replies Mikey, smiling and doing his best to sound confident.

'All of it?'

'Every penny.'

'Hand it over then,' says the tall man, his hand outstretched.

'It's at me dad's,' explains Mikey. 'You don't think I'd bring that sort of money into a *speiler*, do you?'

'A what?'

Mikey jabs a thumb behind him. 'Betting shop,' he explains.

'Right, then, let's go.'

Each of the men grabs one of Mikey's jacket elbows and he's spun round. They start marching him back across the car park.

'No, no! That ain't gonna work. It'd kill me dad.'

Mikey drags the men to a halt.

'Why's that, then?'

''E's got terminal cancer. Honest, 'e's really sick; probably ain't got more than another coupla days.'

The two enforcers look at one another over Mikey's head. The one who hasn't spoken nods affirmation.

'Fine,' says the taller one, releasing his hold. 'Bring it round the shop tomorrow morning. No later than ten.'

'Easy.'

The other man speaks for the first time. His accent is different, Yorkshire, guesses Mikey. 'We know where you live, Mikey. If you aren't there by ten tomorrow morning, I'll be round straight away. And I'll take the money out of you. And your dad.'

'Got it.'

The two men turn and leave Mikey in the car park being watched by an elderly couple loading shopping into the boot of their Austin 1100. Mikey waits for the thugs to disappear before retracing his steps.

'Amateurs,' chuckles Mikey under his breath.

The district nurse is just walking back down the garden path as Mikey brushes past her. She smiles and starts saying something to him, presumably about his father, but he ignores her, opens the front door and slams it behind him. He runs up the stairs to the small box room, and throws everything worth taking into a holdall. Within ten minutes he is striding up the road towards the bus stop. He takes the first bus that arrives without worrying about its destination.

CHAPTER 14

Charles looks up and down the windswept platform of Seascale Station, Cumbria. It's barely a station: two deserted platforms and a wind shelter surrounded by rusting chain-link fences, with an empty car park beyond. The sky is an uninterrupted blue, but the breeze off the beach is surprisingly cold for July. It whistles over a small terrace of houses, across the railway tracks and eastwards towards the lakes, threatening to take Charles's trilby with it.

Charles spins on the spot looking for assistance. Only a handful of others descended from the train, campers or hillwalkers to judge from their equipment, but all have disappeared, collected by friends or family or disappearing into the few waiting taxis. There's no one else to be seen and no taxis now remain outside.

'Where the fuck is he?' he mutters under his breath.

It's been nine hours since he left Euston, with three changes, one delayed train and nothing but a cardboard sandwich courtesy of British Rail since breakfast. Dusk approaches, and Charles is not in the best of tempers. Jones insisted that he visit the *locus in quo* before the trial began. Charles sees no point; he has minutely studied roadmaps of every potential route that Steele might have taken from Kent via Somerset to Wasdale; ordnance survey maps of the area around the lake; dozens of photographs, even some of the underwater shots, for what they're worth; and all the witness statements, with which he is now so familiar, he can almost recite them backwards.

Furthermore, Wastwater was not actually the *locus in quo*. Charles has already been to the house in Kent where Lise Steele met her death, so there's even less reason for him to travel to the far end of the country to see where her body ended up. However, when one's instructing solicitor insists, on such a high-profile case as this — and one which will almost certainly lead to Charles's name appearing in the list of new silks the following April as long as he doesn't muck it up — discretion usually prevails.

So, with as much graciousness as he could muster, he agreed to waste the best part of two days on trains, separated by a night in a local B&B, to satisfy the diminutive solicitor that every possible "I" had been dotted and "T" had been crossed before the trial.

Charles hears a faint voice carried by the wind from the far end of the platform.

'Charles!' it repeats.

Charles turns again and sees Jones, waving energetically. He lifts a hand in reply, hefts his overnight bag over one shoulder and, other hand clamped on his flighty hat, sets off down the platform.

By the time they reach Wasdale Head in Jones's rented car, night has fallen and Charles's stomach is grumbling loudly. Jones changes his original plan of exploring the lake that evening and agrees to do it the following morning, even though rain is forecast.

They check into the Wasdale Head Inn where Jones has booked rooms and just manage to order a meal from a surly local with a dislike of Londoners and Americans before the kitchen closes.

Despite the fact that the hotel is seedy, run down and in need of renovation, the bar is packed with climbers, walkers and locals. The food is indifferent but Charles is so hungry that he clears his plate. He is relieved when Jones, who is not a natural conversationalist and with whom he has little in common, proposes retiring to his room. He leaves Charles in a corner of the bar enjoying the end of his pint of Hartley's Ale, which provides the only pleasant surprise of the day. After a few minutes of eavesdropping drunken competitive accounts of near-death experiences from the fell-walkers around him, Charles also decides to turn in. He is unaware of being studied by a thickset man nursing a half pint of beer on the other side of the bar.

In bed, Charles reads his battered *Times* for a while but even the shooting of Freddie Mills, whom he knew well, can't prevent his eyes drooping after only a minute, so he turns out the light.

Despite the sagging mattress and the bri-nylon sheets, Charles sleeps well and is woken by light penetrating the curtains which do not quite close. He rolls out of bed and dons his dressing gown, opening the door to the corridor to take his place in the queue for the bathroom, when he notices an envelope which has apparently been slid under his bedroom door. From Jones, thinks Charles, as he picks it up.

There is nothing written on the front of the envelope. Charles tears it open and takes out a single sheet of A4 paper. On it, in irregular letters cut from a newspaper, is the message: *Murderer. £10,000 ensure silence.*

'Excuse me,' croaks a large man, also in his dressing gown and bearing a plastic bathroom bag, as he squashes past Charles in the narrow corridor.

Charles steps back into his bedroom and shuts the door, leaning back on it. He's aware that he's holding his breath and his heart rate has doubled. For so long he has dreaded the fall of one axe, and now he hears the swish of a much more ancient blade swooping towards his neck. He turns the letter over: nothing on the reverse. It's a sheet of cheap paper torn along perforations, apparently from an exercise book. Charles realises that his thumb and forefinger are slightly sticky, and he takes the letter to the window, opening the curtains fully to let in the maximum amount of light. The glue fixing the letters to the notepaper is still damp in places. Charles sniffs the paper and the envelope: cheap gum, the sort he used to use at school; it can take a couple of hours to dry completely, even on a porous surface.

He peers closely at the tiny squares and rectangles of newspaper print. The words have been compiled with letters of different sizes and fonts, and appear to have been taken from random pages of newsprint, with one exception: the word "murderer" is a single rectangle of paper and has been lifted complete from its source. It also appears to have some coloured ink, perhaps, red, on the reverse. Someone got lazy, or was in a hurry.

Charles re-folds the letter, replaces it inside the envelope, and slips the envelope into the back of his Archbold, the criminal practitioners' bible that he carries everywhere when on a case.

Having bathed and dressed, he descends to the ground floor and locates the hotel reception. A young woman he has not seen before greets him.

'Good morning,' says Charles, 'my name's Holborne. Has anyone left a message for me?'

The woman turns to the pigeonholes behind the reception desk, scans them quickly, and shakes her head. 'Not that I can see, sir.'

'Is the main hotel door locked after a certain time?'

'Yes, from midnight until six o'clock in the morning. But we can give you a key if you're planning on coming back late.'

Charles thinks back to the previous night; no, he was still reading in his room until after midnight, and the letter certainly wasn't there when he put the lights out. So, someone from the hotel itself? Or possibly another guest?

'No, that's fine thank you,' he replies. 'Do you mind me asking what time you came on duty?'

'About an hour ago, why?'

'Does the hotel deliver newspapers to guests?'

'Yes. Would you like one? We usually have a few spares —'

'No, thank you, but is it possible to speak to whoever was responsible for putting them outside the rooms?'

The woman frowns, puzzled, but nods. 'I should think so.' She turns and calls behind her into an office. 'Spencer?'

An elderly man appears, in the act of cleaning his gold rimmed spectacles. He is smartly dressed in waistcoat and plaid trousers, and wears elasticated metal sleeve holders. Charles addresses him directly. 'Did you take the newspapers up to the bedrooms this morning?'

'Yes, sir. Did I miss you out or get it wrong perhaps? There was a gentleman who wanted *The Telegraph* —'

'No, there's nothing wrong. What time did you distribute the newspapers?'

'Why do you ask, sir?' asks Spencer.

'Someone slipped a letter under my door, and I was wondering if you saw who was responsible.'

'What room are you in?'

'102.'

Spencer shakes his head. 'I came on duty at ten past six, and did the papers straight away. I got to your floor by six fifteen or six twenty and there was no one there then.'

'I don't suppose you saw if there was an envelope sticking out from my door?' Spencer shakes his head again. 'OK. But once you come into the hotel, the doors are open?'

'Don't follow you, sir,' says Spencer with a trace of irritation.

'What I mean is that once you come in, guests can come and go because the doors are then unlocked for the day.'

'Yes, that'd be right.'

So perhaps not a guest after all, just an early bird.

'Thanks for your assistance,' says Charles.

He turns to enter the dining room for breakfast. 'One last thing,' he says, playing a hunch. 'Do you have a local newspaper by any chance?'

The young woman reaches under the reception desk and comes up with a newspaper. 'There's Tuesday's *Cumberland News* if you're interested. I wouldn't have thought it of much interest to someone from London, though.'

'That'll be perfect,' replies Charles, taking it from her. 'I'll return it after breakfast.'

Charles looks around the dining room; Jones isn't yet down for breakfast. Charles orders coffee while he waits for the solicitor and opens the newspaper. He strikes lucky, finding what he's looking for on the inside of the front page. The word "murderer" appears in the middle of a report of a court hearing involving a Seascale man, and the font and size seem identical to that on the letter. Moreover, on its reverse is the corner of a box advertisement on the front page for men's patent leather shoes, in red ink.

Charles closes and folds the paper with a small satisfied smile. The damp glue, the hurried compilation of the demand, its arrival that morning — all point to someone in a hurry, an opportunist. Charles guesses that he was spotted by someone in the bar the night before, presumably someone from his past — and it would have to be someone from almost twenty-five years in the past — who recognised him. Furthermore, he guesses, probably someone who is now a local. Visitors from out-of-town are unlikely to be interested in a local newspaper containing out of date parochial news. Then he reconsiders that last conclusion; on the other hand, someone just looking for an old newspaper to cut up might use the first that came to hand.

In any case, Charles can do no more for the present. He's not certain how seriously to take the threat. Maybe whoever recognised him just thought it'd be fun to frighten the tearaway they used to know as Charlie Horowitz, now an uppity London barrister. On the other hand, he can't afford to be complacent.

Charles mulls it over while drinking his coffee. It'd be a mistake to act the private detective in a rural part of the country where he knows no one; he'd stand out like a sore thumb. In any case, he's due to return to London in a few hours' time; if the mis-spelling putative blackmailer is serious, he'll have to make his next move quickly.

Jones arrives, his hair wet and slicked to his small round head, and the two lawyers eat breakfast in an otherwise deserted dining room, the other guests having hurried off in their windcheaters and walking boots to enjoy the Lakes while the weather is favourable.

Jones drives them out to Wastwater and parks in the gravel carpark. The two men descend to the water's edge and wander round the lake for a while, comparing the witness's descriptions of the topography with their ordnance survey maps, but as Charles had predicted, the visit reveals nothing they don't already know.

Charles accompanies Jones while he returns the hired car and they take a taxi directly to the station. As their train pulls out of Seascale on the first leg of the journey south, Charles wonders if he might not be worrying unnecessarily. Whatever; the rest of the game, if it continues, will be played out on his turf in London, where he has home advantage.

CHAPTER 15

Charles jogs through the traffic on Queen Victoria Street towards the extraordinary four-storey building which houses the City of London Magistrates Court. Built in the Italianate style in 1873, it resembles a triangular slice of cake constructed of ornately decorated, honey-coloured stone. Charles is always struck by the contrast between the edifice itself, its classical columns, balustraded balconies and pointlessly pleasing pediments, and the quotidian display of venality accommodated within: beautiful exterior icing hiding interior putrescence. From the pointy end of the slice in which are set gracious double doors, the court opens its lovely mouth to chew up, digest and then defaecate into the waiting prison vans the worst examples of flagitious humanity the Metropolis can offer.

Charles climbs the stone steps and pushes open the doors to be assailed by a wall of sound. The entrance hall, stairs and galleries are packed to overflowing with journalists, photographers, members of the public and lawyers, and the air is thick with cigarette smoke. He pushes and shoves his way through the throng to force his way to the courtroom.

It's little better here. The bench usually reserved for solicitors and their clerks has been usurped by the press too and barristers and solicitors are squeezed onto benches too small for their ample rumps on the front bench alone. Charles sees a hand waving above the heads of the pressmen and steers towards it. Jones is gesticulating wildly from the front bench where, amazingly, he has managed to reserve space for Charles.

'Morning,' he shouts, his squeaky voice almost wholly lost in the din.

'What a circus!' shouts Charles, dropping his papers on the desk. 'Why on earth did they let all this rabble in?'

'I think some of them'll have to move. There's a six-hander on after us, and nowhere for the lawyers to sit at all.'

'Any sign of the Defence?' Jones shakes his head. 'Still the "dream team"?' asks Charles.

'As far as I know, yes: Beaverbrook and Day. I tried to speak to James Day this morning but he'd already left his chambers.'

Steele's legal team have instructed Robert Beaverbrook Q.C., one of the most formidable silks in the profession. The head of the very set of chambers to which Jones had originally thought of sending the prosecution brief, the set in which Steele had himself practised as a silk, Beaverbrooks's instruction finally proved to Jones that the Crown's choice of an outsider like Charles was essential.

Beaverbrook, a ponderous man with a low, cultured voice and an unerring ability to smell the weakness in an opponent's case, is the very essence of uprightness and probity. His record of prosecuting for the Crown in countless high-profile cases makes him the perfect defence advocate in this case. The jury will recognise him as the straight, honourable, establishment man who, for years, has been protecting them from gangland murderers, serial rapists and Russian spies. If he says Steele's innocent, he probably is.

His junior, James Day, is the same call as Charles. Practising from the same high-profile set as Beaverbrook, as long as he's not caught kerb crawling or doing anything else stupid, Day will almost automatically get silk within a year or two.

Jimmy Day and Charles have been mates since Cambridge and Bar School and have a healthy respect for each other. In fact, in Charles's opinion, Jimmy is a better advocate even than Beaverbrook. His advocacy style is more like Charles's own, more modern, peppered with references to the Beatles and the Stones, football gossip, and gentle ridicule of the other side's witnesses. Like Charles, he has a deft understanding of how juries think and can reduce an opponent's well-constructed arguments to rubble with a single rhetorical question. Thus the Crown has a noted defence junior to present its case, and the defence has a team of establishment prosecutors, an odd circumstance, and one not missed by the tabloids which have been running profiles of the main actors ever since Steele was arrested.

A door behind the magistrates' bench opens and silence spreads out from that quarter of the court like ripples on a pond. But it's only an usher, who descends into the well of the court to order the journalists out of the solicitors' bench. They comply, reluctantly and complaining, and gather at the back of the court to stand with their backs to the wood panelling. They are forced to move again as the main doors open and in sweeps Robert Beaverbrook Q.C. followed by James Day and their solicitor. Beaverbrook ignores the shouted questions from the reporters and takes his seat at the other end of the bench occupied by Charles. Jimmy winks at Charles, a signal spotted by Beaverbrook, who turns and glares briefly at his junior.

'Morning, Holborne,' says Beaverbrook.

So that's how it's going to be, thinks Charles.

Beaverbrook, chosen for his moral rectitude, will be playing his part on and off stage. He let it be known, in one of his very few reported comments, that he views the charges brought against his client as the most scurrilous slur against the very fabric of the English judicial process, and Charles leads the most mistaken prosecution it had ever been his misfortune to encounter. Accordingly, to hob-nob with Charles while British Justice stands, defenceless, in the dock of public opinion, would be an indefensible levity, a scandal. He has no intention of condescending to Christian names. Accordingly Charles understands the rebuke Jimmy receives for his wink and smiles to himself. It will be "Beaverbrook and Holborne", and not "Bob and Charles". So be it.

'Still no leader?' asks Beaverbrook, one eyebrow raised archly.

'No, not at present.'

'Do you not think that a Queen's Counsel is more appropriate for a case of this significance?'

Charles smiles grimly. 'That depends on how one views the case. If British justice were indeed on trial, as your friends in the press insist, you might've had an argument. But as it's a grubby domestic quarrel that ended in bloody murder, any competent advocate could present it. Indeed, I've advised Mr Jones here to conduct the trial. Advocacy overkill risks distracting the jury from the evidence, don't you agree?'

Jones laughs slightly hysterically. He often instructs Beaverbrook and doesn't want the grand man to think he agrees with Charles, but he can't quite bring himself to reprimand his own counsel in public.

Further embarrassment is avoided as the usher calls 'All rise!' and the magistrate enters the court. Sir Winston Kinsey, formerly a judge of the Court of Appeal, has been persuaded out of retirement to resume his former role as stipendiary magistrate for this case alone.

The Lord Chancellor's department decided that a safer pair of hands would be required for such a sensitive case than might be offered by the lay magistrates in Maidstone and, in any case, the public interest was so great that the court facilities in Kent were completely inadequate. Thus the case was moved to London. Charles was grateful; he'll avoid the usual British Rail frustrations involved in commuting to and from Kent.

Everyone takes their seats and the courtroom subsides.

'The first case on the list,' says the clerk, turning in his chair to speak to Sir Winston, 'is the police against Steele. Mr Holborne represents the police, and the defendant is represented by Mr Beaverbrook and Mr Day.'

The clerk turns to the usher and nods. The usher climbs two steps to a door set in the wood panelling and opens it. 'OK,' he calls.

The clinking of keys can be heard echoing in a stairwell beyond the door, and footsteps approach the courtroom. Sir Anthony Steele appears in the doorway and steps into the dock. He is accompanied by a prison officer but apparently deference to his rank was sufficient to prevent him being manacled, as would usually be the case for a man brought up from the cells. The door closes behind him and he is left standing in the dock, facing the magistrate.

Forty-eight hours have elapsed since he was charged. His silver hair is dishevelled and rather greasy and his suit creased and marked. He looks as if he hasn't slept, for his eyes are bloodshot and ringed with heavy circles, and he's evidently not been given facilities to shave.

'Are you Anthony Michael Steele?' asks the clerk.

'I am,' replies the judge, his voice clear and strong.

The clerk makes sure that his papers accurately record the accused's address, and sits.

'What are you seeking today, Mr Holborne?' asks Sir Winston.

'The Crown are not ready to proceed this morning, sir,' replies Charles as he stands. 'There are further investigations to be made, and we still await the results of some scientific tests. We therefore request a short two-week remand. At the end of that period, I expect the papers to be ready for committal.'

'Two weeks?' asks the magistrate in surprise.

'Every effort is being made to ensure the case proceeds as soon as possible, bearing in mind the circumstances. The accused was in fact in the middle of a lengthy trial which has had to be adjourned at great inconvenience to all concerned.'

'Are you seeking a remand in custody?'

'I am,' affirms Charles, waiting for the expected hubbub to die down before continuing. 'I shall call an officer to assist the Bench, but in a nutshell, this a very serious offence by a man of some wealth, who has close contacts abroad where, for example, his brother lives. The principal prosecution witness is the nanny of the accused's children. She and the accused enjoy a very close relationship, and it is feared that he might try to influence her —'

Charles gets no further before Beaverbrook stands to interrupt him.

'This is utterly outrageous!' he booms in his deep bass tones. 'The "accused" is one of Her Majesty's most senior judges with a glittering career of thirty years behind him! As I am sure you are aware, sir, many of the decisions which guide and bind this court were actually his! He is known throughout the English-speaking world as a judge of incomparable fairness and integrity. To suggest that this man would interfere with a witness is —'

Charles interrupts in his turn. 'The allegation made against the accused is that he strangled his wife in a fit of jealousy, and in a most carefully planned and executed crime. He painstakingly obliterated the damning evidence, cleaning up his wife's blood which had been sprayed all over their bedroom in her struggle for life, painting the room, rehanging the wallpaper, and scrubbing and staining the floors to hide the bloodstains. Blood was found on the walls, on the ceiling and under the floorboards. Then he loaded her trussed-up body into his car and drove half way round England with it stinking in the boot while he went to his son's school. There he had tea with the headmaster and took part in a sports' day presentation. Then, we say, he climbed out of the window of his accommodation, drove to Wastwater, loaded the body into a boat and dumped the body over the side tied to a kerb stone. Finally, a few days later, he coolly walked into the police house in his village and reported her missing, supposedly having run off with a lover. There, the Crown say, is your man of integrity.'

Charles's resort to gore and sensationalism is quite deliberate. He knows he has to take control of the presentation of the case from the outset, and it's essential for the magistrate to focus on the crime and the evidence, not on the judge's hitherto impeccable record. It will also do no harm in the court of public opinion to get the Crown's version of events out as soon as possible.

Beaverbrook is about to explode again when Sir Winston holds up his hand.

'Gentlemen, gentlemen, please, this is not helping. Mr Beaverbrook, leaving aside the issue of bail do you oppose the further short adjournment?'

'No, sir.'

'Very well. But you wish to make a bail application, is that right?'

'Yes, sir.'

'Which is opposed, correct Mr Holborne?' Charles nods. 'Very well. If you're calling any evidence, let's hear it.'

'Certainly, sir.'

Charles calls Superintendent Hook. The tall policeman steps into the witness box and takes the oath. With little prompting from Charles he explains the background. In clear dispassionate tones, and with no hint of sensationalism, he explains to the court the relationship between Steele and Jenny and the judge's connections with Argentina where his brother lives. He makes an impressive witness. Beaverbrook rises to cross-examine.

'Jenny Sullivan is a woman of good character, is she not?'

'She is, sir,' answers Hook.

'You have been shown her building society passbook, have you not?'

'Yes, sir, I have.'

'And it shows that over the last twenty years, she has saved over twenty thousand pounds.'

'It does.'

Beaverbrook turns to the Bench. 'Some from her wages, and some from the estates of her parents, now both deceased,' he explains. 'Are you aware, officer, that she has offered to deposit the entire sum in court to secure the attendance of the accused?'

'I understand that she has.'

'And that she will herself stand surety for his attendance.'

'Yes.'

'She is a most suitable person to be a surety, is she not?'

'In other cases, she would be ideal, but we believe that she and the accused have a very close relationship.'

'What's unusual about that? Parents frequently stand surety for their children, don't they? That's an even closer bond.'

'Yes, they do, but my fear is that she might even run off with him.'

'What, and leave the children?'

'Well, the oldest is twenty-four, and the middle child, a girl, will soon be twenty. Only the youngest still lives at home, and he is fifteen. She has no other ties here at all. Both parents are dead and she has no other close family.'

'Are those your only objections to her standing as surety?'

It is a foolish question. Charles has not mentioned any other reason, but Beaverbrook shouldn't have asked it when he didn't know the answer.

'No. She has herself been interviewed regarding an offence arising out of this investigation.'

The quality of the silence in the courtroom changes subtly, as if the court is holding its collective breath. This is fresh meat.

'Has she been charged?' asks Beaverbrook.

'Not as yet,' answers Hook. 'Legal advice is being sought on the subject.'

Beaverbrook has no further questions and resumes his seat. Charles expects him to call the nanny to give evidence — Charles certainly would have done so and he knows she's present, as he glimpsed her sitting in a small room guarded by a police officer, looking pale and beautiful — but for some reason Beaverbrook doesn't do it.

When the QC addresses Sir Winston it's more of the same: a lifetime of public service by a devoted family man who would never dream of abandoning his children; a man so well-known that there's nowhere in the world he could hope to hide undetected; a man who is innocent until proven guilty and who — even if the charges are true — poses no threat to the community whatsoever.

Normally the QC would be wasting his time. Magistrates do not generally allow accused murderers out on bail; they may have the legal power but in truth it's above their pay grade. They know that an appeal may always be made to a High Court judge, and if that judge wants to take the risk, so be it.

In these unusual circumstances, however, the magistrate is already a High Court Judge, indeed more senior still, and a man well-used to taking the big decisions. Sir Winston announces that he will retire to consider the application.

Fifteen minutes later he returns and, to Charles's surprise, remands Steele in custody. As the prisoner is led back down the stairs he turns to Beaverbrook with a look of despair on his unshaven face and, for the first time, Charles feels a flicker of sympathy for the man who is to spend the next fortnight banged up in Brixton with so many of the men he himself incarcerated.

Beaverbrook leans towards Charles. 'I wouldn't crow if I were you, Holborne. I'll be before another High Court judge by this afternoon, and he'll be out by teatime.'

'I'm not crowing, believe me,' replies Charles. 'I know better than most what the poor man's suffering at this moment. As for an appeal, I'd do the same in your place. I'll be in Chambers if you'd like to tell me the judge and the time.'

The magistrate rises to permit the court to be cleared and for the less sensational business of the day to start. Charles seeks out Superintendent Hook and beckons him over.

'They say they're going to appeal, so he could be out by this afternoon. If you have any further searches to do at his house, now's the time.'

'OK, sir.'

He disappears through the crowd, taking two detective constables with him. Charles turns to Jones.

'Is there anywhere we can chat?' asks Jones urgently.

Without waiting for an answer, he leads the way out of court and slips inside an empty consultation room. Charles follows him. The room smells unpleasantly of cigarette smoke, sweat and fried food. As soon as the door is closed, the solicitor turns to Charles.

'I still think the nanny should be charged,' he insists.

This is the third time Jones and Charles have discussed this. Jones wants her charged with being an accessory after the fact or obstructing the coroner; Charles does not.

'On her admissions alone, we have a cast iron case,' presses Jones, 'and if she'd been charged, there could've been no suggestion of her standing surety.'

'I don't think that matters; they'll get him out on bail this afternoon anyway.'

'You think so?'

'They're going to a High Court judge! One still in practice, this time. Steele is the second most senior Supreme Court judge there is; he's their boss! What do *you* think the decision will be? That's the least important consideration in my view.'

'What about as an accessory? I mean, she confessed to it, for God's sake! We have to charge her!'

'Do we? OK, she's an accessory; she helped him obstruct the coroner by buying wallpaper. So what? We could never prove assistance in causing the death, because we can't prove she was there at the time and she acted purely on what the judge told her. And what will her sentence be? Probation? A suspended sentence at worst.'

'That's no reason not to charge her.'

'But she's far better as a prosecution witness,' insists Charles.

Jones shakes his head. He resisted instructing the burly barrister initially, having had good relationships with a number of criminal chambers whose practitioners would have been entirely adequate for the case. There was also Holborne's baggage; his past was a little too colourful and his reputation for fierce independence too often an excuse for what Jones would call insubordination. Nonetheless Jones was persuaded and, since then, has developed a grudging respect for Charles's sharp intellect and his gift for lateral thinking. Charles has the unusual ability to turn a piece of evidence on its head so it reveals new possibilities. But he's unconventional, too informal and you can never predict what he'll do next. Charles makes the solicitor uncomfortable, and on this subject Jones is convinced he's wrong.

'We've been over this,' he says. 'Whether she's charged or not, she's still an accomplice. So the trial judge has to warn the jury that it'd be unsafe to convict him on her evidence alone as she might have a motive for lying. So she's worthless as a prosecution witness.'

'It won't be her evidence alone. We have lots of other, independent, evidence. But *if* we charge her as an accomplice,' explains Charles, again, patiently, 'the court has no option. It *has* to give the warning. Why gift that card to the Defence and weaken her evidence when we don't have to?'

'She might even prove hostile and go back on her statement!'

'Yes, that's a risk, but not a significant one. I'm convinced she'll stick to her evidence, and that could still be the key to convicting him,' insists Charles. 'Her evidence demonstrates that he lied, repeatedly, to the police. She reveals his character. But there's another reason too.'

'Which is?'

Charles hesitates before answering. 'Well, it's a gut feeling.' Jones starts to interrupt but Charles holds up his hand. 'Please, listen to me. Imagine the effect on the minds of the jury, seeing her sitting in the dock, day after day. You saw her — that beautiful woman, quietly, patiently in love with Steele. All these years, she's carried that terrible burden of secret love and guilt, never saying a word, burying her feelings. And there she sits, in the dock, still strong, still loving him, still silent. A martyr. The jury'll lap it up — God, it almost makes me weep! Someone will make a film of it! And it would create an atmosphere of sympathy for both of them which we need to avoid.'

Jones pauses and considers Charles's words. Eventually he shrugs. 'Well, I can't say I agree with you, but your experience before juries is much greater than mine, and I'll abide by the decision. I'll have to record this discussion on the file as your affirmative advice not to charge Miss Sullivan,' he warns.

'Understood.'

'But it goes against the grain to have someone admitting they covered up the disposal of a body, and walk free.'

'I know. But we have bigger fish to fry. Anything else we need to discuss?'

'No. I'll be in touch.'

Pipsqueak, thinks Charles, as Jones departs. Arrogant chancer, thinks Jones.

CHAPTER 16

Charles is right about the appeal. By six thirty that evening he is walking down the steps of the Royal Courts of Justice in the Strand, bail having been granted on three conditions: Steele mustn't contact Miss Jenny Sullivan; he can't go to the family home, and he must live and sleep at a London address, which is going to be his judge's accommodation in the Temple. Charles returns to Chambers briefly, clears his desk and strolls out of the Temple to the tin of tomato soup waiting for him at the flat, wondering if Mr Justice Anthony Steele's lonely supper will be any better.

As he crosses Fleet Street, Charles notes a figure by the front entrance to the apartments, a short man with his back to him. As Charles gets closer he is able to see by the grey hair, the slope of the shoulders and the way in which the man's trousers hang loosely about thin legs that he is old. He wears a heavy overcoat, far too warm for the weather, which disguises his shape and he is turned away from Charles, looking towards Holborn Circus. Nonetheless, there's something familiar about him.

At a point when Charles is almost within speaking distance the man turns, squints in Charles's direction, and turns away again. In that short moment, Charles realises with an intense shock that the man is his father. It's not only the unexpectedness of seeing Harry, alone on an empty pavement, seeming so lost in the middle of the City where his usual routine never takes him, that is so startling. Harry Horowitz looks weak and vulnerable, and Charles is suddenly conscious for the first time that his father is becoming an old man.

Charles walks swiftly up to him and touches him on the shoulder. Harry turns unsteadily, his face full of uncertainty, and for a second Charles doesn't think he's been recognised. He takes his father by the shoulders. 'Dad? What're you doing here?'

The old man stares up at his son and Charles sees that his eyes are red and watery. He's not seen his father cry since his grandfather's funeral twenty years before, and Charles fears the worst.

'Is it Mum? What's happened?'

'Take me upstairs, Charlie,' replies Harry, his voice weak and hoarse. 'I'll tell you there. She's fine. I just need to sit down.'

Charles pauses, wanting information immediately, but realises that his father is close to collapse. 'Come on, then,' he says, taking Harry's arm.

They enter the mirrored entrance hall and Charles sees a battered suitcase by the side of the lift. Harry tries to reach down to it and almost topples sideways.

'I've got it,' says Charles, stooping, and with his free hand he picks up the case.

They get in the lift and travel to Charles's floor. Harry leans against the wall, his eyes unfocused, as Charles fishes in his pocket for his keys and opens up. He almost has to carry his father to the settee and, leaving him there, Charles rushes straight into the kitchen and brings Harry back a brandy. Harry takes it without comment and sips.

'Nice place,' he says, even then not forgetting his manners.

'You've seen it before,' says Charles.

'No, I haven't. When would I have seen it?'

Charles ignores the comment. 'What's going on Dad? How long have you been waiting for me? Why on earth didn't you come down to Chambers?'

'I did, but I couldn't remember which building or which floor anymore. They all look alike.'

'But my name's on the board outside.'

Harry shrugs helplessly. 'I was confused.'

Charles sits next to his father. 'Is Mum all right?'

'Yes, she's fine,' he replies, but Charles detects a note of qualification.

'But?'

'We had a row.'

Charles shakes his head, uncomprehending. 'And? That's why you're here?'

Harry nods and takes another sip of brandy. Some of the pastiness had gone from his face, and he's beginning to look slightly less frail. 'Are you sure that's all?' asks Charles.

'It's not enough?'

Charles has to admit: he's never witnessed a row between his parents. Theirs is not a modern marriage, one in which communication and the right to self-expression are at a premium. Instead, it's founded on common values, respect and Harry's quest for a quiet life. Millie Horowitz is the absolute ruler in their household, a situation neither of them questions. Charles has always thought there'd only be one way for his father to survive: by keeping both his head down and any dissentient views to himself.

'What about?' he asks.

'Everything,' says Harry with finality.

Charles waits for some further elucidation but is disappointed.

'So, how was it left?' he asks.

Harry takes a gulp of air. 'We're separating.'

If it wasn't for the fact that Harry's eyes fill with tears as he speaks, Charles would have laughed. 'People your age don't separate, Dad. How would you live, either of you? You've been together forty years.'

'Forty-two.'

'You can't throw away forty-two years of marriage because of one row.'

'You don't understand.'

'Then explain it to me, and I'll understand.'

Harry looks down at the glass in his hand, and shakes his head.

Charles perseveres. 'Have you discussed this with Mum?' Harry shakes his head. 'Then don't you think you should? It's rather an important thing to decide without speaking to her.'

Charles can't keep the levity out of his voice, and his father looks sharply at him, hurt.

'Oh, Dad, I'm sorry!' says Charles, cursing his insensitivity. He puts an arm round his father's shoulders. 'It's just a bit difficult to take on board, you know? David and I have never seen you row in all our lives, and now you appear here and say you're separating, but you haven't spoken to her about it. Are you sure this isn't just a misunderstanding?'

'It's no misunderstanding. Believe me.'

'Then what's it all about?'

Harry shakes his head. 'It's private.'

'Oh, Dad,' says Charles sadly. 'Does she know where you are?'

Harry shakes his head again. 'No. We had words, I said I was leaving, and she said "So, go already." Then I left.'

'You realise she's probably worrying herself to death. Can I ring her and say you're safe?'

Charles stands and goes to the telephone. Harry makes no effort to stop him. Charles dials the number and stands waiting for a while. 'She's not there.'

'Yes she is. She's sulking.'

Charles waits a while longer and hangs up. Before he has time to move away from the telephone, it rings.

'Hello?' he answers.

'Charles? It's Davie. Is Dad there by any chance?'

'Yes, he is. I just got in and he was waiting outside. Do you know where —?'

'She's here. She arrived half an hour ago with a suitcase, asking to stay. She's in the spare room. Sonia's trying to talk to her.'

'Is she all right?'

'As far as I can tell. And Dad?'

'All right.'

David senses that Charles can't talk. 'Is he in the room? Don't answer; there's nowhere else in that cubby hole he could be. What're we going to do?'

'I haven't the faintest. I thought it might have been … I wasn't sure how serious it was till you phoned. Are you going to let Mum stay?'

'What choice do I have? She refuses to go home. What about Dad?'

'He's brought a suitcase too.' Charles pauses. 'If neither of them is going to use their house, maybe we could move into it.'

David laughs sadly. 'This is crazy.'

'At least she can stay with you for a while. There's nowhere here for Dad to sleep. The bed's a foldaway, and much as I love him…'

'Has he told you what's wrong?'

'No.'

'Mum won't speak about it either. Charles, I think this is serious.'

Harry gets up in search of the bathroom. Charles takes the opportunity to speak quickly. 'Maybe, but I doubt it,' he says, his voice low. 'They're both getting old and cranky, and I guess they're each waiting for the other to apologise. In any event, we won't find out tonight. It might do some good if they're apart for a night.'

'I don't think they've spent a night apart since I was born.'

'Precisely. It might bring them to their senses.'

'OK. I don't think I've a choice anyway; I can't get Mum out of our spare room. What'll you do?'

'Sleep on the floor, I guess. The couch wouldn't sleep a ten-year old.'

'Best of luck,' says David.

'And you. I think you'll need it more than me.'

'Call me tomorrow, Charles, eh?'

'Will do. Bye.'

CHAPTER 17

At just after opening time, *The Grave Maurice* is almost empty. Mikey McArthur nurses half a pint of mild at a corner table as he idly leafs the pages of a newspaper extricated from under the foot of his wobbly table. It's a day old and half the pages are glued with dried beer, but Mikey's never been interested in the news — reading, even newspapers, has never been his strong suit — and right now he's not even focusing on the stained pictures. It just gives his hands something to do as he ponders his next move.

He's cross with himself at the waste of nine pence ha'peny; he should have known there'd be no one around at this time of day, but he had to get away from the old woman's huffing and glaring, and he'd hoped to bump into someone he could touch for a couple of nicker, now that his welcome on Deala's lounge sofa looks to have expired.

He tapped up Deala for a couple of nights on the couch the previous Sunday, but it's now Friday of the following week. Deala's missus has a face like a cold steel vice at the best of times, but the look she gave him as he ate his toast that morning made it clear: time to make other arrangements. However, he now has less than four quid of his dad's pension money left in his trouser pocket, he needs a change of clothes and things are becoming a bit desperate.

Mikey avoids the barman's suspicious glance from the other side of the bar. He realises that, once he got within sniffing range, he narrowly missed being ordered back out of the saloon bar, but the barman changed his mind once Mikey showed him the price of a pint.

Mikey has run out of ideas. Over the last few days, he's discovered that most of the faces he knew from the forties have moved on, and those who haven't aren't keen to renew his acquaintance. The plan to squeeze that Jew-boy Charlie Horowitz had come to nothing. It was never really a *plan*, so to speak. Mikey'd just glimpsed him across the bar, recognised the face and taken a punt. But he'd no idea where the geezer had gone now nor how to get hold of him, and in retrospect it'd been a daft idea. Still, fancy bumping into him so far from the Smoke, and after so many years, eh? Last time Mikey heard anything about him, he'd become some sort of war hero, gong and all, but that was over twenty years ago.

The saloon bar is briefly illuminated as the street doors open and a noisy group of young men enters. They order drinks and take them upstairs from whence Mikey soon hears the click of snooker balls being racked.

Mikey knocks back the last of his drink, stands and closes the newspaper. He puts the empty glass on top of it, looks down and there, right in front of him and as large as life, is a black and white picture of Charlie Horowitz.

He's in a group of suits descending the steps of a building that Mikey knows well but can't, at that second, quite place. Horowitz's head is turned away from the camera as he speaks to someone next to him who's largely hidden by other figures, but Mikey has no doubt at all; it's him! Mikey's heavy unshaven jaw drops and he slowly lowers his bulk back onto the chair, his mouth hanging open slackly. *What are the chances?* he asks silently, full of wonder and disbelief.

He has a sudden vivid memory of the day his mother died. It was during the 1918 pandemic and Mikey was eight, a permanently hungry and grubby boy with, even then, unusually large hands and knees. He'd been called in off the street to sit

169

reluctantly at one side of her bed, trying to avoid eye contact with his weeping aunt at the other, as the dying woman wheezed through her last minutes, her glistening body trembling with fever and the intervals between each painful breath growing steadily longer. Near the end, in a rare moment of lucidity, Dot McArthur opened her eyes, recognised her only son beside her, and reached up to stroke his hair.

'Don't worry, Mikey,' she whispered. 'I'll always be with you. I'm your guardian angel.'

Mikey silently thanks his long-dead mother, because he cannot otherwise explain how the very man he was thinking about should suddenly appear before him in this way. Maybe she *was* his guardian angel, after all, because this surely had to be a sign.

He leans forward and pulls the newspaper closer to him. His stubby forefinger slowly traces the text beside the photograph, his mouth moving soundlessly as he deciphers the words. He's not sure he's understood it properly, but it seems that Charlie Horowitz now calls himself "Charles Holborne". One fact emerges clearly, however: Horowitz is now a brief, and he's on a big case. And everyone knows what briefs earn.

Mikey sits back in his seat. Fuck me, what a turn up, he thinks, as a slow grin spreads across his lumpy features.

CHAPTER 18

Charles spends a third night back in his familiar bed, and again sleeps wonderfully. No doubt it's still exhaustion; he barely slept at all for the first two weeks after Harry's arrival. Night after night he tossed and turned on the lounge floor with only a scratchy blanket and shifting sofa cushions beneath him. Finally acknowledging that his father wasn't going to return to Golders Green any day soon, Charles took a taxi to one of the army surplus shops on Tottenham Court Road and returned with the most expensive foldaway he could find. He intended to use it himself in the tiny living room, but Harry insisted that Charles must return to his own bed, now there was an alternative. He'd be perfectly happy on the foldaway, he said.

Much to Charles's consternation, Harry seems to be settling in for the long haul. He has already revolutionised both Charles's kitchen and his eating habits. Separate crockery and cutlery — two of each item, just enough for father and son — have been acquired from somewhere, and now the proper kosher division of utensils between "meat" and "milk" meals has been made. Over the first couple of days, Charles worked his way through the pork sausages and bacon rashers in the fridge without a word from his father, but they have not been replaced. Food stocks are now rigidly demarcated into meat and milk, and bright new kitchen towels, red for meat and blue for milk, hang on the rail behind the door. Almost without his noticing it, Charles's flat has become kosher, or at least sufficiently kosher for Harry not to object to cooking and eating in it.

To Charles's surprise, despite the cramped living conditions, adjusting to life with his father has not been difficult. Harry seems to make do with only five or six hours' sleep a night, retiring late and rising early. By the time Charles comes out of the bathroom in the mornings the living room has been cleared, Harry's night things are stowed away and a pot of tea usually awaits on the tiny kitchen table. During the day while Charles is at court or in the Temple Harry amuses himself by taking gentle walks through the city, revisiting old haunts, reading the newspapers at Holborn Library and buying odds and ends of food from kosher butchers and greengrocers.

Charles has always known that his father is well loved within his community — he's never heard a bad word said of him — but he's not before seen, close-up, the effect the little tailor has on those around him. He befriends everyone. Despite having known him for no more than a fortnight, Harry has somehow already received an invitation to the home of Dennis, the concierge, in Plaistow, something Charles hasn't managed in several years, and he appears on first name terms with half the Jewish shopkeepers in the City.

Twice Harry has taken a bus and dropped into his little factory in Mile End to keep an eye on things. Now he's in the City it's a lot less tiring than coming down on the Northern Line, he says. In truth, the place has been running smoothly without his daily attendance for several years now, and although the staff are always delighted to see him, Harry, who is now 79, knows they're merely being polite and his visits are interrupting their work. The business of manufacturing dress hats and fur coats for the carriage trade, to which Harry and his father gave, together, over one hundred years of their working lives, now runs perfectly well without him.

Harry doesn't always eat in the evenings, but on a couple of occasions he has prepared something for them both and so, for the first time in a long while, Charles feels as if he's coming back to a home at the end of the day.

Despite Charles's gentle but persistent probing, Harry refuses to be drawn on the issue of the rift with Millie. Whenever Charles raises it, Harry thanks him for his concern but politely declines to enter into any discussion on that subject. He tries not to mention Millie's name, even in innocuous contexts, in case he is drawn into deeper waters. At first Charles concludes that his father's reticence must be caused by pain, but after a while he realises that it's more a sense of delicacy. Harry is of the traditional view that a couple's matrimonial difficulties are no business of anyone except the parties themselves. They are most particularly not subjects for the children, who might be forced or, worse, choose, to take sides. It's private.

After a few days, Charles's frustration is replaced by an appreciation of his father's wisdom. Whatever they may be doing to address the impasse, Harry and Millie will have to be allowed to get on with it in their own time. Charles only discovers that negotiations are afoot with Millie by virtue of a chance remark about a forthcoming visit to David and Sonia's house.

So, as the days lengthen to weeks and the glorious weather of that summer begins to fail, the two men settle into a relaxed and easy companionship. Charles begins to look forward to the hour or two late at night when Harry makes them both a hot drink and they sit chatting in the semi-darkened lounge, the sound of vehicles outside becoming less and less frequent as the City falls asleep.

Charles begins to appreciate that he has never really known his father at all. As a child he saw a quiet, authoritative figure, a distant, reasoning mediator in a household of emotional traumas. Almost as soon as he left home for university, he perceived a narrow, rigid man who couldn't grasp the value of anything outside his own inward-looking culture. There was no intermediate period for Charles to learn what Harry Horowitz thought, what he liked, why he was liked — which Charles knew he was, with great warmth, by everyone who knew him — or what he had wanted for himself.

As Charles hears stories of life in Stepney before the First World War when Harry was himself a young man, of a large and noisy family, its friendships and feuds, its successes and failures and, most particularly, of Harry's warm and close relationship with *his* father, Charles starts to realise how barren and lonely his life is in comparison. Charles is approaching his fortieth birthday, still with no wife, no children, not even a proper home. His relationship with *his* parents has been bitter and angry, especially compared to the intimacy of a family whose children lived in the family home until they married, sometimes even afterwards.

But this *family* thing; it has always been so painful, so raw. His childhood and adolescence were a constant battle to be himself and not to conform with what his religion, culture and, most importantly, his mother, wanted of him. At the time, marrying Henrietta and putting behind him all that archaic Jewish mumbo-jumbo had been a relief, like amputating an infected limb. Now, as he listens to Harry speaking of Shimon Horowitz, Charles's grandfather, he wonders if anyone would ever speak of *him* with the same respect and affection. For the first time in his life, the possibility occurs to him that he has taken a wrong turn somewhere along the line; thrown out something that, in retrospect, was important.

Harry watches his troubled son, deep in his thoughts. 'Charles? Son?'

'Sorry, Dad. Miles away.'

'I saw.'

Harry leans forward, frowning, something evidently on his mind.

'What's up?' asks Charles, rousing himself from his reverie.

'I want to say something to you, Charlie, and I don't want you to get upset or angry, or shout me down.'

'I wouldn't do that.'

'Well, you might. For years I was frightened to open my mouth to you.'

'It's not like that now.'

'With your clever words you used to leave me feeling confused and frustrated, so I couldn't make my point.'

Charles grins in acknowledgement. Henrietta and, more recently, Sally, used to say the same.

'I promise to listen.'

'OK then. I have watched you and your mother fight like cats in a sack for almost forty years,' he starts.

Charles holds up a hand. 'I promise to listen, and I will, but is this a safe subject, Dad?'

'Hear me out. You think I've been unaware of what's been going on? Two of the people I love most in the world constantly at one another's throats? The whole household ruled by the warfare between you two?'

He shakes his head sadly, turns away and falls silent. When he finally does speak again, it is quietly and with profound sadness.

'I used to come home from the factory with my heart in my mouth, wondering what I'd find. The two of you used to suck all the joy out of the place. I sometimes wonder how Davie managed to survive at all, but it was no thanks to your mother, because so often she had no space left for him, or...' He tails off, backing away from expressing that thought, but Charles is certain he was going to add the words "or me."

This is the first time Charles has ever heard either of his parents criticise the other, even obliquely, and he is shocked. He wonders again if this may be what lies behind the present rift.

Harry appears to change subject. 'You didn't know your mother's parents, did you?'

'Not really, no.'

Harry shakes his head. 'They were pillars of the Jewish community, especially her father. A real Torah scholar, too. But not warm.'

'Warm?'

'Your mother once told me that never, not once in her whole life, can she remember either of her parents cuddling her, holding her hand, stroking her hair and so forth.'

'What, not even grandma?'

'Esther Cohen was an invalid for much of her life. The family had money, and she was always being sent off for rest cures here and there. They had a housekeeper for as long as I can remember.'

'What was wrong with her?'

Harry shrugs. 'I always thought she was a hypochondriac, but then she went and died in her early forties of TB, so what do I know? The point I'm making is that your mother had very little experience of living in a loving home. Your grandfather was very strict. *Very* strict. So, I think your mother had no examples of how to praise or encourage.'

'Have you spoken to her about this?' asks Charles.

'Not really. When you were first born I could see her struggling with you. You wouldn't feed, you cried a lot and she had no one to turn to, to ask for advice. She thought she could discipline you out of it.'

Charles puts his hand on his father's, and speaks gently. 'Why didn't you say something, Dad? Do something. *Intervene.*'

Harry sighs and shrugs again. 'Now, I wish I had. But what did I know? I'd never been a father, never had a baby, and I grew up in a household full of boys. Your mother's ... well ... a woman of strong opinions, as you know. She said she knew how to manage it, she was the woman, and so I let her get on with it. She ran the household and I went to work. In the end, I suppose I hoped that her love for you would soften her.'

'Her love for me? I don't think she ever loved me.'

'Son, you couldn't be more wrong. You are the apple of her eye.'

'It's a funny sort of love, then, when it can be turned on and off at will. She could be cold and distant to me for days on end, and I never knew what I'd done wrong. Just that I *had* done something wrong.'

'I know. She didn't know how to manage your disobedience, your independence. But I promise you, Charlie, that doesn't mean she didn't love you. She just did the best she could, with the hand she was dealt. And you have to remember, you did test us. In marrying out, in abandoning your Jewishness, you broke a thread that goes back thousands of years, father to son, mother to daughter. I don't think you'll ever understand how much pain that caused us. All the milestones your mother and I foresaw, a big Jewish wedding, years of festivals and family celebrations with you and our grandchildren, their bar mitzvahs, all that … well, it just disappeared.'

Charles hangs his head. 'I didn't mean to hurt you, Dad. Or Mum. It just wasn't for me.'

Harry nods. 'I see that now.'

'And you sat *shiva* for me!' cries Charles, old hurt resurfacing.

'Yes, I did. And I see now that it was wrong. You weren't just acting out of defiance; we were to blame, too. Perhaps if things had been different at home when you were little, you might have chosen a different path. But this isn't really what I wanted to say to you.'

Charles laughs. 'This'll do! You've said quite a bit.'

Harry laughs too. 'Let me just add one other thing. It's taken us a long time to accept the choices you've made, but in the end what matters most to us is that you're happy.'

'"Us"?'

'Certainly to me. Your mother is … slow to change. But I think she's coming round. We *both* see how miserable you've been, and that's the last thing we want. And you have been unhappy, haven't you, son?'

'I suppose so. Since Sally and I split up in particular.'

'She's a lovely girl.'

'I know it. I'm still not really sure how I mucked that one up.'

'Because it frightened you,' replies Harry simply.

'How did it frighten me?'

'The big lesson you learned from your mother was not to trust anyone to love you. You always believed it would be torn away again, so you kept yourself at a distance … built a protective wall around yourself. If you don't commit to loving someone, you can never be hurt. That's why Sally gave up on you.'

'But we bought the house together! I did commit to her!'

'Did you? Really?'

Charles falls silent and turns away, staring out of the windows at the yellow sodium light on the pavements outside.

After a while Harry pats his son's arm. 'Just think about it, OK?'

Harry stands, looking down on his elder son in the half-light. 'I'll use the bathroom first and get out your way.'

'Sure,' replies Charles, distracted.

'But, before I do, do me a favour?'

Charles looks up. 'What's that, then?'

'Stand up, and give your old man a hug, would you?'

CHAPTER 19

On the Monday before Steele's trial is due to start, Charles rises early. Despite the fact that it's still before seven, Harry is already up, pottering in the kitchen and humming to himself. Charles recognises a tune from his childhood: part of the liturgical service from the Day of Atonement. It reminds Charles that the Jewish High Holy Days are only a few weeks off. He'll have no choice but to discuss arrangements with Harry, which is bound to involve mention of Millie. Deciding to leave that for a more appropriate moment, he declines breakfast and heads to Chambers.

The roads are still largely deserted and it's a sparkling late summer's morning. Charles enters the Temple by Mitre Court and on impulse decides to take a detour. He walks down the slope to the bottom of Kings Bench Row to look over the Embankment at the Thames. A black smudge of smoke from the funnel of a tug chugging into the distance, too far downwind for its engine to be heard, is the only sign of river traffic. The summer breeze blowing off the water ruffles Charles's curly hair, and he tastes salt air on his lips. He gazes for a while at the sequin-flecked blue waves, feeling calm and at peace.

On his desk he finds a large cardboard box marked for his attention. He has just opened it and settled down to examine its contents when the door opens.

'Hello, Charles,' says a fair-haired man in his early thirties.

'Hello, Peter,' replies Charles, with a broad smile directed at his ex-pupil. 'Not seen you in ages. Busy?'

This is a familiar greeting in the Temple. Everyone claims to be "busy". The opposite, being "quiet" — not having enough work — is every barrister's fear, but given the competitive nature of the Bar and the cauldron of rumour that is the Temple, few will admit to it. Confessing to being "quiet" risks word getting round that one's practice has failed, that one is out of favour, or, worst of all, past it. On the other hand, being genuinely "busy" often means working until midnight six nights a week, sometimes preparing cases for the following day at the last minute and doing without sleep at all. Charles knows of half a dozen marriages that failed through "busyness", including his own. It's one of the handicaps of a system in which clerks run their guvnors' diaries: there's no way the barrister can turn off the tap, even when he's drowning.

Bateman shuts the door behind him, dumps his robes bag on the floor despondently and sits at his desk. He looks weary.

'Completely fucking overloaded,' replies Peter in his perfect upper-crust English. 'I was still here 'til almost three this morning. Managed an hour's sleep, a shit and a shave, and here I am again.' Peter yanks the ribbon off a set of Instructions. 'I met this lovely girl a few weeks ago and I was — well, I *am* — quite smitten. I think she was, too. But since the second date, I've had to cancel her three times, once at the last minute. Now she won't return my calls.'

'Sorry to hear it. Sounds all too familiar,' comments Charles grimly.

Peter, engrossed in reading, focuses belatedly on Charles's response and looks up. 'Oh, course you do. Sorry,' he says, remembering Charles's travails with Henrietta. 'Didn't mean to be insensitive.'

Charles waves away the apology. Peter hurriedly opens his desk drawer looking for paper and unscrews his fountain pen. He looks despairingly at the papers in front of him and then at the clock.

'Fuck,' he says again. 'I don't think I'm going to have time for this. Got to be in Aylesbury by nine.'

'The Assizes? A bit early, isn't it?'

'No. Day One of a five-day fraud and I've never met the client, so I need to squeeze in a con first.'

Charles checks the clock. 'You'd better get going. If you miss the quarter past, you'll be screwed.'

Peter hesitates a moment longer, stands and grabs his bags. 'You're right. Look, you couldn't do me a favour, could you, Charles? I need an indictment drafted by this evening, not straightforward, four or five potential counts. I can leave a note for Barbara to find a pupil to do the legwork, but if it's finished this afternoon, any chance you could cast an eye over it before it goes out?'

'Of course.'

'Thanks. I owe you one.' He turns to leave. 'Oh, by the way, there was a bloke downstairs asking for you.'

'A bloke?'

'Yes. Well, he wasn't asking *for* you, more *about* you. Wanted to know if you worked here. I showed him your name on the board, he seemed satisfied and off he toddled. A client, I guess.'

'Probably. What did he look like?'

'Didn't really pay much attention. Fifties maybe? Not fat, but a bit beefy. Your height. Anyway, better run. Thanks again.'

The door closes and Charles listens to Peter's footsteps running down the stairs. Charles stands and peers out of the window at the cobbles below the main entrance. Other than Peter sprinting towards Fleet Street, there's no one to be seen.

Charles had almost put the amateurish blackmail letter out of his mind. It's several weeks since his return from the Lake District and there's been no follow-up to the ill-spelt letter. Charles briefly considers running downstairs in the hope of catching sight of the man seen by Peter, but decides against it. If it *was* the putative blackmailer, he thinks, I'll let him make his move.

Charles returns to the box on his desk. Opened, it seems to contain jumble of miscellaneous items, some unused prosecution material but, more intriguingly, items which appear to be the contents of Steele's desk, presumably from the Royal Courts of Justice. There are also documents seized from the chambers where Steele was in practice at the time of his wife's disappearance, the most important of which are his court diaries. Charles thumbs through them quickly to the days immediately following Lise's return from her dirty weekend with the lover. If the defence were able to call three Court of Appeal judges to say on oath that the accused was appearing before them at the time when, according to the nanny, the body must have been disposed of, that would be the end of the Crown's case. Charles is relieved to find that the two days, a Thursday and a Friday, are blank; wherever else he was, Steele was not in court.

Charles digs further into the box and finds some loose additional statements from prosecution witnesses. In the first, the boy's headmaster confirms that he remembers Steele presenting the rugby trophy. He can't remember the year, but it has to be the relevant one as in earlier years the boy had not played rugby at all, and by the end of the next term he'd left the school.

Charles gets out his pen and starts creating a timeline which immediately highlights another difficulty. If Steele was in the West County presenting prizes, he couldn't at the same time have been tying his wife's body to a kerbstone and pitching her into Wastwater. So, was the nanny wrong about the timing? Or could she be lying?

Charles turns to Carr's notes of his interview of Jenny Sullivan and the formal interview that followed it and reads them again. If there is one thing of which Charles is sure, it's that Jenny Sullivan is in love with her employer. Why then had she rendered a *possibility* that he would be charged into a *certainty* — and, what's more, dragged herself into it? What motive could she possibly have in lying to Carr? So, her statement's likely to be true, and she's unlikely to have made a mistake about such a memorable event. Charles's experience tells him that memories laid down by witnesses in a state of emotional stress, as Jenny Sullivan must have been when presented with the fact that Steele had killed his wife, are usually the strongest and often the most reliable. Her statement is almost certainly accurate as to this, meaning that somehow Steele had got from Kent to the school in Somerset, from there to Cumbria — either with a dingy or small boat, or finding one by chance at the lake, which seemed very unlikely — and then back the length of the country to Somerset, before returning home to Kent. But in the time available … how?

Charles turns to the personal belongings and goes through them carefully. Steele is evidently a methodical man. Bills for household services are tied in chronological bundles, the family insurance policies are in card envelopes inserted into a ring binder, each labelled on the front with the monthly payment, the maturity date and the sum payable, and the man's entire professional life as a barrister is logged in neat handwritten columns in a ledger, with date, name of client, name of solicitor, the type of work, fee charged and the date when it was paid. Again, Charles looks at the two particular dates and finds that the judge apparently did no work of any sort on them. No court appearances, no advices for troubled solicitors, no pleadings. Then there's a separate file of the documents bearing the numbers by which the state identifies its citizens, birth certificates, National Insurance Cards, National Health Service cards and, finally, a marriage certificate.

Charles puts the file to one side and digs right to the bottom of the box. The last item he finds is a photograph in a wooden frame. It's the one taken from the judge's study wall and it does, as he claimed to the police, show him shaking his son by the hand. The boy is muddy and there's a smear of what might be mud, or perhaps blood, on his upper lip, but he looks triumphant. Underneath the photograph, in a neat oval cut-out in the mounting card, is the date and the words "Man of the Match". With their free hands, father and son hold a silver trophy aloft between them. Behind them are the rest of the rugby team and a few members of staff, all applauding. It is a posed photograph, but they both look natural and happy, their smiles exactly alike and their penetrating eyes with identical expressions. The boy will have become a good-looking man by now, thinks Charles.

Fathers and sons again, he muses, without completing the train of thought. He looks for some trace of evil, some knowing look, to corroborate the appalling fact that had to be true if the prosecution case is sound: that as the man stood there, pride and happiness shining from his eyes, his dead wife, the mother of the victorious rugby player, lay, stiff and stinking, in the boot of his car in the school car park. But there's nothing. Steele looks as if he hasn't a care in the world, as if his mind is full at that moment of pride and happiness to the exclusion of all else. He's either the coolest killer Charles has ever seen, or he's innocent.

Charles replaces all the items and shoves the box onto the floor behind his desk. The perusal of the box's contents has left him unaccountably sad. His discussion with Harry has been much on his mind over the last few days. How can one family be so unhappy and another, without any obvious effort, able to create an atmosphere of loving, nurturing support from which children grow into balanced, happy adults? Tolstoy's *Anna Karenina* principle comes to his mind: *All happy families are alike; each unhappy family is unhappy in its own way.* He sits, staring at the ceiling for a while, and then throws himself violently to his feet.

'Bollocks!' he shouts, in a successful attempt at dispelling his mood. He retrieves his transistor radio, which someone else has moved to the windowsill, and tunes to the nearest pop station to find The Byrds telling him that it's "a jingle jangle" morning. Satisfied with that sentiment, Charles strides to the shelf on which he keeps the rest of his briefs and throws himself into a buggery defence by way of light relief.

At the same time, only a hundred yards away across Fleet Street, a stocky middle-aged man stands on Fetter Lane, accurately identifying the block housing Charles's flat from the description given by an Inner Temple car park attendant who he'd conned into revealing more than he should. The man pushes open the front door, darts inside and leaves on Dennis's unattended reception desk an envelope marked for the attention of "Mr Charles Holborn".

Within seconds the man is out of the building and striding northwards towards Smithfields and a cooked breakfast, whistling as he goes. Mikey McArthur likes being back in the Smoke. He particularly likes having a plan; it always invigorates him. And he's made his move.

CHAPTER 20

September, and autumn, enter with a bang. August was characterised by prolonged hot spells, frequently up to 80°F, but on 1 September, London feels definitely autumnal. On the Sunday almost an inch of rain falls, and it's so chilly that Charles finds himself digging out jumpers that have been in the back of the wardrobe since April.

The trial in *The Crown versus Steele* is listed to start during the third week of September, the precise date to be specified nearer the time. Charles has heard nothing further from Jones. All the pre-trial manoeuvring and circling are over; there remain no more tactical games to be played and everyone concerned is anxious to get on with the main event. The absence of any news hasn't prevented the newspapers from continuing to run stories on all the main players, including Charles. He has been door-stepped twice in the last fortnight, once outside his flat and once as he left Chambers.

Harry is still at Charles's flat and Millie remains with David and Sonia. The sons take turns visiting their parents' vacant home to collect the post and check that all is well. The High Holyday season looms, and Charles has a growing sense of foreboding.

Jewish religious festivals have always been important landmarks. To a greater extent than in a Christian family, they form the structure of the year, and the passing of each season is always marked by a festival, a family gathering, particular foods and songs. The New Year and, ten days later, the Day of Atonement, are the most sacred events in the calendar. For five thousand years, Jews the world over have come together

188

on those days to pray, to reflect on their sins and to seek forgiveness. Even those who ignore their religion for the whole year feel the call of the race memory and few resist it. For almost fifty years, Harry has prayed from the front row at synagogue and sat at the head of his table to take and break his fasts, surrounded by his family, supported by his wife. At these times he is the head of the family in more than just name. The rift with Millie, barely supportable at any other time, threatens now to break a tradition that seemed inviolable, and Charles isn't even sure his parents' marriage can survive it. He broaches the subject once, only to be sharply rebuked.

'Have you thought about Yomtov?' he asks.

'What about it?'

'Where will you go?'

'Where I always go. To *shul*.'

'What about Mum?'

'She'll go where she pleases.'

'But —'

'No buts.'

'Dad —'

'No.'

Charles watches as his father's blotchy hands start to tremble, with anger or distress he can't tell but, in any event, he retreats.

That afternoon he telephones David at his office. Millie's anger buoyed her through the first few weeks of separation, but she has since become silent and depressed. David reports that she spends most of her time in her room, even refusing telephone calls from her sister and friends. She's begun to lose weight and she looks frail. David is seriously worried about her.

He and Charles discuss how to resolve the problem. Both Millie and Harry have refused marriage guidance. Sonia invited their Rabbi to the house to counsel Millie. The old lady listened civilly over two glasses of lemon tea, nodded when the Rabbi, who was David's age, spoke about compromise and understanding the other's position, and after thanking him for taking the trouble to see her, returned to her room. Not a word was said about the visit until the next evening, when she commented in passing that she thought she might, perhaps, give Golders Green Synagogue a try. There at least the Rabbi had respect for his elders.

'If only they'd make a decision,' says Charles. 'They've been in limbo for months now.'

'It's not months, Charles. It just feels that way,' laughs David.

'Whatever. Nothing seems to be happening. They're not moving forward and they're not moving back.'

'But what is there to go forward *to*?' asks David. 'Separate old-age homes? They're both terrified of life apart, and utterly obstinate about a reconciliation. Do you know what Dad's doing about Yom Kippur?'

'He says he's going to *shul* as usual.'

'On his own?'

'Well, you'll be there, won't you?' points out Charles.

'Yes. And Mum will be upstairs with Sonia and the other women.'

'So, in fact, everything will be as usual. The fact that they're not talking will make no difference.'

'Except that the family will be apart in spirit, and in taking and breaking its fast, for the first time since they married. Imagine the emotional impact it'll have on them.'

'Maybe it'll shake them out of this obstinacy.'

'I doubt it. Of all the problems I anticipated for their declining years, this was not one of them. I really don't know what to do.'

And that's how the brothers leave it.

Over the following days, Charles starts to take fewer cases of substance to guarantee his availability for the Steele trial. He spends more time in Chambers, poring over the depositions, re-reading the interviews, making notes, chronologies, points for cross-examination and speeches, preparing himself for the biggest case of his career. Barbara is already wondering aloud about Charles taking silk on the back of the case, and the more approachable colleagues in Chambers, particularly the other juniors, take to calling him "Mr Attorney-General" at teatime. For the first time, Charles wonders aloud if the tradition of taking afternoon tea might not, after all, be dispensed with.

As he is leaving Chambers one evening in another sudden squall of rain, he is approached by a man with his raincoat collar up and a dripping trilby hat pulled low over his eyes. Charles moves to one side of the pavement to allow the man to pass but feels a hand grabbing the front of his coat. Charles leaps back into a defensive stance, his fists raised, and then peers more closely at the man.

'Deala?' he queries.

'Sorry Charlie, didn't mean to make yer jump.'

Charles pulls the man under the arch leading into Pump Court to shelter from the rain.

'What the fuck, Deala? You're lucky I didn't punch your lights out!'

Wheeler Dealer, or Frederick Wheeler as he was christened, is a second-hand car dealer, so the moniker was obvious from the start. He's been a face in the East End for longer than Charles can remember; so long in fact that Deala jokes that his earliest deals were for one horsepower vehicles, namely, old nags. Now in his late seventies, his sons have been running the business for years. It's a good business too, comprising six forecourts and garages in the East End and Essex.

However, Deala remains solely responsible for one niche part of the enterprise, the importation of flash American cars, all chrome and fins, for select clients, principally Ronald and Reginald Kray.

'Yeah, sorry 'bout that, Charlie. I've been waiting a bit, and when you rushed past I almost didn't recognise you.'

'Waiting for me? What for?'

'Got a message from the twins.'

'Which is?'

'Word is, that someone's been asking questions about you. In the boozers and *speilers*. 'Spect you've heard?'

'Who's been asking questions?'

'Well, that's the funny bit. I put 'im up for a few days. He just turned up on the doorstep, and I didn't feel I could refuse. He worked for me for a bit, donkeys back.'

'Who?' repeats Charles.

'Remember a bloke called Mikey McArthur?'

Charles nods, dripping water from his hat brim down his face. 'I remember.'

'I thought he must've died years ago. Disappeared completely soon after the war. After that night at the *Prospect* … well, you know. He only stayed a while, and then he fucked off without a word. I thought nothing of it at first, but then I 'eard his name again one night down the Royal, and I mentioned it to Reggie. The boys reckon it can't just be a coincidence he's suddenly resurfaced and started asking questions. They think he means to cause trouble.'

'They're right.'

'But the twins say not to worry; they'll sort it. Reggie says you'll know why. He says to tell you they don't want nothing interfering with their plans.'

'Look, Deala, tell Reggie I'm very grateful but I've got the matter under control. I can manage this one without their support.'

'Yeah, I thought you'd be on top of it. You always was one step ahead.'

'Well, make sure they get that, OK? I've got a plan. If that goes wrong, I'll let them know. Got it?'

'Got it.'

'Right then. You go back up Middle Temple Lane, and I'll skirt round to Sergeants Inn. McArthur was hanging around a while back, and it'd be best if he doesn't see us together.'

'Gotcha,' says the old man, pulling up his raincoat collar again. 'Be lucky, Charlie.'

'And you, mate. Thanks for the heads up.'

Charles makes his circuitous route back to the flat, lost in thought. At least he now knows who's blackmailing him, which is a start. But despite having had the second letter for several days, and examining his options from every angle, he *doesn't* have a plan.

CHAPTER 21

Charles checks his watch again: ten minutes short of seven o'clock. McArthur is now twenty minutes late. Charles guesses the time and place were chosen because, at 6:30 p.m., Essex Street would be thronging with workers heading home in the rush hour, but even in the forty minutes Charles has kept watch from his corner table in *The Three Brewers* the press of commuters has begun to slacken. Perhaps it's now too late; he begins to doubt McArthur will show.

In McArthur's telephone call to Chambers, during which the blackmailer made no attempt to disguise his voice, Charles feigned ignorance of his identity and demanded his name several times. Otherwise, however, he'd been compliant, agreeing without quarrel to the drop details prescribed by McArthur.

In return for McArthur's silence, Charles is to leave a holdall with £10,000 in a waste bin at Essex Road Underground Station, the Canonbury Road exit. During the call, McArthur twice referred to the station as "Canonbury and Essex Road", apparently unaware that that name hadn't been in use since 1948. Charles hopes that McArthur's unfamiliarity with the present name also implies ignorance of the fact that two of the old exits are no longer in use. Were he in McArthur's place, he'd have picked a station or other public place with as many exits as possible to provide the widest choice of potential escape routes. McArthur now has only one: he can go underground via the Canonbury Road entrance, or he might move off on the pavement. In either case, Charles is confident he can follow.

Charles's main purpose today is not to engage with the blackmailer, but identify and assess him. Charles needs to know if he's working alone and, if he's lucky, where he's staying.

Another ten minutes elapse.

Finally Charles sees a heavily-built middle-aged man walking swiftly, almost jogging, along Essex Road towards the station entrance. Charles studies him from behind his newspaper. There's a vague familiarity about him, but nothing more and Charles isn't sure if it's McArthur. The man is dishevelled and sweating and is looking about himself anxiously. *Just someone running late?* wonders Charles, but then the jogging stops abruptly at the waste bin and Charles's doubts are resolved. The man looks inside briefly and then, with almost comical furtiveness, leans against the railings within sight of the waste bin. He takes a rolled-up newspaper from under his arm, over which he looks, his head swivelling this way and that, as he attempts surreptitiously to evaluate the passing commuters. After a further few seconds he rolls the newspaper again, looks around himself once more, approaches the bin and digs deeply into it with his left hand.

He comes up a moment later with the holdall Charles left there an hour earlier, spilling half the contents of the bin onto the pavement in a cascade of old newspapers, orange peel and other detritus. He bends to pick up a few of the items, stops with the tidy-up half completed, drops his newspaper into the bin and strides off down Canonbury Road.

Charles swallows the dregs of his Scotch and leaves the pub in pursuit. He's held up for a few seconds, unable to cross the road for fast-moving traffic in both directions in front of him. Diagonally across the junction he sees McArthur actually break into a run. Charles doubts the beefy man can keep it up for long, but he skips through the traffic and increases the pace of pursuit. Charles is still in good condition, having been in training for his last boxing match until only a few months earlier, and his brief observation of McArthur suggests that the sweating man is pretty unfit.

McArthur disappears into Canonbury Gardens to his left, a hundred yards or so further down the road. The Gardens are a small triangular park formed between the junction of Canonbury Road and Canonbury Villas. From here McArthur has a choice of several potential routes and Charles increases his pace still further.

He needn't have worried. Charles almost blunders into plain view because McArthur has halted at the first park bench. Charles stops in his tracks, watching McArthur testing the zip of the holdall as he realises that Charles has closed it with a small padlock. McArthur yanks furiously at the padlock.

Shit! Charles only used the padlock to ensure the zip didn't fall open, revealing the torn-up telephone directories within. It's a tiny padlock, a toy really, and could be broken open in an instant with a screwdriver, perhaps even a metal nail file. Charles didn't foresee the idiot trying to open the bag and examine £10,000 in cash in public and during the rush hour! But McArthur's either so impatient or so anxious he keeps pulling at the padlock, merely moving the zips from one end of the holdall to the other without ever getting it open, and getting increasingly incensed. Finally, he utters an inarticulate roar of frustration and throws the holdall onto the bench beside him. Charles steps sideways swiftly, heading for the nearest tree, but not in time before McArthur turns. Charles faces the other way, presenting McArthur with his back, but it's too late; he's been recognised.

'You!' calls McArthur, and Charles hears footsteps running towards him.

For a second or two Charles maintains the pretence of being an innocent pedestrian, and he moves nonchalantly back the way he came, but McArthur's not buying it. Charles decides not to run. He turns back towards McArthur, preparing a story, but is astonished to find McArthur literally in mid-air, feet off the ground and almost horizontal, having launched himself into a sort of rugby tackle.

Charles spent an entire day planning, anticipating every possible outcome of the drop, including those where everything went awry, and devising stratagems to deal with each, but one scenario he hadn't predicted was a very public fist-fight with a thwarted blackmailer. A well-known aphorism amongst advocates is that *You can rely on the stupidity of your opponent only so far; sooner or later they get the point,* and the half-formed thought flashes through Charles's mind that perhaps he should have applied it rather more widely. But he has no time to chide himself before McArthur's solid bulk clatters into him. Charles is knocked off his feet and he finds himself sailing backwards, landing heavily on the scrubby grass with McArthur on top of him. Charles is assailed by unwashed body odour and beer fumes.

'Where's my fucking money, you cunt!' screams McArthur, aiming a wild punch at Charles's face.

Charles manages to get an arm up and blocks, but another punch comes in from the other side, and he realises that he is going to have to fight back or take a beating. At the same instant as McArthur lands a blow on Charles's cheek, Charles head-butts him heavily, making good contact with his nose. As McArthur rears up, Charles swings his arm at the other's face. He misses, but his elbow catches McArthur's chin as it flies past. McArthur's attempt to avoid the blow shifts his body weight and Charles heaves the man off him. The two of them are now wrestling on the floor, watched by an elderly woman with a shopping trolley and a small dog. Part of Charles's mind floats above the fray and he would laugh if he weren't quite so occupied — they must look like a couple of street urchins wrestling in the gutter — but McArthur now has his hands around Charles's throat and is squeezing hard.

Although a skilful Marquis of Queensbury boxer, Charles learned his trade on the streets, and he hasn't forgotten the tricks. He responds by clamping his hands around McArthur's head and pressing his thumbs hard into his eye sockets. McArthur howls in pain and releases his grip on Charles's neck, and Charles shifts his weight again and rolls on top of him.

Now he has the upper hand. He swings a punch at the left side of the man's face, and another at the right, his knuckles coming away red with McArthur's blood. He's about to land another punch when McArthur speaks.

'You gonna kill me too?' Charles's arm halts in mid-air. 'Beat me to death 'n' all? Ain't that your MO, Jew-boy?'

Charles feels the body underneath him relax and he realises that McArthur's offering no further resistance. Instead of landing the blow, Charles brings his knees up to straddle McArthur's chest, pinning his wrists against the grass on either side of his head. He turns his head to address the elderly woman, who has now been joined by two or three other passers-by. They are frozen into a still tableau, watching, mouths open.

'I'm going to call the police!' shouts the old lady.

'It's OK,' Charles shouts back. 'He's my brother. He escaped from St Anne's mental wing this morning. He'll calm down in a second, I promise. You're OK, aren't you Mikey?' Charles drops his voice. 'You want the police? Or do you want the money?'

'You fucking —' starts McArthur, beginning to struggle again.

'Think about it, Mikey,' says Charles through gritted teeth. 'Let them call the police, and it's over. You won't get a penny. So, revenge or money?'

Charles's eyes bore into the face of the man underneath him.

'Let me go, then,' snarls McArthur, but quietly enough that only Charles can hear him.

'Are we good?' asks Charles.

'Yeah.'

Charles sits up cautiously, releasing the pressure on McArthur's arms. He climbs off and stands, brushing the gravel and dust off his knees and shoulders. Then he offers a hand to McArthur to pull him up. McArthur hesitates, but takes the offered hand. Charles hauls him upright and starts dusting him down.

'See?' he calls over his shoulder at the bystanders. 'It's all over. No need for the police, is there, Mikey?'

McArthur's face contorts into an unconvincing smile. 'No,' he calls across. 'I'm OK. Charlie here's just looking out for me.'

The bystanders remain stationary, still unsure.

'We're just going to sit on the bench together for a few minutes,' says Charles, pointing to where McArthur had been sitting. The holdall is still there. He puts a fraternal arm around McArthur's shoulders and steers him towards the bench. After a few further seconds of hesitation, most of the bystanders disperse.

Charles and MacArthur sit, the holdall between them.

'You locked it so I couldn't see inside, dincha?' accuses McArthur. 'What's in there, then? Newspapers?'

Charles leans forward, brushing grass and mud off his knees. 'Phone directories.'

'You cunt,' repeats McArthur. He speaks quietly, glancing at the remaining onlookers, a couple of whom are still keeping a watchful eye on the two men sitting on the bench as their dogs investigate scents around the trees. 'You think I weren't serious?'

'I think you're serious, Mikey, but I don't think you've thought this through. £10,000?' he scoffs. 'I can't get hold of that sort of money. So what choice did you give me?'

'You're a fucking brief! You lot are loaded. You'll find it.'

'I *am* a "fucking brief", but if you'd bothered to do your research you'd have seen that I'm a fucking *Defence* brief. We work on legal aid rates. Ever heard of legal aid, Mikey? Criminal barristers are not the fat cats they're portrayed in the press.'

This isn't altogether accurate, as Charles has been doing well-remunerated high-profile work for the last year or two, and recently for the Crown, but there's more than a little truth in it, and his voice is persuasively sincere. He sees doubt flicker in McArthur's eyes.

'How much can you get then?' asks McArthur, and now Charles knows he has the upper hand. He doesn't answer McArthur's question but changes tack.

'That's not the only thing you haven't thought about. Do you really think the police are going to believe you, twenty years after the event?'

'They'll believe me. I thought you was dead, didn't I? Killed in the war. And then — would you believe it? — you just popped up in the Lake District and I recognised you. Oh yes, they'll believe it!'

'You've got no body, you've got no independent witnesses and you've got no credibility. I reckon you've seen the inside of a prison, haven't you?' McArthur darts a sidelong glance at him, and Charles has his confirmation. It's not difficult for a prosecution barrister to access the Criminal Records Office, but without McArthur's date of birth, address or other details he wasn't sure until now that he'd identified the right man. 'What's more, you and Bledsoe were looting and in the middle of beating another man to death.'

'You're the one who beat someone to death, Horowitz. You know it, and I know it.'

'I didn't beat anyone to death. The poor man was crushed when that wall fell on him in the air raid,' says Charles blithely.

'Is that the story? I always wondered what you did with him.'

'Look,' says Charles. 'We can kick this around all night, but it won't get us anywhere. I might be able to get something together if you give me a bit of time.'

'How much?'

Charles hesitates, calculating. 'A monkey, perhaps.'

'Five hundred nicker?! You gotta be joking. It's got to be worth a grand, minimum.'

Charles pretends to chew it over. 'I might be able to get a grand together, but I'll need time.'

'How long?'

'A fortnight, minimum. Gotta call in some debts.'

'I'll give you till Friday week,' says McArthur, standing. He turns to look down on Charles's head.

'The rozzers don't have to believe me. From what I hear, you're on fuckin' thin ice as it is. It'd only take one more accusation, and you'll be finished as a brief anyway.' Perhaps not quite as stupid as he appears, then, thinks Charles. 'Be here, Friday week, at 6 p.m. OK? If you don't show *with the money*, I'll walk into the nearest nick and tell 'em what I saw. No skin off my nose.' Something else occurs to McArthur and he puts out his hand. 'And I want a tenner now. I'm boracic.'

Charles look up at McArthur and stares at him for a moment before opening his wallet and handing the man two five-pound notes.

'A grand, Horowitz,' repeats McArthur. 'No less.'

'I understand.'

Charles watches McArthur disappear into the gloom under the trees. *Well, that went well*, he thinks. *Now what?*

CHAPTER 22

The Crown v Steele is finally listed to start the last week in September, on the day immediately before *Rosh Hashana*, the Jewish New Year. For some reason, the coincidence in timing seems ominous to Charles. He hasn't celebrated any Jewish festival since he left for university, more than twenty years ago, and he'd been drifting away from his family's religious beliefs and observances for years before then, since even before his bar mitzvah. He's usually completely unaware of the Jewish calendar unless, perhaps, he stumbles over something in the newspaper or overhears some rabbi intoning meaningfully on the Home Service as he eats breakfast.

This year however, with his father sharing his cramped living quarters, it's impossible to avoid it. His religion nudges and whispers to him, calling for his attention. Charles tries out the justifications: *I gave that up years ago … I don't believe in God … this is the biggest case of my career and no one could expect me to return it … it would be professionally improper anyway, so close to trial …* but he can picture Harry's face as he departs for synagogue, suppressing his disappointment, leaving Charles to go to work as usual.

In truth, the excuses taste dry and dusty even to him. For the first time since he was a child, his family's religious celebrations seem rich and inviting, a sparkling river passing him by within earshot. He catches himself humming a tune from the *Rosh Hashana* evening service, a haunting melody in a minor key, one that always brought a constriction to his throat as a child, and instantly turns on Radio Caroline. Thus, he deploys twentieth century pop to drown out the siren calls of the millennia before Christ, and forges on with his preparation.

The morning before the trial is to start Charles orders a minicab from a reliable company used by Chambers and arranges to transport his father from the City to his synagogue in the suburbs for each day of the forthcoming festival. Harry has never before used transport to travel to or from his *shul* — in God's eyes that is work, and work is forbidden — but even he accepts that he'd be unable to walk the eight miles each way. God will have to understand or turn a blind eye, he concedes. For the rest of the day Charles is fully occupied with last-minute conferences, deciding the order of witnesses, agreeing a chronology with his Defence opponents and bundling the legal precedents Xeroxed by the clerks on which he expects the Defence to rely.

The following day he wakes at 7.27 a.m., three minutes before the alarm. He calls the cab company to make sure the driver arrives at the flat in time to collect Harry by half past five that afternoon for the evening service. Satisfied that he's done all he can, he bathes and dresses, shouts a goodbye to his father who is still in the bathroom, hefts his robes and a suitcase full of case papers, and leaves the flat. On the landing he experiences that feeling of having forgotten something important and he stops, his finger on the lift button holding the doors open, trying to pin down whatever it was but, if there was something, it eludes him. He shakes his head and enters the lift.

'Best of luck, sir,' calls Dennis as Charles emerges onto the ground floor.

Dennis has kept abreast of the case by chatting to Harry and reading the newspaper reports, occasionally asking Charles which parts of them are accurate.

'Thanks, Dennis.'

He walks across Fleet Street to Chambers, potters about there for half an hour, only really killing time, and heads down Fleet Street to Ludgate Circus. As he crosses the junction onto Ludgate Hill he sees, ahead of him, two barristers he knows, deep in a discussion of their case in progress. Behind him is another, louder, group of young barristers none of whom he recognises. The route to the Old Bailey, particularly at 9.30 a.m., is the place to meet members of the criminal Bar.

Charles turns left up Old Bailey. He hoped that by arriving early he'd avoid the cameramen and reporters, but the pavement is already crowded with them. He has to push his way through the group to reach the doors, but before he reaches the safety of the building someone has recognised him.

'Mr Holborne! Mr Holborne, sir! Any comment on today's case?'

Charles ignores the question and continues into the relative quiet of the court building. He gives himself over to the searching and security checking, his mind on the prospect of bacon and eggs upstairs in the Bar Mess. One of the best breakfasts in London is to be obtained on the top floor, with a view over most of the City to accompany it. He rides in the lift to the fourth floor, dumps his robes and briefcase in his locker and walks up the final staircase.

'Hello, Charles,' says a familiar voice.

Charles turns. It's James Day, smiling and looking a great deal friendlier than at the Magistrates' Court.

'Hello, Jimmy. Been let off the leash, or is this a change of tactic?' replies Charles, not breaking his stride towards food.

Day, at five and a half feet tall, has to skip every now and then to keep up, and the fact that he does so confirms to

Charles that the Defence wants something, or perhaps have something to offer.

'All ready?' he asks, joining the short queue behind Charles.

'I expect so. I haven't seen my solicitor yet, but as of yesterday all our witnesses were ready. How about you? Any last-minute offers?'

'Ha, ha,' replies Day with heavy sarcasm. 'You don't expect one of Her Majesty's top judges to cave in just before trial, do you? *It's a fair cop, guv, I done it. Sorry to have wasted the time of the court'*?'

'You never know. That might depend on whether he's guilty.'

'Don't be silly, Charles.'

'Then what can I do for you?'

'Nothing. Just being sociable, old chap.'

'Balls.' Charles turns to Day with a grin. 'Come on, Jimmy, I know you too well. What's up?'

'Well, we just wondered what your attitude would be to a plea to the second indictment alone.'

'What, obstructing the coroner? Come off it.'

'Aren't you being a little over-confident? It's really all you've got. And if the nanny doesn't come up to proof, you might not even get that.'

'She'll come up to proof, I've no doubt on that score.'

Charles takes his tray, thanks the waitress serving him and moves to a table by the window. Day follows and sits down. When he speaks again, it's with a lowered voice.

'Have you asked yourself what you're trying to achieve? Even a plea to obstructing the coroner will finish his career for good. He's no risk to society, even you must see that, especially if you've read all the depositions from the neighbours and friends. He'll be sent to an open prison, serve his time and go into retirement. Think what a conviction for manslaughter or, even worse, murder, will do to the profession. Who the hell's going to believe in anything we do anymore?'

'Are you representing him or standing for Parliament?' replies Charles, with a grin. 'No, I'm sorry for the levity. For your information Jimmy, I *have* thought about it, but I've come to exactly the opposite conclusion. What'll the public think if the Crown accepts obstructing the coroner, and doesn't even try him on the other counts? "*One law for the rich…*" etcetera? A profession closing ranks yet again? I would personally like nothing more than to see him tried and acquitted to loud fanfares and joyous flag waving. That'd prove that no one, absolutely *no one*, is above the law; that we have the nerve to use the system even against one of our own; and that it works. If *we* trust it, so will the public. But if we circumvent it, there'll be no respect left for it at all. It's bad enough that the Met's institutionally corrupt and that London's ruled by the likes of the Krays and the Richardsons. But the judiciary, and the Bar, well, surely *we've* got to be beyond reproach?'

Charles looks around, suddenly conscious of the depth of quiet near their table, and finds several of the lawyers looking their way and eavesdropping unashamedly. A sprinkling of applause, only half in jest, makes him grin again. He bows from his sitting position, and turns back to Day.

'Sorry, old chap. I think we're just going to have to go through with it.'

Day looks at him hard, and then nods. 'I expect you're right. I was told to ask, and I have.' He rises, leaving his coffee untouched. 'By the way, have you seen who our judge is?'

'Someone with no career ambition, I hope. Poor sod's in a no-win position.'

'It's the Recorder.'

'Well, at least we're sure of a fair trial. That's something. It would have been just like the Lord Chancellor's office to have wheeled in some old duffer who'd have summed up for an acquittal — and got just the opposite.'

'My views exactly. See you in court.'

There's an eerie hush in the packed Number 1 Court as Charles enters just before eleven o'clock. The Defence team, both barristers, a solicitor and a clerk, huddle with their heads bowed in quiet consultation at the barristers' bench. Jones sits one row behind in the solicitors' bench with a member of his staff, his back to Charles. The public gallery and the reporters' seats have been full for over an hour, no one daring to leave their places for fear of losing them. Charles noted the long line formed of members of the public queuing around the corner of the Old Bailey, hoping for a front-row vantage point to watch the trial of the decade. Two of the dailies have identical headlines that morning: "*British Justice on Trial*" which, Charles thinks, is both a clever pun and entirely accurate.

The Judge, the Recorder of London, has dealt with a short matter and risen for the parties to ready themselves. As Charles walks to his seat, his arms laden with files, bundles of precedents and law books, and his wig perched on top of the uppermost, he looks at the accused who, having already surrendered to custody, sits in the dock.

Anthony Steele is the very caricature of a judge out of his court robes: a kindly, handsome, patrician face, surmounted by well-cut grey hair, silver at the temples; a quietly expensive charcoal-grey suit of conservative cut; a blue silk tie with a thin gold stripe in it, a matching folded handkerchief protruding from the breast pocket; a white creaseless cotton shirt, fastened at the wrists by simple gold cufflinks. He sits with his manicured hands clasped gently in his lap, his head erect and slightly to one side, his eyes unfocussed, as if concentrating on some interesting but rather baffling point of law that requires all his attention.

'Morning,' says Charles to the solicitors as he takes his seat.

'Morning, Charles,' replies Jones. 'Anything you need?'

'No, thank you. Oh, there is one thing: I appreciate why you wanted absolute confidentiality at the outset, but now the press of the entire western world knows that a senior British Judge is to be tried for murdering his wife, do you think I might know your real name now?'

'It's Jones,' replies the solicitor with a slight blush. 'That's why I haven't bothered to correct you.'

'Fine. Somehow, I guessed. Are the witnesses here?'

'I've had a call from the pathologist's office. He was doing a post-mortem in Leeds first thing this morning and he's been caught in traffic. He'll be here by lunchtime. Apart from that, they're all outside.'

'We may not reach him at all today in any event.'

Charles is about to tell Jones about his conversation in the Bar Mess when the usher calls 'All rise!' and the Recorder enters.

Charles leaps up and grabs his wig, just getting it into position on his head as the judge turns to the barristers and bows. The barristers all bow in unison and then they and the judge take their seats.

Charles sizes up the man on the bench before him. His Honour Judge Mackey QC was appointed to the office of Recorder of London only six months before. Although the senior judge sitting at the Old Bailey, he's of the new generation, scarcely ten years older than Charles. Charles has not appeared in his court before but has heard that he's a fair man, not, as many of his predecessors were, overtly prosecution-biased. The Recorder addresses the barristers' bench.

'Good morning gentlemen.' The three barristers rise. 'Interesting reversal of roles,' he says with a smile. 'Trying our hand at gamekeeping, Mr Holborne?'

'Not for the first time, my Lord.'

'Well, are we ready? Mr Holborne?'

'Yes, my Lord.'

'Mr Beaverbrook?'

'Yes, my Lord.'

'Let us proceed to arraignment, then.' He nods to the court clerk, who rises, the indictment in his hand. 'Please stand,' he asks the accused. 'Are you Anthony Michael Steele?'

'I am,' replies Steele. His voice sounds tired but calm and measured.

'On count one of this indictment you are charged with murder, in that in or about April 1953 you did murder one Lise Helene Steele, contrary to common law. How do you plead?'

'Not guilty.'

The clerk moves to the second count, manslaughter. Charles decided to add this as an alternative. He doubts he'd have accepted a manslaughter plea even if offered, but he wanted to keep his options open. The question proves academic, as Steele pleads not guilty to that charge too.

The clerk continues to put a second indictment, this one containing only one count, that of obstruction of the coroner in the execution of his duty. This is Charles's fall-back position. More importantly however, its inclusion is dictated by tactical considerations. Until his conversation with Jimmy Day, Charles had no indication whatsoever from the Defence whether they were going to accept any part of the nanny's account. The plea to this count will give him an early indication: if the plea to obstructing the coroner — in short, disposing of the body — is "Not Guilty", Charles will know that the Defence intend to deny Steele's admission to Jenny Sullivan that he killed Lise in self-defence; they have no alternative.

If that's their position, it sets Steele's evidence against hers and, in that contest, Charles expects Jenny Sullivan's evidence to prevail and Steele to be shown to be a liar. On the other hand, if Steele pleads "Guilty" to this count, it means that Jenny told the truth about at least part of the story, and that helps the Crown too.

The clerk finishes reading the particulars of the offence and, in contrast to his response to the other charges, there is a fractional pause before Steele answers.

'Guilty,' he responds, and lowers his head.

There's a collective intake of breath in the courtroom. With that one word, uttered in less than half a second, Lord Justice Steele's glittering career comes to an end. It all vanishes: his profession, his way of life, his ambition for the one remaining judicial elevation before him, to the House of Lords, his good name — even his pension. Whatever he might now say; whatever defence he places before the jury; however much they might believe him, even sympathise, with him; and however lenient the trial judge might be; he has admitted to disposing of his wife's bloody body, to tipping her with a weight attached into a lake at the dead of night. Now it is revealed to the whole world that his feet are, contrary to all expectation, made of clay like everyone else's.

Whispering begins as the realisation of what the plea means gathers pace in the court. The expected defence of "*It wasn't me; this is all a terrible mistake*" can no longer be run. Steele has no alternative: he is going to have to tell everyone how his wife met her death.

Ever since he was charged, the story has made headlines, in England and abroad. It has been the subject of two questions in the House, several leading articles and innumerable documentaries, chat show discussions, and jokes by comedians and newspaper cartoonists. Battle lines have been drawn. Some refused to believe that one of the country's top judges could possibly be guilty of murder; in their opinion, this was a conspiracy to undermine justice, the government and the jury system. Others, the cynics who always knew there was corruption and evil at the top of the system, merely expressed surprise that no one had been caught with red hands before. The ground has now been cut away from under that debate. It's no longer a question of "*Is he guilty?*" but "*How guilty is he?*"

The clerk of the court calls twice for silence but to little effect. Then the Recorder intervenes.

'Unless there is silence immediately, I shall clear the court and conduct the entire trial in camera,' he says with quiet authority.

The conversations gradually cease and silence resumes. The clerk addresses Steele. 'You may sit.'

'Jury, Mr Holborne?' says the Recorder. By his question he asks Charles if the Crown is satisfied with the pleas tendered, or if it wants a trial.

'Yes please, my Lord.'

Charles listens with only part of his attention as the jury in waiting is brought in. Neither prosecution nor defence challenge any of the first twelve whose names are called, and the jury members, six men and six women, are all sworn in. While the clerk directs the unused jurors to follow the jury bailiff, Charles leans across to Beaverbrook.

'What's your view about telling the jury that your client has pleaded guilty to impeding the coroner?'

'I have no objections. They'll find out as soon as I start cross-examination in any event.'

'OK.'

The court clerk is telling the jury the charges faced by the defendant. He finishes and sits down, and the Recorder nods at Charles. Charles opens his notebook and rises, gathering the wings of his gown about him.

'Ladies and gentlemen, I appear on behalf of the Crown in this case. The Defendant is represented by Mr Beaverbrook, who sits nearest to you on the front bench, and, behind him, Mr Day. My purpose is to tell you something about the case that you will hear. What I say — indeed, what any of the barristers say — is not evidence, and you will not decide the case according to what we tell you. The outline I give is intended to assist you when you come to hear the evidence, so that you can put it in context. It's the evidence you hear from that witness box —' and Charles points across the courtroom at it — 'or that you hear read to you by the court clerk, that will decide this case.

'That's particularly important in a case like this. You'll all have heard television and radio reports about this trial. I am sure some of you will have read accounts in the newspapers. All of that you must now put out of your heads. Some of you may know (and I suspect you all will, by the end of this trial) that reporters and commentators deal in speculation, gossip and opinion. Sometimes they've part of the truth; often they've none of it. The only people who hear everything, that is, all the evidence from beginning to end, are we in this court. And the only people who have any part in the decisions that have to be reached on the facts, are you twelve, as assisted by his Lordship. Your job is to hear the evidence, sift it, decide what you and you alone think about it and then, subject to his

Lordship's directions as to the law, reach verdicts. It is critically important to put aside anything you may have heard about the case already, or anything that you may hear about it, *unless you hear it in this court.*'

He pauses to see if the jury are following him. They are. Two or three nod slightly and the others have all their attention on him.

'You know that the defendant is a very senior judge. He is also a knight of the realm, as are all judges of the High Court or higher. That should neither count for him nor against him. He is, of course, a man of good character, and his Lordship will direct you as to how you should treat that fact when he comes to sum up. But let me say this now: everyone, whether humble or mighty, has a good character at one time, and every man or woman who is convicted of any offence loses it. The fact that a judge's fall from grace may be from a greater height does not affect that.

'I now propose to give you an outline of the case before I turn to some of the detailed evidence you will hear. As the court clerk just told you, the defendant faces two charges, murder and manslaughter. Also, before you were sworn in, he pleaded guilty to a third count, that of obstructing the coroner in the execution of his duty, by failing to report the death of the deceased, his wife, and by unlawfully disposing of her body.'

Several members of the jury turn their heads towards the dock suddenly, shocked at Charles's words. He waits a few seconds and continues.

'You can see therefore that each of the three charges against him represents a different level of guilt. He may, firstly, be guilty only of having unlawfully disposed of his wife's body. Secondly, he may be guilty of having killed her, albeit without malice aforethought, or for some other reason which reduces the charge to manslaughter. Thirdly, he may have killed her, intending to do so, or to do her serious harm. That is murder.

'He has admitted the first to you by his plea; it is for you to decide if he has committed the second or the third or neither of them. The Crown's case is that he is guilty of the highest level of guilt: that he murdered his wife in cold blood.

'Why? Firstly, he had a very strong motive. His wife was an adulteress, many times over. She taunted him with her affairs, conducted them right under his nose, and repeatedly embarrassed and humiliated him in public. Furthermore, she was dependent on alcohol, and her outrageous behaviour was such that his career — he was, at that time, a very successful junior barrister — was unable to progress while he was married to her. Divorce was something he would not consider, firstly because of the scandal but, perhaps more importantly, because it would mean losing his three children, of whom he was extremely fond.

'Secondly, opportunity. He was the only person in the house on the afternoon the deceased disappeared. The last person to see her before then was her lover, some hours before, whose evidence you will hear, and who himself has an unassailable alibi that has been verified by numerous witnesses. The defendant admits that there was a terrible row that afternoon. The deceased was never seen again alive after that row. However, when the body was discovered, thirteen years later, it was wearing the very clothes in which the lover had last seen the deceased and which, the Crown say, she must have been wearing at the time of the row.

'Thirdly, the scientific evidence. The bedroom in the house that was the matrimonial home, the very bedroom where this terrible row occurred, has been minutely examined. The floorboards were stained in huge areas with human blood. There was so much blood that it dripped though the floorboards and ran down a light flex where it collected in a brass lamp hanging from the dining room ceiling. Blood was found under paint and wallpaper on the walls, on the cornices and on the ceiling of that bedroom. Tiny droplets and splashes of it, suggesting either that it sprayed out of the deceased's body through some wound, or that it was flung off as a result of violent blows.'

Charles sees the winces of some of the members of the jury, and one or two of them turn again to examine Steele in the dock as if asking themselves if it was possible for *this man* to have done *that*. Charles presses on, his voice forceful but not dramatic, trying to make a jury, hardened by newspaper and television portrayals of violence both true and fictional, see the real horror of real crime.

'As to blows, you'll hear evidence from the pathologist that there were marks at the side of the deceased's neck consistent with strangulation. He was unable to find any other injury, illness or disease that would account for Lise Steele's death.

'Finally, you will hear from a witness who was at the time, and remains to this day, a nanny at the house, a Miss Jennifer Sullivan. We do not suggest she had anything to do with the death of the deceased. What she has said however, is that the defendant came to her, highly distressed, and admitted killing his wife, albeit, so he claimed, in self-defence. She says that she was asked by him to go out and buy paint and wallpaper so that he could cover up the evidence. Having done that, she left the house with the children for a few days to let him get on with it. Now, obviously, her statement cannot help you decide if the defendant is guilty of murder, as she was just repeating what he told her, but it constitutes an admission by the accused that his wife met her death in that bedroom at his hands. Now, and this is important: when he was asked by the police, he *denied* any such event. He claimed instead that his late wife stormed out of the house after the argument, alive and well. The Crown rely on the evidence of Miss Sullivan to prove, firstly, that the accused lied to the police when challenged about the events and, secondly, that Mrs Steele met her death at the accused's hands, in their bedroom on that afternoon.

'What makes us say that you can be sure he's guilty of murder? Well, in addition to the fact that he's the only person with both motive and opportunity; in addition to the blood and other scientific evidence — the clothing, the plastic and the wire which you'll hear about, and which he used to truss her up; in addition to the lies he told the police; we rely on the planning, the intricate, careful, scrupulously-executed, planning.

'Two complete rooms in the house were redecorated, the floors scrubbed, stained and re-varnished, the walls repapered, the ceiling repainted. The body was somehow smuggled out of the house, wrapped up so that, no doubt, no blood would drip from it. It was then taken from the home to Wastwater. The accused must have obtained a kerbstone from somewhere, and a boat, as you cannot get a body into the middle of the deepest lake in England, weighted down with a kerbstone, without a boat.

'Why go to all this trouble if her death occurred at someone else's hands, or, perhaps, at your own hands but by accident or in self-defence? Surely the sensible, lawful, and obvious thing to do is to telephone the police immediately and tell them what happened. This is a barrister we're speaking about, a man who knows the law, and what's more, is likely to be believed. The Crown says that the most obvious indication of the accused's guilt is the very fact that he covered up the death. Had he been innocent of his wife's death, it was something he had no need to do — indeed, it was an illegal, dangerous, career-threatening thing to do.

'That, members of the jury, is the basic outline of the Crown's case. I shall now tell you a little more about the witnesses and their evidence, so that you will know who each of them is when they come before you.'

'I think, perhaps, Mr Holborne, that you'd best do that at five past two,' interrupts the Recorder, nodding at the clock, which says a minute past one.

'Certainly, my Lord.'

'All rise!'

The court rises while the Recorder leaves the bench, and Charles turns to speak to Jones. Something makes him look up at the public gallery. Waving shyly from the front row is his father. Harry points to the door questioningly. Charles nods and puts up one hand, five fingers splayed, to indicate five minutes. Harry nods understanding and leaves his seat.

'Anything we need to discuss?' asks Charles of Jones.

'No, I don't think so. Nice opening, Charles. Put like that, it seems an almost impregnable case.'

'Don't you believe it. There's a long way to go yet.'

'Did you have any idea about the plea to count three?'

'Day said something to me in the Bar Mess, but I wasn't sure if he was serious or just sounding me out. I assumed that it wouldn't be acceptable?'

'You assumed right.'

'Good. My father's somehow got himself into the public gallery, so I thought I'd have some lunch with him.'

'Fine. I've got to call the office anyway. See you at two.'

CHAPTER 23

'Do you think he did it?'

Harry and Charles sit at a small table in the *Magpie and Stump*, the pub in Old Bailey so close to the court and usually so full of barristers and solicitors that it's known to everyone in the profession as "Courtroom No 10". Harry will, of course, eat nothing as the food isn't kosher, but he sits with an untouched glass of water while Charles munches his way through an egg sandwich, wishing he'd had the courage of his convictions to order the ham, which looked better.

'I really don't know, Dad. You never really know until all the evidence has been heard. And not always then.'

'I don't suppose anyone ever really *knows*, do they? Not unless they're the accused...' muses Harry, 'or God, I suppose.'

'You think He knows?' asks Charles.

'I sincerely hope so, son,' says Harry.

'It's nice of you to come down, Dad. What made you?'

Harry shrugs and smiles gently. 'I don't know really. I've never seen you in action before, so that's one thing. And I've watched you get nervous and distracted over the last few weeks, and I wanted to see for myself what the fuss was about.'

'I've told you what the case is about, and how important it is.'

'I know, and I read the newspapers. But that never gives you the real answer, the truth.'

'The truth? Now there's a rare commodity. And how on earth did you get a front row seat in the gallery? It was packed hours before we started.'

'I told the man in uniform…'

'The sergeant at arms.'

'Yes, him … I told him I was your father, and that you'd promised me a seat.'

'And he believed you?'

'After I showed him photos from your bar mitzvah, then your graduation, and then your Call night. *Then* he believed me.'

Charles laughs. 'Good for you! Will you stay for the rest of the afternoon?'

'No, thank you. It's *Erev Rosh Hashanah*, as you know … I need to get changed and ready for *shul*.'

Jewish days run from sunset to sunset, so the New Year begins at sunset on the eve of New Year's Day.

They fall silent and Charles finishes his sandwich. Harry watches his son patiently. After a while he speaks.

'*Nu?*' he asks.

Charles looks up.

'You think I don't know when you've something on your mind, Charlie? So, spit it out.'

'Well…' Charles starts haltingly. 'I have been meaning to say something.'

'I know. Say it, already.'

'OK. But, Dad, I've not really worked out exactly what it is, so bear with me if it takes a couple of goes. OK?'

'OK.'

'You know how sorry I am about everything … between you and Mum —' Harry holds up his hand; *this* he doesn't want to hear, but Charles presses on. 'No, it's not what you think. I just wanted to say that … well, two things, really. Firstly, although I'm so sorry that you two are living apart at present … I've really enjoyed your being with me. The silver lining to all this is that I've got to know you better. I wish I'd done it sooner, but I thought … well, you've disapproved of me so much that … anyway… And, secondly, I think you've been taking my part with Mum, and … if that's part of the reason you two have fallen out … well, your support means a lot to me, but I don't want it to continue at that price. You two belong together, and I couldn't bear to be part of the reason you're not. On top of everything else.'

Harry smiles sadly, but says nothing. He leans forward and takes Charles's square hand in his veined and spotted ones, and squeezes.

'Maybe … maybe there were three things, actually,' continues Charles. He leans forward to ensure that no one at the adjoining tables can hear him. 'I don't remember saying it for a long time actually, but I love you.'

Harry's rheumy eyes lock onto Charles's and fill with tears. He squeezes Charles's hand again. 'I know,' he replies. 'I love you too.'

He releases Charles's hand, takes a handkerchief from his pocket and blows his nose noisily. He catches sight of the clock above the bar. 'Haven't you got to be back at five past two? You've less than ten minutes.'

'Shit! Yes! Let's go.'

'No, I think I'll pop into St Paul's — it's years since I've been in the cathedral — and then go back to the flat to get changed.'

'Will you be all right?' asks Charles, standing.

'I know this city better than you, boychick. I got here without your help and I'm sure I'll find my way back. I'll be fine.'

Charles downs the last of his half-pint and wipes his mouth with the back of his hand. 'OK, then. I'll see you after *shul* this evening. Give my love to … everyone.'

'I will. Oh, Charles, I meant to tell you.'

'What's that?'

'Sally telephoned the flat this morning, after you'd gone. She wanted to wish you luck.'

'Really?'

This is the first time Sally's made any contact with Charles since they split up. He ponders the news, wondering if he should read anything into the call. Probably not.

'That's kind of her.'

'We had a nice chat, actually. If you want my opinion, the girl misses you.'

Charles shakes his head. 'No. She's got a new bloke.'

'Did you know that she's back living with her mother in Romford? I may be wrong, but I got the impression she wasn't with that chap any longer. Anyway, it's almost two.'

Charles casts another look at the clock, swears again softly, and runs out of the bar.

Back in No 1 Court, Charles's opening only takes another hour. He senses the jury becoming restive; they've had enough of being told what evidence they're *going to* hear; they want to hear it. So he cuts short his overview and by three o'clock is calling his first witness.

The divers are the first to give evidence, starting with the woman from the club who found Lise Steele's wrapped up body, and then the police frogmen who got her to the lakeside. The Defence told Charles they wanted the witnesses to be called live rather than having their statements read as agreed evidence, but after Charles finishes taking each witness through their evidence in chief, to his surprise, Beaverbrook stands briefly and announces that he has no questions. The same occurs with the dentist who matched the jaws of the deceased to her dental records and the succession of police officers who dealt with the chain of custody of the exhibits, the clothes, the body and the cord used to tie it. Charles has the clerk read as agreed evidence the statements from the companies that produced the plastics and the cords, but by four fifteen he has run out of live witnesses to call, and the pathologist has still not arrived. He rises to explain to the Recorder, but the latter puts up his hand.

'Before you address me, Mr Holborne, I have a question for your learned friend.'

He turns to Beaverbrook, who also stands.

'Much as I am delighted at the speedy progress we've made this afternoon, Mr Beaverbrook, I am concerned at the waste of public money. None of these witnesses needed to have given evidence at all. Their statements could have been agreed months ago. Would you mind telling me what's going on?'

'My Lord, I am extremely conscious of the way in which matters have proceeded, and I apologise. I regret that I am not able to explain to your Lordship. Your Lordship will, I hope, understand my position, which is a difficult one.'

Jones leans forward and tugs at Charles's gown. Charles half-turns in his seat. 'What the hell is he saying?' whispers the solicitor.

'I'm not sure. I *think* he's saying that he's in professional difficulties.'

'Meaning?'

'Meaning, he has good reasons, but he can't explain them because that might entail revealing that his client is guilty of something. Or something more.'

'Wow!'

Charles turns back to the Recorder, who is pondering Beaverbrook's response, doodling on his notebook.

'Very well,' he says, looking up. 'I would however like you to speak to Mr Holborne before tomorrow and decide whose evidence may be read as agreed, and whose evidence may be led in chief for you to cross-examine. That way, poor Mr Holborne won't run out of witnesses.' Beaverbrook bows and resumes his seat. 'Have I covered what you were about to say?' asked the Recorder of Charles, with a smile.

'Perfectly,' replies Charles.

'Good. Then we'll rise for the day. Members of the jury, you have heard little evidence as yet, and none that is disputed, but all the same I must ask you not to discuss this case with anyone outside your number. Your family and friends will all no doubt be very excited and will want to know what's been happening, and it will be a great temptation to tell them. The risk is that they'll say something which, even unconsciously, affects your mind, and then the decisions made by you are not just made by you twelve, but by everyone you've spoken to who's expressed an opinion. The safest thing is to say nothing, at least until the case has ended.'

He addresses the barristers' bench. 'There are no problems over bail, are there?' Counsel shake their heads. 'Very well.'

'All rise!'

As if a door to a boisterous party has suddenly opened, loud talking begins the moment the Recorder disappears through the panelled door. The events of the day, the failure of the Defence to ask a single question and the enigmatic answers of Robert Beaverbrook QC all tighten the ratchet of tension and speculation. It's the possibility of "professional difficulties" that particularly interests those who understand the code. Is there to be a surprise change of plea? Or has Steele's story already changed, as explained by his late plea of guilty to obstructing the coroner?

'What do you think?' asks Jones of Charles.

Charles shrugs. 'I don't know. We'd better assume it's a fight 'til they tell us otherwise. Beaverbrook?' he asks, turning to the Defence silk.

'Yes?'

'What about witnesses for tomorrow?'

'Are you still following the order you gave to Day?' asks Beaverbrook, peering down his extremely long and very fine nose at Charles.

Charles knows he can't help it; at six foot three, Beaverbrook is forced to look down that nose at almost everyone, but Charles thinks he detects an extra scintilla of superciliousness when the silk is addressing him. The two men could not look more different: Beaverbrook, tall, thin, blue-eyed and Aryan; Charles, five inches shorter, dark, broad, and the olive skin of a Mediterranean. "*Jew*", Beaverbrook's look says, at least to Charles, which is perfectly unfair, as the thought hasn't entered Beaverbrook's head.

'Yes.'

'Very well. For the present, please assume that I'll want to cross examine all of them except the police officers. I'll make a decision about them by close of play tomorrow.'

'Thank you. See you tomorrow.'

Beaverbrook turns away from Charles to talk to his solicitor, but remembers something. 'By the way, Holborne, you know that one of the defendant's conditions of bail was that he didn't contact prosecution witnesses?'

'Yes.'

'In view of the fact that Miss Sullivan has stayed with the family to look after the children, the bail condition has entailed the defendant living elsewhere for the last two months. There's a problem with the younger son I understand, and the defendant wants to go to the house tonight to resolve it. Would the Crown have any objections?'

'Will that entail the defendant speaking to Miss Sullivan?' asks Charles.

'I expect so.'

Charles considers this. In reality, had the two decided to speak they'd already have done so. If Steele wanted to get her to change her evidence or not give evidence at all, he wouldn't risk leaving it until the night before she step into the witness box. On the other hand, they can't have spoken about that day's events, and that's not a card Charles wants to give away.

'In view of the fact that she's about to give evidence, it would be better for them not to speak tonight, don't you think?' he says. 'I'm afraid that if you want the bail conditions relaxed, you'd better call the Recorder back and make a formal application.'

'I understand. No, I shall make no application.'

'Fine.'

Charles raises his eyebrows to Jones for confirmation of his views, and Jones nods back vigorously.

'See you tomorrow then?' says Charles to the solicitor.

'I'd proposed to leave you in Shane's hands here,' replies Jones, indicating the young solicitor next to him, 'but I think the way things are going, I'd better be here.'

'I agree. I think we could be in for some surprises.'

CHAPTER 24

Charles returns to an empty flat echoing with Harry's absence. He feels in need of company and considers going into Chambers, but it's five-thirty and most of his colleagues will soon be on their way home. Those that aren't will be settling down for the nightshift and won't have time for gossip.

He pours himself a scotch and wanders about the tiny place, six paces to the kitchen, six paces back to the lounge, turns the television on and off, goes to the bedroom, throws his clothes on the bed and has a wash. He feels irritable with nothing to do, no work for the next day, no preparation required for the case.

He returns to the lounge with a towel tied about his waist and pours another drink. His eye lands on the black Bakelite telephone and he pauses, wondering if he might call Sally, and decides against. After a few more seconds of random pacing, he resolves to get dressed again and go into Chambers anyway. He reaches for some slacks, hesitates, looks at the clock and changes his mind again. He pulls out instead a clean shirt and freshly laundered suit. Dressed as if for court, he picks up his car keys at a run and closes the flat door behind him. Five minutes later, he sits in his battered orange MG Sprite sportscar, manoeuvring it out of the Temple car park and into rush-hour traffic, heading for north London.

Traffic is lighter than he imagined it would be, probably explained, he conjectures, by the fact that the Jewish workers in the City, of whom there had to be many thousands, had all left early to arrive in synagogue before sunset. He weaves his way northwards, in and out of the familiar back streets to avoid

227

the worst of the jams, and by twenty past six he's at the back of Hampstead; by six-thirty, Temple Fortune; and six forty-five, Hendon. Here there is very little traffic on the road, almost Bank Holiday-like, but the pavements are crowded with families in their best clothes, all making their way purposefully towards their annual audit with their God.

Charles parks a short distance past his parents' synagogue to avoid drawing attention to the fact that he's driven there.

He joins the stream of people walking towards the building and only then realises, as he sees the stewards checking tickets, that he's wasted his time; he won't be allowed in. The short-lived annual return to religion of hundreds of congregants never seen in prayer for the other fifty-one weeks of the year means that most synagogues have to issue tickets for the High Holydays. No ticket, no entry.

Charles stands, helpless and frustrated, as people move round and past him, display their permissions to pray and enter the building. He's about to give up when a hand lands on his shoulder. He turns. It's David, Sonia next to him.

'Hello, stranger,' says his brother, a huge smile on his face. 'Good Yomtov.'

'Good Yomtov,' replies Charles, the greeting tasting unfamiliar in his mouth.

'Good Yomtov, Charles,' says Sonia gently, kissing him softly on the cheek. 'It's lovely to see you here.'

'Make the best of it,' replied Charles wryly. 'I've no ticket, so I can't get in.'

David's smile flags momentarily, but he taps the side of his nose conspiratorially.

'Look after Charles for a sec,' he instructs Sonia, and he moves past the queue of people waiting to enter. The two men checking entrants greet David warmly as he reaches the front, shake his hand and incline their heads as he explains something confidentially. They both glance over at Charles as David speaks. The queue behind David grows and congregants lean forward to learn the cause of the delay, some looking back inquisitively at Charles standing with Sonia. Finally, the officials both nod and resume their job. David excuses himself back through the crowd.

'No problem,' he announces. 'You can sit with Dad and me.'

'How did you do it?' asks Charles.

'I reminded them of their duty,' replies David with a smile. 'I asked, who were they, on this day more than any other, to impede the return of an errant sinner to his God? They regard it as a *mitzvah*, a holy obligation to assist you to repent.'

'They're saving my soul, eh?'

'You never know.'

Charles enters synagogue with his brother and sister-in-law. He recognises no faces, this being the Horowitz's new synagogue since their move to the suburbs, but the babble of greetings, kisses, children pushing in and out of the adults, all is so familiar.

The women separate from the men in the entrance hall and climb the long curving staircase to what the Horowitzes had always impiously referred to as "the Circle", an upper tier of seats looking down on the men. Women are still not citizens with full rights in orthodox Jewry, a fact which Charles finds uncomfortable. Sonia waves goodbye to them and falls in with a group of other young married women whom she obviously knows well.

'Do you have a head covering?' asks David.

'Yes,' answers Charles, hands delving into jacket pockets and coming up with a skullcap in one and a prayer shawl in the other.

'Good. And a book?'

'No, that you'll have to get for me.'

David takes a book from a pile on a nearby table and rejoins Charles.

'Where's Mum?' asks Charles.

'She went back home today.'

'What, permanently?'

'She wouldn't tell us. She left mid-afternoon, saying she needed some other clothes. I offered to drive her, but she said she'd enjoy the walk and come to *shul* under her own steam. She's probably upstairs now.'

'Does this mean…?'

David shrugs. 'Who knows?'

'Have the two of them been in touch?' asks Charles.

'I think so, but I know better than to ask.'

The two brothers walk from the entrance hall into the synagogue itself. Charles pauses as he catches sight of the decorated ark containing the ancient handwritten scrolls, the glittering silver decorations and the arched stained-glass windows, and he struggles to identify how it all makes him feel.

David is greeted by half a dozen other men, some with the traditional New Year greeting, some with a handshake and a pat on the back, one or two putting their heads close to his to talk business for a moment or two.

Charles has always found orthodox synagogues a distasteful, even hypocritical, amalgam of spirituality and marketplace, but to his surprise he finds it less annoying than he remembered. He leaves David in one of the aisles and scans the rows of skull-capped men for his father, just spotting him as the choir stands and starts to sing.

The congregation quietens swiftly, rising to its feet as the rabbi enters, the cantor a few paces behind him. David slips into the row where Harry stands from one end, just as Charles arrives at Harry's side from the other. As the rabbi starts to pray, Harry realises who is next to him. He looks from one son to the other and then back again. The beam of pleasure he radiates is alone enough to make Charles glad he came. Harry leans towards him, his eyes moist for the second time that day, and whispers.

'It's good to see you. What changed your mind?'

'I'm not really sure. Maybe I'm looking for the truth too.'

'You'll find more in this court than at the Old Bailey. How did *you* get in?'

'You're not the only one with family connections, you know.'

Harry pats each of his sons on the back. He twists to look up at the gallery to see if Millie is there, but his failing eyesight is not up to the task. At that distance he identifies people by the colours of their clothes, but not knowing if she's there at all or, if so, what she's wearing, makes it impossible on this occasion. He opens his prayer book, his face still ceased by a smile from ear to ear. Charles and David share a look behind Harry's back and David winks.

The service takes a little over an hour. Charles finds himself prey to exactly the same emotions that left him disaffected years before. The proceedings are conducted in Hebrew and at such a frantic, breakneck, pace that most of it's incomprehensible. Even where he can follow the prayers and psalms in the prayer book, neither Charles nor most of the congregation can understand the Hebrew, let alone, in some cases, ancient Aramaic. Furthermore, and to his irritation, conversations periodically break out in pockets of congregants. At the same time, some of the prayers touch him and made him look deeply into himself if only for a moment or two, and some of the songs are hauntingly beautiful.

After it is over he, David and Harry wish one another Happy New Year and together walk outside, Harry and David shaking hands with the many congregants they know. When they reach the foot of the staircase, all three hesitate as if by an unspoken accord. David sees Sonia coming down with the crowd and points her out to Charles with a nod. Millie is with her. They descend the staircase without speaking and stop when they reach the bottom. Sonia kisses David and would have greeted Charles and Harry too had her husband not restrained her gently by the elbow. Millie and Harry look at each other for a moment, standing an arm's length apart, a rock in a moving tide of congregants which opens briefly round them and closes again once past the obstruction. Several cast glances at the Horowitzes, knowing the situation.

'Good Yomtov,' says Millie politely to her husband.

'Good Yomtov.'

'Are you all right?' she asks stiffly.

'Fine. You?'

'I'm OK.'

She turns to Charles. 'Good to see you, Charles. It's been a long time since I saw the three of you praying together. Come, Sonia, walk with me.'

And that's it. She takes Sonia's arm and, without a backward glance, merges into the crowd, allowing herself to be carried along with it. Sonia spins round briefly and gesticulates to David, and he apparently understands, for he nods and waves in reply.

'Are you taking Dad back to your flat?' he asks Charles.

'Unless things have changed. Dad?'

'No,' he says softly.

Charles can't decipher the layers of meaning or emotion in his father's response. Then, rousing himself, Harry says more firmly, 'We need to pay the cabbie, but I'll go back with Charlie.'

'OK. I'll catch Sonia up,' replies David.

He moves off, but shouts back to Charlie over the heads of the people between them. 'Call me!'

'Will do!'

Harry remains stationary for a moment longer, takes Charles's arm, and they move into the now thinning tide of congregants. Charles spots the taxi, pays the cabbie, and rejoins Harry. They walk slowly, at the pace of the remaining crowd, towards Charles's car.

Charles opens the passenger door for Harry, helps him sit in the unsuitably low sportscar and fastens his seatbelt for him.

'The Days of Awe,' says Harry as they move off.

'What's that?'

'You don't remember? That's what these ten days are called, the Days of Awe. Ten days between *Rosh Hashanah* and *Yom Kippur* in which to look afresh at our lives, to re-evaluate, to recognise our sins. "*On* Rosh Hashanah *we consider how judgment is formed; on* Yom Kippur *we consider how judgment is sealed*".'

'A very legal concept, that.'

'Yes indeed. It means we're given ten days to repent and seek forgiveness.'

'Not long enough,' says Charles flippantly. 'I'm not sure I could list all my sins in ten days. And as for repenting them all…'

'Long enough if you're sincere. God will forgive you if you forget a few.'

Charles hears something disquieting in his father's tone and turns to him. Harry is staring out of the passenger window at the houses flashing by. Compared to his happiness in the synagogue, he now seems deflated and depressed. Then, in a flash of unaccustomed insight, Charles realises that the sins to which Harry was referring were not those of his errant son; they were his own.

CHAPTER 25

'Call Commander Ferguson!' shouts the usher.

The door at the back of the court opens immediately and in walks a slender man. Charles, standing in counsels' benches, follows his progress down the aisle and into the witness box. Turned out in the full uniform of a commander, one rank below ship's captain, Ferguson looks impressive. He wears a double-breasted, navy blue jacket with four rows of brass buttons, gold braid on his cuffs and multicoloured medal ribbons on his chest; matching trousers; white shirt, black tie and black leather shoes. He carries his peaked hat under one arm. He makes a Technicolor splash amid the monochrome ranks of lawyers. His gait is halfway between a walk and a march and when he reaches the witness box, Charles fancies that he almost salutes the judge.

In trawling through Steele's life, the police turned up dozens of witnesses who spoke of the state of his marriage. Their statements all gave examples of Lise Steele's appalling behaviour — helpful in establishing motive for murder — but equally demonstrated Steele's saint-like patience and gentleness. Almost unanimously, the witnesses stated that the man they knew would never be capable of murder.

So sharp is this double-edged sword that Charles eventually decided against calling any of those he privately calls the "village witnesses". Instead he told Jones to hand over their statements to the Defence; let Beaverbrook decide whether or not to use them. That at least freed Charles to cross-examine any called for the Defence if he saw any profit in it.

Commander Ferguson RN was the exception. Formerly a colleague of Anthony Steele's during the war, it didn't appear that he and Steele had actually been friends or even liked one another very much when they served together. After the war, Steele returned to his legal practice and Ferguson remained in the Navy, doing reasonably well. The two men maintained a desultory correspondence over the years and, according to Ferguson, during one shore leave in 1953 he was invited to spend a weekend at the Steeles' home. There he was able to observe them over the space of three days, and his evidence had a different flavour. His evidence, untainted by sympathy or friendship, was accordingly more dispassionate. Having read Ferguson's preliminary statement, Charles asked to see him in conference to make a final decision.

He found Ferguson odd. He presented as a fussy, precise man who spoke quickly and never smiled, and Charles wondered if it was anything more than politeness that persuaded Anthony Steele to continue writing to this strange man over the years. Nonetheless, he gave his account clearly and with authority, and of course he was well turned out in his naval uniform, something that always appeals to juries. Charles expected the jury to trust him. He therefore concluded that it was worth taking the risk in his case.

At Charles's request, Ferguson gives his name and rank to the judge. Charles deals swiftly with his wartime and post-war relationship with Anthony Steele and then moves directly to the weekend Ferguson spent in the Steeles' home.

'Do you remember a particular night when you and Mr and Mrs Steele were preparing to go to a party?'

'Yes I do. It was at a neighbour's house in the village. Because I was staying at the Steeles', I was invited too.'

'Do you remember any of the events that occurred before you left for the party?'

'Yes, very clearly, because they were so extraordinary.'

'Please tell us what happened.'

'Mrs Steele had finished dressing and was downstairs. I was the last down. I arrived in what they called the "morning room", a sort of family room. Mrs Steele was pouring herself a drink.'

'Did you see what sort of drink?'

'Rum. She drank a tumbler-full of neat rum. I watched her pour it.'

'What was her mood?'

'She was already drunk.'

'How could you tell?'

'From the way she moved and from her speech, which was slightly slurred. She was also acting peculiarly.'

'Peculiarly?' asks Charles.

'She was very uninhibited. It was quite shocking.'

'Can you expand on that?'

Ferguson frowns, framing his answer carefully. 'Lise Steele was a very attractive woman, and she knew it. She always dressed provocatively, but on this occasion … well… I was shocked, like I said. She was in high heeled shoes and a backless cream cocktail dress, cut so low at the back that it exposed her skin from the nape of her neck to the cleft of her buttocks. It was obvious she was wearing nothing underneath.'

'Was Mr Steele present?'

'Yes, he was in the room when I arrived. He was remonstrating with her, asking if she hadn't already drunk enough. She said "Not nearly enough". He also wanted her to change into something more suitable for an English garden party. I remember it very clearly. He said, "This is Kent, not

Guadeloupe." She came from there, or somewhere close by, perhaps Martinique.'

'What happened then?'

'Lise carried on drinking. She put the gramophone on and started dancing on her own. She was singing, to a Josephine Baker song. She said something about seducing Anthony with it when she first met him.'

'Seducing him?'

'Yes. I was there when Anthony first met her in 1940. We were both serving on *HMS Moreton Bay* when we intercepted a ship full of prisoners being transported to Casablanca, which was then occupied by Vichy. We commandeered the ship and returned to Martinique. Lise and her father were amongst the prisoners we freed. They'd have been in a concentration camp otherwise, and she was very grateful. We met her and a few of the others later in a bar, the *Café de Paris,* and she sang for us all. She looked dangerous then, but in a playful way. She's what in those days we called a "man-eater". I never understood what she saw in Anthony.'

Ferguson's delivery is calm and measured. He gives his evidence looking throughout at Charles, and speaks almost in a monotone. He reminds Charles of a tickertape. The contrast between his lack of expression and the content of his evidence is striking, and somehow makes the evidence all the more powerful.

'Please explain.'

'Well, he was rather buttoned up, shy, maybe a bit repressed. His nickname on board the *Moreton* was "Virgin". He used to blush when she flirted with him, which made her do it all the more. He fell completely in love with her. Irrationally so, some thought. Some of us tried to talk him out of it, point out the obvious difficulties.'

'Difficulties?'

'Well, she was black for a start. From a very poor family, and not well educated. We told him to have a fling with her by all means, but she wasn't wife material.'

Charles cringes at this description but reminds himself of the period. 'This was in 1940?' he asks, making sure the jury are reminded too.

'Yes.'

'Bring us back to 1953 then, please. Was Lise Steele still a "man-eater"?'

'God, yes. She'd had three children by then, but she still looked amazing.'

'Describe her for us, if you please?'

Ferguson answers immediately, without having to think. 'Coffee coloured skin, very good figure, voluptuous; regular features, wide lips, flashing dark eyes and thick brown hair falling over one eye.'

'What happened next?'

'You see, she was taunting him. That song of Josephine Baker's was called "I Found a New Baby". She was talking about her lover, and I found the whole scene extremely embarrassing. I could see him getting more and more angry, but he controlled himself and walked away. He was just reaching for the door handle to leave when he ducked. I don't know if he heard something or it was just instinct from years of marriage to her, but she'd thrown her glass at him. It was a heavy tumbler, and it only missed his ear by an inch or two. It shattered on the wall by his head. He paused for a second, and just carried on walking out of the door. That was when she launched herself at him. She was going to kick him in the back I think, but her foot skidded on the broken glass and liquid, and she fell over. That's when the nanny came in.'

'Do you mean Miss Sullivan?'

'Yes. She'd been getting the children ready for bed. She had the youngest wrapped in a towel in her arms. Then the other two appeared in the doorway in their pyjamas.'

'How old were they then?'

'The oldest, Stephen, would have been about ten or eleven I suppose. He was an absolute spit for his father. The girl, Charlotte, was four or five years younger, darker-skinned and with the same black eyes as her mother. The baby was probably about two. I'm not good with children's ages I'm afraid. Anyway, Anthony always tried to make things look normal in front of the children. He reached down to help Lise up, but she slapped his hand away and screamed at him in French. Anthony nodded at the children and asked her to stop shouting, but it had no effect. The girl started crying and the son, Stephen, tried to protect her.'

'How do you mean?'

'He put his arm round her and told his mother to stop shouting at her. He had a bad stammer, worse when speaking to his mother. She taunted him about it, mimicked him. I thought it was cruel, to a little boy. Anthony told him to take Charlotte upstairs because Lise was not feeling well. So they went, with the nanny.'

'Did you all go to the party, after this?'

'Oh yes. Anthony tried to persuade her to stay at home but she refused. He said her behaviour was intolerable, and she said something like "Well if you don't like it, divorce me." But then she threatened him that if he tried, she'd tell everyone he was a child molester, which would ruin his career. Stop him becoming a QC.'

'What was his reaction?'

'He took a step towards her with his fists clenched and she stepped back. For a second I wondered if he was going to hit her and I was about to intervene, but he controlled himself again. He said something like he couldn't believe she'd threatened that. He said he'd never laid a finger on the children, and she knew it. She wasn't cowed, though. She said something like "Just so you know where we stand, OK." She said she liked things as they were, and wouldn't let him divorce her. So we all went to the party. It was very odd. As we got into the car, Anthony apologised to me for the scene.'

'Commander, the jury may wonder how it is you remember these events with such clarity. It was, after all, over ten years ago. Yet you remember almost the precise words.'

'I agree, but it was such an extraordinary performance, I've never forgotten it.'

'Thank you. Did everything calm down at the party?'

'Initially, yes. We all went in the same car. No one said anything. But then when we arrived and the door was opened by our hostess — I forget her name … just a moment … it'll come to me … yes, Marie, that's it, William and Marie — Lise was all smiles and hugs, perfectly charming. She just walked in; sailed through the hall into the kitchen and then onto the patio at the back of the house. Everyone watched her, especially the men, but there was no trouble at all for a while.'

'For a while?'

'Yes. She went and helped the other women get the buffet food ready and we, that is Anthony and William — he was a barrister too, a colleague I think — we just chatted in the garden. It was a balmy evening and there were lots of children running around. Everyone was having a good time. But then Anthony looked round and couldn't see Lise and went looking for her. I remained in the garden. The men I was with — I didn't know any of them — were being very unkind about Anthony. They were suggesting that Lise was very … promiscuous … that he was a cuckold. Talking about her as if she was a prostitute.'

'Did the accused find her?'

'Yes, we watched through the French windows. She was in another room sitting at a bar chatting to another man.'

'Chatting?'

'Yes. But she'd taken off one of her shoes and as she was sitting on her bar stool, she was using her foot to stroke the leg of the man she was talking to.'

'Do you think the accused saw that?'

'It looked as if he did. He was about to go to her when the hostess, Marie, put her hand on his arm and stopped him. She handed Anthony the tray of drinks she was carrying and she went to speak to Lise. I didn't hear what she said, but Lise got up and returned with Marie to the kitchen, so it all looked OK.'

'What happened then?' asks Charles.

Ferguson looks uncomfortable and his gaze moves from Charles to the judge. 'I'm afraid this isn't the sort of thing I'd like to say in front of ladies,' he says, looking pointedly at the female members of the jury.

'Don't worry about that,' replies the Recorder. 'You might be surprised, Commander Ferguson, by the sort of evidence we hear every day in these courts. Please continue.'

'Well, later that evening, towards midnight I guess, Lise went missing again. Anthony searched the house for her but couldn't find her. He asked me to help. We looked again, in the house and in the gardens. I even walked up the road a little way but we still couldn't find her. Then someone came to us and said we'd better come upstairs.'

'What did you find?'

'We heard her voice first, calling a man's name. "Mark" I think it was. When we got to the hallway, we could see her looking in one of the bedrooms. She was naked.'

Ferguson pauses. The courtroom is utterly silent, everyone straining to hear his next words. 'She was looking for this chap. When she saw Anthony ahead of me in the corridor, she accused him of spoiling everything, of frightening the man off.'

'What did the accused do?'

'He told her to get her clothes on because they were going home. She refused, said she was going to stay, and I think she would have, but then Marie came up the stairs with two or three of her friends and said they would deal with her. Marie was furious. She said something like she was tired of Lise spoiling her parties, and that she was a selfish cow. They got her dressed and half-carried her downstairs. She was almost asleep by then. We put her in the back seat of the car, and Anthony and I got into the front.'

'Was that the end of the evening?'

'Almost. As we pulled into the drive of their home, she was sick in the car. The nanny must have seen the car's headlights because she arrived on the doorstep. When she saw what had happened, she went and got a bucket and some gloves. Lise was unconscious by then. We cleaned her up a bit and Anthony and I carried her up to the spare bedroom. She woke up as we were leaving the room. Started calling for "Roddy".'

'What was the accused's response to that?'

'He'd obviously been very angry earlier that evening but, now, he just seemed … sad. He said Roddy wasn't there. She said she didn't want him, she wanted Roddy. His response was that, if this was the alternative even *he* would prefer Roddy, but he'd gone back to his wife, so that was that. He also said that if she was going to drown her sorrows like this every time one of her lovers jilted her, she'd end up killing herself.'

'Did she reply to that?'

'Yes. She told him to fuck off.'

'Did you see her again that weekend?'

'No, I left after breakfast the following morning and she didn't surface.'

'Did you speak to the accused about the events of the night before, before you left?'

'Briefly. He wasn't keen to talk about it. I offered the opinion that it really couldn't go on, not least because of the children. And he agreed.'

'Did he explain what he meant when he agreed with you?'

'No. But I had the definite impression that he had reached the end of his tether. He seemed determined. As if he'd made up his mind.'

'Thank you, Commander. Please remain there.'

Charles resumes his seat and Beaverbrook stands.

'So what you are telling us, Commander, is that despite this appalling provocation, Mr Steele controlled his feelings.'

'Yes, he did.'

'He showed Mrs Steele no violence?'

'Absolutely not.'

'According to your account, he didn't even raise his voice.'

'That's correct.'

'And although Mr Steele seemed determined the following morning, you can't tell us what, if anything, lay behind that.'

'Well…'

'He might have been determined to seek a divorce, for example?'

'Yes, I suppose that's possible.'

'He might have been determined to separate from his wife?'

'Yes.'

'He might merely have been determined to buy no further rum.'

'Well, it seemed more … significant than that, but I suppose that is possible.'

'Thank you. I have no further questions for this witness.'

CHAPTER 26

'Call Roderick Batchelor!'

The door opens and Lise Steele's former lover — her final lover — enters court.

Charles has not met the man before, having seen no need to interview him, having read his statement. He knows that Batchelor still works for a large bank in the city of London and assumes he will see a confident and imposing man striding towards the witness box, but if Roddy Batchelor was ever confident or imposing, his best days are clearly long behind him. Now in his early sixties, he is of average height, slightly paunchy and has a disappointed air. He walks hesitantly down the aisle, as if unsure where to go. His only feature of note is his nose, which is long and aquiline. It might once have been described as fine; now it just makes him look like an unhappy bird of prey.

He makes his way to the witness box and reads the oath from the card handed to him, holding the New Testament in a hand that moves around slightly as he speaks, as if flapping away a troublesome insect.

He hands the Bible and the card back to the usher and looks vacantly around the court. When Charles calls his name, he jumps slightly before turning to face the barristers' benches.

'Mr Roderick Batchelor?'

'Yes?'

'Please give your full name, address and profession to the court,' requests Charles. Batchelor does so.

'Do you understand why you are here, Mr Batchelor?'

'Yes. You want to ask about Lise.'

As he answers, Batchelor's eyes flick upwards, towards the public gallery, and Charles follows his gaze. Sitting in the front row is a woman in a floral dress and a hat. She is staring fixedly at the witness, her brow contracted into a frown. Charles looks back at Batchelor who casts his eyes down, embarrassed or ashamed. *So*, thinks Charles, *that's the long-suffering wife.*

Charles returns his attention to his notes. 'What was your relationship with Lise Steele?' he asks.

'We were friends…' His voice drops, but then he adds '…lovers.'

Charles can see the man trying hard to avoid the gaze of Anthony Steele in the dock. Steele is staring at him dispassionately.

'How long did your affair last?' asks Charles.

'Two or three years, on and off.'

'On and off?'

'Yes. We broke up repeatedly.'

'At whose instance?'

'Sometimes hers but, towards the end, mine. I was trying very hard to break off all contact with her. It was difficult.'

'Why?'

Batchelor's face reddens slightly. 'She was always able to persuade me back.' He flicks another shame-faced glance at the gallery.

'When did you last see her?'

'The Sunday before she disappeared.'

'In what circumstances?'

'I'd told her I couldn't see her anymore, about two or three weeks before then, but she wouldn't accept it. She besieged the house with telephone calls. Eventually my wife insisted on answering the phone to tell her to desist.'

'Your wife knew about the affair?'

Batchelor hangs his head. 'Yes,' he says softly.

'Tell us what happened on that Sunday.'

'She called the house, at a time when she knew Wendy would be at church. I guessed it would be her. I nearly hung up, but she said she had the letters I sent her, and I wanted to get them back.'

'Did you meet her?'

'Yes.'

'Where?'

'At the telephone box from which she rang. It was on a deserted country road.'

'What was your purpose in meeting her?'

'I just wanted the letters back. I didn't want Wendy to read them ... she would have found them very upsetting, and I was ashamed. I wanted to destroy them, and never see her again.'

'What happened when you met her?' Batchelor doesn't reply. 'Mr Batchelor? Did you hear my question?'

Batchelor sighs and draws a deep breath. When he answers his voice is quiet, timid. 'She got round me. Like she always did.'

'So what was decided as a result of that meeting?'

'I was persuaded to give our relationship one last try. Like I said, she could be very persuasive. She wanted to go away for a few days, to a cottage we had rented in the past.'

'Did you go?'

'Yes. We went back to our respective homes to pack some overnight things, and we left that evening.'

'How long were you away?'

'Three days, or two nights.'

'And what happened when you returned?'

'What do you mean?'

'Well, did you see her again?'

'No. We arranged to meet but she didn't turn up. Nor did she call.'

'What did you do about that? Did you call her?'

'I didn't do anything. It was a relief. Wendy was prepared to have me back as long as I promised never to have anything to do with Lise again, and I promised. We expected her to call or even turn up at the house, but as the weeks passed and we heard nothing, we gradually realised that it was over.'

'Were you not worried about her?'

He shakes his head. 'No. She was very … flighty. I just assumed she'd met somebody new. Several of the early breaks in our relationship occurred when she met some other man to whom she took a fancy for a short time.'

'Finally, Mr Batchelor, were you in any way involved in the death of Lise Steele, or the cover-up of that death?'

'Mr Batchelor you don't need to answer that,' intervenes the Recorder. 'You are under no obligation to answer any questions that might lead you to implicate yourself in a crime.'

'But I want to answer it, my Lord. I had absolutely nothing to do with Lise's death or any cover-up.'

'Thank you, Mr Batchelor,' says Charles. 'Please remain there. There may be some further questions for you.'

'Before you rise to cross-examine, Mr Beaverbrook,' says the Recorder, 'I have a question for Mr Holborne.'

Charles stands again. 'My Lord?'

'What is the purpose of this evidence from Mr Batchelor?'

'My Lord, the Crown have not yet heard any of the Defence case. Although Mr Steele has admitted disposing of his wife's body, we still have no idea what his case is regarding her actual death. He has pleaded not guilty to both murder and manslaughter. He might, for all we know, point the finger elsewhere, and the obvious choice would be Mr Batchelor. For that reason, it was essential for the jury to hear Mr Batchelor's account of the days before the deceased's death. They've now heard it; they've heard him deny any involvement whatsoever. Accordingly, unless Mr Beaverbrook cross-examines him and suggests to the contrary, the jury will know that, whatever the Defence case may be, it is no longer open to them to suggest that Mr Batchelor might have been the culprit. Mr Batchelor will no longer be of any relevance. But until we hear from Mr Beaverbrook, the Crown cannot leave the matter open for the jury to speculate on.'

'I see. Yes, thank you, I see your point. Well, let us find out, shall we? Mr Beaverbrook?'

'Thank you, my Lord. I have no questions Mr Batchelor.'

'Do you accept the point made by Mr Holborne that, in giving up your chance to cross-examine Mr Batchelor, you are accepting that he was in no way involved in Mrs Steele's death?'

'I do, my Lord.'

'Very well.' The judge turns to Batchelor. 'Thank you for your evidence Mr Batchelor. You are free to leave.'

CHAPTER 27

'Call Inspector Murray!'

A policeman in the uniform of the Kent Constabulary enters court. He's a tall man in his late thirties with sandy hair and a freckled complexion. He steps into the witness box and, without being prompted, picks up the Bible in front of him. Without looking at the card, he recites the oath in a clear voice. He then turns towards the Recorder of London, gives his name, rank and collar number and says 'My Lord'.

'Thank you, Inspector,' says Charles. 'Now, in May 1953 I believe you were a police constable at the local police house in the Kent village of Ash, is that correct?'

'That's correct, my Lord. It was my first posting.' Murray speaks with a soft Scottish accent.

'Did you ever have occasion to meet the accused, Anthony Steele?'

'Yes. I'd been called away urgently to Canterbury, and I'd actually locked up when Mr Steele arrived. I had to unlock the door and put the lights on again.'

'Do you remember the date of that event?'

'Please may I refer to the records I made at the time, my Lord?'

'What records are those, Inspector?' asks the Recorder.

'I completed a missing person's record while I was speaking to Mr Steele. I recorded what he told me in this book —' he brandishes a large index book with a hard cover — 'which is what I was trained to do. I would not be able to remember the exact time or date without refreshing my memory from the book.'

'Any objections Mr Beaverbrook?'

Beaverbrook remains sitting in his seat but shakes his head and mutters 'No, my Lord.'

'Very well,' says the Recorder, 'you may refer to the book insofar as necessary.'

'Thank you, my Lord. Yes, on third May 1953, at 19:05 hours, I recorded an entry regarding a missing person, a Mrs Lise Steele. The person making the report was Mr Anthony Steele.'

'Other than the content of your record, Inspector, do you remember anything else about your exchange with Mr Steele?'

'I do. He was quite well-known in the village and because he was in my line of work so to speak, I had noted him. He looked tired and very worried, which I put down to the anxiety of having a missing wife.'

'Do you remember what he told you, if anything, about his wife's disappearance?'

'I have a short note here, my Lord, which says that they had a row and she stormed out, four days earlier. I asked Mr Steele why he waited that long to report his wife's disappearance, which is unusual, and I remember him saying that she'd run off before. There was a boyfriend, he said, in fact there had been several, and she usually turned up again after a few days. So I didn't think the delay was suspicious.'

'Do you recall anything else?'

'Only that I asked if he thought the lady wanted to be missing, and he said it was quite likely. I tried to reassure him how common this situation was, even in a quiet village such as ours. I'd recorded several such reports myself. Mostly the person would turn up again, usually when the money ran out.'

'Thank you, officer.'

Charles had been undecided whether or not to call the inspector. The contents of the record were admitted by the Defence, so it was not disputed that Steele had reported the deceased as missing. But he wanted the jury to hear a first-hand account of Steele's playacting. Now he had admitted disposing of his wife's body, it demonstrated that he was not only a liar, but a convincing liar.

Charles is about to resume his seat when the inspector starts speaking again. 'May I add something, please, my Lord?'

'As long as it's admissible, yes.'

'As I explained, I was already on my way out when Mr Steele arrived, and I left the police house with him. After I'd finished taking his report, we walked down the path together towards my police car, and because I was passing his house on the way back, I offered to drop him off. He accepted, and we drove the five minutes or so in the car to the other side of the village.'

'Yes?' asks Charles. None of this was in the inspector's statement, so Charles is anxious about what the officer might be about to say.

'When we arrived back at Mr Steele's house, the three children were playing in the garden with a young woman who I believe to be Miss Sullivan. As Mr Steele approached, they all gathered round him. I couldn't hear what he was saying, but the two older children rushed into his arms, looking excited. The nanny put her hand on Mr Steele's arm and was looking up at him. It looked obvious to me that she had great affection for him.'

'Why are you telling us this, Inspector?' asks the Recorder, impatience edging his voice.

'Well, my Lord, I remember thinking to myself that they looked like such a happy family. Which seemed a little strange, given the circumstances.'

CHAPTER 28

Jenny Sullivan can't sleep.

The prospect of giving evidence in the morning terrifies her, fills her tummy with butterflies and makes her sweat. She trusted that awful Inspector Carr, spoke when she shouldn't have, and as a result made everything much worse for Anthony.

Charles was wrong; in fact Jenny's had no contact with her employer since the afternoon he was arrested; she for fear of doing more damage, he for fear of being accused of influencing her evidence. As a result, Jenny is certain that he must now hate her.

Worried about over-sleeping and missing the London train, she went to bed early, desperate for a good night's sleep, read for a while and turned the light out shortly after 10 o'clock. It's now well past midnight, and sleep still eludes her.

She decides to make herself a milky drink. She rises, pulls on her dressing gown and creeps down the hall. The faint sounds of Radio Caroline come from behind Bobby's bedroom door, but he plays music as he drifts off, and the radio is often still playing in the morning when he wakes for school, so she slips past his door quietly.

Bobby has also struggled to sleep over the last few weeks, so worried is he about his father's case. He envies his older siblings, Stephen, now a civil servant in Northampton, and Charlotte, away at university. They've been as worried as he over the charges faced by their father, but they have busy lives in distant towns and haven't been brought face-to-face with the reality of it every evening when they return home. Both have said they'll be at court tomorrow and Bobby's looking forward to seeing them. He's been lonely in the family home since they left.

The conditions of Anthony's bail have kept him away from the house for over three months and Jenny has been unutterably miserable and anxious. She pauses by his open bedroom door. The room is clean and tidy, awaiting his return. She has continued with her routine of changing his bed linen every week even though it's not been used. She won't allow herself to think about what will happen if he's convicted; if he never comes back.

In the kitchen she puts a saucepan of milk on the gas to warm up and sits at the table, not thinking of much. Above the table is a photograph of the whole family, the three children, Anthony and herself. It was taken by a helpful fellow-tourist on the island of Kos a decade earlier. Anthony stands in the middle of the group, his arm resting on Stephen's shoulders. Charlotte stands just in front of Jenny who has Bobby, then aged five, in her arms. She remembers that he wriggled and didn't want to be picked up, but he had to be lifted if he was to be in the photograph. Blue sky merges with blue sea behind them.

On impulse she stands and goes to a bookcase in the corner of the room. It's cluttered with the usual detritus that gathers in a kitchen, bills to be paid, some pages torn from Bobby's maths exercise book with his working out in pencil, and the keys to the shed, which she forgot to hang up earlier. She pushes it all to one side and reaches for a photograph album, taking it back to the table.

She flicks through the pages of holidays, birthdays and graduations. She's had to make compromises with life, yes, but overall, these snaps remind her how happy she's been. Her eyes arrest on a photograph taken two or three years after the holiday in Greece. That page, and those that follow, are full of photographs from a particular event, the party in 1958 to celebrate Anthony being "made up" — becoming a judge.

Unlike most judges, Anthony decided not to have a stuffy "lawyers" party in the Temple. He wanted to celebrate his success with the people who were most important to him, and while that did include a handful of barristers, solicitors and other judges, the guest list was mostly made up of family, friends and neighbours from the new village where they'd put down fresh roots. The lives of everyone in the family were neatly divided into two: the period when Lise lived with them and the period afterwards. These are all "after Lise".

Jenny peers at the face of her employer, now The Honourable Sir Anthony Steele QC. In almost every photograph he is smiling or laughing, completely at ease whether speaking to a senior High Court judge or to the village postmistress. Shortly after moving into the house, when the demands of his practice allowed, he began to drop into the local on Friday evenings, something he'd never done before, for a quiet pint and to show his face. Within a couple of years he was completely immersed in village life, helping his neighbours with their bales of hay, pushing their cars in winter mornings when their batteries were flat and writing references for their children when they sought their first jobs. He wouldn't tolerate any of the "my Lord" or "Sir Anthony" nonsense; he was, simply, "Tony".

The photographs show their crowded back garden, full of adults laughing and chatting in the sunshine, drinks in their hands and children everywhere, some being entertained by a magician at the back of the garden. She remembers how happy their children were, particularly Stephen. Shortly after Lise's disappearance, Anthony brought him back from boarding school, and by the time of this party he was a changed boy, happy and popular at the local school, studying hard for his A-levels.

Jenny catches sight of herself in several of the photographs as she hands plates of food around with other village mums. She flicks ahead quickly through the pages of the album — she dislikes photos of herself — and is about to close the album when she sees one last photograph, from the end of that evening.

She guesses it must have been taken by Stephen or perhaps one of the other guests who remained to help tidy up. She and Anthony are shown in the kitchen, he washing up and she drying. It's not a good photograph — Anthony must have been moving slightly just as the shutter opened — and it portrays a common and ordinary household scene. Although Anthony's hands are still in the soapy water, he is caught in the middle of saying something, as his head is turned to look at her over his left shoulder. Jenny looks closely at her own face. She is staring up at him, a quiet smile on her lips, and her eyes locked onto his. *My God!* she thinks to herself, *Was it really so obvious how I felt about him?*

She thinks back to the end of that evening, and sighs. By the time they had finished clearing up it was gone midnight and everybody else had departed. The children were in bed and the house was silent. It had been such an enjoyable day that neither of them wanted it to end. He lifted the last clean platters to the top shelf of the dresser while she hung up the saturated tea towels to dry. She turned to find him looking at her. The intensity of his gaze made her self-conscious, and she remained still, afraid that any movement would be awkward and reveal her emotions. His regard of her lasted so long that she had to break it.

'I'll lock-up, then,' she said and, in speaking, disrupted his scrutiny.

He hesitated and then simply said, 'OK. Goodnight,' before leaving the room and climbing the stairs to his bedroom without a backward glance.

Jenny still remembers the aching disappointment.

She closes the album firmly and returns to the hob, just catching the milk before it boils over. She pours it into the waiting mug, washes up the saucepan and is about to carry the hot milk up to her bedroom when she is startled by a noise behind her. She whirls around, slopping hot milk onto her fingers.

There is a dark shape outside the back door leading to the garden. Her heart leaps, and she is suddenly afraid, but then there is a quiet tap at the glass.

'Jenny!' comes a hoarse whisper. 'Jenny!'

It's him! She scrambles to unbolt the door.

Anthony is almost unrecognisable. He wears a woollen hat and thick-rimmed glasses. His nose is red from the cold night air and he needs a shave. For a second she is puzzled but then she realises. Of course! He's disguised; his face is all over the evening papers.

He stands there for a second on the threshold, as if a stranger waiting to be invited in.

'Oh, Anthony!' she cries. 'I'm so sorry!'

He takes a step into the kitchen. He stares at her, his mouth working, but no sound emerging. Then he reaches for her, enveloping her in a tight embrace, as if his life depended on never letting her go. She feels him sob and her body shudders in sympathy. She finds herself crying into his chest, long, deep gulps of air being drawn painfully into her lungs.

'Hush, darling,' he soothes, the unfamiliar endearment sounding wonderful to both of them. 'It's all going to be alright.'

His words have an immediate calming effect. He is holding her, stroking her hair, his hot breath in her ear and suddenly the case against him seems unimportant. This, *this* is all that matters.

'I'm so, so sorry!' she manages. 'I'm so, so sorry! I had no idea!'

'No, really it's all right!'

'N-no ... it's *not* all right ... I've done nothing but damage! I thought I was helping but ... they said they were going to charge you with murder! I couldn't let them do that! But I see now: I should've said nothing. Absolutely nothing! I was trying to help. Please forgive me.'

He disengages from her but holds her fast by the upper arms, staring hard into her face.

'Why?' he demands. The intensity, the urgency in his voice, startle her.

'Why what?'

'Why couldn't you let them do that?'

'Don't you know? How can you not know? Because I love you! I've loved you for years! Don't tell me you didn't know?'

'No ... yes ... oh, yes!' And he hugs her again and kisses her furiously on the cheeks, the eyes, the forehead, everywhere he can reach her skin. 'I knew, I knew ... I just ... couldn't allow myself to know.'

'I don't understand —'

'It doesn't matter now.'

'But of course it matters! I've ruined everything!'

'You haven't. Believe me, you haven't.'

'What should I do tomorrow, then? Tell me. Should I refuse to give evidence?'

'No. That's why I've taken the risk of coming — I was so afraid you'd do something rash. Give your evidence exactly as it happened, understand? Just answer their questions honestly, plainly and simply.' She nods. 'I'm just sorry you got dragged into this at all. I should never have asked for your help.'

She reaches for him and snuggles her head into the warm hollow between his neck and shoulder, her sobs subsiding. 'It's not your fault,' she says. 'You didn't know what to do.'

'But I miscalculated. I should've told the police the whole story as soon as I was questioned. I thought they'd charge you for helping me, so I denied the whole thing. I still can't understand why they haven't charged you but, thank God, they haven't. But of course, now they can prove I was lying.'

'What a mess!'

'Yes, it is a mess. How are the children?'

'Holding up. Stephen and Charlotte have both been down when they can manage it, and they'll be there from tomorrow, until the end of the case. Stephen's strong and silent, as always. Charlotte alternates between anger and tears, but she'll be fine. I'm mostly worried about Bobby. He's gone into his shell, and I can't reach him. You know how sensitive he is.'

Steele frowns with worry. 'He's such a sweet boy.' He flicks a look at his watch. 'I'm going to miss the last train back to London.'

She draws back and holds his face tenderly between her hands. 'Do you love me?'

'Yes,' he replies. 'I do love you. More than I can express.'

'Then I can cope with anything. Even the worst.'

'Let's hope it doesn't come to that. Keep your voice up, speak slowly, look the jury right in the eyes, and you'll be fine.'

She smiles, for the first time in weeks. 'Ever the lawyer.'

'And don't tell *anyone* you've seen me tonight, okay?'

'Okay.'

She waits for him to make a move but he doesn't, so she leans forward and kisses him on his cold lips. It's a short kiss, but in it is all the pent-up love and longing of fifteen years.

'Worth waiting for,' she says.

CHAPTER 29

Dr Butcher, forensic pathologist, gives his oath in a slow, deliberate, fashion, holding the Bible high over his head. Then he looks down at Charles and, without prompting, gives his name, professional address and qualifications. Charles leads him through his evidence, dealing with the deceased's clothes, the state of her body and how long, in his view, she had been immersed in water. Then Charles turns to the cause of death.

'As part of the post-mortem examination, did you examine the deceased's internal organs?'

'I did.'

'Did you find anything of note?'

'They were all substantially damaged by her long immersion in water and putrefaction. However, the temperature of the water had, unusually, caused their structure to be preserved. They tended to disintegrate on touch, but I was able to make quite a detailed examination.'

The courtroom is completely silent, those in the public gallery leaning forward to catch every word.

'What, if anything, did you find?'

'There was no sign of injury or disease, certainly none that could have contributed to death.'

'Were you able to analyse the stomach contents?'

'No. They were too damaged by putrefaction. But had she taken drugs, for example, there would have been other signs, and there were none.'

'Were there any signs of injury to the body?'

'There were no lesions.' Dr Butcher turns to the jury. 'No cuts or lacerations,' he explains for their benefit.

Charles follows the pathologist's gaze to the six men and six women in the jury box. They are riveted to the evidence, three of them taking notes.

'Any broken bones?' he asks.

'None.'

'Did you find anything therefore that can throw any light on the cause of death?'

'Yes, one thing. There were two areas of discolouration of the flesh, one on the left side of the forehead and one on the left side of the hyoid bone. The first one was about here.'

He indicates by pressing a finger to his own forehead and, while holding the pose, angles himself first to show the Recorder and then the jury.

'And the second was about here.'

This time he indicates a point to the left of his voice box.

'Thank you,' says the Recorder, making a note and a quick sketch of the places indicated.

'What does that discolouration mean?' asks Charles.

'It does not necessarily *mean* anything. What it *suggests*, is bruising at those points. The discolouration was beneath the skin, and wouldn't have been visible on the surface. When someone is bruised, tiny blood vessels under the skin are ruptured. A small amount of blood leaks into the tissues. Normally, the body's repair mechanisms cause it to disperse in a few days or weeks. But if the person dies, that process does not occur. What I found were small deposits of haematoidin, one of the breakdown products of blood. It's brown in colour and crystalline in nature.'

'Would such bruising suggest blows sufficient to cause death?'

'Well, the bruise to the forehead would not have caused death. It would have been quite minor. The bruise to the left of

263

the hyoid bone is more significant. It is consistent with strangulation.'

Charles pauses long enough for the answer to sink in. 'Bearing in mind all your findings, what, in your opinion, was the cause of death?'

'Manual strangulation.'

'Thank you, doctor. Please wait there.'

Charles sits. This time Beaverbrook stands and spends thirty long seconds arranging his notes on the lectern in front of him. The tension grows as the jury and the gallery appreciate that at last they are going to hear some contested evidence.

'Now, doctor,' he begins, his weighty, rounded tones booming across the court. 'No disease, and no illness?'

'None that I could identify.'

'No broken bones?'

'None.'

'No cuts or lacerations?'

'Not that I could find.'

'And you looked carefully?'

'Of course. You must understand, however, that when a body has been in the water that long, even if, like this one, it is in a remarkable state of preservation, putrefaction has set in. That makes it impossible to be certain. All I can say is that I found no wounds that could have contributed to death. There may have been small lacerations which would have been impossible to identify with any certainty after this length of time.'

'I understand. Thank you. So there might have been a small cut to, for example, an eyebrow.'

'That is perfectly possible.'

'Can a person bleed after death?'

Dr Butcher frowns and shrugs. 'Of course. Just as with any carcass, gravity will work to drain the blood out.'

'So, in simple terms, if I cut a vein in your foot which does not kill you, and then I kill you by shooting you in the head, were I able to keep you upright, all your blood would drain out of the wound in your foot?'

'Very likely.'

'So, if the deceased had a cut, say on her eyebrow, and that part of her body just happened to be at the lowest point following her death, she could lose a lot of blood through it, even if her heart had stopped beating. Is that correct?'

'It is.'

'Thank you. Let us move to the marks on the forehead and neck. Are these definitely bruises in your opinion?'

'I would say that they are very likely indeed to have been bruises.'

'But not definite bruises?'

'Nothing is ever definite, particularly after so long.'

Beaverbrook pauses, surveying the members of the jury one by one. With his eyes fixed on the last member, a bulky man in a suit a size too small for him, he asks, 'How much force does it take to strangle someone with one's hands?'

'Usually considerable force. One has to close off the windpipe.'

'How long for?'

'That will depend on the extent to which the victim struggles. The more they struggle, the more oxygen they use up. Also, it would depend on how fit they were, whether they had taken alcohol, whether the obstruction to the windpipe was complete or incomplete, many factors.'

'Shall we assume that most people when being strangled will struggle?'

'That is a fair assumption if the person, the victim, is conscious. It is of course perfectly possible to strangle someone who is unconscious.'

'Let us also assume that no alcohol was taken, as there is no evidence of the deceased being drunk before her disappearance, and she drove to the house without accident. Let us also assume that, as a young woman of slim build, she was fairly fit. How long in those circumstances?'

'It's difficult to be precise. There are few witnessed incidents as you can imagine. However, Taylor's Jurisprudence, which is one of the standard texts, would suggest up to a minute or so for unconsciousness, and perhaps a further minute to two minutes for death to result thereafter — assuming that the pressure is continued, of course.'

'So, say three minutes during which the pressure on the windpipe has to be maintained?' persists Beaverbrook.

'Yes. It might be less, however.'

'It is almost certain that in such circumstances, severe pressure being applied for two to three minutes, one would find bruises on the windpipe, in the region of the hyoid bone.'

'It is. In many cases the hyoid bone is broken. It is quite fragile.'

'Would it be possible to strangle someone with one hand?'

The pathologist considers this for a moment, his eyes turning towards the vaulted ceiling as he imagines the mechanisms involved. 'Yes, it would, but it would be unusual. The hands of the strangler would have to be very large, or the neck of the victim unusually thin. Even then, I imagine it would be difficult to maintain the grip.'

'Did the deceased have an unusually thin neck?'

'No. In fact, she was sturdily built.'

'Have you seen the defendant's hands? Are they what you would call "very large"?'

Dr Butcher peers over the edge of the witness box. He turns to the Recorder. 'May I go to the dock to have a closer look?'

'You may.'

Two hundred or more eyes follow Dr Butcher's progress from the witness box to the dock. He takes Steele's right hand in his and examines it carefully, turning it over, looking at the fingers and feeling its strength. He thanks the judge quietly and returns to the witness box.

'The accused is a tall man, but he has very fine hands, quite narrow and not particularly strong. I think he'd have had great difficulty in strangling the deceased with one hand.'

'So, if he strangled the deceased, he'd have had to have used both hands.'

'Very likely.'

'And that would have broken the hyoid bone?'

'Not "would"; *might*.'

'But there *would* have been bruises on both sides of the windpipe.'

'Almost certainly.'

'Whereas here there was one *possible* bruise, on one side only.'

'That is correct.'

Beaverbrook's tone changes, and it seems as if he is moving to another subject. 'Now, doctor, when someone is strangled, there are often other tell-tale signs, are there not?'

'Yes.'

'Such as petechial haemorrhages, protrusion of the tongue, cyanosis, intense venous congestion ... have I missed any?'

'Bruising of the deeper tissues of the neck, prominence of the eyes, marks on the skin, from fingernails, perhaps.'

'I shall not ask you to explain all of these. I have a simple question: were any of them present in this case?'

'Some would not necessarily have been visible after the length of time —'

'Were any present that might have been visible after the time spent by the deceased in the water?'

Dr Butcher answers a shade reluctantly. 'No.'

'There were no such signs at all?'

'No.'

'So, we have no signs of strangulation except one *possible* bruise on *one* side of the neck only.'

'Yes.'

Beaverbrook pauses to let that sink in. 'As a result of the points I have put to you, do you not agree that your diagnosis of cause of death, "Manual Strangulation", might be wrong?'

'It is not certain that that was the cause of death, I accept.'

'Not only was it not a certain cause of death; I suggest to you that it was not even a likely one.'

'I still think that it was the most likely cause. No other cause could be identified.'

'"*Most likely*"?' For the first time, Beaverbrook's tone changes to one approaching scorn. 'This jury has to decide how the deceased met her death so that they are sure. *Sure!* How can they be *sure* she was strangled on the basis of "*most likely*"?'

'Well, something killed her.'

'But that's irrelevant! What's relevant for the jury is whether or not the Crown can establish *beyond reasonable doubt* what caused her death and that this man was responsible for it.'

Beaverbrook points dramatically across the courtroom to his client. Steele sits upright in the dock, his face calm, as if listening to an interesting debate between two experts in a trial he is hearing. Dr Butcher's round face pinks at the reprimand.

'So, let me rephrase the question, doctor: are you *personally* sure beyond reasonable doubt that this woman was strangled?'

'No. I'm not. Of the various possibilities that is the most likely, but I cannot say I am sure.'

'Thank you. The fact is, there were no clear, obvious signs to point to the cause of death at all, were there? The high-water mark of your evidence is that, of all the possibilities, strangulation is the most likely, but even that is not *very* likely.'

'Well, it *is* the most likely of all the possibilities.'

'What is "vagal inhibition"?'

Dr Butcher looks slightly startled at the apparent change of tack. 'It's ... it's an inhibition of the vagal nerve.'

'Where is the vagal nerve?'

'In the neck.'

'To be precise, it is in the neck, almost exactly where you found the discolouration, is it not?'

'It is.'

'Vagal inhibition can cause death, can it not?'

'It can, in unusual circumstances.'

'What are those circumstances?'

'A blow or, more likely, pressure would have to be applied to exactly the right spot.'

'And would such pressure need to be applied for long?'

'That would depend. There are cases in which only fleeting pressure has resulted in death.'

'Fleeting?'

'A second or so.'

'Could a single blow do it?'

'If it was an extremely lucky one.'

'Or an extremely unlucky one.'

'Er, yes ... that's what I mean.'

'Thank you, doctor. I have no further questions.'

There's a communal exhalation of breath as Beaverbrook resumes his seat. Charles silently congratulates the Queen's Counsel for keeping the smugness out of his expression. Charles weighs up whether or not to re-examine. He might be able to repair some of the damage, but the risk is he'll make it worse by emphasising it. Beaverbrook has undermined the Crown's theory of cause of death, probably fatally. Furthermore, Charles reminds himself, he is prosecuting, and as a prosecutor he has a duty to assist in getting at the truth, not strive for a conviction. It's not his job to make the pathologist sound sure when he isn't.

He rises. 'Thank you, doctor. Does your Lordship have any questions?'

'No, thank you. Dr Butcher may be released, unless there are objections?'

Both barristers shake their heads.

'Thank you, doctor,' says Charles to the pathologist, who steps out of the witness box. Charles looks down at his notes. Here we go, he thinks; everything now turns on this last card.

'Miss Jennifer Sullivan, please,' he says.

All eyes turn to the door as Jenny's name is called outside. There's a short delay, the door opens again and she enters the courtroom. She keeps her eyes lowered as she passes the packed reporters' bench, the solicitors and finally the barristers. She climbs the three steps into the witness box.

She wears a plain, royal blue suit of silk, a cream blouse underneath and little makeup. Charles sees a suggestion of peach-coloured lipstick on her soft wide mouth, and her hair is tied in a simple ponytail. The effect is to make her look younger than her years and attractive, thinks Charles, in a wholesome way. Only the pinched, drawn look about her mouth, and the hazel eyes encircled by dark rings reveal the damage done by the events of the last months.

She takes the Bible offered to her in one hand, the card with the oath printed on it in the other, and reads the oath in a clear voice. She returns the Bible and the card to the usher and settles herself, hands on the brass rail and head lowered, awaiting the onslaught.

In answer to Charles she gives her name, address and occupation without looking up. Charles asks his questions slowly, in a gentle voice, as if dealing with a wild deer that might at any moment be startled into flight. He moves to the early part of her employment, her duties, how the house was run. Then he moves to the deceased.

'Were the accused and the deceased happy, do you think?'

'I don't think so.'

'What did you see that gave you that impression?'

'They argued a lot or, to be more precise, she argued and he listened.'

'Was there ever violence between them?'

'She was sometimes violent. He was never so.'

'In what way was she violent?' asks Charles.

'When she was angry, or drunk, she would throw things around, smash furniture or ornaments. She would also shout and scream at everyone.'

'Everyone?'

Jenny looks up, a hard look in her eyes. 'Yes, everyone, including me, the children, the neighbours. Anyone who came within range. But particularly Stephen and the other children.'

It's the children, realises Charles; that's what brings out the protectiveness, the anger in her. 'Was she drunk often?' he asks.

'In the year or two before she … before … her death, she was. It went in patches. There might be weeks when she was fine, followed by periods of non-stop drinking. It was often caused by problems in her … extra-marital friendships.'

'Do you mean affairs?'

'Yes.'

'How did you know of these affairs?' asks Charles.

'Everyone knew; it was no secret. In fact, I think she deliberately publicised them.'

'What makes you say that?'

'I think she loved the drama. Being the centre of attention, like the heroine in her own film. And of course, so she could hurt him.'

'The accused?'

'Yes.'

For the first time since stepping into the witness box, Jenny risks a tentative glance at the dock, but Steele has his elbows on his knees and is staring at the floor.

'What were relations like between them shortly before you last saw her?'

'Poor. Her latest boyfriend had ended their relationship, or had tried to —'

Beaverbrook stands swiftly. 'I object, my Lord, to this witness giving evidence of what may or may not have occurred between the deceased and any other person. It's hearsay.'

The Recorder addresses Charles. 'Mr Holborne?'

'Yes, my Lord, it is hearsay, although in light of the uncontested evidence from Mr Batchelor, it's not disputed. Nonetheless I shall attempt to prevent any more being given.'

'Thank you.'

'You said,' continues Charles to the witness, 'that relations had been poor. Perhaps you could tell us what that meant in practice at the house?'

Now, for the first time, Jenny's feelings begin to be revealed. As she starts reciting the catalogue of unpleasantness, her colour rises, her voice grows louder and her sense of outrage and bitterness is displayed for everyone in the court to see.

'It meant that she drank heavily, created scenes, shouted at the children for no reason, taunted and demeaned them, played cruel mind-games with them, threw tantrums and objects around the house, vomited in the bedroom once and the car once, picked fights with everyone around her and treated me like filth.'

The Defence barristers, who had until then been concentrating on taking down her words, stop writing to stare at her. A heavily charged silence falls at her last words. Her head drops again, but her voice continues, firm and clear.

'I hated her then. Before, I thought of her as unhappy and lonely and I felt sorry for her. But what she did to the children, particularly the eldest boy, was cruel and hateful.'

'Do you know how the accused felt about it? Did he say anything to you?'

'No, he didn't. He was very ... proper. He would never discuss his marriage with me. But he didn't need to; it was obvious to anyone who lived in that house.'

'When was the last time you saw Mrs Steele?'

'Three days before she ... disappeared.'

'Please describe that occasion for us.'

'It was tea-time and I was sitting with the children in the kitchen. We heard her car on the drive. We were all holding our breath, because she'd been in a foul mood for days, and we weren't sure what to expect. Stephen held my hand. But she bounced into the house, singing. She almost skipped into the kitchen. She kissed the top of the children's heads, one by one. They were astonished. Then she put the kettle on to boil.'

'Did she say anything to explain her mood?'

'Yes. She volunteered that she'd "got him back" and that he was giving them "one last chance."'

'Did you know who she meant?'

'I assumed she meant Roddy. He was the man she was seeing at the time, and it was the end of their affair that had made her so unhappy.'

'What happened then?'

'Well, there was a bit of a strained silence, and when no one said anything she asked why couldn't we all be happy for her. I said I really couldn't say what I thought about it, not in front of the children. She said "Oh, they want me to be happy, don't they?" and she ruffled the hair of the two older children as she said it.'

'What happened then?'

'She lost patience with the kettle and switched it off. She said she had to go and pack. Charlotte asked if she was going away again and she said "Only for a couple of days". She said she needed a break. That caused Charlotte to start crying, and that set Lise off again.'

'Set her off?'

'Everyone had to share her joy or her sorrows. She hated it when the children were unhappy when she was on one of her "upswings". She couldn't see that she was responsible. So she rounded on Charlotte, shouting at her, demanding her to explain why she was crying. That just made Charlotte cry all the more.'

'What happened then?'

'She told Charlotte she was too old to be a cry-baby, and ordered her to stop. Of course, that did no good, and she raised her hand as if she was going to slap her. Stephen intervened.'

'What did he do?'

'He got off his chair and ran round to his sister. He shouted at Lise to leave Charlotte alone, that she was always bullying her. It was foolish, but it worked.'

'Did Mrs Steele stop?'

'No, but it worked in the sense that it diverted her anger away from Charlotte. He was stammering so much he could barely get the words out, and Lise mimicked him, poking him in the chest as she did so. She threatened him that if he didn't watch out, he wouldn't be coming home at all over the holidays — he was in a boarding school, you understand — and he hated it, but Anthony … Mr Steele … felt it was the only way to protect him from Lise when she was in this frame of mind. He worked away a lot on cases, so he couldn't be there to protect Stephen.'

'And you? Couldn't you protect him?'

Jenny shrugs. 'I tried, of course I did. But I was just the nanny. She could've sacked me at any moment. I think the only reason she didn't was that I was prepared to put up with more of her behaviour than the previous staff.'

'What happened then?'

'She ran upstairs and I took the children into the garden to get out of her way. That was the last time I saw her before she disappeared.'

Charles thinks for a moment, framing his next question carefully. 'You say "before she disappeared", but the truth is that she didn't disappear, did she?'

Jenny looks at her feet and gives no answer.

'Did she?' repeats Charles.

Jenny shakes her head and almost whispers. 'No. At least, I don't think so.'

'What makes you think that she didn't just "disappear"?'

Everyone in the court strains to hear her next words. 'Because he told me.'

'Who told you, the accused?' She nods. 'May I ask you to give a spoken answer?'

'Yes. Anthony. The … accused.'

'What did he say?'

'He told me that she came at him with a knife, and that as he was defending himself, he killed her by accident.'

'When did he say this?'

'The day after she came back from her few days away with the boyfriend.'

'Where were you when you had this conversation?'

'In my room.'

'Your bedroom?'

'Yes.'

'Did he say why he was telling you this?'

'Yes. Because he didn't know what to do. He was terrified that if he went to the police, they wouldn't believe him. Everyone knew how awful she was, and he thought he'd be suspected of killing her deliberately.'

'Did you talk about it?'

'All night.'

'Did he make a decision?'

'Yes. I told him that —'

The Recorder intervenes. 'Excuse me, Mr Holborne, but I think I must interrupt you. Am I not obliged to warn this witness against self-incrimination?'

'Well, my Lord, I have no intention of bringing out anything to her detriment, but I suppose she may stray over the line.'

'It sounded as if she was about to do that very thing,' says the Recorder. 'What do you think, Mr Beaverbrook?'

'This is not really the province of the Defence, but I would submit that the warning is appropriate.'

'Yes. I think so.' The Recorder turns to Jenny. 'Madam, you are entitled to be warned that you need answer no questions, the answers to which might tend to incriminate you of any offence. Do you understand? You are not on trial, and you have a right to protect yourself by not answering any question that suggests that you are guilty of any offence.'

'I understand, my Lord,' she replies.

'Continue, Mr Holborne.'

'Thank you, my Lord.' Charles pauses before addressing his next question. 'You need not tell us about any action you took. Just tell us what, if any, decision the defendant took as a result of your discussion.'

'He decided to … hide her body, rather than tell the police.'

'Where did you understand from him that the deceased had met her death?'

'In their bedroom.'

'Where was she when he came to talk to you?'

'I didn't look, but he said she was still in there.'

'Did you ever see her, alive or dead, again?'

'No, I didn't.'

'Thank you. I have no further questions for you. Please remain there.'

Beaverbrook gathers his gown around him and rises to his feet. This time he uses no notes. He tries to keep the boom out of his voice and to speak in the same manner as that adopted by Charles.

'Are you a single lady?' he starts.

She sighs deeply to steady herself. 'Yes.'

'Are you still the nanny of the accused's children?'

'Yes.'

'And how long have you lived as part of the family?'

'About fifteen years.'

'Do you love the children?'

'As if they were my own. I have been their mother in all but name since long before Lise Steele … died.'

'In the last ten years or so, you have lived in that house with the defendant, just the two of you and the children?'

'Yes.'

Beaverbrook lowers his voice further, and when he speaks he sounds almost apologetic. 'Has there ever been any intimacy between the two of you?'

If the listeners expect outrage at the suggestion they are surprised, for she answers with the simplicity of truth, and with obvious sadness in her voice. 'If you mean, have we had an affair, the answer is no.' She smiles sadly and her cheeks regain some of their natural colour. 'No. Nothing of that sort has ever happened.'

'He has behaved with complete propriety towards you, at all times?'

'There were times when I wished he hadn't, but he has.'

'How do you feel about him?'

Her eyes move from the QC asking the questions to the man in the dock. He looks up at her and their eyes meet for the first time. She half-smiles and her expression softens. She sighs again and says simply: 'I love him.'

A tear escapes from her right eye and drops onto the brass rail of the witness box where it lies, sparkling like a gem.

There are rare moments like this, in Charles's experience, when the truth manages to escape the sludge of lies, obfuscation and half-truths in which the courts habitually deal. When that happens, everyone who hears it recognises it as the truth, and they are united in their understanding. At that moment No. 1 Court of the Old Bailey stands hushed, and the heart of everyone present is touched by an emotion recognised instantly as pure and true. When Jenny continues, she speaks directly to the man in the dock. 'And I wish I'd told him long before now, because now, when I risk losing him, it's too late.'

She gasps suddenly and stretches out her hand towards the dock. 'Oh!' she sighs.

It's a sound full of compassion and tenderness, the sort of sound that might be made by a mother pitying a grieving child. Everyone's eyes follow the line of Jenny's outstretched arm and see that Lord Justice Anthony Steele QC is holding his head in his hands, and that he is weeping silently too.

Beaverbrook resumes his seat without a further word. No word, no question, could possibly improve upon the effect the scene has made on the jury.

'I shall rise for a moment,' announces the Recorder.

CHAPTER 30

The papers and the news reports the following morning are full of the drama. What was expected to be the highest-profile criminal trial in a generation has developed an unexpected new dimension: now it's a love story too.

The weighty broadsheets remain, reluctantly Charles senses, with the evidence and the constitutional issues, but the tabloids have no hesitation; they carry the day with "*I'll stand by you!' weeps Nanny*" and "*Judge cries in dock for love that never was!*".

Two television programmes have interviews with psychologists who applaud the ability of men to cry, one even venturing the opinion that the tears signified innocence rather than guilt, before the presenter is able to blurt out "*Sub judice!*" and shut her up.

From a week before the trial began, in accordance with his usual practice, Charles ordered not just *The Times,* but *The Guardian*, *The Herald* and *The Mirror* to give himself the widest possible insight into what the jury would be thinking. This morning's reading over breakfast provides him with unpalatable food for thought. If the jury's views are those of the average *Herald* reader, they'll acquit, and he can't blame them. What's more, the Defence haven't even started their task of building Steele into a paragon, a man to whom violence was abhorrent and untruth anathema. Charles knows from twenty years of defending that that's exactly what he'd do in Beaverbrook's place: lay on with a trowel the good works, the humane judicial decisions, the lifetime of public duty and private respectability.

Charles eats his toast and drinks his second cup of coffee while reading the final, and only interesting, report (*"Ten things you didn't know about High Court Judges"*) and throws the paper to the floor. Harry sits opposite him, looking out over the river, a dry piece of toast in his hand.

'Do you think he's guilty now?' he asks without turning around.

'Peculiarly, the surer I become that he murdered her, the more I'm convinced the jury'll acquit.'

'He'll receive his punishment,' responds Harry, as always taking the longer view.

'Sure about that?'

Charles paces around the flat for a while before deciding to walk to the Old Bailey early. He takes his other route for a change, up Fetter Lane and along High Holborn. He turns right into Old Bailey and, for once, it's deserted. He salutes the famous statue of Justice, blindfolded and with the scales in her outstretched hand, and enters the building.

He changes quickly into his wing collar, bands, wig and gown and decides not to go into the Bar Mess, but instead straight to court. The usher, just unlocking the doors, greets him and Charles descends into the well of the court and his bench. A moment later the doors open again, and Inspector Carr enters. Charles hasn't seen him since the committal hearing. The inspector sees Charles and approaches. They shake hands.

'I gather from the papers that it's not going our way,' comments the policeman.

He's had a haircut since Charles last saw him and wears what appears to be a new suit. He looks too nice to be a copper, thinks Charles.

'You gather correctly.'

Carr nods, as if unsurprised. 'I know we all said how awful it was, how we hoped for the sake of British justice he was innocent, but I think we all secretly wanted him to be guilty. It gave us a sort of satisfaction, knowing that they weren't above it all. Now I look at the evidence, I wonder how we let it get so far.'

'The evidence or the tabloids? Anyway, that's a bit defeatist, isn't it?' says Charles. 'He's pleaded guilty to disposing of a body already, and the game's not over so far as murder is concerned. We're not exactly going away empty-handed even if he gets off the other charges.'

'Yes, maybe,' replies Carr, unconvinced. 'Will you get to me this morning?'

'Almost certainly.'

The court begins to fill. The door to the public gallery is thrown open and the spectators rush for the best seats. The journalists and the sketch-drawers start filing in. Charles overhears Beaverbrook asking one if he could have the original sketch made of him as he cross-examined Jenny Sullivan; he wants to frame it. What a bizarre side-effect of cameras being banned, thinks Charles: a trade in court sketches for smug, self-important members of the Bar.

The journalists are looking around, hoping to catch sight of Jenny and the children, but they're absent. Running late or a tactical error? wonders Charles. He'd have wanted Jenny looking tired, pale and beautiful as she waits patiently for her man to be exonerated. He has no more time to consider it as the Recorder enters and the day's proceedings begin.

Charles calls Inspector Carr and, after him, Superintendent Hook. No questions are asked of either of the police officers, except to confirm that the accused was a man of good character. Hook reads through the whole of the interview with

Steele in which he denied any knowledge of his wife's death, and which, if Jenny's evidence is true, is a pack of lies. Not a word of it is challenged, not a question asked, but Charles understands and agrees with the Defence strategy. Cross-examining the police officers would only emphasise the falsity of the statement given by Steele in interview. The man has an explanation, and he'll give it when he goes into the witness box.

Then, just as Charles is about to close his case, he hears a light groan behind him. He and the other barristers all spin in their benches to the source of the sound, and see that the accused is almost invisible, so low is he bent in the dock. He sits with his head in his hands, his eyes tightly shut.

James Day stands quickly, bows to the Recorder and scurries back to his client while everyone waits. He speaks to Steele, who replies faintly, his head still buried, and then returns to counsel's bench. He whispers his news to Beaverbrook; the QC nods and then sends Day back for more information. There's another whispered conference at the dock and Day returns a second time to report to his leader. Beaverbrook frowns, gives a good impression of a man thinking very hard, and rises. The suspicion begins to germinate in Charles's cynical mind that some pretty fancy footwork is being done by the normally ponderous silk.

'My Lord,' says Beaverbrook, 'my client is feeling ill. He warned me this morning before he came into court that he thought that a migraine headache was coming on, and I fear that's what has happened.'

'Would you like me to rise and permit him to seek medical help?' asks the Recorder, already collecting his pens in preparation.

'That's very kind of your Lordship, but it won't be necessary. The Defence is reluctant to hold up the proceedings if that can be avoided. I anticipate that Mr Holborne was about to close the Crown's case…'

He pauses to allow Charles to confirm. Charles's suspicion has now germinated and is putting forth its first roots. He doesn't like the smell of what's coming, and he isn't happy to assist it. He has no choice, however, as the Recorder is waiting for him.

'Yes, my Lord, I was about to close my case,' he says.

'Thank you,' says Beaverbrook, smiling in a way that Charles knows forebodes some ploy. 'My position is this: I have a number of witnesses who've been waiting to give evidence for some time. I doubt any of their evidence will be contested by the Crown. I wonder if it would be possible for your Lordship to break with the usual rule and permit them to give their evidence first? That would give time for my client to recover. These witnesses mainly go to character, although some also deal with alleged motive.'

'What about your client?' asks the Recorder. 'Don't answer unless you wish to do so, Mr Beaverbrook, but are you expecting him to give evidence in his own defence?'

'Certainly, my Lord, but not with a migraine. I'm sure your Lordship would agree that it would be unfair to ask that of him. What I request therefore is permission for him to be allowed to leave court, at least until luncheon, so that he may lie down. I understand there is a first aid room here where he can rest.'

'Does he have any objections to evidence being heard in his absence?'

'Apparently not,' replies Beaverbrook.

The sick accused finds enough strength to raise his head and mouth "No".

Charles's suspicions now burst into full flower and produce a good crop of fruit.

The Recorder turns to him. 'Mr Holborne, do you have any objections? If you insist, I shall adjourn and require the defendant to give evidence first, as is usual.'

Charles curses silently. The Recorder has neatly completed Beaverbrook's outflanking manoeuvre. Of course Charles doesn't want to "insist" that a sick man be forced to the witness box. Equally, he doesn't want to air his suspicions, namely that Steele is faking so as to defer giving his evidence until after the other evidence. Beaverbrook is saving him up for a final grandstanding act, trying to ensure that Steele's is the last voice the jury hears. Charles weighs the disapproval of the jury if he is seen to be openly unsympathetic, against the detriment to his case if Steele gives evidence last.

'Would a short adjournment, perhaps an hour or so, allow the accused to recover?' he hazards.

'No,' replies Beaverbrook firmly. 'My instructions are that once one of these migraine headaches start, it takes a couple of hours at least before they improve.'

'Well, Mr Holborne,' says the Recorder. 'As I say, if you insist, I will of course adjourn. That's your right. But surely in a case where the other witnesses are character witnesses, it makes little difference?'

Under that pressure, Charles is forced to a reluctant decision.

'No, my Lord. The Crown has no objections.'

'Very well. The defendant may leave the dock.'

An usher appears with the court usher's cure-all, a warmish glass of water. The judge takes a weak sip from the glass and allows himself to be assisted to his feet. He does, Charles concedes, look extremely pale, but then so would he if he were on trial for his life.

Beaverbrook waits until his client disappears out of the doors, wringing every last scrap of sympathy from the situation.

'Do you in fact close the Crown's case, Mr Holborne?' asks the Recorder.

'Yes, my Lord. That is my case.'

Beaverbrook rises again. 'Then I shall call my first witness, with your Lordship's permission.'

The QC calls a woman's name, a name familiar to Charles. It belongs to one of Steele's neighbours at the family's last home before Lise disappeared. Charles leafs through his main index of witnesses, which includes not only the witnesses relied on by the Crown but also those whose statements the police obtained but were of no use to the prosecution. He finds her statement.

A tall, elegant woman in her middle years, wearing an expensive Italian suit and a broad-brimmed hat, enters court. Beaverbrook guides her line by line through her statement. She details seven years of patience and forbearance by the defendant in the face of public humiliation and private unhappiness. She was a close friend, originally of the deceased, but then, as she came to know the family better, of the defendant. Her views, she said, were no different to those of anyone else who knew the couple. Everyone was sick of the alcoholic, adulterous wife and sorry for the husband. He coped unbelievably, he was totally devoted to the children and it was inconceivable that he could ever use violence unless, perhaps, in fear of his life. These last words are delivered with a gravity and deliberation that is deeply ominous to Charles's ears. She finishes with an almost-humorous anecdote of a church fete where the deceased disgraced herself again and the accused employed, yet again, tact and diplomacy in diffusing the situation, when, by rights, most men would have thumped her.

She's good, concedes Charles, very good. She gives her evidence with calm assurance, looking every now and then at the jury, with a touch of humour here and there, but always conscious of the gravity of the proceedings. The jury likes her. She's attractive to the men without being fast or loud, and just Woman's Institute-matronly enough for the women to find her familiar and trustworthy. A sound choice for the first Defence witness.

She is followed by four further witnesses, two men and two women, all of whom give evidence in the same vein. To the men, he was a quiet, pleasant companion at the pub and tennis club who suffered the burden of his wife with grace and patience, and who made efforts in the face of a busy professional practice to give as much time to the children as possible. To the women, he was a gentleman, in both senses of the word.

The two female witnesses also have something to say of the deceased. Both experienced her at her worst, witnessing fits of frightening violence to inanimate objects and, once, to the defendant. One uses the word "predatory" of the deceased's relationship with other men, and it sounds a chord.

These witnesses are followed by two vicars whose statements, taken by the Defence solicitor, Charles did not have, one from the old community and one from the village where the Steele family lived until his arrest. Both make it clear that Steele's religion is important to him, that until his arrest he was an active member of the church and that they would trust implicitly anything he says on his oath.

Next, the jury hears from the woman who worked at the deceased's antique shop, two of her relations and another neighbour. Finally, there comes a nanny who worked at the previous address several years before. A woman in her sixties, plump, with red cheeks and white hair curled in a bun, she is almost a caricature of a kindly, goodhearted, old-fashioned nanny. She details the deceased's violent nature, her unreasoning hatred of the older boy, and her affairs. The contrast between her words — of blows, mental torture, smashed furniture and sexual rapaciousness — and her grandmotherly appearance is strikingly powerful, and her regard for Steele and the children, of whom there had only been two during her reign, is perfectly pitched and entirely credible.

Charles has not a single question for any of them. By the time the parade ends, shortly after the luncheon adjournment, Beaverbrook has set the stage perfectly for the return of his client and, on cue, as the kindly, rosy-cheeked former nanny steps down from the witness box, an usher hurries up the aisle and hands a note to the court clerk. The clerk stands, turns and speaks to the Recorder, who nods.

'Mr Beaverbrook, your client is, apparently, recovered. Yes,' he says to the clerk, 'let him return to the dock.'

A moment later, Steele appears at the back of the court. He bows to the Recorder, who returns the compliment — a false note that, thinks Charles; it reveals to the jury the courtly relationship between the judge on trial and the judge conducting the trial — and steps quietly into the dock. Before he can sit, Beaverbrook calls him to give evidence.

Steele walks to the witness box, takes the Bible offered to him and, without needing to read the words on the card presented to him, gives the oath.

CHAPTER 31

Steele's voice is firm and calm, but there's another ingredient, another quality that for a moment Charles struggles to identify. Then, it comes to him: it's sadness. His well-modulated voice is saying: *This is a terrible mistake, but I believe in the English system of justice, and therefore although this causes me pain, I am confident that the truth will prevail.*

In answer to Beaverbrook, Steele gives his name. He could have used "Sir", for all High Court judges are knights of the realm, or even "Lord Justice", but he gives just the name with which he was christened, thus making it clear that he expects no favours because of his rank. Beaverbrook takes three sentences to describe the judge's career and then moves directly to his family life. If any member of the jury does not already know from the newspapers and the wireless about the brilliant young barrister, how he rose with spectacular speed through the ranks to Queen's Counsel, then judge of the High Court, then the Court of Appeal, they're not going to be interested now. They want to hear about his personal life. So Beaverbrook moves directly to that, to Steele's marriage, the birth of his children and the move to their first family home in Kent. Then he pauses.

'Was your wife faithful to you?'

Steele's face is sad, but resigned, as if his late wife's affairs were a chronic illness which, although life-limiting, they had both learned to accommodate. 'No, she was not. To my certain knowledge she had affairs from very early in our marriage.'

'How did you feel about that?'

'They saddened me. At first I didn't think it was too serious. She was much younger than me, and she found marriage very restricting.'

'Did you consider divorce?'

The judge looks surprised. 'No, of course not. I loved her. I could never quite believe that someone so lovely — she really was very beautiful, you know? — could love me, and yet she did. She'd be so sorry after ... one of her ... indiscretions, so apologetic. I was jealous, of course I was, but they never meant anything to her. It was a weakness, that need for excitement, and I hoped she'd grow out of it.'

'Did she grow out of it?'

'No. Well, for a short time they stopped, when she found she was pregnant with our eldest. She was so excited, so involved in it all, that I really thought she was settling down. I believed it was exactly what she needed, a child, someone she could love and who would depend on her totally.'

'Did it work out that way?'

'No. Just the opposite. After the first excitement wore off, she hated everything about it. She hated being pregnant, hated being fat and unattractive — or so she thought — and when the baby arrived, she hated him too. He represented everything that was tying her down, preventing her from enjoying her life.'

'What happened?'

'She started drinking.'

'A lot?'

'I didn't appreciate how much until the health visitor came to see me. She had gone round several times in the mornings and found ... well, my wife wasn't up to caring for the baby at all.'

'How was your relationship with your wife at this time?'

'It was the beginning of a downward spiral. She'd get very angry with me, with the baby, with her whole life. She felt trapped, and her way out was through drink. She was very unstable. She would fly off the handle at the least provocation.'

'Who with?'

'Anyone. We had a succession of people who came to help with the children, nannies, home helps, a cook once,' and he turns to the jury and addresses them directly. 'You've heard from some of them. Not one of them lasted more than a few months.'

Charles observes as several jury members nod. They're lapping it up, he thinks.

'The jury might wonder why you had a second child, if your relationship was so poor,' comments Beaverbrook, asking the very question Charles would have asked at that point.

'It wasn't always as bad as that,' replies Steele.

Charles sees him flick a glance at the Recorder's pen, and his speech immediately slows. He knows very well that if he speaks too fast, and the Recorder misses anything, the jury will not be reminded of it in the summing up, so he's making absolutely sure that he speaks no faster than the Recorder can write. It may look like he's just answering the questions as they come, without guile, thinks Charles, but this is all executed with minute precision. Inside the attractively humane exterior of Anthony Steele there hides a cold, methodical, thinking machine.

'There were periods when she would try to get a grip, she'd stop drinking, tidy up the house, play at being the devoted mother and wife. She'd make romantic meals for us when I came home. She would try very hard for a short time, but then something would happen, she'd have a temper tantrum, and she'd start drinking again. Both the younger children were conceived during her periods of remission, at periods when we both hoped it would work.'

'Remission? You make it sound like an illness.'

'It was an illness. She was sick and, like many invalids, she made the entire family unhappy.'

'You could have left her. Why didn't you?'

'You don't leave your wife when she falls ill. You stand by her.'

Very nice, thinks Charles. He had to hand it to Beaverbrook: this was an admirable piece of examination in chief. Everything that had preceded it had been designed to lead to that answer.

'What, if anything, did you do to help her?'

'I suggested various things, like hypnotherapy and counselling. The self-help organisation, Alcoholics Anonymous, was just starting in this country and I even suggested we went to some meetings. She wasn't interested in any of it. I ended up going on my own. Eventually, I had the idea that maybe we should move, start again. There was a man, a lover, at that time, and he was becoming a nuisance.'

'How?'

'He was very serious about her, but unstable too. He would telephone at all hours of the day and night, they'd have rows. One time she came back from seeing him with her legs bruised. She wouldn't tell me what had happened, but I think he kicked her. It seemed best all round to make a fresh start. So we moved from London to Kent. Right out into the country. I thought a hundred miles would be far enough. We moved into a small village where I thought we could live our lives unobtrusively, and I bought her a small business. I hoped it would occupy her mind and make her more financially responsible.'

'Why "financially responsible"?'

'She never could handle money. Even when we were first married, it went through her hands like water. When she started drinking, however, it became impossible. She spent all our savings, and got us into debt. I'd put aside money for my income tax, several thousand pounds, and when I went to pay the bill, it had all gone.'

'I see. Did it work, the move?'

'No. She wasn't interested in the business except to spend the money. It became a huge drain on our resources. And she started another affair, actually within a week of our arrival. She met him at a party in the village; the first to which we were invited.'

'How long did that affair last?'

'This was Roddy Batchelor. It lasted right until her death.'

'It sounds as if it was serious.'

'I think it was. She had other flings too, but she always went back to Roddy. Maybe she loved him.'

'What was the situation between you two at that time?'

'At its worst. We lived in a sort of armed truce. I had more or less given up any hope of a real marriage, but at the same time I didn't want a divorce — at least, not 'til the children were grown up.'

'Why not?'

'I have seen, in hundreds of cases, what a divorce does to the children. Especially when the parents are at one another's throats. She hated being a mother, and she hated our eldest son, but I knew she'd fight for custody, to spite me. She taunted me with it frequently. And the children were very young. I had a busy practice and was often away from home, so she had a real chance of persuading a judge.'

'But she was an alcoholic.'

'And a very good actress. You have to understand that when she was behaving, she was absolutely charming, and very beautiful. I'd look at her and be baffled by how all that *meanness* could hide under such a wonderful exterior.' He shrugs helplessly. 'I couldn't take the chance that she'd sweet-talk some matrimonial judge and I'd lose the children. They'd have been at serious risk; Lise was utterly incapable of looking after them. So I decided the best thing was to keep her in the home and under control as much as possible. As long as I could keep the rows and tantrums to a minimum, and I could at least limit her consumption of alcohol, I thought that even a bad atmosphere in the home was better than a custody battle and two homes.'

'What was the situation immediately before her death?'

'I've just described it, really. Periodic flare-ups, constant drinking with peaks and troughs, an on-off affair with Roddy.'

'Did that affair bother you, if it was more serious than the others?'

'Just the opposite in fact. He was a good influence on her. He certainly had more control over her than I did, and when she was happy with him, she was much less difficult at home. You could always tell when they'd had a row, because the drinking increased and she'd be even more violent in her mood swings. I actually felt grateful to him and sorry for him in about equal measure.'

'What happened on the day of her death?'

This one question makes it clear at last that Steele is no longer saying that his wife simply walked out. It means admitting that he was there when she died; that he lied to the police.

'She came back from a couple of days away with Roddy. The children were out somewhere, at the park I think. She looked lovely, alive and happy. And she was sober. You must understand that in spite of everything, I did love her. I thought we might have a quiet meal somewhere, just the two of us, but when I suggested it, she laughed at the idea. She said she was going out again, with him. We had a row.'

'What about?'

'About him, about her lack of interest in the shop, about … our sex life, or lack of it. Then she threw the sheets at me, and told me to wash them.'

'Sheets?'

'The ones she took down to their cottage, where they had their dirty weekends. They had to take their own sheets.'

'Where did this row occur?'

'It started downstairs in the kitchen and carried on upstairs in the bedroom.'

'Was it violent?'

'Not at first. She had a way of turning on you — some of the other witnesses have spoken about it — completely out of the blue. Sometimes even in mid-word. There would be something in her eyes, a sort of glazed look, and she would go wild, absolutely wild. She did it once with an au pair, and the poor girl just ran for it, straight out of the house. Never came back, even to collect her clothes. I had to post them to her parents in Germany. I believe the police took a statement from her, as she called me and asked what was going on. Anyway, we were just arguing as normal, just a lot of shouting on her part, and attempts at reasoning on mine, and suddenly she came for me.'

'How?'

'With a knife, from the picnic hamper. She'd taken a hamper away with them to the New Forest or wherever they used to go, and she carried that and her overnight bag upstairs when she flounced out of the kitchen. She was unpacking as we argued.'

'Did you know she had a knife?'

'Well, I'd seen the hamper, but I'd not really thought about it. She had her back to me. I was in mid-sentence, and she just screamed at me and whirled round.'

Charles sees the first glimpse of something more interesting beneath Steele's calm veneer. His speed of response has picked up and the Recorder is having greater difficulty keeping up with the torrent of words. Beaverbrook interrupts to slow him down.

'What did she scream?'

'Not words; it was incomprehensible. Just rage.'

Steele leans forward, his cheeks now slightly flushed and his pale eyes darting. 'As she spun towards me I realised there was something in her hand, but I had no time to identify it. I put a hand up to fend her off, like this,' and he demonstrates to the jury, his right hand held at head height, palm facing away from himself. 'I felt something strike my hand. I didn't feel any pain until it was all over, but she'd cut my hand very deeply between the thumb and forefinger. There's a slight scar, my Lord, which I can show the jury, right in the crease.'

'Yes, certainly, before you complete your evidence, but continue with your account for the present. And, please,' he adds, 'a little more slowly.'

'Sorry, my Lord,' says Beaverbrook. 'It's my fault. Go on.'

'I was backing away from her but she kept coming at me, screaming and shouting, her arms flailing wildly. I realised that, at that instant, she was just crazy enough to kill me.'

Despite the Recorder's request, Steele's delivery is still accelerating. The Recorder's hand is flying across the pages of his red notebook, but Charles sees from his expression that he's losing ground on Steele's account. Beaverbrook is also aware of it and puts up his hand to slow his client down, but Steele's focus is on the jury, urging them to believe him, desperately willing them to enter that bedroom, and see the events through his eyes.

'I didn't think she'd *mean* to kill me, but she was out of control and didn't realise what she was doing. I tried once to get her arm but it was waving too violently. I tried to punch her — I thought I might even knock her out — that's what you see in the films, isn't it? — but I only got one good punch in, and it didn't seem to affect her at all. Plus, I got cut on my arm.'

'Where did that punch land?'

Steele's flow stops suddenly and there's a fractional delay before he answers. He puts his hand to his temple at almost exactly the spot where the pathologist had identified a possible bruise. 'About here.'

'You say it didn't affect her at all. Do you know if you connected with her?'

'Yes, I'm pretty sure I did, because my ring caught her eyebrow, and it started bleeding. It was quite a gash, and I was surprised Dr Butcher didn't notice it. In any event, it didn't slow her up at all.'

'What happened then? And please try to speak more slowly.'

'You must understand that this all took a very short time, seconds, probably.' Steele looks round the court, first at the jury, then at the Recorder, then back to his counsel. A sheen of sweat has appeared on his handsome brow.

'It's difficult to remember the precise order, the precise sequence. My next recollection is of being in the corner of the room, and realising I couldn't get out. She was coming at me, but I remember blood running down her face, into her eye, and she was blinking hard. I realised I had to disarm her, and I lunged at her, got in between her arms. I have this picture of me bear-hugging her, and her arms were behind my back, thrashing away. We both fell over, me on top of her. I let go as we fell, and put my hands out to break my fall. I landed on my forearm, on top of her.'

'Did your forearm connect with her body?'

'Yes, across her throat.'

'Did you leave it there?'

'Momentarily only. I got off her as soon as I could.'

'Wasn't that dangerous?'

'No, because she'd fainted. At least, she was unconscious. I thought at first that she'd banged her head as we went down. I sat up, just trying to gather myself. I was going to get my breath back, take the knife away and hide it, and then get a wet towel or something for her.'

He stops again. His face contorts into an expression of revulsion, as if remembering something deeply disgusting. When he starts again, his throat is constricted. 'It was a few seconds later that I looked at her face.'

He shakes his head. His eyes close, as if trying to shut out the memory. Beaverbrook leaves him like that for a moment, and then speaks softly.

'What did you see?'

'Her eyes ... it was her eyes. They were open ... but I could see immediately that something wasn't right. Blank, like a fish's eyes. I think I knew then that she was dead, but I couldn't believe it. I listened for her breathing, put my ear to her mouth, felt for a pulse. Then I tried artificial respiration. I thought she *had* to be alive, because the wound on her eyebrow was still bleeding ... and I didn't know what I could've done to kill her! I hadn't hit her hard. I leaned on her neck, but for a second, not even that, and I couldn't believe that I'd suffocated her. I thought, maybe she's had a heart attack, but I knew what that would look like, and she hadn't exhibited any of the signs, so ... I just didn't know! Then I saw the room. There was blood everywhere! I looked at my hands, and the right one was completely red. It was the first time I realised that I'd been cut. There was blood on the floor from her eyebrow, a huge pool of it, getting wider as I watched, and flecks on the walls and ceiling where I suppose it had been flung off my hand in the struggle.'

'What did you do?'

'I just sat there, looking at her. I knew she was dead, but I kept expecting her to sit up, like it was some game to frighten me. Then I got a plastic bag to put her head on.'

'Why?'

'Because blood was still coming from her wound.'

'What did you do then?'

'I sat on the floor with her. I don't know how long, but it was dark when I next remember. I heard the door go downstairs and the children's voices.'

'What were you doing while you sat there?'

'I was thinking what I should do. My first impulse was to call the police, but then I began to think what it looked like. Here was a man in an unhappy marriage, his wife having an affair right under his nose, demeaning him and abusing him all the time, and his wife was dead at his hands. I knew prosecutors — I was one myself! — who could make a case out of that. What's more, some people, police officers sometimes, love to put people like me in their place. They work hard for convictions in those cases,' and he looks directly at Charles as he says this.

'What did you decide to do?'

'Nothing at that stage. I got up and left the room, and locked the door behind me. I went straight to the bathroom, took off all my clothes and put them in a holdall, and had a shower. Then I went back to the room, bandaged my hand, took some clean clothes, and locked it up again. Then I went downstairs and helped with getting the children to bed. We had supper, and then I went to my study to think. Later that night I realised that I was going round and round in circles, and I needed to talk to someone, to collect my thoughts.'

'So you went to your children's nanny? The jury might find that rather strange.'

'Jenny was more than just a nanny. She'd been with us for years, was part of the family. She was my friend, she loved the children and I trusted her completely. She at least would believe me when I said it was an accident. There had never been anything between us, but maybe … I don't really know, maybe unconsciously, I knew she cared for me. Anyway, I knocked on her door, asked to come in, and told her the whole story. We talked all night. In the end I decided not to report it. When it got light, before the children were up, I went back into the room. There was a huge pool of blood in the centre of the floor.'

'I think we can move on from —' starts Beaverbrook, but Steele pays no attention and forges on.

'I realised that if I was going to dispose of my wife's body, I had to bend her double to fit her in the car boot. I knew that rigor mortis would set in, but I didn't know when. It'd been a warm night and she wasn't stiff yet.'

Beaverbrook tries again, 'Mr Steele —'

'So I got some polythene sheeting from the loft, bent her knees up under chin, and rolled her up into a package. I couldn't find anything long enough to tie it up, so I got all the bits and pieces from around the house that I could find, cable, rope and so on, and used that.'

The Recorder stops taking notes and watches the accused man talking. None of this evidence is relevant to the charges of murder or manslaughter. He makes eye contact with Beaverbrook and raises his eyebrows, inviting the QC to control his client, but the man in the dock now seems unaware of everyone and everything in the courtroom. He's no longer on trial, no longer choosing his answers. He needs no prompting, no guidance. He's caught up in a story stronger than he, a story with a life of its own that demands to be told. Whether innocent or guilty, he has waited over a decade to tell this story, and now he is going to tell it.

'I had another shower and was already dressed when the children got up. Just the younger ones, you understand; Stephen was at boarding school. They were packed off to some friends for the day, and I got the body down through the house and into the garage. I emptied the boot and put her in. Then I went back up to start clearing up the room. As soon as I started, I realised that the whole room would have to be redecorated — there was so much blood. We never usually locked the doors in our house, so I had to do it immediately, or the children would start asking questions. During that day I stripped all the wallpaper and repainted the ceiling. The skirting board and other glossed areas I washed down. I scrubbed the floor a dozen times. By late that night, all I had to do was repaper. That evening, after supper, I was sitting in the dining room, and I could hear a noise like a tap dripping. I searched for the sound, and found there was blood dripping from the light fitting onto the dining table. It had seeped through the floorboards from upstairs and was running down the light flex. I went upstairs, and, while the children were asleep, I prised up the floorboards. There was more blood underneath them. I thought I could get away with mopping it up until I realised that I had marked the boards when lifting them. They were badly stained anyway, so I decided that I would have to re-stain and re-varnish them.'

'Can we move on —' tries Beaverbrook for the third time.

'The next morning I set about trying to put together an alibi. I'd told my son's headmaster that I might come down for the sports day, and I thought: if I can get there, I can get a lot of people to remember me. I wasn't sure what I was going to do with the body at that stage, but I wanted to put as much distance between myself and the house, and as publicly, as soon as possible. Then I stained the whole of the floor of the bedroom. It took less time than I had imagined. I used a mop and it was done in two hours. While it dried, I went out in the car to look for something really heavy. By then I'd had the idea of a lake or the sea or somewhere, and I knew that I'd need a weight. I found a sort of hollow kerbstone, I think it's the stone under the kerb that takes all the surface water, it looks like a doughnut, with a hole in the middle, which was perfect.'

The Recorder interrupts, fascinated. 'You went out in your car?'

Steele looks up, the words having percolated into the scene replaying his head, and he answers with smile. 'Yes, my Lord.'

'The one with your wife in the boot?'

'Yes. I only had one car, so I had no choice. There was room for both the body and the kerbstone in the boot anyway.'

Steele's expression suggests that he saw nothing surprising about driving round a county town with one's wife's body in the boot of your car.

He continues. 'When I got back, I started to paper the walls. That was the most difficult part. I'd never done wallpapering before. It's very difficult. I did it though,' he says, with evident pride, 'and then I did a final clearance of the room. The bedding for example had to be taken out and washed, the curtains taken to the dry cleaner's and so on, and when I was sure there was nothing left incriminating, I started applying the varnish to the floor, gradually painting myself out into the corridor. Then I closed the door and locked it. Now I was able to do so legitimately, as I told the children that I had redecorated, and I was locking the door so that they wouldn't accidentally touch anything that was still wet.

'That night I got out my old dinghy —' he turns to Inspector Carr who sits at the back of the court. 'Sorry I lied to you, Inspector; I *did* have some experience of sailing — and I put that into the boot too. Even deflated, it was a tight fit but I just managed it. By now, it was two days since her death, and I'd had no sleep. I lay down for an hour, and then set off for Somerset where my son's school was. I didn't dare stop anywhere and leave the car, as she was beginning to smell a bit. I got to the school late that afternoon, just in time to watch the sports. I parked the car at the far side of the car park and kept my fingers crossed. I had a stroke of luck, as the head asked me to present the prizes, so I had lots of photographs taken of me.

'I made an appointment to see him the following morning, and I checked into a local hotel. Straight after dinner, I told reception that I was going to bed and asked not to be disturbed. I made a bit of a fuss about it, saying I was feeling unwell, so everyone would remember me. After a short while in my room, I climbed down the drainpipe.

'Then I set off for Wastwater. I knew it was the deepest lake in Britain, and I thought that it would be better than the sea, where she could get washed up, or caught in a fishing net or something. I had bought a complete spare set of bulbs, windscreen wipers and so on. I didn't want to be stopped for any reason and risk the police searching the car. I drove under the speed limit all the way, stopping every now and then to make sure all my lights were working.'

Now Beaverbrook interrupts forcibly, raising his voice over that of his client. 'I don't think we need to deal with this in detail,' he says smoothly, trying to camouflage his disquiet. 'The jury knows that you've pleaded guilty to obstructing the coroner.'

Steele barely glances at his counsel and continues. Charles looks carefully at the jury members. All are riveted on Steele's animated face. One or two of the women have their hands covering their mouths as if in shock or horror. They don't want Beaverbrook to stop this story; they are there, with Steele, on this wild ride.

'I went via Carnforth and took the southern route to Wastwater. I had to drive around for a while to find somewhere where I could get the car down to the shore. I knew I wouldn't be able to carry the body, the stone and the dinghy very far. You have to understand that this was now my third night without sleeping, and I was incredibly tired, so tired that my hands were beginning to shake.'

Yet again, Beaverbrook tries to halt the flow. 'Can we turn now to your police interviews?'

'Yes, I'm almost finished,' replies Steele dismissively.

Wow! thinks Charles, this is doing real damage to Steele's hitherto perfect performance. The atmosphere of sympathy and understanding Beaverbrook had so carefully constructed is being frittered away, replaced by puzzlement and, on some jurors' faces, revulsion. They can't understand why the accused persists, despite his counsel's attempts at restraint, in going through the cold-blooded and grisly minutiae of the disposal of his wife's body. And Beaverbrook's last attempt to silence his client was desperate and crude. Now the jury is aware that even the QC fears the damage his client is wreaking to his own case.

Beaverbrook tries to look unconcerned, but it's not working. His expression reveals that he too cannot understand his client's obsession with these details.

You don't get it, do you? thinks Charles. He's got something on his chest, a weight as heavy as that which pulled his wife almost to the bottom of Tiffen's Rock. It's been crushing him slowly for years, and *this* is his chance to rid himself of it. It's the most potent evidence so far, at least so it seems to Charles, that the man is guilty of murder.

Steele's still talking.

'I found the perfect spot. It sloped right down to the water's edge from the road. I drove down, slowly, to avoid grounding the car, as I knew it was very heavy, and turned off the lights. I had even taken the lightbulb out of the boot, as I knew that otherwise it would go on when I opened the boot; it's as dark as pitch out there, and it could have been seen. I got out of the car, and I was about to take the dinghy out when another vehicle, a van I thought, pulled up on the road, its headlights pointed out over the lake, above where I was.'

He accelerates again, back in that moment. The Recorder's pen has been lowered again, and he now listens, fascinated, as intently as the jury. Charles scans their faces. A bomb could go off outside, and they'd barely notice. They're being given a point by point lecture in how to dispose of a body, one that but for pure chance would have been completely successful. Steele continues, the pride in his voice unmistakeable.

'I stayed calm. At first I thought it was the police, that I'd been discovered somehow, but the van stayed where it was, and the lights stayed on. Then the engine was turned off. It remained there for twenty minutes, the longest twenty minutes of my life! Then the lights went off, and I thought the occupant was about to get out. I got ready to run back to the driver's seat and drive off, but then I saw that it was only a courting couple. They stayed in the van for another fifteen minutes. Then the lights went on again, it started up, and drove off. I pulled the dinghy out, blew it up with the foot pump and dragged it to the water. Then I rolled the stone to it, and lastly I carried the body down.

'I took the sculls and rowed out. I had put some odds and end of rope and cable in my pocket, together with a knife, as I intended to tie her to the stone once out on the water. I thought there'd be less chance of being seen out there in the black than by the car. What I'd forgotten was that I'd wrapped the body up so tightly that there was no way to attach a rope to it and make sure it didn't slide off. So I had to open up the package at her feet to get a rope round her ankles. I guess that's why part of her foot was missing when she was found. I tied the rope in a figure of eight round both ankles, and attached it to the stone. Then I did the same again with another cable, just in case. It was extremely difficult I can tell you, and more than once I almost went overboard with her and the stone. I had pictures of being dragged down with her.'

He laughs briefly, completely unaware that over a hundred people are staring at him, horrified.

'When I was sure she was tied securely, I tipped her and the stone overboard. I thought I was right at the centre of the lake. I didn't know about Tiffen's Rock; I thought it went straight down. It was pure bad fortune that the body landed there. Then I rowed back. It took three goes to find the right beach — it was so dark that I couldn't see the car at all. Finally I found it, pulled the dinghy up the gravel, and washed it out thoroughly. I couldn't see, but I thought that some blood might have leaked onto it. Then I loaded it back into the car, and set off. After I'd driven for an hour or two, I stopped at a pub. At the back I found a large industrial waste bin. I took out half the rubbish, got undressed, and put the dinghy and all my clothes inside. Then I replaced the rubbish on top. I got changed into a spare set of clothes in the car, and then I set off on the return journey. I got to the hotel much later than I'd hoped — it was after nine in the morning and I couldn't work out how to get in without being seen — but I had a stroke of luck. The back door was open, and a milk delivery was in progress. I slipped by when no one was watching and went upstairs. Then I came straight down again, said "Good morning" at the desk, and went direct to the dining room for breakfast.'

Steele looks up and smiles. 'Then I went to the school, saw the headmaster about taking Stephen out, and we drove home. I told anyone who asked that my wife had gone off with one of her lovers. No one was surprised.'

He stops at last, and breathes deeply. Then he looks across at his counsel. 'Any more questions?' he asks.

'Yes.'

'Oh, the police interviews! Yes, well, I'm afraid I lied in them. I had no doubt that the police would realise it eventually, but at that stage I half hoped to avoid dragging others into it with me. It seemed inevitable that if I admitted to killing her, everyone in the house would be questioned. I wanted to avoid that.'

Beaverbrook pauses. There are other questions he needs to ask, but so uncertain does he now feel about his witness, he decides not to take the chance.

'I have no further questions,' he says, and he sits.

The tension is broken for the first time as people shift in their seats and cough. Charles stands, waiting for the court to quieten again.

CHAPTER 32

Charles stands to ask his first question. 'Your wife was a vindictive woman, was she not?'

'Yes, she was.'

'To use your word, she hated your eldest son, yet she would still have fought you for custody.'

'So she threatened, on many occasions.'

'And you believed her.'

'I did, yes.'

'So you reached a policy decision to stay in the marriage, so as to protect the children.'

'That is right.'

'Would you agree with me that the affair with Roddy was different from the others?' asks Charles.

'To some extent, yes.'

'For one thing, their relationship lasted for three years or more.'

'Yes.'

'For another, your wife claimed to love him, and he to love her.'

'Yes.'

'There were times when your wife pleaded with him to continue their relationship while he was trying to bring it to an end. Is that not right?'

'That is correct.'

'Indeed she seems to have made more effort to keep *that* relationship alive than she did the marriage?'

'I accept that, yes.'

'So, whereas the others were passing attractions, in her mind this was a serious long-term relationship.'

'By her standards, it was serious, yes.'

'And, whereas the other relationships were passing fancies, the one with Mr Batchelor constituted a real threat to you and the family, didn't it? If your wife decided to leave you for him, you might face your custody battle after all.'

'That occurred to me, but not as a serious risk. I doubted Roddy would want to set up home with her. He'd tried to break it off so many times, and I couldn't see him taking on three young children either. His girls were almost grown up by then.'

It's a decent answer, and Charles knows it. He is trying to re-establish a motive for murder, but this feels too tenuous, too unlikely. He feels the case slipping even further away from him, but has insufficient evidence to pull it back. In the last analysis, once Steele pleaded guilty to disposing of the deceased's body, the other charges would stand or fall solely on one question: would the jury believe his account of the events leading up to her death? At present, in Charles's judgement, they would. So he changes tack.

'Your wife frequently embarrassed and disgraced you in public.'

'She did.'

'Her name was often seen in the gossip columns.'

The judge sighs, but whether at the memory of Lise's behaviour or the predictability of Charles's questioning Charles cannot tell. 'Sometimes, yes.'

'She flirted with colleagues, upset their wives, got drunk and created scenes, took her clothes off in public, that sort of thing.'

'There are five questions there, Mr Holborne,' responds Steele, accidentally slipping out of the role of accused into that of a judge trying the case. 'To answer them in order: yes, sometimes, yes, yes and only infrequently. To my knowledge she … undressed at … inappropriate times only twice, and one of those was at a party with a swimming pool. And a number of guests were swimming.'

'Not naked.'

'No, not naked. But many people were drunk, and it was seen as fun; daring, yes, but high spirits.'

'High spirits? It wasn't the "Swinging 60s" then. This happened in 1953. People would have been absolutely scandalised, wouldn't they?'

'It is true that many people were shocked. But others weren't. They'd been drinking heavily too. I remember one or two other women jumped in, wearing just their underwear.'

'Am I right in thinking that the newspapers got hold of that story too?' asks Charles, and to forestall a negative answer, he brandishes a file of newspaper clippings he has compiled.

'They did.'

'She couldn't have done your career any good.'

'I really don't know.'

'Come now. Anyone who knows how the Lord Chancellor's department operates knows that silk and judicial promotion come to sober, establishment, conservative lawyers, not those frequently the subject of gossip columns.'

'Perhaps. You'd know more about that than I.'

Charles's ears crimson, and he smiles. 'Touché. We are both no strangers to unwelcome publicity,' he says. 'Did you apply for silk before your wife's death?'

'Yes,' answers Steele, after a momentary hesitation.

'How many times?'

'Four.'

'Unsuccessful?'

'Yes. But so are many the first times they apply. I know some who've succeeded at the eighth attempt.'

'Did you apply after your wife was dead?'

'Yes, evidently.'

'And you were successful?'

'Yes.'

'At the first attempt?'

'It was my fifth attempt, but the first after my wife's death.'

'How long afterwards were you elevated to the Bench?'

'Two years.'

'And how long after that before you were promoted to the Court of Appeal?'

'Five years.'

'A pretty meteoric rise then?'

'I was fortunate.'

'And very clever.'

'The Lord Chancellor does not habitually appoint idiots to the Court of Appeal.'

Charles swivels to look at the jury in response to that answer, and is pleased to see that their reaction is the same as his own: the sarcasm was misplaced and came across as arrogant.

'You knew very well that your wife was a handicap to your career,' continues Charles.

'Of course she was, but that's no reason to kill her. As the Americans say: those are the breaks. Everyone suffers difficulties in their life, and most think it's unfair. But life is unfair. People do not by and large kill their spouses, or others who cause them difficulties.'

'Most do not have to endure what you did.'

Steele shrugs. 'That's not a question, Mr Holborne. I don't know how to answer you.'

'Do you love your eldest son?'

'I love all my children.'

'He had particular difficulties, did he not?'

'Not for some time.'

'At that time, though, he did,' presses Charles. 'I'd like to read you something, and then ask for your comments.'

Charles picks up two documents, the first the statement by the boy's headmaster, and the second a report from an educational psychologist who saw the boy a year earlier. Charles reads selected passages dealing with the child's stammer, his unhappiness at school, and his relationship with his mother.

'Do you agree with what I've just read?'

'He was very unhappy at that time. That's true.'

'And that unhappiness was caused by your wife?'

'Largely, yes.'

'Has he wholly recovered from those earlier problems?' asks Charles.

'Yes, completely. All the children seem happy and reasonably well-balanced, thank God.'

'So, let's look at the consequences of your wife's death. Your career took off, your children were all much happier, your son's psychological problems resolved, the threat of a public and bitter custody battle was lifted, and your public humiliation at your wife's hands ceased.'

'Yes.'

'Each one of these effects was predicable before she died, was it not?'

'I suppose so.'

'You did have a motive for murder then, didn't you?'

'You might have asked me that right at the outset Mr Holborne, and I'd have saved you the time of this carefully constructed cross-examination. Yes, I *did* have a motive. She was an awful, destructive person, particularly to those close to her, and at times I hated her. But I'm not a killer — at least, not willingly. It's not in my nature. I have been wedded to the law since I was a student and I believe in it. I'm also a Christian. Killing people is just not done.'

One or two of the jury members smile and one laughs briefly.

'If you believed in the law, why didn't you report the death immediately? If you believed in the law, why dump your wife's rotting corpse in a lake at dead of night?'

'Mr Holborne!' protests the Recorder. 'That's enough of that! I won't have you trying to influence this jury with tabloid emotionalism.'

'Sorry, my Lord.'

'I made an error,' continues Steele. 'We all make errors. I was frightened and confused. I had never been in such a situation before, and my faith in the system was not as strong as I thought it was. Once I had embarked on it though, it was too late to go back. It would have been one thing to report her death to the police, quite another to report it and tell them I'd disposed of the body. That would have *guaranteed* a sceptical response and an investigation.'

Charles changes tack again. 'Had it not been for Tiffen's Rock, and an astonishing set of coincidences, you would have got away with it.'

'Is that a question?' asks the Recorder.

'I'm sorry, my Lord, I'll rephrase it. Your cover-up of the actual killing was successful, was it not? The redecorating, the staining of the floorboards, washing all the bedclothes and so on, all that?'

'Yes, it was.'

'And you managed to get your wife's body out of the house without it being seen?'

'So I believe.'

'You set up your alibi — at least for the time of the disposal of the body — and that seems to have worked?'

Steele looks rather puzzled, but continues to agree. 'Yes.'

'And you managed to get your wife, with a heavy weight, all the way to the deepest lake in England, drop her body in, and get back without being discovered.'

'That is correct.'

'Had it not been for the circumstance that you just happened, in the dark, to drop the body over Tiffen's Rock, thirty-five metres below you, and had the body not landed at just the right depth to preserve it, and had the plastic sheeting been just tight enough to prevent the fishes eating the body — had that series of events not conspired against you, you would have got away with it.'

'It's possible.'

'I suggest that the facts show that your disposal of your wife's body was meticulously planned and very precisely executed.'

'I was making it up as I went along, actually.'

'Do you deny that, less than five minutes ago, there was pride in your voice as you described what you did?' shouts Charles, with such volume that the court jumps.

'That's not true!' protests Steele, looking from Charles to the Recorder and then to the jury.

'It *is* true,' asserts Charles, his voice now quiet and deadly. 'I'm sure the jury heard it as well as I did.'

Steele remains facing the jury box, his face a picture of mixed astonishment and horror. They are all examining him closely. Charles knows he's hit a nerve. He's right; the jury *did* hear it.

'I'm not proud of it,' beseeches the accused man. 'Not at all. It was a nightmare. I didn't know what to do. I was in a blind panic. I was so tired at the end of it I couldn't think at all.'

'The truth is that you planned the entire thing from start to finish. You knew precisely how you would dispose of your wife's body long before she was dead.'

'No. No! I had to think it through after it happened. I have a logical mind, and I'm methodical, that's all; it's been my training for thirty years!'

'You'd have the jury believe that you acted in "a blind panic", when you've admitted to a cold methodical clean-up and redecoration of the home; careful manhandling of your wife's body, a kerbstone and a dinghy into the boot of your car; the fabrication of a detailed false alibi involving handing out prizes at your son's sports day; even the purchase of a set of spare bulbs for the car! All that was done in "a blind panic"?'

'No, not all of it. I *was* in a blind panic, but once I had decided on a course of action…'

'I see. Well, I have no further questions, my Lord,' says Charles, and he begins to sit down.

'May I say something further?' asks Steele of the Recorder.

'Yes?'

Steele turns back to the jury and appeals directly to them. 'You have to understand that from the second I realised that Lise was dead, my overriding concern was for the children. Everything I did, I did for them, to spare them. I can't explain it well in words, but if you have children maybe you'll understand. They'd been so unhappy when Lise was alive, and

I hadn't been able to protect them properly. Now they were at even greater risk, and that was my fault too, even if it was an accident. I have no near family, a brother who lives abroad, that's all, and the thought of them going into care or even being split up among distant relatives was unbearable. For hours and hours I couldn't make up my mind what was right, but then, at the end of it, the one thing I had left, the one thing that kept coming back, was the knowledge that they'd trusted me to look after them, and I'd failed them. I'd failed them up 'til then, and I wouldn't... I *couldn't* fail them again. They needed me.'

There is a painful catch in his voice now as he speaks.

'Had they been grown up, I *would've* gone to the police, they could've managed perhaps ... but ... Bobby was just a baby. And Stephen was so unhappy ... so unhappy...'

Charles doesn't need to look at the jury to know what effect this is having. He can hear the love and desperation in the man's voice, and he tries to understand it.

Fathers and sons, he thinks again. Would I have gambled everything for my children? he asks himself. He can't say; he's never felt this sort of love, this unreasoning selflessness of a parent for a child, but he can see that most of the members of the jury have. There are tears in the eyes of more than one, and the faces of the rest tell the same story. Charles suddenly feels deprived, excluded from an understanding that he realises, belatedly, is important.

Steele's voice has now dropped and he speaks with great control. 'You see, it *had* to be planned and carried out meticulously: everything, *everything* depended on it. That's what I'm trained to do, to think calmly under pressure and to carry out a carefully-constructed plan. And if my voice showed pride or something like that, I'm sorry, really I am, because I am not proud of anything I've done.' He pauses, and then adds: 'Except one thing: I *did* manage to protect my children until now, when they *are* grown up, and able to cope alone. I have *that* of which to be proud.'

A heavy charged silence descends on the courtroom. Steele sinks down slowly onto the seat behind him.

'Re-examination?' asks the Recorder of Beaverbrook. Beaverbrook shakes his head, remaining in his seat. He wants no noise to break in upon the emotions now running through each and every one of the twelve jury members.

CHAPTER 33

The following morning, Charles rises to deliver his closing speech. It's short. He relies heavily on the planning and execution of the disposal of the body, the lies to the police in interview, and the inherent unlikelihood of an innocent Court of Appeal judge panicking and deciding to commit a serious criminal offence by disposing of a body. He is fair, reminding them of the burden and standard of proof, making it clear that if the jury thinks Steele is telling the truth, or even that he *might* be, it would be their duty to acquit. It's a powerful speech and Charles delivers it with his usual passion and humour, but his heart's not in it. He already knows the result of the trial and that, no matter what he says, he doesn't think he can influence it.

He feels that sense of deflation and disappointment on losing a case, that sensation all barristers experience even after decades at the Bar. It's a professional risk; in every contested trial there's always one losing barrister, and there are none who haven't experienced that sinking feeling in the pit of their stomachs when the jury returns with the "wrong" verdict, confirming that a winnable trial has slipped away.

Somehow this feels worse. It's not even the fact that this is such a high-profile case or that its loss might affect his chances of promotion to silk. Plenty of barristers get silk on the back of losing big cases; it's the prominence that counts and having done a good job despite all. On top of the deflation there's a sense of … sadness.

As he sits, Charles's attention is drawn to a movement at the back of the court. He sees the door closing, but he's convinced the person slipping out of the courtroom was Sally. Part of him is pleased that she'd want to be there, to see him in action again; it might mean she still has feelings for him. On the other hand, another part of him is sorry; she'll have witnessed his failure.

Beaverbrook's speech takes longer. He reminds Charles of a bulldozer: not fast or pretty, but strong, and he just keeps coming. He runs through most of the evidence, returning time and again to the standard of proof: how could the jury be *sure* the defendant killed premeditatedly, or even intended serious harm? Although it wasn't possible to group it, some of that blood in the bedroom could have been, almost certainly was, that of the accused. The Crown cannot prove otherwise. And if so, the Crown cannot disprove self-defence or accident. Either way, how can anyone say they're *sure* it didn't happen as Steele claims?

Finally, the QC moves to Steele's evidence. This is what the jury's been waiting for. Charles has seen it many times before: the jury reach their own conclusions on the evidence but they, the most important of all the actors in court, have no voice until the verdict. So they wait for a champion to put into words, in public, what they've been saying to one another in their private discussions in the jury room. Then they will nod and smile their agreement, almost with relief. Charles terms it "*jury catharsis.*" Beaverbrook doesn't disappoint.

'Lastly, I want to say a few words about the accused's evidence. You heard it; it is for you to judge it, but did it not resound with the truth? Can anyone in this court not have heard the love, the *desperation* in his voice? Can't you *feel* just what he felt in those crucial hours as he paced that bedroom, torn between doing what was right in the eyes of the law, and what he believed was right by his young children? Those of us who have children, especially very young ones, we know this feeling. We know that sometimes ... sometimes, there is no risk too great, no sacrifice too much.'

Again Charles feels excluded from a club whose rules he doesn't understand.

'Mr Holborne says that from the careful, well-executed disposal of the deceased's body, you may infer that the accused killed his wife in cold blood. He says that all that care and attention to detail point only to cold, calculating evil. I say that it was just the opposite: it was love, love for those children, a love which shone so clearly from every word of his evidence.'

He pauses, and when he continues, his voice is slow and deliberate.

'There is only one possible verdict in this case, and we all know what it is: *not guilty.*'

He resumes his seat, staring hard at the jury, challenging, defying them, to disagree. The silence in the courtroom crackles like static electricity. Then, his voice low, as if not wanting to disturb the atmosphere, the Recorder of London starts his summing up.

The judge begins with an explanation of the law of murder. It is skilful and scrupulously fair. He explains in a clear, sensible way that no jury could misunderstand and he summarises the evidence simply, drawing together the threads of the Crown's case and then doing the same for the Defence. Had the jury been hoping for some hint of how he viewed the evidence, they'd have been disappointed. The entire summing up takes less than two hours. Then he asks the barristers if either of them has any points they believe he should have addressed but omitted, and on being informed that there are none, he has the jury bailiffs sworn in and the six men and six women file out to start considering their verdicts.

The Recorder rises to allow the court to clear. He is to hear a guilty plea while he waits for the jury. Charles turns to Jones.

'What do you think?' asks the solicitor.

'I think I need a coffee,' replies Charles, so they go to the public restaurant.

The room is full of solicitors, barristers, witnesses, defendants and their families. The air is heavy with cigarette smoke, talk of evidence and chances and tension. Jones finds an empty table by the door while Charles collects two cups of coffee. He puts them on the table and takes off his wig, rubbing his hands vigorously through his dark curls.

'He'll be acquitted,' he says simply as he sits. 'I don't know if I believe him, but I'm bloody certain the jury does.'

'It looked better before the trial.'

'As I said then, we had powerful evidence of disposing of the body, but only just enough for trial on murder or manslaughter.'

'Well, it hasn't been a waste of time. Judges shouldn't go around dumping their wives in lakes, even if they didn't mean to kill them.'

'I agree. It sets a bad example.'

'How long do you think the jury'll be?' asks Jones.

'God knows. Ever read A. A. Milne?' Jones shakes his head. 'You should. Anyway, juries are like Heffalumps, and as Pooh says of Heffalumps, "*You never can tell.*" I gave up predicting what juries would do years ago.'

'I don't think they'll be long. It's pretty straightforward, one way or the other.'

'Yes, but what if there's six one way and six the other? Or even eleven one way and one the other?'

'They should allow for majority verdicts. Having one single juror disagree and cause a retrial is crazy.'

'I agree. It's also an invitation to corruption. It's very easy to bribe one or two jurors. There's talk of a change in the law soon. But not soon enough for us, today.'

At a quarter to one, the lawyers drift towards No. 1 Court again. The guilty plea has finished and the Recorder has retired to his chambers. An usher approaches Charles and shakes her head.

'They've asked for sandwiches. The Judge says he'll not take a verdict until after two-thirty at the earliest.'

'Thanks,' says Charles. He turns to Jones who heard the conversation. 'I think I'll pop back to Chambers for a while. I've done no other work for the last two weeks, and I'll try to return a few phone calls.'

'Fine. See you later.'

Charles changes and walks back down Fleet Street to the Temple. Two or three members of Chambers are in, and they stop Charles to ask about the case. He answers shortly, takes the pile of telephone messages waiting for him, and goes to his room to starts working through them. The last surprises him; it's from his mother. He can't remember the last time she rang him at work. On the very rare occasion when she does call Charles, she usually rings the flat where she can leave a message with Dennis if necessary. The message is dated from three days before. Charles dials David's number and his mother answers.

'Hello, Mum, it's me.'

'Charles. Good of you to call,' the subtext of which six words say: "I've waited three days for you to return my call, but there was no hurry. I'm only your mother, after all."

Despite himself, Charles feels impelled to give excuses. 'I've only just got your message. Why didn't you phone the flat? Is anything wrong?'

'No.'

Charles senses her struggling with herself. She wants to continue to criticise him — that's what their relationship is about — but she evidently wants something else too. Immoveable object meets irresistible force, and irresistible force wins. 'I need your help.'

My God, thinks Charles, what those words must have cost her!

'How can I help you, Mum?'

'Are you going to *shul* on *Yom Kippur*?'

Yom Kippur, the Day of Atonement, the holiest of all holy days.

'I hadn't thought about it. I doubt it. I went last week on impulse.'

'Well, if you could have another such impulse, I'd be grateful.'

'Why?'

'Because you'd be doing me a favour, that's all.'

'No, I mean: why do you want me to go?'

'I need a reason? I can't ask my eldest son to do something for me without explaining the whys and wherefores?'

Charles draws a deep breath. 'I'll do what I can Mum. No promises, but if I can get there, I will.'

'Fine, so don't do me any favours, OK?'

'Got to go, Mum. I'm due back in court.'

'So, go already,' she says, as if he has been detaining *her*, and she hangs up.

Charles makes a further call before leaving Chambers. He picks up a bacon sandwich from Mick's on Fleet Street and eats it while walking back to the Old Bailey.

He replays the conversation with his mother in his head. The last time she called with such urgency in her voice was when

Harry had a suspected heart attack, a couple of years before. She never does anything without a motive, reasons Charles. And the motive here? Charles isn't sure, but maybe an olive branch?

At the Old Bailey, before going upstairs to change, he puts his head into the courtroom. There's another case in progress. The usher spots Charles at the door and shakes her head. Charles waves in acknowledgment and heads to the fourth floor.

The robing room is almost deserted, most barristers having returned to their courts by two o'clock. He walks up the staircase to the fifth floor to get himself a coffee, but the pot is still empty after the lunchtime rush. He asks for a fresh pot and installs himself in his favourite seat by the window.

He picks up a discarded newspaper and opens it, but only pretends to read. He hates this part of the case. Some barristers bring other papers with them and work away industriously while waiting for their juries. Charles can't do it; he's unable to concentrate. Particularly on important cases, his mind is invariably drawn back to the trial: to the points in his speech that he might have made just a little more powerfully; to the one question in cross-examination that he could have pursued a bit further; or, more often, to the one question he shouldn't have asked at all. When he started in practice over twenty years ago, he used to wonder if more experience would end these mental inquests, but it hasn't. No matter how skilled he becomes, he can always find something he wishes he'd done even slightly differently.

So he sits there, cursing, because he said something in his speech that hadn't received its customary nod of approval from a single jury member and he couldn't work out why. As the waiter brings out a fresh pot of coffee and calls his name, so the tannoy announces that all parties in the case of the *Queen versus Steele* should return to No. 1 Court.

Sod's law again, he thinks. Often, when juries are taking an inordinate time to return with a verdict, he tells all the barristers waiting to order a drink; it invariably prompts an announcement requiring them to return immediately to court.

He thanks the man for the coffee and starts the descent to the ground floor. Verdict or question? he wonders.

'We've a verdict,' says Jones as Charles enters court.

Charles looks at the clock. Only four and a quarter hours. He is one of the last to arrive. The gallery and the journalist's bench are already packed and there's a hushed intensity about their whispers. The barrister's bench is full of members of the Bar who'd suddenly found a few minutes to spare from their other duties. Charles squeezes along the bench. A couple of barristers he knows, and on whose toes he is treading, pat him on the back or wish him luck as he goes past. He reaches a space and pulls his papers towards him. He glances over his shoulder at the man in the dock. Steele looks thin, and every one of his sixty-one years sits heavily on his shoulders. The usher calls everyone to rise, and the Recorder of London enters court. He sits immediately, as does everyone else in court except the accused. He stands at the rail of the dock, gripping it with both hands, his knuckles showing white.

The clerk stands, indictment in hand. Charles's heart pounds, as it always does in the seconds before a verdict is delivered. Despite his predictions, one never knows...

'Would the foreman of the jury please rise?' asks the clerk.

A woman from the back row has been transplanted to the front, nearest to the clerk, and she stands. She's in her thirties, with a sharp intelligent face. She took notes in shorthand throughout the trial, and Charles had guessed she'd vote to convict. The clerk addresses her.

'Please answer my next question either "Yes" or "No". Has the jury reached a verdict or verdicts on this indictment upon which they are all agreed?'

'Yes,' she replies in a firm voice.

'On Count 1 on the Indictment, do you find the defendant guilty or not guilty of the charge of murder?'

She pauses for a second. 'Not guilty.'

There's a sharp intake of breath round the court, but no one speaks.

'On Count 2 on the Indictment, do you find the defendant guilty or not guilty on the charge of manslaughter?'

'Not guilty.'

A sigh erupts from the court, which grows instantly in intensity and then crashes, like a wave, over the heads of everyone present. Everyone speaks at once and the clerk bangs his gavel to no effect. Some of the journalists race out of court to phone through the verdicts, and parts of the gallery erupt into applause.

Charles turns to study Steele. He remains in precisely the same position as he was before the verdict was delivered, his knuckles just as white, his face expressionless. Then gradually his knees bend and buckle, and he sinks to the seat behind him, his hands still hanging onto the rail.

'I shall rise for a moment!' calls the Recorder over the din. 'Take Mr Steele down until order has been restored!'

An hour later, Anthony Steele emerges, blinking into the glare of flashbulbs and spotlights, onto the pavement of the Old Bailey. Jenny Sullivan is with him, and the children, and they pose momentarily together, a happy family group, Steele's arm round Jenny's waist. Questions hurtle in from all sides and Steele bats back answers as if returning tennis balls.

'What do you think of the verdicts, sir?'

'I have always had complete faith in the English jury system, and that has been vindicated once more.'

'What about the sentence for obstructing the coroner? It's a heavy fine.'

'What I did was wrong, and I accept that. Fines are supposed to hurt, and if, like me, you're wealthy, it's only right that the fine is heavy.'

'What are your plans, my Lord?'

'I shall be handing my resignation to the Lord Chancellor tomorrow morning.'

'What will you do then?'

'We shall see. I've always wanted time to devote to writing my memoirs.'

'Will you two marry?' ask two reporters in unison.

Steele and Jenny look, laughing, into one another's eyes, and everyone knows the answer. Half a dozen flashes go off simultaneously as the tabloid press gets the photograph that will adorn all the front pages the next morning.

'Can we have one with the children, too?' they shout, and Steele is happy to oblige.

A large car pulls up swiftly at the kerbside and its passenger door opens. A man jumps out and swiftly ushers the family in. Amid protests from the reporters, the doors slam and the car speeds off.

CHAPTER 34

Dusk is falling, it's raining hard and there's nowhere to shelter.

You'd think that blackmailers collecting their money would be on time, thinks Charles.

He started on the bench where he last sat with McArthur, but when the heavens opened he ran to the shelter of a large tree. Even here he's getting soaked. The large manila envelope under his arm is almost saturated, and he begins to worry that its contents will spill out of the sodden paper.

Charles looks up and down the park again but he remains the only person visible. Everyone else, the dog walkers, the mums with prams and the homeless man who apparently lives on an adjacent bench, all have disappeared. Another peel of thunder cracks above Charles and is followed immediately by lightning so bright that it creates a fleeting chiaroscuro outline of the trees on the grass.

Charles looks again at his watch and resolves to give McArthur another ten minutes. He pulls the collar of his raincoat up further, hunches his shoulders and leans against the bole of the tree. A sudden gust of wind bends the branches towards him and he is drenched further.

He sees a figure enter the park from the main road, take a few steps down the gravel path and hesitate. Charles identifies McArthur's solid shape and steps out from the tree to make himself visible.

McArthur stops and waves impatiently to Charles to join him. Charles starts towards the other man, and it's as if he's walking, fully-clothed, into a shower. Out in the open he is assailed by sheets of rain, harried this way and that by the wind.

They cause McArthur's appearance to be oddly blurred, ghost-like.

Charles calls as he nears the blackmailer. 'Can we get out of the rain to do this?'

'No need,' comes McArthur's shout in reply. 'Just hand it over.'

'No. I want to get a few things straight. You're not just walking off with a grand without a word.'

Charles now stands before the man. Both have water dripping off their noses. 'Look, there's a café just round the corner. It'll take two minutes. I'll even throw in a cuppa.'

'I ain't drinking tea with you, Horowitz. We ain't mates.'

'Fine. I'll drink the tea and you can drip. But I'm not doing it here.'

Charles takes the initiative and strides past him towards the exit. McArthur whirls round, trying to grab Charles's arm as he goes past, but misses. He remains stationary for another moment and then reluctantly follows.

The café is in a small parade of shops a hundred yards from the station. The plate glass windows are obscured by condensation, but the lights are on and the place glows with comfort and warmth.

As Charles pushes open the door a bell jingles and the aromas of fried food, toast and cigarettes greet him. The place is only half-full, mainly with people nursing cups of tea while sheltering from the torrential rain.

Charles strides to the Formica counter behind which a West Indian woman and a white man are busy buttering toast and pouring tea from a large stainless steel pot. Charles hears the bell ring a second time and looks over his shoulder to see that McArthur has followed him in. He points to an empty corner table and calls.

'You sure about the tea?'

McArthur nods, and navigates the narrow gaps between the tables to the corner indicated by Charles.

Charles orders a cup of tea and a slice of buttered toast, the manila envelope clamped firmly under one arm.

This is better, he thinks. McArthur has already demonstrated a tendency to impetuosity and carelessness for consequences, and that's less likely to occur here, in close proximity to members of the public, than in a darkening and rain-swept park.

Charles pays and takes his plate to the table. He pulls off his saturated raincoat, hangs it on a hook on the wall beside him, and does the same with his hat.

He sits and places the envelope in front of him. McArthur, still in his coat and hat and dripping onto the table, reaches across immediately but Charles leans back out of reach and holds the envelope fast.

'Just wait a minute,' he says, smiling, and in the tone he'd use to chide a toddler for grabbing at a birthday present. 'I've something to say first.'

McArthur's eyes swivel round the small café, estimating his chances of grabbing the envelope, perhaps punching Charles and running for it. He evidently decides against. 'What?' he challenges.

'There's less in there than you wanted, but there's also something else. And before you fly off the handle, I suggest you have a look and think. Hard. Because this is the one and only offer you're going to get from me.'

'How much?' demands McArthur, managing to control his voice with difficulty.

Charles doesn't answer but pushes the envelope across the table.

McArthur grabs it and tears the sodden paper. Inside he finds a small bundle of banknotes held together with a rubber band. There is also a thick sheaf of typed paper. He ignores the paper and flicks through the banknotes.

'There can't be more than £100 here!' he hisses, leaning forward dangerously.

'Spot on. There's *exactly* £100 there. And before you say anything else, I suggest you look at what else is in that envelope.'

McArthur glares at Charles and places his palms flat on the sticky tabletop, about to stand and launch himself across it.

'Look at it, Mikey,' repeats Charles. 'Before you make a major mistake.'

Charles watches the man battle with himself. The habits of a lifetime, which for forty years or more have led him in and out of fights and prison, vie with a slender residue of better judgement and caution. In the end, it is the unconscious fear that Charles is cleverer than he is and might possibly have something dangerous up his sleeve that prevents an explosion of anger and frustration.

McArthur relaxes slightly in his seat and pulls the bundle of papers towards him. He has seen this type of document many times before over the years, since his first arrest in his early teens for assault occasioning actual bodily harm: prosecution depositions.

'What the fuck…?'

'Just read, Mikey. You can read, can't you?'

Mikey McArthur reads.

Deposition of May Carter
Occupation: Nurse
Address:

Magistrates Court Rules 1952: This deposition of May Carter, Nurse, of [insert address], was sworn before me, [   ], Justice of the Peace, on [   ] 1965 in the presence of [   ] at the [   ] Magistrates' Court.

Signed:
Signature of deponent:

May Carter WILL SAY AS FOLLOWS:

I am a staff nurse employed at the [   ] hospital at [insert address]. I have been asked to recall an event which occurred in December 1940. I remember it very well because it was so frightening. In fact, I had nightmares about it for years afterwards and still have occasional flashbacks to it.

I do not remember the precise date, but it was about two weeks before Christmas 1940, and was during the Blitz of London. I was with a friend, Louise Silvester, on Commercial Road in the City of London when an air raid started. We found ourselves surrounded by incendiaries, and were going to run for it when a van pulled up and a young man opened the door. He threw an air warden's hat over the nearest incendiary and grabbed us. We got in the van and it drove off. We decided to go to the Prospect of Whitby pub to shelter from the air raid. I had been there before to shelter in the cellars. The man who drove the van was named Izzy and the younger man who jumped out of the passenger seat was called Charlie.

We got safely to the Prospect and Izzy dropped the three of us off. He said he was going to park the van somewhere safe and would come back in a minute. I went down to the cellar with Louise and Charlie. After a while Izzy had not returned and Charlie went upstairs. He said he was going to look for Izzy. Only a minute or two after that the all-clear sirens sounded. We all went up the stairs into the saloon bar. The electricity went back on and we could see that a fight was in progress in the bar. Izzy was tied by his wrists to the bar and was taking a beating from two men. I recognised both. One was a Blackshirt called Bledsoe, and the other was Mikey McArthur. They both lived and worked near my family in the East End and I had known them for years. I have no doubt about their identities.

They were beating Izzy so severely that I thought they were going to kill him. Bledsoe was doing the punching when I first saw them, but McArthur was urging him on. Then I saw Charlie intervene. He hit McArthur with a bar stool and knocked him out. Bledsoe then attacked Charlie. Charlie was forced to defend himself. He finished up straddling Bledsoe's chest and we pulled him off.

I am convinced that if Charlie hadn't intervened, Izzy would have been killed or very seriously injured. His face was completely mashed and there was blood all over his shirt.

I am prepared to give evidence in respect of this matter.
Signed: May Carter

'What the fuck is this?' demands McArthur.

'You can see for yourself. They're depositions taken from other witnesses in the *Prospect* that night. The witnesses' addresses have been blanked out so you can't get at them. Read on.'

McArthur leafs at random to another deposition.

Deposition of Andrew Felsted
Occupation: Publican
Address: [   ]

Magistrates Court Rules 1952: This deposition of Andrew Felsted, Publican, of [insert address] was sworn before me, [   ], Justice of the Peace, on [insert date] 1965 in the presence of [   ], at the [   ] Magistrates' Court.

Signed:
Signature of deponent: Andrew Felsted

Andrew Felsted WILL SAY AS FOLLOWS:

I am the licensee of the [   ] public house in [   ]. In December 1940 I was 18 years of age and was about to be called up to the Royal Navy. At the time I had some temporary part-time work as a barman at the Prospect of Whitby public house at Wapping Wall, London, E1. It was several hundred yards from the Prospect to the nearest air raid shelter, and we used to allow customers and other local residents to shelter in the cellars of the pub during air raids. I was on duty in the fortnight before Christmas when the bombing of London by the Luftwaffe was very intensive. I remember a night during that period when there was an air raid. The cellar was, as usual, full of people sheltering from the bombs. When the all-clear sounded we all went upstairs. The pub was in darkness because the electricity had been cut, so when we reached the bar area it was still dark. Then the power was reconnected, and all the lights went on.

We were faced with a scene I shall never forget. Two men who were known to me as local people and regulars in the pub, called Alec Bledsoe and Mikey McArthur, were in the saloon bar. They had tied another man to the bar by his wrists and were giving him a real thrashing. He was powerless to defend himself. I knew this man as well. He was a lighterman and a regular at the Prospect. His name was Izzy Conway, although he was known to me by his river nickname, which was "Merlin". Merlin looked as if he was unconscious. His head was hanging down and he was only held upright by the ropes tying his wrists to the bar rail. His face was

335

a complete mess with blood all over it. Bledsoe was standing in front of him repeatedly punching him in the face and body, and McArthur was right next to him, encouraging him on. We all came to a halt at the head of the stairs. Then another young man, who I didn't know, intervened. He was very strongly built with dark curly hair, and he swung a bar stool at McArthur, who fell to the floor. Bledsoe rushed at the young man, throwing punches, and the young man defended himself. He eventually knocked Bledsoe down.

I am sure that if the young man had not stopped the fight, Bledsoe and McArthur would have killed Merlin or at least done him very serious injury. I do not know why they were attacking Merlin in the way they were.

I am prepared to give evidence in respect of this matter if I'm asked to do so. It was a very shocking scene and one that I have never forgotten.

Signed: Andrew Felsted.

'There are sixteen statements there, Mikey, and they all say the same thing: you and Bledsoe were beating Izzy to death and that I was acting in self-defence. Every one of them will give evidence against you.'

McArthur leans forward. 'Yeh, but they don't say you killed Alec, do they?' he says triumphantly.

'No, they don't.'

'Well they're all fucking liars, then.' He almost shouts this, causing others to turn and stare at them.

'The point is, Mikey, it's going to be your evidence against seventeen other witnesses. You say I killed Bledsoe. They say I was defending Izzy and if I hadn't intervened you'd have killed him. They say Bledsoe attacked me and I had no choice but defend myself.'

'Bledsoe's still ended up dead, with you on top of him.'

Charles waves his hand, dismissing the point. 'Bledsoe died when a wall fell on him. Bombs were dropping everywhere. If you go to the police, it's going to be you answering the difficult questions. Like, what were you and Bledsoe doing, beating the shit out of some young lighterman? There are sixteen witnesses there, not including me, who say you were going to kill him. Attempted murder? With your record? Who do you think the police will believe?'

'They're never going to turn up and actually give evidence after all this time,' says McArthur defiantly, but Charles sees doubt in his eyes.

'They were perfectly happy to give me statements. Not a single witness turned me down. And do you know why? 'Cos they still hate you. Yes, after all this time. You and Bledsoe made their lives a misery during the war — walking into shops and taking what you wanted; smashing shop windows; terrorising people — and not just Jews. East End folk have long memories. You should know that.'

McArthur's face contorts as he tries to think his way out of the problem Charles has presented to him. He brandishes the wad of banknotes.

'What's this for, then?'

'Travel money. Go back to the Lake District. Go anywhere, I don't care. But just fuck off out of London. If I see you again, it'll be me going to the police, with this lot,' and he jabs his finger on the statements.

McArthur sweeps the documents off the table and into his clutches, momentary triumph in his eyes.

'Yes, keep them, by all means,' says Charles with a smile. 'I have copies, of course. They're with my solicitor. If anything ever happens to me, he has instructions to send them to the Met.'

Charles waits patiently for McArthur's decision. He takes a sip of hot tea and a bite of warm buttery toast.

Without another word, McArthur stands and throws the draft depositions back onto the table. He shoves the £100 into his jacket pocket.

'You're a fucking smug, Jew-boy cunt!' he shouts, and he reaches over and flips Charles's saucer up, spilling tea over his jacket and into his lap. He then whirls around and storms out of the café, slamming the door behind him and leaving the little bell jangling. Charles reaches for some paper napkins and starts dabbing tea off his front.

'Not hot enough for him,' he explains to the spectators with an insouciant smile.

Charles grimaces as he pulls on his saturated raincoat and squelchy hat. He gathers together the draft depositions and rolls them into a tube to keep as a souvenir. Concocting them had not taken long, but he'd never learned to type, so his clunky two-fingered creation of the false statements on spare deposition sheets found lying around Chambers had taken him several evenings. Worth the effort, however, he thinks. He pops the last bite of toast in his mouth, raises his hat to the people behind the counter, and heads back out into the rain.

CHAPTER 35

'Is he in?' asks Charles.

'Yes, sir,' replies Mr Justice Steele's clerk. 'You're lucky you caught him. He's packing up to leave. I'll just announce you.'

The clerk moves off down the wide corridor, his footsteps muffled by the thick blue carpet. Charles examines the oil paintings on the wall: originals, he guesses. Very different from the Royal Courts of Justice's *public* corridors, he thinks. The clerk, a thick-set man with black hair glued horizontally to his scalp by half a jar of Brylcreem knocks deferentially on a door marked "Sir Anthony Steele" and waits to be invited to enter. A few moments later, he steps back into the corridor and beckons to Charles.

'His Lordship will see you now,' he announces.

Charles enters and the door closes softly behind him. The room is beautiful: large and well-lit, with a tall, ornate ceiling and a chandelier hanging from an impressive ceiling rose. Two walls are lined with bookcases, a third with oak panelling surrounding a tall marble fireplace, and the last containing a large window overlooking a courtyard. The furniture, upholstered in red leather, looks and smells expensive and comfortable. The floor and desk are dotted with boxes and books.

To Charles's surprise, Steele wears a green and blue check shirt and corduroy trousers. He looks a decade younger than he did five days earlier when the trial ended. His arms are full of books.

'Holborne. To what do I owe this pleasure? Come to say goodbye?' He speaks easily, without rancour.

'Partly, my Lord.'

'It's "judge" when in chambers, and it's not even that now. So "Mr Steele" is probably sufficient.'

Charles stands uncomfortably by the threshold. Steele mistakes his hesitation, and is cheery and welcoming.

'Well, come in, take a seat. I hold no grudges. You did your job, well and fairly. I couldn't have asked for a straighter closing speech.'

'I did it fairly perhaps. But not very well.'

'You do what you can with what you're given.'

Steele continues to potter about, stacking books on the floor, selecting some to go into boxes and some for the bin, but then something about the quality of the silence makes him look up. Charles is staring at him, his eyes narrowed, his lips set in a hard line. Steele suddenly becomes uneasy.

'Look, I don't know what you've come here for, Holborne, but as you can see, I'm very busy…'

His voice tails off as he watches Charles hold out his hand. 'The police will return everything else, I expect,' says Charles. 'They collected what I had in Chambers yesterday. I wanted to deliver this in person.'

Steele hesitates and then lowers the books in his arms. He takes the paper bag offered by Charles, opens it and draws out the photograph of himself and his son, each holding one handle of a large silver cup. 'Oh, that is kind. You could have given it to the police, I'm sure.'

'I had it all the time. It was among the things taken from your study when it was searched.'

'Thank you —'

'You never did show your scar to the jury, did you? You took a dreadful risk there. Got carried away, I suppose.'

Charles now has Steele's undivided attention. The disgraced judge lowers the photograph to his crowded desk.

'Do you want to show it to *me*?' asks Charles. 'The scar from the terrible wound your wife inflicted on you? The one that splashed blood all over the room?'

Steele doesn't answer. He leans back against the stone window sill, the noise from the Strand just audible in the background, and stares at Charles, waiting. His body is intensely still, every muscle frozen, and his clear blue eyes are narrowed almost to slits. He is frightened, sees Charles; far more so than before the jury delivered its verdict.

'The photograph's a good one isn't it?' comments Charles conversationally, almost enjoying the fear he is causing. 'I was looking at it yesterday, marvelling how alike you and your son were then, the same fair hair, lean faces, cold hard eyes. Even the way your hands each grasp a handle of that cup. And then, just as I was about to put it back in the box with the diaries and the papers and all the rest, I realised: no bandage; no cut. You can see your hand very clearly. It's unmarked.' Steele continues to stare at Charles silently. 'Are you going to say anything?'

Steele shrugs. 'What would you have me say?'

'Perhaps that you murdered her? Or maybe that it was, after all, manslaughter; you lost your temper, you were provoked into an uncharacteristic outburst. Something like that, perhaps?'

'You think I killed her, deliberately?'

The question puzzles Charles. 'Of course!'

For a split-second, Steele's expression reveals something so unexpected that Charles can't identify it. For an instant, he seems to be on the verge of smiling, his posture relaxes, and he starts to breathe again. Then the frown reappears, but there remains something about him that is different, an inexplicable confidence that makes Charles hesitate.

'What are you going to do?' asks Steele.

'What does it matter? You know the law as well as I; you can't be tried again for it. Double jeopardy. You got away with it.'

'If you say so.'

'I think you *did* murder her. The blood all over the room was not yours, it was hers. There was no knife — or, if there was, it wasn't your wife who used it. But that wasn't the best part, was it, my Lord? The best part was your "confession" to that poor woman.'

Steele shakes his head slowly. 'I don't know what you're talking about,' he says, averting his eyes.

'No, sorry, that doesn't have the right ring to it at all. Do you want to try again? It's a cliché, that one; I wouldn't use those words if I were you. In a way, I find that the most venal thing you've done. You've shamelessly used Jenny Sullivan for the last ten years. You even risked her prosecution as an accomplice, but that didn't bother you. She was your insurance policy. Insurance against the day when the improbable, the almost impossible, occurred, and the body was found and identified.

'You even planned for *that*. You knew she loved you, that she'd never knowingly betray you. So you gave her a story about a knife, about self-defence and a terrible accident. And you cried, and you made her believe it. And then for ten years you kept her at arm's length because as your wife, she wouldn't be compellable as a witness against you. The law says a wife can't be forced to give evidence against her husband. But I *can* force an employee to give evidence against her employer, can't I? And you *wanted* her to be a witness against you; you *needed*

342

her to testify for the prosecution. Such a tragic figure she'd make in the box: a woman in love, forced to betray her heart. How could any jury not believe her, or the false account you'd planted in her?'

'You deduce all this from that one black and white photograph? How do you know I didn't make a mistake and get the date wrong? It could be from the year before!'

'The cup you presented, the one you're holding between you and Stephen, is the inter-house rugby trophy,' replies Charles, pointing at the photograph. 'Stephen's house only won it that year. I checked with the sports master this morning. It didn't win the cup in the eight years previously, and hasn't won it since.'

The judge laughs briefly, a short bark devoid of any mirth. 'I repeat: what are you going to do then?'

'Nothing. You're retiring. I suppose I could have you charged with perjury, but for what purpose? To destroy the woman who stood by you all this time?'

'Then we have nothing more to say.'

Charles wants to say something more, even if it's useless and inadequate. Someone had to say it. 'You're an evil calculating man, and a disgrace to your profession,' he says.

Steele smiles. 'Now who's using clichés?'

He strides to the door and opens it for Charles. Charles stares hard at the older man, thinking seriously about knocking him down. Then he sweeps past Steele and leaves.

CHAPTER 36

It's the day after Charles's interview with the disgraced former judge, and it is *Kol Nidre*. Everywhere throughout the diaspora and in the Holy Land, Jews are preparing to fast for 25 hours. No food, no drink; nothing. Harry makes himself a light lunch, preparing for a large early evening meal, around five or five-thirty, he calculates. He hasn't asked Charles about his plans, but he cooks enough for two anyway. Charles hasn't mentioned his conversation with Millie. Earlier that morning he went into Chambers, read the papers in an armed robbery defence, got bored and returned to Fetter Lane.

The smell of freshly-made soup now fills the flat, making his mouth water. The kitchen in the Horowitz household was always Millie's domain, and no one else was allowed to touch anything in it, let alone do any cooking, but in fact Harry has always been an accomplished cook. He and his sister were both taught by Charles's grandmother, and if anything, Harry had shown the greater aptitude.

The table in the corner of the lounge is laid for two, and without saying anything, Harry ladles out two steaming bowls of soup, less salty than usual — one gets thirsty enough after 25 hours — and places them on the table. Charles sits and eats with his father.

For the first two days after the trial ended, he talked of nothing else, and Harry, realising that his son needed to get it off his chest, listened and tried to make appropriate comments. Now it's talked out. So they chat about David and Sonia and the forthcoming addition to their family. Harry is anxious to have grandchildren before he dies. His peers' grandchildren are all approaching their teens and bar mitzvah age. That's a joy he fears may not be reserved for him, but he'd like a grandson or daughter to crawl all over him, play with his glasses and sit on his knee.

When the soup is finished, Harry collects the bowls and returns to the kitchen. He takes a baked side of salmon out of the oven and re-enters the lounge, brandishing a fish slice and fork, one in each hand.

'Well? Are you eating or not?' he demands.

'Sure, I'll keep you company. I can't remember the last time I ate home-cooked salmon. I don't think I've eaten it here, in the flat, at all.'

Harry serves the meal and they eat in companionable silence. Charles offers to clear up while Harry gets changed. He is only gone fifteen minutes. As he returns to the lounge in his best suit, the intercom buzzes. Charles answers it. 'It's your cab,' he announces.

Harry pulls on his coat while Charles opens the door for him and calls the lift. The two men face one another in the doorway. Harry guesses what's going through his son's mind.

'You can still come, if you want.'

'No thanks, Dad.'

'Got nothing to say to your Maker? No sins you would like to be forgiven?'

'Plenty, but what if there's no one there to do the forgiving?'

'But what if there is?'

Charles shakes his head. 'If there was, the world would be a more just place.'

'Who said the world was going to be fair? Maybe that's the whole point. You've got to learn to cope with it as it is, and maybe do a little to make it better. Well?'

'I don't think so.'

Harry shrugs sadly and enters the lift.

Charles is in bed by the time Harry returns that night and, the next morning, he creeps out of the flat early. Charles eats no breakfast because, he assures himself, he's not hungry. He works with half his mind on the robbery papers until four and then makes a decision.

The synagogue smells of bodies that have not eaten or moved for several hours. Charles sees his father and brother from the back, and goes to sit beside them. Both smile at him and Harry grips his hand for a moment.

'I kept your place for you,' he whispers.

'Thanks, but I could have sat anywhere.'

'I don't mean your seat. I kept your *place*,' and he raises his eyebrows to the heavens. Then he winks, but Charles knows he's only half-joking. If Charles won't save his own soul, Harry will do it for him.

Charles cranes his neck to look up to the gallery but can see neither Millie nor Sonia. He opens his prayer book, finds the page and allows the songs and chants of his childhood to wash over him like a balm as he examines his conscience.

As he prays and sings, his mind keeps drifting back to Steele, not to the trial or even their interview afterwards, but to two photographs taken a decade apart: that of the prize-giving which had revealed the former judge as a liar and probably a murderer, and that taken on the steps of the Old Bailey with his family surrounding him. It was a good photograph, the recent one, so natural, so happy; it made every single national daily. Jenny, looking up into the eyes of the man she could now marry after all those years of waiting, the two younger children, half-laughing and half-crying with relief in the sunshine, and Stephen, the unhappy eldest son.

Charles's mind returns to Stephen. In both photographs, he and his father are staring at one another across the heads of others: two tall, handsome men with identical eyes and identical expressions. It is odd though, Charles muses, that at the very moment of triumph, immediately after his acquittal, Steele should look with such intensity at his eldest son. This was the first time that Steele and Jenny had been in touching distance since, in the full glare of the public eye, they had declared their love for each other, a love suppressed for fifteen years. Yet Steele was not looking adoringly at the woman he could now marry; instead the photographer had caught him staring at Stephen, and their shared glance brimmed with silent communication, the participants' expressions uncannily similar to those in the earlier photograph.

Fathers and sons, thinks Charles again.

Such love there was in that look, such protectiveness, such — and the word flashes into Charles's mind with such an electric clarity that it blots out everything going on around him, the choir, the rabbi and his father's quiet singing beside him — such *sacrifice*!

Charles lowers himself slowly to the bench as the realisation of how mistaken he had been strikes him with a physical impact. The memory of the earlier photograph comes back to him as clearly as if he still held it in his hand. He remembers the cup held aloft between father and son and the revealing lack of bandage on the father's hand, but … then his mind's eye travels across the convex curve of the shiny silver cup until it rests on Stephen's hand; Stephen's *bandaged* hand, the hand that Charles assumed without thinking must have been injured in the victorious game of rugby, but which Charles now knows, beyond any reasonable doubt, had borne a deep cut between thumb and first finger. A cut inflicted by his mother.

347

Harry sits next to Charles. 'Are you all right?' he whispers.

Charles shakes his head. So stunned is he that he cannot speak for a moment. 'He was innocent all along.'

'Who? Your judge?'

Charles nods. 'It was his son … he was covering up for his son.'

Harry thinks about that. 'There you are; justice *was* done after all.'

'But he almost went to prison for murder … his career is finished…'

'So? You think I wouldn't do the same for you or David? How old was the boy, eleven, twelve?'

'Something like that.'

Harry shrugs.

'But … my God … he risked everything!' whispers Charles.

'But you, of all people, should understand,' explains Harry. 'There are those for whom you'd do anything. Lose your job, give up your freedom, even sacrifice your life.' He takes Charles's hand in his. 'You're not going to do anything about it, are you? You'll leave them alone now, surely?'

Charles nods. 'Yes. Of course.'

'Good. Enough damage has been done to that family already, don't you think?'

Charles doesn't answer. For the rest of the service he sits with his prayer book open on his lap, staring into the middle distance, his eyes focused on something invisible to anyone else.

The end of the service is marked, as always, by the blowing of the ancient ram's horn, and, as always, it brings goosebumps to the arms, and tears to the eyes, of many in the congregation. For more than five thousand years it has been the Jewish call to prayer, to war, to life; it has become a race memory, buried deep in the unconscious of Jews throughout the world. The congregation stands en masse, tired and hungry, while the cantor blows his trumpet blasts and the rabbi asks for the last time, on behalf of his community, for forgiveness for the year that is past, and strength for them to be better people in the year that is to come.

Then Charles kisses his brother and his father, and they file out. Again they wait, without speaking, at the foot of the stairs. Sonia and Millie approach and greet them. Millie addresses Charles.

'Thank you, son,' she says. Then she turns to Harry. 'Will you take me home, Harry?' she asks simply.

'Why?'

'Because I was wrong. You're my husband, and my place is by your side. I am truly sorry, and I ask your forgiveness.' Harry smiles at her, his eyes and his heart melting. 'I've prepared a meal, and the house is warm,' she continues. 'Can we be a family again?'

David and Sonia, looking on, beam with pleasure.

'Sure. Let's go home,' he says. He takes her arm.

'And Charles,' she says, turning again to her eldest son. 'I owe you an apology too. Your father's right; I've not treated you fairly.'

'It's fine, Mum.'

'Will you break your fast with us?'

Charles knows that Millie's post-repentant glow of love for all men probably won't last beyond the main course and might even falter at the chicken soup, but he smiles nonetheless.

'I'd be delighted,' he says. 'But I have a call to make on the way.'

Harry turns to him, eyebrows raised.

'You're right. I need to speak to Sally.'

HISTORICAL NOTE

Some of you may remember the case on which *The Waxwork Corpse* is based. A respectable airline pilot killed his wife in the 1970s and dropped her body into Wastwater from a dinghy at the dead of night. I have written his book with his permission, hiding his identity in that of Sir Anthony Steele so as to protect his family. However, the basic facts of the case, in particular how the body was disposed of and most of the pathology evidence, come directly from the court documents.

A NOTE TO THE READER

Dear Reader,

Thank you for taking the time to read the fifth Charles Holborne legal thriller. I am following Charles's story through the 1960s and another book is in the pipeline.

Those of you have been to my one-man show, "My Life in Crime", will know that Charles and his history are based upon me and my own family. Mine was the first generation of Michaels to be born outside the sound of Bow Bells (as you will know, the test for being a "true Cockney") since 1492, when they arrived in the Port of London as refugees from the Spanish Inquisition. Much of the series is autobiographical. Thus, Charles's love of London and the Temple are mine; at the start of my career I experienced the class and religious prejudice faced by him; the plots are based to a greater or lesser extent on cases in which I was instructed as a criminal barrister; many of the strange and wonderful characters who populate the books are based upon witnesses, clients and barristers I have known, represented and admired respectively. I try to take no liberties at all with the operation of police procedure, the criminal justice system or the human heart; the books are as true to life as I can make them. If you find any mistakes, I shall be delighted to hear from you. I always reply, and if you're right, I will make sure future editions are changed.

Nowadays, reviews by readers are essential to authors' success, so if you enjoyed the novel I shall be in your debt if you would spare the few seconds required to post a review on **Amazon** and **Goodreads**.

I love hearing from readers, and you can connect with me through my **Facebook page**, via **Twitter** or through my **website**.

I hope we'll meet again in the pages of the next Charles Holborne adventure.

Simon Michael

www.simonmichael.uk

Sapere Books is an exciting new publisher of brilliant fiction and popular history.

To find out more about our latest releases and our monthly bargain books visit our website:
saperebooks.com